ON *the*
RECORD

Also by K.A. Linde

ON *the* RECORD

RECORD SERIES BOOK 2

K.A. LINDE

Text copyright © 2014 K.A. Linde
All rights reserved.

Published by Montlake Romance, Seattle

www.apub.com

ISBN-13: 9781477823880
ISBN-10: 1477823883

Cover design by Laura Klynstra
Library of Congress Control Number: 2014901936

Printed in the United States of America

To The Campaign.
For yard signs, Ye Olde, and meta conversations.

Chapter 1

ELECTION DAY

I can't believe you dragged me to this party," Victoria said.

Liz's best friend was standing against the bar with a drink in her hot-pink-manicured hand. She looked as gorgeous as ever in a skintight black dress covering her voluptuous body, and bright red heels to match her cherry red lips.

"You're the one who said that you wanted to go out with me tonight," Liz reminded her.

"I didn't know it was to a newspaper party . . . on election night." Victoria tossed her dark brown hair off her shoulder and looked at Liz beneath thick black lashes coated in mascara.

"I've only been working toward this, oh, I don't know, all year."

Victoria shrugged. "Some things are important to you and some things are important to me. At least we both agree on alcohol," she said, holding up her glass.

Liz giggled and took a sip of her drink. "Liking the effects of alcohol and liking alcohol are two different things."

"That's like saying liking the way Hayden kissed you and liking Hayden are two different things."

"Coming from the girl who will kiss anyone!" Liz cried. Gah! Did Victoria have to bring this up again? How often had they had this conversation since she and her editor at the paper had shared that heated kiss over the summer?

Giving up Brady had been bad enough.

Her affair with the State Senator Brady Maxwell had lasted the length of the summer, and in that span of time she had fallen unequivocally in love with him. In love with a man whom she couldn't be with because she was a reporter, a liability to the campaign, a liability to everything he had worked for. And then on the night of his primary victory Brady had given his acceptance speech, proclaiming her, in all but name, as the person who had made him believe completely in this journey he was on. It was in that moment of clarity that she had known what she had to do.

If she forced Brady to decide between her and the campaign, it would have hurt him; and if he chose her and lost the campaign, he would resent her. She hadn't been okay with either of those scenarios. So Liz had taken the choice into her own hands and walked out on him, and she hadn't heard from Brady in the two and half months since she had left. Two and a half agonizing months.

"I can kiss whoever I want, Liz," Victoria said.

"Like the Duke Fan?" Liz chided, shuddering.

"Yes, I can't believe you are so freaked out that I went on a date with someone who goes to Duke." Liz just shrugged. "And anyway, you're the one swooning over your Hayden Lane."

Liz's eyes shifted from Victoria to Hayden, standing only a few feet away lost in conversation. If he heard a whisper of this, Liz would kill Victoria.

She wasn't ready for a relationship or really anything else with Hayden—or anyone. Victoria didn't understand why, but then again, she didn't know that the guy Liz had been seeing over the summer had been Brady Maxwell. No one did. Certainly not Hayden. He didn't even know she'd been seeing someone.

That had made it difficult to explain why she wouldn't go out with him. It wasn't like she could just come out and say she was too emotionally bruised by a certain sitting State Senator and was stupidly hoping that he might come find her. She had tried sidestepping Hayden when he had asked her out, but then she'd had to tell him something, and none of her excuses seemed to be good enough. How long could she keep a guy at bay after kissing him the way she had in front of the Lincoln Memorial in D.C.?

"Swooning?" Liz shook her head, trying to keep her voice down. "Are you serious?"

"He's been flirting with you all night, Lizzie." Victoria batted her eyes at Liz.

"Oh, stop calling me that."

"He won't."

That was the truth. Hayden hadn't stopped calling her Lizzie since that night they'd kissed over the summer. Victoria found it hilarious and always poked fun at Hayden whenever she could.

"You're insufferable. You know that, right?"

Victoria smiled in a way that said more than even her perfectly arched eyebrow. Liz didn't know why she let her best friend get to her so easily. She wasn't ready to move on. She wasn't over Brady Maxwell . . . as much as she wanted to let go. Their relationship had been too important for her to just easily move on to someone else. Perhaps that was silly.

"Well, if you won't make a move, then maybe I should," Victoria suggested, like she had just thought of it.

"Hayden's not even your type."

"Type?" Victoria asked. "What is this thing you speak of?"

"He's not currently working toward or already has a PhD."

"Well, yeah, he's not smart enough for me. That's obvious," Victoria said.

Liz rolled her eyes.

"But I think I wouldn't mind a piece of a tall, fit runner for a change," Victoria said, taking a step forward.

"Victoria!" Liz snapped, blocking her path. "Cut it out."

"Oh, come on, Liz. Have some fun."

"Not that kind of fun." The last thing she wanted was for Victoria to embarrass her in front of all of her colleagues. And, well, even if she wasn't sure she was ready to move past what had happened with Brady, that certainly didn't mean she wanted Victoria to make a pass at Hayden.

"Why not? Just go home with him. Have a good fuck and move on from the summer. The summer is *over*. You can't change anything that happened, but you don't have to let it make your decisions for you."

"I'm not," Liz said, but there was no conviction in her voice. How could she ever explain? Letting Brady go felt like a bigger loss than just walking out of the primary party. But she *had* walked out. She had made her own decision, and it didn't sit well with her that Victoria implied that she was still allowing Brady to control her.

Tristan, one of her freshman helpers at the college paper, came running into the room and broke through her thoughts. He craned his neck around, and Liz waved her hand in the air to signal him. He darted over and stood before her in perfectly pressed khaki pants, a navy polo, and a black jacket. The only thing giving away that he had been in a rush was the wave at the crest of his typically flawless hair, and the bead of sweat forming at his temple.

"Dougherty," Tristan said to Liz in greeting. She had been able to break him of the formal Miss that had gone before that for the first month or more of his working for her. But now, even when they were just out with friends, she couldn't break him of the habit of addressing her simply by her last name.

"What did you find?" Liz asked.

"I have the results for the precincts you requested."

Liz looked over Tristan's shoulder to find Hayden only a few feet away from her. "Hayden!" she called. Their eyes locked and he smiled that heart-stopping smile before hurrying over to stand just a bit closer.

"Does he have the results?" he asked Liz. He was all business too. It was why they worked well together. It was why they had always worked well together. And it was one of the reasons she had liked him the past two years. She would have given anything for Hayden to make a move before Brady.

Before Brady.

It was like a constant mantra. She forced those thoughts out of her mind and focused on the business at hand.

Tristan nodded, pulled a piece of paper out of his pocket, and handed it to his bosses.

Liz scanned the list, her stomach somersaulting. She couldn't believe what she saw. "All but one precinct," she whispered.

Hayden flashed her a smile. "Just like you predicted."

"Not Meriweather precinct, because they always run opposite the Maxwells," she murmured.

"You said that too," Hayden encouraged.

It wasn't the entire fourth district by a long shot, but the few precincts that they had been watching in Chapel Hill had swung for Brady. Maybe that would swing the whole district, if the boost in student voting on campus was any indication.

She would find out soon enough.

"This is great, Tristan," Liz said. She was close to shaking, she was so emotional and conflicted. She wanted Brady to win. She didn't want it to all be for naught. It just felt like this day had taken forever to get to . . . and they still had to wait for the official announcement.

"You said from day one that our politician would win," Hayden said.

"Well, he hasn't won yet. Tristan, will you write up something short for tomorrow with this information, along with the official results?"

"Of course, Dougherty. On it." With that Tristan turned and started for the door.

Liz sighed and ran after him. "Hey, you don't have to go now," she said, modulating her no-nonsense tone. Sometimes she forgot that Tristan was just a freshman, the paper wasn't his real job, and she wasn't his real boss. He wasn't getting paid for this, and he probably wanted to celebrate too.

"Don't you want that article?" Tristan asked.

"Why don't you stay and wait for the election results to come in? You can party with the rest of us."

He looked at her in wonder, like Liz had just given him a huge privilege. She really must have been working her staff hard if he was this appreciative. "That sounds great, Dougherty. I'll still be sure to get that article to you. I could run out and get my computer while we're waiting, if you think that will help."

"Maybe you should just get a drink," Liz suggested.

He laughed and shook his head. "I don't drink, but thanks for the offer. I think I'll grab my computer anyway."

Liz watched him depart, wondering if she had been that determined and strong-willed as a freshman. She didn't remember it quite like that, but she probably had been.

"Hey," Hayden said, coming up behind Liz.

"Hey." She swiveled in place and came face-to-face with his intriguing hazel eyes. They were leaning more toward green rather than brown tonight. He looked good in gray slacks and a green button-down, loose at the neck. Dressy but casual.

"You've done a great job with your team."

"Thanks," Liz said, flushing.

"Do you know what you want to do next semester?"

Liz scuffed her foot on the floor. She hadn't wanted to think about that yet. The campaign would be over and she would have to fall into place somewhere else on the paper.

She shrugged. "I'm not sure. Where do you want me?"

His answering smile made her flush even further, but she didn't dare break eye contact.

"On the paper . . . that is," she muttered. *Way to make it even more embarrassing.*

"I was thinking of moving you and your team over to Massey's Washington division. I'd still like some focus on whoever wins these races, and your team already knows them."

He wanted her to continue to follow Brady . . .

Hayden must have seen something on her face, because he started backpedaling. "Unless you don't want to work with Massey . . ."

"The Washington division sounds great," she quickly corrected. She didn't want him to think that she didn't like Massey or that she wasn't serious about her role at the paper.

"I had thought . . . that you might work with me some too," Hayden said.

Liz arched an eyebrow.

"I still think you could be editor after I leave."

Liz's breath caught in her throat. Editor. It was her dream, what she had been working toward. But was he giving it to her because he liked her or because she deserved it? "Are you sure you want me for the job?"

"Yes, I'm sure I want you," he answered quickly. "For the job."

"All right. Well, I could work with you then," she said, her head buzzing.

Liz couldn't believe how much a few months had changed everything. She remembered her first press conference. The anticipation had killed her as she waited for State Senator Brady Maxwell III to walk out onto the stage. She'd had no thought that she would get to ask a question, or that that very moment would change her life. She had just been an untested reporter hoping to catch a break.

Now Hayden was pushing for her to be editor after he graduated. She knew that he had said she was capable of it that same day after the conference, but it was different hearing that he wanted to start preparing her to take the job. The very notion sent a shiver down her spine.

Liz caught Victoria eyeing her from the bar. She was sure she knew what Victoria was thinking . . . that Liz was taking her advice. It would be easy to return Hayden's flirtatious smiles and cute comments. It wasn't like she didn't like Hayden . . . hadn't always liked Hayden. But still, she stepped away from him instead of into him when he moved toward her.

Hayden's smile didn't falter, but she could see him straining to keep it on his face. Liz didn't know why he hadn't given up on her yet. One kiss wasn't enough to keep a guy's interest for this long. The way he looked at her, though . . .

Liz shifted her attention back to the television screens just as the announcers started broadcasting the latest results. She held her breath as she waited for them to show North Carolina.

"The Cunningham-Maxwell race that we've been following still doesn't have full results in just yet," the news broadcaster reported. "From the looks of what we do have it's a pretty tight race down there. The front-runner, Cunningham, appears to have the lead by a small margin, but it's a toss-up if I've ever seen one. We'll keep our eye on that one, but in the meantime, let's take a look at the open seat race in Pennsylvania."

Liz breathed out heavily. She wanted the results, and the waiting game was frustrating.

"Going to be close," Hayden said, walking with her back to the bar.

"We always knew that."

"Those results Tristan had make me think Maxwell's going to pull it out. You said it from the beginning, but it's different having the proof in my hands."

"Yeah," she whispered. The culmination of a lot of hard work and ambition on Brady's part. He'd been born and bred for this role . . . born and bred to be president. He had convinced her of that. Liz shook her head. She needed to get Brady Maxwell out of her thoughts. After tonight that would be her mission. After he won . . . He had to win!

"Are you two going to have a shot with me or what?" Victoria yelled. She reached out and latched on to Liz's arm and dragged her back to the bar. "Come on, Lane. Hurry up!"

Hayden shuffled forward with a barely suppressed eye roll. "Whatever you say, Vickie."

"Liz, make him stop," Victoria whined just before shoving a shot into both of their hands.

Liz turned her back to the bar, cocking her head to the side as she stared at him. God, he looked good tonight! "Hayden, play nice."

"I always play nice, Liz."

Victoria thrust her shot glass up into the air between them and they both followed suit. "I'll toast this one to Liz."

"Me?" Liz asked, widening her eyes.

"To the chick who worked her ass off for this moment. May the best man win," Victoria said with a flourish.

Liz cringed at the ill-timed toast. Victoria was talking about the congressional race, but to Liz it was more between Brady and

Hayden. Brady had been her world, but then her world came crashing down. Now she had to keep moving, keep living despite the destruction. It was self-inflicted . . . after all, she and Brady couldn't be together. She had written negative articles about him before she had gotten to know him, and anything that could hurt Brady's chance of winning was a danger to the campaign. Brady hadn't left her mind a single day since she had walked away.

As she tipped the shot back into her mouth, the burn down her throat reminded her of exactly how she had felt every day since she had left him. It might have been the right decision, but it wasn't easy, and it constantly left her with a bad taste in her mouth . . . and feeling a little sick.

But Hayden was always there too. Slowly but surely trying to pick the pieces back up . . . pieces he didn't know existed. Liz had just refused to let it go further than that. The last thing she wanted was to start something with Hayden and look back and see that it had been a rebound.

"Looks like the results are in on that Cunningham-Maxwell race down in North Carolina," the anchor said, slashing through all Liz's coherent thought.

She froze with her eyes glued to the television. It was finally time. The next moment felt like an eternity, as if Liz were watching the whole thing in slow motion. The crowd quieted all around her as heads turned to the screen to hear what had happened. Victoria collected shot glasses from Liz and Hayden and slammed them down on the counter, then turned to listen to the reporter. Even she was interested . . .

Hayden's hand landed on the small of Liz's back and he drew closer to her. She felt his breath hot on her ear as he whispered softly, "Go out with me."

It wasn't a request, but not quite a command. And he said it so faintly, so decidedly, and at just the right time that she didn't even have time to process what was going on. In a split second she was going to find out if Brady had won. But now her mind was lost in Hayden's comment.

"And it looks like State Senator Brady Maxwell has pulled it off by an even slimmer margin than his primary race, with just over seven hundred and fifty votes over that threshold. Truly amazing. Congratulations, Senator Maxwell. We'll be analyzing this victory more thoroughly later on tonight . . ."

Liz couldn't hear anything else as the bar erupted. People all around her were screaming and cheering for their hometown hero. And she just stood there gaping.

He had done it! He had pulled it off. Seven hundred and fifty votes had pushed him to victory. That was such a small margin. Any precinct could have tipped the balance.

Then Hayden had his arms around her middle and was spinning her in circles. Liz giggled, threw her arms around his neck, and pressed her thin frame against his chest. He slowed to a stop and then lowered his mouth down to her lips. Without even a second thought, Liz let herself get caught up in the moment—get caught up in Hayden.

Her eyes closed and electricity shot between them as they melded together. The more she had pushed him away, the more the heat built between them. And now it had all released into one celebratory kiss. She hadn't even known that she wanted this until it happened, and her heart fluttered.

Hayden pulled away first, and she knew her breathing was uneven as his hazel eyes looked deep into hers. "Go out with me," Hayden repeated with that same smile that had won her over from day one.

Liz bit her lip. Brady was going to D.C. to be a congressman in the House of Representatives. He had just won everything he wanted and was likely celebrating that victory. He wasn't celebrating with her, and he wouldn't be. November didn't mean anything to her anymore, and she had to move on. She had to forget Brady Maxwell. She would never regret what had happened between them, but she couldn't keep obsessing.

Maybe if she just let herself like Hayden again instead of putting all of her energy into pushing him away, that would make it all that much easier.

She wanted this. She was ready to start over, and Hayden was giving her that opportunity. A smile broke out onto her face to match Hayden's.

This was good. This was the right direction.

"I'd love to," she murmured before finding his lips again.

Chapter 2
CHRISTMAS BOMB

Liz had skipped the newspaper holiday party the past two years. Walking into the upstairs of a downtown bar that the paper had rented out for the night with Hayden, she realized she hadn't missed much. Cheap Christmas decorations filled the room, and a tiny tree was set up in the corner. A table was filled with platters of holiday treats and punch. Most people, not surprisingly, weren't dressed up for the occasion. Some had on tacky sweaters, but Liz had clearly outdone them all.

She had on an oversize sweater that looked like it had stepped out of the back of a grandma's closet, complete with a Christmas tree with working lights and hand-painted ornaments and presents. She had paired that with tight black leggings and Rudolph tennis shoes she had snagged from the kids' section. A strand of jingle bells was wrapped around her neck, and she even had a couple red and green plastic bows stuck in her hair. Victoria had jokingly told her that it looked like a bomb went off in the Walmart Christmas aisle.

People mingled around the food table and the bar on the adjacent wall, or danced awkwardly to the Christmas music playing through the speakers. Liz picked out Massey talking to the rest of the Washington division. She was gesturing profusely to her captivated audience. Tristan was tucked into a corner working on his laptop. That kid seriously needed to take a break or have a drink. Liz noted that Brady's sister, Savannah, wasn't in attendance yet, and breathed a slow sigh of relief. She didn't mind that she and Savannah worked together on the paper, but the reminders of her brother Brady were bad enough when it wasn't the first time Liz was out in public with Hayden.

"Hayden! Liz!" Meagan said, rushing up to greet them. She was wearing a tacky sweater that Liz couldn't even begin to explain. It was like an explosion of red, green, and white glitter in random designs that was both terrifying and hard to look at without squinting.

"Hey, Meagan," Hayden responded amiably. "Great job with the party this year. I think this is way better than last year."

Liz was sure he was just being nice. Typical Hayden.

"Liz, you look so cute. I'm glad you really dressed up! I was worried I was going to be the only one," Meagan said cheerfully.

"Thanks. I thought more people would be dressed up than this," Liz said.

"At least some people did it this time. Last year it was only me and a couple other people. I guess Calleigh told everyone else she wasn't dressing up . . . so no one else did," Meagan said with a shrug. Then she seemed to quickly correct herself. "Nothing against Calleigh, of course. She looked fabulous as always! Love her!"

"Well, thanks for putting this all together," Hayden said. Liz glanced up into his face when she heard the strain in his voice.

Huh. Seriously, what was the deal with Calleigh and Hayden? He had said that he and the beautiful reporter had dated briefly and that it was over. Liz had never pushed further than that. Whatever they had been had clearly never been something public, because she was sure she would have noticed that, at least. Maybe she would find a time to ask him that didn't make her sound jealous. So . . . never.

Hayden wrapped an arm around her shoulders and directed her away from Meagan. They didn't take more than a couple steps before Massey darted into their path. She was on the shorter side with shoulder-length blond hair. A die-hard sorority girl who even wore her letters to a Christmas party.

"Oh my God! Look at you two! So flipping cute. I can't even handle the cuteness. So glad you're not like hiding your relationship anymore," Massey said, linking her arm with Liz's and dragging them into the center of the group.

Massey had told Liz earlier that week that she wasn't going to dress up, because she didn't want to wear the tacky sweater she had gotten for her sorority date night more than once. She couldn't be photographed in it or she might die. Liz had just laughed. Oh, the woes of having an active social life.

"Y'all, aren't Hayden and Liz like the cutest couple ever?" Massey asked as introduction.

Liz smiled, fighting the blush of embarrassment that was surely creeping up her cheeks. Hayden just drew her in closer. Though she didn't look up at him, she was sure he was smiling. He might have been nervous earlier about how people would react, but not now. Right now he was in his element. This was his paper. These were the people he worked with, the people who worked for him. He was going on four years of their camaraderie and respect. Hayden owned this group with nothing more than a smile.

The total control pouring out of him pulled the tension right out of her shoulders. Why was she worried about what these people thought? It was her relationship, not theirs. She and Hayden had kept the past month of their relationship private. Even though they had snuck glances across the office and left the newspaper at the same time, this was their first official appearance out together. Liz just had to remind herself that it didn't interfere with work in the slightest, and apparently everyone already knew. She needed to get ahold of herself.

She wasn't some cowering girl hiding behind a man. She wanted to be editor next year, and then she would be commanding the same respect Hayden had currently. Liz visibly straightened, ignoring the jingles that came from her necklace.

"Thanks for that, Massey," Liz said.

"It's just good to see you guys out," Massey said.

"It's not like you all didn't already know," Hayden said.

The group shrugged and hid their smiles behind their drinks.

"Well, y'all were *not* subtle," Massey responded.

Hayden laughed and brushed his hand back through his blond hair. "Why would I ever want to hide Liz in the first place? Just look at her."

She glanced up at him and swallowed. That was all she had ever been with Brady—hidden—and it had ripped her heart open and scattered it into a million little pieces. But the adoring look on Hayden's face at least momentarily stopped the destruction and seemed to bandage the wound.

"Okay. Oh my God, we get it. You don't have to be so flippin' disgusting," Massey drawled. "Like, get a room or something."

"Don't be jealous, Massey," Liz said.

"I'm so not jealous, but can we talk about this adorable outfit for a second?" Massey asked. And with that the tension about Liz and Hayden being together dissipated.

Nothing to see here, people. Move along.

Liz sidled up closer to Massey, who apparently was super jealous about Liz's jingle bell necklace. She promptly handed it over for

Massey to wear and insisted she keep it for her date night. Then Liz made her way to Tristan's table to try to coax him to come out of his corner. He stared up at her doe-eyed and shared a few words with her about the party, informing her he was having a great time. She couldn't get him to leave the table, though, and as soon as she walked away, he started in on his laptop again.

Time seemed to fly, and Liz realized with a start that she was having a really good time. Her anxiety had been for nothing. She kind of wished that she had come to the event the previous two years. Either way, it was nice to mill around with her friends and colleagues and just relax a little instead of being constantly on deadline.

Hayden was also nearby, never too far away but certainly not hovering. And . . . it felt right.

The room quieted as Hayden called everyone's attention to where he was standing. Without even thinking she moved to stand next to him, and he squeezed her hand.

"Hey, y'all! Thanks so much for coming out to the annual holiday party. I don't have a long speech or anything, but I just wanted to thank everyone for your hard work and dedication this semester. You've all really put in the time and effort it takes to propel this paper into the forefront of college journalism," Hayden said to a chorus of applause.

Liz smiled up at him. She felt a familiar excitement spread through her body at the words. She was proud. Proud of Hayden, proud of the paper, proud of everything they had accomplished. She was part of something worthwhile.

"I know I would never be able to stand here today and talk about so many achievements without every single person here right now. From our three-person campaign division, taking on the midterm elections, to our kvetching column, keeping the student body entertained, to the photojournalists, chronicling the activities around campus, we are the heartbeat of the university. We only have one week left this semester, and I know it will live up to my high expectations for this paper. I can't even wait for next semester, which always brings in new people, new challenges, and new chances to shine. So thanks for coming out tonight, and happy holidays!"

Hayden held his glass up and everyone followed his lead, yelling out happy holidays and merry Christmas, then tipping their drinks back.

The chatter resumed as soon as Hayden finished his drink, and he turned to face Liz, pulling her into him. She slid her arms around his middle and leaned her head against his chest. It felt totally normal, as if she had been doing it for much longer than she actually had.

"That was a good speech," she told him thoughtfully.

"Thanks. Made it up on the spot."

"I could tell," she joked.

Hayden poked her side playfully until she giggled and tried to pull away. She looked up at him to tell him to stop, and his lips found hers. The kiss was brief, but heated, and when he released her, she seemed to have forgotten what she was going to yell at him about.

"Are you ready to get out of here?" he asked.

"Where are we going?" She wasn't sure why it mattered, with the way he was looking at her.

"Well, we could go back to my place," he said softly. "Or we could go to that party with my friends."

Hmm. Going back to his place sounded like a good time. A really good time. But was she ready for that?

"Party? I'm not tired yet," Liz said quickly. As if he wanted to take her back to his house to sleep.

They had been dating a month, and still she changed the subject whenever the subject of sex came up. God, she loved sex, but a small part . . . okay, a large part of her screamed that she wasn't ready for that.

She still associated Brady with so many of the emotions and feelings that came with sex. It wasn't fair to jump right into bed with Hayden when she couldn't even tease apart her own thoughts on the subject. Sometimes she thought that she wanted to, and she knew Hayden wanted to—what guy didn't?—but she wouldn't until she was sure she was ready, and Hayden didn't push her. Ever the upstanding gentleman.

"All right. Your call. I'll let the guys know," Hayden said, reaching for his phone and hiding the slight look of disappointment that crossed his face.

When Hayden got on the phone, they moved over toward the entrance so he could hear the phone conversation. Liz took out her own phone to see if she had heard from Victoria. The screen came up blank just as Savannah Maxwell walked into the party.

As usual, she looked gorgeous, tonight in a red sweater dress, thick black tights, and black heels. Gold jewelry dangled from her ears, and a long chain hung around her neck. Her dark brown hair was sleek and straight well past her shoulders. And still . . . she reminded Liz of Brady. They had the same shape eyes, the same overconfidence, and the same poised stride.

Liz had fought with herself every day this semester while working with Savannah. She liked the girl, and Savannah wasn't her brother. That was for damn sure. But sometimes it was all wrong, and Liz just wished over and over that things could be right again.

"Liz," Savannah said with her effortless politician's smile. She really should consider running for office, though Liz knew she had no interest whatsoever. "Sorry I'm late. I got held up. What did I miss?"

Liz had a moment where she wanted to ask her where she had been. It wasn't that it was likely that she had been with Brady. And it wasn't that it made a difference if she had been.

Christ, Liz needed to get ahold of herself. Everything in her life did not revolve around Brady fucking Maxwell.

"Not much. Hayden made a speech. We all just hung out," Liz told her.

"Cool. I'm going to go say hi quickly. I have a physics test in the morning," she said, rolling her big brown eyes.

Liz cringed. "That sucks. Good luck."

"Thanks. See you at the paper."

"Bye, Savannah."

Liz watched her walk away, a weight lifting off her chest. Her relief at the other girl's departure was totally irrational, but it happened all the time.

"You ready?" Hayden asked, slinging his arm over her shoulders again.

She diverted her attention back to Hayden. "Yep."

They walked down the street briskly to try to keep back the biting cold. The first week of December was usually pretty chilly, but this was too much. A cold front had just run its course through Chapel Hill. With North Carolina's mercurial weather it would be in the eighties tomorrow or something equally ridiculous. She seriously missed her parents' house in Tampa right now.

When they reached the bar where Hayden's other friends were gathered, Hayden held the door for Liz and she quickly passed through. Rubbing her hands together to try to bring life back into them, she waited for Hayden to follow her. He planted a kiss on her forehead and then took up warming her hands for her. Then he laced their fingers together and pulled her through the crowd.

His track friends were clustered around the back end of the counter with beers in hand. She had met most of them at the beginning of the semester when she had helped Hayden move, and had gotten to know them a little better over the last month.

When she got close enough, Hannity greeted her with a hug and pulled her into the center of their group. Three of the guys on the team were named Andrew, so they all went by their last names: Bynum, Cush, and Lightsey. The other guys in attendance were Jake Morgan and Henry Evans, who also went by their last names. It was confusing and had taken her a while to get used to.

"Glad you showed up, Lane," Bynum said, as they clapped each other on the back.

"Yeah, how was your cute holiday party?" Hannity asked. He poked at the bows still in Liz's hair and she rolled her eyes. She had completely forgotten those were there.

"It was great. Free food. Cheap drinks. About what you can expect," Hayden told them.

"I like your outfit, Liz," Lightsey said with a wink. He was the youngest of the bunch and a known flirt, but with little success.

"Thanks. If you'll all excuse me, I'm going to go find the restroom," Liz said. The guys parted to allow her to pass and pointed down the dark hallway nearly right behind them. She darted away from them and found the women's restroom at the end of the hall.

After relieving herself, Liz pried the Christmas bows out of her hair and finger-combed the waves into submission. She didn't think it really did the trick, but she didn't have another option. At least Massey had taken her jingle bell necklace, and Liz had switched off the lights on her sweater. There was nothing she could do about the tennis shoes. Why hadn't she thought of a change of clothes?

Deciding that was as good as it was going to get, Liz walked out of the restroom and back down the hallway. She stopped short of the exit when she heard her name from one of the guys.

"No, seriously, she's really fucking hot," Hannity said.

Liz peered around the corner and saw all of the guys nodding, agreeing. Hayden just shrugged. They hadn't seen her, and while it felt wrong to eavesdrop, she was curious.

"Are you telling me you still haven't slept with her?" Bynum asked, gesturing with his hands.

"It's not a big deal," Hayden told them.

Liz's cheeks burned even as Hayden defended her. She knew guys talked about this shit. She and Victoria were ten times as vulgar, but somehow it embarrassed her in this context. They didn't know that she was merely steps from them, but how long did they think she took in the bathroom?

"I mean, we thought you were gay when you claimed you were hung up on this girl all year," Lightsey said with a shrug.

"You're one to talk, Lightsey," Cush yelled, punching him in the arm.

"Back the fuck off, Cush."

"Fucking make me!"

"Christ," Hannity cried, knocking Cush back. "You sprinters need to get off the juice."

The guys all laughed. Steroids were banned even for the club team, but everyone joked that the sprinters used it to take seconds off of their time.

"Is she a virgin or something? What's the hang-up?" Hannity asked. "You guys have been hanging out for weeks and you haven't even tried anything? She doesn't seem like a prude to me. So, what's wrong with her?"

"There's nothing *wrong* with her, you asshole," Hayden said, shaking his head. Whatever else he said was lost to her as she took a few steps back toward the bathroom and leaned her head against the wall.

It didn't matter. It didn't matter. It didn't matter.

It had only been a month. Why were guys such dicks about that shit? She and Hayden didn't have to sleep together in the first month. It was a perfectly reasonable amount of time. Hayden wouldn't push. He respected her and her decisions. Plus, he had defended her to his friends.

They were just being dudes. They never would have said that shit if they knew she had been listening. She just needed to calm down, laugh it off. There was nothing wrong with her.

Liz took a deep breath and walked out into the bar with her head held high.

"Lizzie," Hayden said, reaching out for her. She let him draw her into him. "You took out your bows."

"I figured I didn't need to look as much like a Christmas bomb away from the party."

"I thought you looked cute."

"Thanks," she murmured, unsuccessfully stifling a yawn. She hadn't even thought that she was tired, but all of the energy had drained right out of her at those comments.

"Hey, do you want to get out of here?" Hayden asked.

Liz nodded. She really did want to get far, far away from this moment. "Are you okay to drive?" She hadn't paid attention to how much he had been drinking, but after her friend Justin's DUI, she wasn't going to make the mistake of getting in the car with someone who had been drinking ever again.

"Yeah. I only had one at the other party," he told her as he placed his mostly full beer back on the bar.

"Y'all aren't leaving, are you?" Bynum asked.

"Yeah, man, we're going to head out. Liz has class early on Fridays."

"All right. Y'all take care."

Hayden shook hands with all of the guys. A glint of mischief was evident in Hannity's eyes as he stared between them. He gave her another hug that she tried to escape, making him laugh. And then they were free and walking back toward Hayden's car, getting inside, then driving to her house.

Liz let Hayden open the door for her, and she trudged inside, exhaustion taking over. She grabbed a pair of yoga pants and a sweater from a drawer and walked into the bathroom to change out of her silly Christmas attire. She returned a minute later to find Hayden looking at the pictures on her dresser.

He turned around when she walked back into the room and shot her a dazzling smile. "Hey, gorgeous."

She bit her lip and walked over to him. Hayden wound his finger through her hair and her eyes closed of their own accord. He ran his hands along her scalp and over the tense muscles in her neck. She couldn't help it when a moan escaped her lips.

God, she just wanted to let herself get lost in this moment. She wanted to feel his lips against hers, have him press her back into the bed, to just give in to the emotions warring through her. But thoughts of Brady crept in, coupled with the words of Hayden's friends, and it all just felt so wrong. She had never had this happen before. She usually just let romance run its own course, but every time it seemed to begin with Hayden, she felt a Brady stumbling block cross her path. Her body stiffened and she couldn't continue.

Reading her body language, Hayden pulled back to look at her. "Are you all right?"

Liz nodded and then after a second shook her head. No point in keeping it from him. That wouldn't help anything, and she wasn't ever going to go further with him if she kept this feeling bottled up inside of her. And she liked Hayden.

"What's going on?" he asked, drawing her toward her bed. It had a big comfy queen-size feather-top mattress that she sank into when she sat down. She scooted closer to the center.

"I heard what your friends were saying at the bar," she said in a rush.

Color drained out of Hayden's face. She had never seen him look so ashamed and uncomfortable.

"I don't know what you think about . . . this relationship," she said. "But I didn't know that there was anything wrong with me for waiting."

"Liz, there's nothing wrong with you."

"I know. And I feel stupid for even bringing this up or feeling bad about it . . ."

"Please don't feel stupid," he said, taking her hands in his. "The guys are the stupid ones. They don't know anything about a real relationship, and they don't know anything about *our* relationship."

"They seemed to know quite a bit about our relationship." Liz arched an eyebrow.

"I would never want you to feel bad for your choices, Liz." He paused as if deciding what to say next, and then he moved closer to her on the bed and brought her hands to his lips and placed a kiss there. His hazel eyes, almost green in the dim light, stared back up at her then like he couldn't ever convey enough with just words. "If you don't want to have s . . . go further with our relationship, then we can wait. I'm not in a rush."

"I'm not in a rush either," she whispered, lost in his gaze, in his sincerity, in that smooth voice.

"Good. Because I don't plan on letting you go."

Chapter 3

ALL THAT MATTERS

Liz spent the long holiday lounging on the beach at her parents' place in Tampa and catching up on reading. It was a nice break from reality. Normally she liked to stay in Chapel Hill for breaks, as she had over the summer. But by the end of winter break, she was more than ready to come home to see Hayden, who had been in D.C. with his family. He called every day and they chatted for hours, long into the night, but the phone calls weren't enough. Liz had gotten used to him coming over to her apartment, seeing his smiling face at work, and spending time with him late into the evening.

She missed him. A lot.

The realization hit her all at once one afternoon right before Christmas. She had been home for two weeks and Hayden had called her like normal to wish her good night, which always resulted in a marathon phone conversation.

"I miss you." It was the first thing out of his mouth. Not *hey, Liz* or *Lizzie*, as he had grown accustomed to calling her. Simply *I miss you.*

Liz knew that she hadn't given her relationship with Hayden a hundred percent from the beginning. It was her own fault. She had let her own problems hold her back. She had clung so fiercely to her previous relationship with Brady—the late-night rendezvous, the intense passion, the adrenaline of the secret affair, falling blindly in love—that she hadn't been able to see what was right in front of her. But in that moment, it didn't matter what had happened before. She knew that if she wanted this to work—and she did—she needed to actually try to put some emotional distance between her and Brady and concentrate on the person who was putting in the effort.

Which was how she ended up convincing her parents to move her plane ticket to D.C. so she could spend New Year's with Hayden. Better yet, the very next day his sister, Jamie, had the grand opening of her new art collection. After selling out of every single painting in her fall show, she had been commissioned for another, more prestigious exhibition.

Hayden picked her up at baggage claim at Reagan National Airport on New Year's Eve. Liz dropped her heavy carry-on bag on the ground at his feet when she reached him and threw her arms around his neck.

"Hey, gorgeous." He pulled her tight against him and she stood like that for a minute, just breathing him in.

"You smell so good," she whispered.

Hayden chuckled. "Thanks. It's good to have you back. Don't go so far away again, okay?"

"Okay," Liz murmured, surprised at how easily she agreed with him.

They picked up her oversize suitcase from baggage claim and Hayden wheeled it out to his car. They drove the short distance into the city, and Liz smiled as she started recognizing the familiar brownstones near where Jamie lived. It seemed so long ago that she had come up to D.C. for a weekend to see Hayden practically on a whim. And yet . . . so much of what had happened last summer always seemed to be fresh in her mind.

The last time she had been here, Brady had just confessed to loving her. Not to her, of course. He could never let himself slip like that. He had told his press secretary, Heather, and his attorney, Elliott. Liz shook her head. She didn't really want to think about it, but memories of Brady never seemed to care. They just cropped up unbidden.

Maybe it would be okay to remember them once they didn't do so much damage to her heart. Until then she would continue to wrestle them down.

Once they were parked, inside the brownstone, and up the three impossibly steep flights of stairs, the door practically burst open. Jamie grabbed Liz and yanked her into the apartment with way more force than someone with such a small frame should possess. Jamie immediately launched into a full-on excited question-and-answer session about Liz's trip, flight, ride over, and more.

Hayden walked into the back and deposited her bag in the spare bedroom, leaving her alone to Jamie's barrage. Liz tried to keep up with all of the questions, but Jamie was so enthusiastic, her black bob bouncing as she seemed to dance in place, that sometimes she would start asking another question before even letting Liz answer the previous one.

"Geez, Jamie, lay off," Hayden said, appearing in the doorway again. "She just got here. Take a breath."

Jamie shot him a death glare, but when she looked back at Liz, her giddy smile was back. "It's so good to have you here again. I was so happy when Hayden told me you would be here for the opening of my exhibition!"

"I'm glad it worked out too," Liz told her.

Liz greeted Jamie's boyfriend, James, who was never too far away from the brilliant artist, and her roommate, Meredith, who was a Pilates instructor and had a killer body because of it. Apparently James had moved into Jamie's room during the fall, so they wouldn't have to fill the spare bedroom with another unfamiliar body. Liz was sure that Jamie just liked having James close all the time. Liz had had the same feeling at the airport when she saw Hayden.

Her flight had gotten in relatively late, and they didn't have much time to get ready. Jamie had scored them some comped tickets from one of her art buyers to a private party downtown. Her paintings were picking up steam among high-end clientele and politicians, and these perks seemed to keep dropping into her lap. The event was a black-and-white affair, but not black tie, which meant that the guys didn't have to wear tuxes and the girls didn't have to go for formal wear. That was lucky for Liz, who certainly hadn't packed a floor-length dress.

Instead, she changed into a long-sleeved black sequined dress, thick black patterned tights, and shiny black heels. She wrapped a white infinity scarf around her neck and paired it with matching white gloves and her trusty black peacoat. The temperature difference was stark compared to the balmy seventy-five degrees she had been relaxing in in Tampa.

The five of them piled into James's Expedition and drove into town. They normally would have taken the Metro, but Jamie had been given a parking pass too.

James pulled up in front of the Gaylord Hotel at Washington National Harbor about thirty minutes later. When Liz laid eyes on the building, she was blown away. It was a colossal structure that looked more like a compound than a hotel, with a glass greenhouse and full Bellagio-style water display inside the waterfront structure.

A valet handed James a ticket and then they were whisked away into the giant hotel. An attendant checked their tickets and directed them through the red-carpeted lobby to a massive ballroom. Hayden wrapped an arm around Liz's waist to hold her close to him as they stepped over the threshold together.

The room was already packed nearly wall-to-wall with people dancing to the DJ's beats. She could see that the space had been divided into different areas depending on whether you wanted a DJ, live entertainment, or a slightly quieter environment. A set of stairs led up to a secluded VIP area that had her mind drifting off and away to a time when she had walked up similar stairs in Charlotte the very first time she had ever met Brady.

After depositing their jackets at the coat check, Jamie led the way through the crowd, bouncing along like no one was elbowing or running into one another. Finally they found a slightly quieter area and sent the guys to go get drinks.

Jamie spotted an available table near the corner and skipped over to grab it before someone else did; then she waved Liz and Meredith down as if they hadn't been following her. Free spirit simply did not do Jamie justice. Sometimes Liz wondered how she and Hayden were related.

"Oh my God, Liz, I am so happy that you're here. Aren't we, Meredith?" Jamie asked without waiting for Meredith to respond. "I just *knew* that you and Hayden would start dating. He's so much cooler when he's with you. Do you think I could have dragged him to this without you? No way. He's too uptight."

Liz laughed softly and took a seat at the table. "Well, I'm glad I could oblige you."

"Plus, I totally love you as a person. Doesn't she have such a great presence, Mere?" she asked. Meredith opened her mouth to say something, but Jamie just kept right along. "I'm just so glad that he brought you for New Year's this year. The snobby bitch he brought last year drove me nuts."

"What?" Liz asked, before she could think better of it.

"I mean, we weren't even going to the same party, and I was ready to ditch her before dinner ended. Do you remember her, Mere?"

"Wait, what girl?"

"I remember her," Meredith said, getting a chance to speak up. "Redhead, right?"

"Yes! That's her. I don't remember her name, but I'm glad she's gone. And I'm glad you're here!" Jamie cried with a practically buoyant smile.

"Her name wouldn't happen to be Calleigh, would it?" Liz asked. She heard her heartbeat in her ears when she asked the question. It had to be Calleigh. Who else was a redhead that Hayden had been involved with? But Liz hadn't thought it was serious. Certainly not enough to bring Calleigh to D.C. with him for New Year's Eve.

"Calleigh! Yeah, that was it. Do you know her?" Jamie asked.

"She was editor of the paper last year."

"Oh, yeah, I remember her going on and on and on about that. When Hayden made editor, I was hard-pressed to be happy for him, because she was so annoying about it."

Liz shrugged, trying for nonchalance. "I didn't know they were serious."

Jamie paused as if realizing for the first time what she had just walked into. "Oh, I don't know if they were. And anyway, that was a long time ago. They broke up when she moved."

"To Charlotte?" Liz offered.

"Yep. That sounds right. It's been long, long, long over," Jamie said with a reassuring squeeze to Liz's arm.

Liz wasn't sure why she even let this bother her. She was certain it had something to do with the fact that she just did not like Calleigh anymore. She had once idolized her, but now she realized how misguided that had been. Why had she thought it was ever genius that made the other woman turn down her job offer in New York for the paper in Charlotte? Maybe she had simply wanted to stay closer to Hayden.

The thought struck Liz so clearly that she almost knew it for a fact.

Hayden and James reappeared just then, drinks in hand. Liz couldn't keep her brain from working overtime, and Hayden gave her a quizzical look. It was as if he could see the wheels turning.

Liz snatched her drink up and grabbed Hayden's hand. "Come on. Let's go dance," she said, drawing him away from the group.

Jamie bit her lip in concern, but Liz turned her back on her. She knew that she should probably talk to Hayden about Calleigh. She had been curious about it since May, when Calleigh had confronted the two of them outside of a club in Raleigh, and it had only intensified since they had started dating. Sure, it was old news. Calleigh and Hayden were over and done with, but the thought of them together made her sick. The thought of Calleigh staying close by because she wanted to be near Hayden made it even worse.

"This way," Hayden said, moving ahead of her. She followed him and they walked into another room. A band was playing and people were dancing around, but it wasn't as packed as the dance floor she had been heading for. Liz started to veer toward the center of the room, but Hayden tucked her arm into his and walked her to a far wall. He circled her and pushed her back against the wall softly.

"What did Jamie say?" he asked with a sigh.

"What?" Liz asked, playing dumb. She didn't want to talk about this. She just wanted to go dance and forget.

"I seriously hate leaving her alone with people. Her big mouth always manages to say the exact *wrong* thing. And she said something to you, didn't she?"

"Hayden, it doesn't matter." She tried to put a smile back on her face and push away from the wall, but he stopped her with a sharp kiss on the mouth.

"It matters," he breathed when he pulled back. "I haven't seen your gorgeous self in three weeks. I couldn't care less about the party. I don't like to see you unhappy. And I can't make it better if you don't talk to me."

Liz swallowed. "You brought Calleigh here last year."

Hayden's brow furrowed. "So?"

"You told me it wasn't serious. And yet she keeps coming back up."

"It wasn't serious," he said calmly, brushing a hand back through his hair.

"Okay," Liz said with a shrug.

"Is something else wrong?"

"I just . . . I must have been oblivious last year when she was at school. I didn't even know you guys were involved. And now I feel like I'm blindsided by her memory at every corner," she told him honestly. "And then you said it wasn't serious, but you brought her here and it makes me think maybe . . . we're not that serious."

Since when had she pushed for it to become more serious?

"Hey," he said, placing his hand under her chin and tilting her head up to look at him. "It wasn't serious with Calleigh. She wanted more than I did. It is serious with you and that's what matters. That's *all* that matters."

Liz stared up into those compelling hazel eyes in the darkness. They were almost brown with intensity. He meant every single word. She didn't know why she had gotten so flustered about the whole thing. Calleigh got under her skin; that was for sure. But

Hayden . . . the thought of this relationship with Hayden being a sham was even worse. It made her heart constrict to realize how much he really meant to her. They had been dating for nearly two months now, and while she had liked him for much longer, she hadn't even realized that she had given away so much of her heart.

Calleigh was still in Hayden's life as little as Brady was in hers. And it wouldn't be fair to hold it against him when she was still trying to get her own feelings under control.

"I like that we can talk about these things, Liz," he told her. "I don't like to bottle up my feelings, and I don't want you to feel like I'm ever hiding anything from you. I'll always tell you everything."

"I know," she said, pushing his words away. There were too many things in her past that she couldn't tell him about. She had been hiding from Brady and she wasn't about to share that secret. Not now . . . maybe not ever.

Hayden's hands found the curve of her waist and slid down to her hips. He gripped her through the thin material of her dress, and Liz leaned forward into him. His mouth came down on hers softly at first, gaining momentum as he rested her back against the wall again. Her hands dug into his black dress shirt, willing him to keep going.

Their tongues volleyed and she could feel her own breathing quicken. It had been so long since she had gotten completely wrapped up in a kiss. This new level of passion seemed to encase them like a cocoon.

Their bodies were pressed flush together, and she released a moan when he took a breath. She could feel the outline of him through his pants, and she pushed her pelvis up against him. His eyes shut and he groaned deep in his throat.

"Lizzie," he said, fighting for words. "We're in public."

A thrill shot through her spine at the possibilities. The thought of people watching them should have made her stiff and uncomfortable, but it didn't. It made her want to keep going. When her last relationship had been completely predicated on secrecy, it was exhilarating to have these moments.

"So?" she whispered.

She dropped her hands to the waistline of his pants and teased her fingertips along the material. His quick intake of breath told her more than his words ever could. She didn't know how ready she was to push the limits, but the look of lust on his face sure made her want to continue.

"I'm not . . . inclined to . . ." He stopped speaking when her hand moved a little farther south. "Lizzie."

The way he said it was an encouragement rather than a reprimand. But when her hand slipped farther down the front of his pants and skimmed the outline of his dick, he grabbed her wrist and pulled her away. His breathing was uneven.

"I want you," he told her simply. "But not here . . . not like this."

She sighed, disappointment hitting her. She quickly covered it up. He was right. They shouldn't do this here anyway. "Okay," she said. He released her hand and she dropped both of them to her sides.

He kissed her once more on her lips before moving out onto the dance floor to find their friends. Meredith was grinding on a guy hot enough to be a model, and it looked a bit like she might not be returning with them. Jamie squealed when she saw them, and tried to yell over the music, but Liz couldn't hear anything. They all danced until sweat dotted their foreheads, alcohol coursed through their veins, and their legs and lungs burned.

As the evening came to the apex, champagne began to be passed out among the attendees and everyone cheered the countdown to midnight as they watched the ball drop in Times Square.

10, 9, 8 . . .

Hayden grabbed Liz around her waist and they raised their champagne flutes high.

7, 6, 5 . . .

Jamie sloshed half of her glass on the floor, but just laughed hysterically and leaned into James. He was sober and practically holding her upright.

4, 3, 2 . . .

Meredith was already making out with her model guy, their champagne nowhere in sight.

1 . . .

The entire ballroom erupted with applause, and balloons rained down on them from all directions. Liz released the laugh that bubbled up inside of her as the ball hit the bottom, ringing in the New Year. Hayden bent down and lowered his lips to hers. Their earlier discussion lost from her mind, she reveled in the feel of his lips on hers, knowing it was the very first thing she would remember about this year.

"Happy New Year, Lizzie," he whispered, resting his forehead against hers.

"Happy New Year, Hayden."

Chapter 4
VISION

Everyone except James awoke with a hangover from hell. Apparently mixing champagne, vodka, and tequila was not a good idea. Ever.

Liz was glad that she didn't have to do anything but lounge around in the spare bedroom with Hayden until the art opening. Jamie was running around the house like a chicken with her head cut off, despite the constant expletives about how terrible she felt. James just followed behind her, helping where he could, and chuckling softly under his breath, reminding her that he had told her not to drink so much.

Hayden channel surfed, stopping every few stations to see what was playing. His other arm was wrapped around Liz's waist, and she leaned into his chest, watching the shows flash by. It was nice to just nurse her headache with his body pressed against hers.

He finally stopped on a news network and tossed the remote onto the nightstand. Liz stared forward indifferently. She hadn't been paying attention to the news since she was on break. It had been a reprieve from her day job. She loved journalism and couldn't wait to start her career as a reporter, but sometimes it was nice to forget that anything else existed in the world.

Hayden kissed the top of her hair and stroked it back with his hand. She sighed, wishing she could have done this all break, minus the hangover, of course.

As the media recapped some of the biggest New Year's Eve parties and the gorgeous gowns, images of politicians and their dates flashed before her on the television screen. Most of the men were in plain black tuxes, but the women's gowns definitely stole the show. Some of the older wives were drab and boring, but others looked runway ready.

And then he appeared on the screen. Her heart plummeted. She didn't care how ridiculous it was, but she couldn't seem to avoid Brady Maxwell. Even here, when she was safely wrapped up in Hayden's arms, Brady was showcased on the news. Standing next to him was a diminutive brunette sheathed in layers of emerald-green silk that only accented her tan skin. They said the creation was a three-thousand-dollar Oscar de la Renta dress—one of the best they had seen all night.

As quickly as Brady was there, he was gone. The girl hardly mattered. Liz was sure it was just another one of the women Heather used for his public appearances. But he'd looked so . . . happy. It was wrong for her to be sad about that. She was dating Hayden, and they'd had a good time last night, but still she couldn't shake the feeling.

Liz rolled away from Hayden and off the bed. "I'll be right back."

"Hey," he said, reaching out and grabbing her hand. She turned back to face him. "Hurry back."

She smiled softly and nodded. "Just using the restroom."

He released her reluctantly, and she scurried down the hall and into the bathroom. She shut the door and locked it before sinking helplessly to the floor. Tears sprang to her eyes fast and hot. A sob racked her chest and she slapped her hand over her mouth.

No.

No. No. No. No. No.

She would not cry over Brady. She would not.

No matter how many times she had told herself all semester that she wouldn't cry over Brady Maxwell, the man still brought her to tears.

It had been months. They were long over. Brady probably didn't even think about her anymore. And yet the thought of walking away from him still made her feel like someone was repeatedly beating the shit out of her.

She had made the right choice. Brady hadn't been willing to give her what she needed, because she couldn't continue with their relationship as a secret and he wouldn't budge on that. So she refused to let him choose between her and the campaign, and made the choice for him. Now she knew that Hayden was the right choice. He was sensible, attentive, handsome, caring, and he would never hide her. He was as fucking perfect as Victoria described him.

But still . . . he wasn't Brady.

Liz cringed just thinking that thought, but it was the truth. In some ways that was a good thing. She couldn't ever see Hayden bringing her to gut-wrenching tears, but Brady was only capable of that because he elicited such strong emotions from her.

That only made the tears come harder.

Why couldn't she just be rid of Brady? Why did he have to keep popping up everywhere? She wanted him to plague someone else's life, because she couldn't keep going with her heart perpetually shredded.

She knew that she had been in the bathroom too long, but she couldn't leave without composing herself. Taking a deep breath, she flushed the toilet even though she hadn't used it and then turned the faucet on. She splashed her face a couple times and hoped the red splotches disappeared before Hayden saw her. There wasn't much more she could do without makeup.

Praying that Hayden wouldn't say anything, but knowing he likely would, Liz left the bathroom and returned to the bedroom. As she expected, he arched an eyebrow when she entered the room and he saw her puffy face, eyes red-rimmed from tears.

"Are you okay?" he asked, pushing himself out of bed and standing hastily.

"Yeah. I'm okay." She didn't want to lie to him, but she couldn't tell him the truth. Not yet. He couldn't know about Brady. What would he think about her? What would he think about both of them?

She already knew that he didn't like Brady. He had confessed that he had voted for his opponent in both the primary and the election. Their joke about Brady being "our politician" was only because that had been her first press conference.

No, she couldn't tell him. It was still too fresh. Plus, Brady had just won. He wasn't even inducted into Congress yet. She couldn't risk news of their relationship getting out. Any scandal was a problem for a politician, but one with a reporter seven years younger who wrote negative articles about him . . . ? She could just see their relationship plastered on headlines and following him around the rest of his career. Not to mention it killed her credibility as a journalist, risking her job as much as his.

"You look like you've been crying," Hayden said.

"I just don't feel well." There. That was the truth. "Hangover."

Hayden's lips tugged down at the corner. "Do you need me to get you some medicine?"

"Nah. I think I'm just going to lie back down," she said, walking to the bed. "Come lie with me?"

Maybe it was wrong to take comfort in Hayden's arms, but she wouldn't find comfort anywhere else.

———

A couple hours later, Liz walked into Jamie's art expo. Her hangover had finally subsided and she had changed into a burgundy strapless dress that hugged her curves, paired with a black cardigan and the same heels from last night.

Liz had never been to an art exhibition before, so she only had a vague idea of what to expect. She assumed the gallery would look sort of like a museum, with high ceilings and winding hallways that led to different exhibits. She didn't think she would quite *get* what the artist was trying to convey. But then again, she didn't always get Jamie either.

Her vision wasn't too far off. The room was stark white, with three walls dividing the paintings into the different types of work Jamie was showcasing. Refreshments were set up next to a bar, and a small line had already formed. Everyone was drinking wine or champagne, nothing hard, and certainly not beer. Most of the people in attendance were in suits and nice dresses. Liz was glad she had gone with her burgundy dress.

"Let's tell Jamie we're here," Hayden whispered.

Jamie had left for the showcase over an hour before them to prepare. Liz wondered if it was just jitters.

"Liz! Hayden!" Jamie cried as soon as they made it through her welcome line. "It's so good to see you!"

The best part about Hayden's sister was that she was completely and entirely genuine. It didn't matter that they were staying at her apartment and she had seen them an hour ago, Jamie was just as excited to have them here. Maybe even more excited, since this really meant something to her.

"I wouldn't miss it for the world," Liz told her.

"Feel free to mingle around. I have so many new pieces that you haven't seen," Jamie told them.

"My sister, the artist," Hayden said with a shake of his head.

"Don't listen to Hayden when you go through the displays," Jamie said, smacking him on the arm. "He doesn't appreciate art. He once told me it all looked the same. How exactly can a portrait and a landscape look the same?"

Liz chuckled softy. That sounded like the Hayden she knew. He was so . . . square. Everything had a place and an order. His world was ruled by that. Art was ruled by no one, and it explained why he didn't understand it.

"I'll just get us some alcohol to dull the pain of staring at Jamie's vision of the world on every wall," Hayden joked. "Go ahead and look around." He kissed her cheek before giving his sister a bemused look and walking over to the bar.

"Don't listen to his condescension any more than I do," Jamie said in an incredibly upbeat tone. "We've been having these discussions since we were kids and he preferred to count blocks while I liked to finger paint the ones he was using and call it art."

"I can totally see that happening," Liz said, covering her mouth with her hand to try to hold back the laughter bubbling up in her.

"Now go! Go have a good time. I'll see you later," Jamie said, ushering her into the exhibit.

Liz followed the crowd into the first room and a huge smile broke out on her face. In a way, Hayden was right: Jamie's vision of the world was artfully reflected back to them in every single picture. She was such an exhilarating person to be around. So different from her brother, yet they were more similar than either would admit. Both could hold an audience with just a smile, and wow a crowd with their unique abilities.

She wanted to see the other two rooms before taking a closer look, so she squeezed past the crowd and into the next section. Liz couldn't pretend to know much about art, but she did know that these paintings were beautiful.

Jamie used color and light to create the tone and mood in her paintings. Some were landscapes, others portraits; but each one of them was more awe-inspiring than the next, until Liz found that she couldn't even compare the splendor of one to another. Liz could write, and the written word could move people to tears or cause them to go to war. But if a picture was worth a thousand words, than Jamie's were worth ten times that. No wonder she was being thrust into such prominent circles.

As she walked into the last room, what struck Liz wasn't the brilliant paintings, though they certainly were incredible, but rather the person standing at the center of the room. She had met the woman only once, but she had made an impression that Liz would surely never forget. From her perfectly coifed platinum-blond hair, to the diamonds in her ears and around her throat, to the excessively expensive dress on her fragile frame, there was no doubt in Liz's mind that she was staring at Clay Maxwell's girlfriend, Andrea.

Liz had met her briefly at Hilton Head while staying at a resort on the coast right before Brady's primary victory. She had left the resort only long enough to get lunch and had run smack-dab into Brady's younger brother.

If Andrea was here, did that mean that Clay would be here? They had first met over the Fourth of July weekend, when he had helped her during her panic attack over Brady—though he hadn't known the cause—and then he had tried to take her home at Brady's gala event later that same summer. His charming cocky personality and incredible good looks made him both appealing and irritating. Liz's heart fluttered, and she wasn't sure if it was his connection to Brady or fear of him being in the same vicinity as Hayden, who knew nothing about Brady.

But when she turned to flee, because the thought of encountering Andrea ever again made her a bit nauseous, she ran right into Clay. And Christ, he looked handsome. She was sure her imagination had contrived how attractive he was, but no, definitely not. If anything, she hadn't done him justice. He wore a navy-blue suit coat, khaki pants, and a blue button-down that made his baby blues pop. His blond hair was styled, and man, those dimples when he smiled. The waves of arrogance that radiated off of him sure knocked him down a few pegs, though.

"Liz Carmichael," Clay drawled.

Oh, shit! Sandy Carmichael had been the fake name that she had used with Brady when they had been hiding their relationship, and Clay was the only person who knew that Carmichael was associated with her, even if he had no idea what it referred to.

Liz sighed heavily, not even able to hold it in. "Clay Maxwell."

His smile only brightened. Was she smiling? No way. She wasn't happy to see him. He was just another reminder—

Liz stopped herself and focused on the present . . . like how to get far away from this situation.

"I haven't seen you in a long time," he said.

"If you missed me, Clay, you could have just called," she said with a nonchalant shrug. Clay had never used the number he had begged her for back at Brady's fund-raising gala late last summer. For some reason, besides the blonde bimbo he called his girlfriend standing behind her, it wasn't a surprise.

Clay chuckled at her comment, and opened his mouth to say something, but she cut him off. Her last thought had made her painfully aware of exactly where she was. Andrea could come over any second, and Liz didn't want to deal with her. Not to mention Hayden could walk up. How was she supposed to explain all of this?

"We're in the way," Liz said, walking into a corner on the other side of a wall from Andrea. She didn't know what to do about Hayden, but she had to eliminate her problems one at a time.

"Already hauling me off to a corner alone."

Liz shook her head. "What are you doing here? I wouldn't have guessed that you were into art."

"Andrea's a big fan of the artist. She keeps buying her work," Clay said with a shrug. "What are *you* doing here? I haven't seen you since Hilton Head. I thought you were going to be my date for the primary after-party, but you never showed."

Liz swallowed hard. Shit. She could not handle this right now. Not after just seeing Brady on TV and having a mental breakdown in the bathroom. She needed to keep the banter light and move away from the topic of Brady. But then again, all they had ever talked about was Brady.

"You were probably there with your girlfriend anyway. Hardly matters." Clay opened his mouth for what Liz assumed was going to be another arrogant remark, but she kept going. "Anyway, I happen to know the artist. She's my boyfriend's sister."

"Ohhh," Clay said with that same knowing smirk. "Is that why I haven't seen you at any of Brady's events?"

"Something like that," she said noncommittally.

"Is the boyfriend here now?" he asked, his eyes searching the room for the prime suspect. "I'd love to meet the guy who is going to be knocking down my door after I take you home with me."

Liz bit her lip and laughed softly at Clay. It was strange to feel as if she had missed him and his antics, when she hadn't ever really spent all that much time with him. But staring into his handsome face, she realized that she definitely had missed him. It made her stomach clench and roll at the life she had given up.

"So full of yourself," she murmured.

"Oh, come on. You've been dying to get in my bed since the first time we met."

"The first time I met you I was having a panic attack."

Brady had just given a speech at a Fourth of July festival and Liz had suddenly realized how much he meant to her, how much the campaign meant to Brady, and that he had won her vote. The feeling had overwhelmed her and Clay had found her, though she hadn't known he was Brady's brother at the time.

"I did say you were dying," Clay said, reaching out for her hand. She took a step back, letting his hand just barely graze her before retreating out of arm's distance.

"You never cease to amaze me." Her tone was light. It wasn't as if she was actually angry that he was here. She just needed to get away before Hayden came looking for her.

"I've heard that before."

Liz rolled her eyes. As cocky as they came, and yet she still hadn't walked away.

"Well, I'll let you get back to your girlfriend," Liz said, the emphasis on *girlfriend*.

"Are you really going to turn me down again?" he asked, stepping closer to her once more.

"One day you'll get the hint."

"But not today," Clay said with a smirk.

"There you are, Lizzie," Hayden said from behind her.

Her face fell. She had been so close to leaving, but not close enough.

And the way Clay was looking at her just then spoke volumes. He knew that something was up, or at the very least that she didn't want to be seen with him. She could punch him for that smug look, and she just hoped he kept his goddamn mouth closed.

Hayden wrapped an arm around her shoulders and planted a kiss on her lips. Huh. Was he showing signs of jealousy? Oh, it was so cute on him.

"Who's your friend?" Hayden asked.

"This is Clay," Liz said.

Hayden stuck his hand out in introduction. "Nice to meet you. I'm Hayden Lane."

"Clay Maxwell," Clay said, shaking Hayden's hand firmly.

Hayden looked back and forth between Clay and Liz in surprise at the name. Liz bit her tongue. She would let him figure it out, and hope he didn't ask her questions later about how she personally knew Clay Maxwell.

"Maxwell. Like Senator Brady Maxwell's brother?"

"Ah. Representative Maxwell," Clay corrected.

Oh, so now he was going to defend his brother?

"Well, it's great to have you here," Hayden said, producing that smile that always won everyone over.

"Thanks. You're the brother of the artist, correct?"

"Yes, that's right. Jamie is wandering about here somewhere," Hayden said. He glanced around the room as if thinking about her would make her materialize before his eyes. And that was when it hit her: Hayden had stopped the jealous-boyfriend act as soon as he realized that Clay was potentially influential.

"I'm sure my girlfriend would love to meet her," Clay said.

"I'd be happy to introduce the two," Hayden responded.

And that was how Liz's night turned torturous. She could see written all over Clay's devious face that he was going to use the opportunity to stick close by.

They located Andrea, who didn't seem to remember Liz from that chance encounter on Hilton Head back in August. That was lucky. Then they went to find Jamie, who was incredibly excited to finally meet her favorite fan. Apparently they had been chatting back and forth between the curator of the gallery who had procured Jamie's artwork for Andrea.

Liz followed them around for another hour as Andrea gushed over Jamie's talent. Clay and Hayden spoke cordially about everything from the newspaper to Brady's election to Clay's experience at Yale to the weather. Liz interjected only when she thought that it was veering too close to talk of Brady, but Clay didn't know that she had been with Brady over the summer, so it wasn't like that could come up. It turned out by the end of the conversation that she had freaked out for nothing.

Andrea purchased ten of Jamie's paintings out of a single collection, and told Jamie that she would be a collector for life. Liz couldn't even think of ten walls in her house where she could hang artwork. Then again, Andrea had a trust fund, and was dating a man who would most certainly move on to become a very prominent attorney . . . she probably had a bigger house than the one Liz lived in.

Clay shook Hayden's hand as Andrea started for the door. Liz moved forward to say good-bye, but Clay pulled her aside. Hayden moved to talk to Jamie and didn't even object to his girlfriend being taken away. She figured Clay must have charmed him in a way that only the Maxwell men were capable of.

"So," Clay said as they walked slowly toward the exit.

"So," she repeated.

"He's in love with you."

"What?" Liz snapped. She hadn't been expecting that *at all*. Which was likely why he had said it.

"Yeah. I'll be in town the next two days. We should find time to meet up again."

Liz shook her head, still dazed from his assumption. "I'm not going to meet up with you. I know what that entails."

"But you don't love him," Clay said, turning to face Liz.

"We haven't been dating that long. Ugh! Why am I even justifying any of this to you?" she asked, turning to go.

"Hey. Don't be angry." He grabbed her elbow. "It really is good to see you."

"Still not going home with you, Clay."

He smiled in that way that made his dimples appear. "Next time then."

Liz rolled her eyes. "Good luck."

"I don't need luck," he said with a wink as he walked back toward Andrea.

Liz watched him walk out of the art exhibition. Her whole body trembled with the exertion of keeping herself together. Clay riled her up so easily, but she wouldn't let him get to her.

So she didn't love Hayden. She didn't have to love someone she had only been dating for two months. It didn't matter that she had fallen for Brady in a similar amount of time. She couldn't compare the two men. She needed to stop doing it. Right. Now.

"Hey," Hayden said, walking up behind her and whispering into her ear. She nearly jumped out of her skin and he just laughed. "Come with me."

"All right," she said, taking a deep breath and turning away from the exit.

"Thanks for introducing me to Clay. He seems like a good guy."

Liz held in her *hmph*.

"Jamie is freaking out about his girlfriend's purchase."

"That's good," she said. At least someone had gotten something out of the day's events.

"Will you just stand over here with Jamie for a minute?" Hayden asked.

"Why?"

Hayden smiled and wrapped his arms around her waist, drawing her into a hug. She breathed into him, feeling every ounce of what Clay had said washing over her.

Christ, he loves me.

"Just trust me," Hayden said softly. "I'll be back in a minute."

"Okay," she agreed.

Liz walked over and stood next to Jamie, who was chatting enthusiastically with Meredith about the event. Liz heard Andrea's name come up at least five times while she was waiting.

The room had cleared out already. Liz hadn't realized it was going to be such a short event, but apparently the exhibition stayed open for a couple months. The grand opening was just the initial preview. Jamie said that she had never sold more than one piece opening night. And besides Andrea's purchases, two other couples had each bought a painting from the collection. Jamie was stunned and excited that her work was finally gaining momentum, and she couldn't stop bouncing from foot to foot like a little fairy.

Hayden reappeared a couple minutes later with James, holding on to a nice bottle of champagne and some glasses. He popped it open and handed out the glasses. Jamie giggled the entire time, glowing radiantly from the celebration and forgetting how badly champagne had treated her the night before.

"I would like to propose a toast," James said, his hand shaking lightly as he held his flute out. Everyone followed his lead and raised their glasses into the air. "To my beautiful girlfriend . . . and her successful art exhibition. Just the start . . . to a long-lasting career for the . . . brilliant artist I have come to love."

Liz smiled at the glowing couple. James had had trouble getting some of the words out; he was practically stammering. It was the most adorable thing she had ever seen. He was so proud of her that he could barely even speak. Jamie let out an *aww* at his speech.

"To Jamie!" the group chorused, and they all tipped their champagne glasses in a toast.

"Y'all are too sweet," Jamie crooned.

James handed Hayden his glass of champagne and then sank to his knee right in the middle of the art exhibition. Jamie stared at him, shocked, and then looked around as if she couldn't believe what was going on.

"Jamie," James began softly, "I've loved you since the first day I met you. I have loved you every day since. And I want to love you every single day after that. Would you do me the honor of marrying me?" he asked, producing a black box from his pocket.

Jamie screamed at the top of her lungs and launched herself at him. Her glass toppled to the ground, discarded in her haste. It landed on the wood and shattered, but Jamie didn't give it a second glance. Her arms were wrapped around James's neck and he was struggling to stand as he laughed at her enthusiasm. Liz could see that through her excitement, Jamie's body was shaking with tears.

"Oh my God. Oh my God. Oh my God," Jamie said over and over again. "I can't believe this. Yes! I want to marry you. Yes!"

He laughed and kissed her full on the mouth.

Without even knowing it, Liz had moved closer to Hayden. He was looking straight at her and Liz just smiled. "You knew," she whispered.

He nodded. "Of course."

Liz watched as James plucked the ring out of the box and slid it onto Jamie's finger. Jamie jumped around in circles before thrusting her hand out to Meredith and then Liz in between squeals.

Liz couldn't think of a couple that she thought should be married more than Jamie and James. They just worked. They weren't rushing into things, and they weren't doing it for the wrong reasons. Liz could tell that it was going to really last. And she was so happy to have witnessed their moment, even if she had this strange feeling creeping through her . . . as if she couldn't imagine herself going through that anytime soon.

She shook that thought away. It was probably just residual jitters from Clay's comments. Who really knew whether they wanted to marry someone after only two months anyway?

Chapter 5

ALL THE WRONG REASONS

Thank you all so much! Next week we will be discussing the new digital age, so please be sure to read chapters six and seven in the textbook and the three articles assigned on the syllabus," Professor Mires yelled over the shuffling of students stuffing everything into their backpacks at the end of class. "Please remember to turn in your assignment here on my desk. I've graded last week's papers and they are sitting in alphabetical order over here." She placed a stack of papers, likely bleeding red ink, on the other side of the desk. School had started three weeks ago and this was already their third round of papers.

Liz closed her computer with a sigh. Professor Mires had recommended that she take her upper-level political journalism class in the spring after Liz had excelled in the news writing and editing prerequisites and then the special topics class she had taken over the summer. She had wanted to take the professor's class anyway, so it was an easy yes, but she wasn't quite prepared for how much extra time she would be spending.

Professor Mires had also engineered an extra three-hour course as a field credit to prepare for the political journalism colloquium that she and Liz were orchestrating at the university for the end of the semester. Plus Liz had research hours assisting the professor with the papers she was sending out for publication. Add aiding Massey with running the Washington division of the newspaper and Hayden's insistence on pushing for her to be editor, and it was no surprise that Liz was a bit overwhelmed.

The only thing that really bothered her was her slacking on tennis practice, but school and her career came first.

Liz pulled her paper out of her backpack and placed everything else back inside. She walked down to the front of the classroom and waited as everyone rifled through the stack of papers to claim theirs. She smiled at Professor Mires and handed in her draft.

The benefit of seeing her professor all the time was that sometimes she gave Liz ideas for what to write about or looked over the copy before she turned it in. A lot had changed since last summer, when Liz had been terrified of getting a C in her class.

"Thank you, Liz," Professor Mires said, taking the paper out of her hand. Her professor had dropped the formality of calling her Miss Dougherty once Liz started working for her, but Liz still couldn't get used to calling her Lynda. "Will you stay after so we can review the incoming submissions for the colloquium together?"

"Sure." She had been expecting that. Last semester they had put together panels, and the call for papers had gone out near the end of the semester. Professor Mires had also sent some personal invitations to prominent professors in the field, journalists at top newspapers and news broadcast venues, as well as some politicians. Since then they had been flooded with inquiries and responses to their call, and Liz had been tasked with sifting through the mountain of messages.

The rest of the class slowly filtered out, leaving only the papers of students who hadn't shown up. Liz's was sitting at the top, and she grabbed it, reading through the notes. She had received an A. From the looks of the students who had left before her, not many others had. Another benefit of taking Professor Mires's summer course.

Once everyone left, Liz followed the other woman back to her office. She took a seat across from the professor and waited as the computer booted up.

"That was great work this week," Professor Mires said.

"Thank you," Liz said cautiously. Those words normally came with a *but*.

"Do you feel challenged in my class?"

Oh boy! It wasn't that she didn't feel challenged, but she enjoyed the subject so much that it didn't feel so much like work.

"Um . . . yes?" she said, it coming out more like a question. "This is the subject I want to move into. I find it very interesting and valuable for my future."

"Good. Good," Professor Mires said absentmindedly as the computer brightened before her eyes. She took the distraction to filter through her emails and Liz just waited. "This colloquium is very important to me and to the university. It is truly part of my life's greatest work to be able to bring together my colleagues along with prominent journalists and politicians to foster more research and development, as well as the potential for great educational and networking opportunities for everyone involved. I want everyone to benefit from this, and I want you to participate."

Liz sat frozen. How could she participate more than she already was?

"I would love for you to present some of your own research at a special topics in undergraduate research in political journalism on Friday afternoon."

"Me?" Liz asked, excitement bubbling up in her chest.

Professor Mires looked back at her from behind her horn-rimmed librarian glasses with a smile. "Yes. I thought I would include your final research paper for the semester. Of course, that would mean it would be due a couple weeks early, but we could work with the preliminary drafts, if that suits you."

"That would be . . . wow," Liz said, speechless.

"I'll take that as a yes?"

"Yes! Absolutely."

Professor Mires's face brightened further. "Are you sure you're set on becoming a reporter? You would do wonderfully in graduate school."

Liz's head buzzed with the compliment. "I'm open to different options, but I've always wanted to be a journalist."

"Well, don't rule grad school out," she said with a nod of her head. "Now go on. That's all I wanted to talk about. You can respond to these emails tomorrow during your research hours."

Liz blew out a sigh of relief. She really just wanted to get home and see Hayden. Massey was covering the paper this afternoon, so Liz had the night off.

"Thank you again," Liz said, before darting out of the room.

When she left, she was walking on cloud nine, with a bounce in her step and everything. Liz took the stairs two at a time and pulled out her phone to text Victoria. She was supposed to meet with her after class to walk home, but she had forgotten to let her know she would be late. She jotted out the message to ask her to wait.

As she hit Send, her phone started ringing. Shit! Had she had that on loud all class?

Then Liz noticed the name flashing on the screen. Justin. That wasn't a name she had seen in a while. After he had gotten a DUI last summer, lost his scholarship, and left the school, no one had really heard much from him except to know that he was taking a semester off to "get his life back together." Sometimes he didn't even return the messages she left for him, which was why she wasn't expecting him to call back now.

"Justin, hey! How have you been?" Liz asked.

"Hey, Liz. Not too bad actually. Yourself?"

"Good. Professor Mires is working me into the ground and Hayden wants me to be editor-in-chief next year, but you know, nothing big."

Justin laughed. "You still dating Lane?"

She hadn't heard from Justin in weeks. "Yeah. We're still together. What's up?"

"I'm coming into town for work in a couple weeks. Do you want to catch lunch next Friday?"

"Sure," she said immediately.

Liz's classes were over early on Friday, but she usually had plans with Hayden. No biggie. He wouldn't care if she rescheduled. She almost laughed at the thought. Only a couple months ago she had gotten out of a similar lunch with Justin at the thought that she might see Brady, and now she was dropping her lunch with Hayden with equal ease.

"Sounds good. Aren't you back in school? What has you traveling to Chapel Hill for work?"

"Yeah. So about that," Justin said. She could practically see him shrugging through the phone. "I got a job with a software company. I'll tell you all about it when I come into town."

"Just text me when you get here and we can figure out where to meet."

"Sounds good, Liz. Catch ya on the flip side."

"Bye, Justin," she said, trying to hold back an eye roll.

Liz dropped her phone into her purse and rounded the corner. Victoria was standing under the tree in the middle of the Pit, talking on her cell phone. She hadn't even noticed Liz walking directly toward her.

"No, seriously, you're ridiculous," Victoria said into her phone. "I am never going to do that."

"Hey," Liz said, waving at Victoria as she approached. Victoria still ignored her.

"You can try if you want." Victoria tapped her foot impatiently. "Yes, I might be amenable to that, but that doesn't mean I'm going to let you bring one of your friends in on this. If I'm having a threesome, I want some double penetration." Victoria glanced up then, smiled and waved. "Hey, Liz is finally here. I'll call you later." Victoria snapped her phone shut. "Ready to go? I've been waiting all fucking day for you."

"Trouble in paradise?" Liz asked.

Victoria shrugged. "I'm giving Daniel a hard time. He wants to threesome with some other chick, which I'm down for, but not one of his friends. Ew. Gross. Let me find the chick if it *has* to be a chick. You know?"

"I just can't believe you are still dating the Duke Fan," Liz said the name with disdain, "let alone sleeping with him."

"Oh, lay off. He's not that bad. And anyway, at least I'm sleeping with someone. How come you haven't fucked Mr. Perfect yet?"

Liz shrugged. "Not ready." How many times had they had this conversation? Victoria didn't want details if she did sleep with Hayden. She just wanted it to happen already so that she could tease Liz.

"It's been a couple months. It's kind of weird. You're not going to fucking save yourself for marriage or anything, are you? I might disown you."

"Oh my God, no. I'm not saving myself. I just . . . I don't know. I'm not ready."

"How are you going to know when you're ready? When he puts his dick inside of you and you don't tell him no?" Victoria asked. "I think you should just let him fuck you and then you'll know if you were ready or not."

"That does not make *any* sense. At all, Vic."

"Try it out and then it'll make sense." She stopped midstride and gasped. "Oh my God, is he impotent?"

Liz rolled her eyes and picked up her pace. "I'm never talking to you again. We've ceased being friends."

Victoria laughed boisterously and jogged to catch up in her mile-high heels. "I'm fucking with you. Slow down. Slow down."

"You're a real bitch. You know that, right?"

"Class A act. The one and only."

"Class A tramp."

"I love you, Lizzie," Victoria said, trilling the name affectionately.

"I love you too, Vickie," she said, in the most annoying singsong voice she could muster.

They turned the corner onto their street with a relieved sigh from both of them. It wasn't a far walk, but in chilling temperatures and high heels, it sucked. Liz changed the topic and told Victoria about her conversation with Professor Mires. Victoria was happy for her, and even managed to hold in her sarcastic comments until the very end. Victoria knew how important this was to Liz, because Victoria's success was just as important to her in her genetic research laboratory. Both girls were on the right track to getting any job they wanted after graduation.

Once they finally made it to the house, Liz dropped her backpack in her room and quickly changed into a pair of jeans, a black tank top, and black sweater with her black riding boots. She was glad she had the night off to hang out with Hayden. It had been a while since they had just relaxed together. School was sucking the life right out of her, and he was loaded down with coursework, the newspaper, and applying to jobs at the same time.

"Heading over to Hayden's," Liz called out to Victoria.

"Tell Mr. Perfect I said hello and to fuck your brains out," Victoria yelled back.

She cringed. Liz had used the phrase with Brady the first time they were together. She did not want to think about Brady. It felt wrong to even think about them in the same sentence. But Victoria was kind of right. It had been a long time since she and Hayden had started dating, and why was she holding back anyway? She should want to be with Hayden like that. Maybe if things felt right tonight . . . maybe.

Rushing out the front door, Liz hopped into her car and drove the short distance to Hayden's house. His car was in the driveway, but his roommate, Kevin, was missing.

Liz parked behind Hayden, and then walked up to the front door. She knocked and then walked inside without waiting for him to answer. He was halfway to the door when she stepped across the threshold.

"Hey, gorgeous," Hayden said with a bright smile plastered on his face.

"Hey," she said, closing the door behind her.

She walked right up to him and wrapped her arms around his neck. He pulled her against him and dropped his lips to hers. Liz let him take over, feeling the energy of his kiss and losing herself in the electricity that passed between them. She let her mind wander to that moment at the Lincoln Memorial, how her body had reacted, how a part of her even then had wanted that kiss. She had wanted that kiss for a long time, and now that she had it, she let the tingles run up her spine and opened her mouth to him eagerly.

Their tongues met and massaged each other. His hands gripped the thick material of her sweater and pulled it up so he could feel her skin. She clutched the longer strands of his medium brown hair, not even thinking for a second of letting him go.

But slowly his kisses became pecks and he stepped back, laughing, as if he was surprised he had lost himself so completely in the moment. "I guess you missed me," he said, keeping a hold of her hand and walking her toward his bedroom.

"I think you missed me too." Her eyes darted to the outline of him now visible through his jeans.

He chuckled again and nodded. "I always miss you."

She walked into his room and kicked off her boots while he closed the door. "How was Professor Mires's class?" he asked, as he flipped on a side lamp.

Now was not the time for talking, but that was what made Hayden, Hayden. He was not an act-now-and-think-later, fly-by-the-seat-of-his-pants kind of guy. Normally she really liked that about him. It was definitely different from most guys, who thought with their dicks and wanted to talk only after they got it wet.

"Good. I got an A on my paper. After class she told me that she wants me to participate in the political journalism colloquium and include my research paper in the undergraduate research panel," she told him proudly.

Hayden broke into another huge smile. "That's awesome, Lizzie," he said, wrapping her in a hug.

Not an ounce of jealousy. If something similar had happened to him, Liz knew she would have been jealous. But Hayden wasn't like anyone else. He was genuinely happy for her.

"What a great opportunity for you."

"Yeah, she's trying to get me to go to grad school, I think. She told me she thinks I'd conduct great research."

Something did flash in his eyes that time. Anger? Frustration? Liz wasn't really sure.

"You'd give up being a reporter after working on the paper all this time?"

Oh. That.

"No. I wasn't planning to."

"I just . . . well, I wouldn't want to put in all of this time preparing you to be editor after I graduate if you're going to drop out of the paper after I leave."

After he leaves. She hadn't really thought about him leaving in a while. It didn't sit well with her. She didn't *want* him to leave.

"I have no intention of going to grad school if I can get a job as a reporter," she consoled him. "I just thought it was a nice compliment on my work."

"It is," he agreed.

She reached out and took his hand, stroking it gently with her thumb. "Don't talk about you leaving."

"What?" he asked, staring down at her pressed into his bed. She saw his eyes take in the position of her body in a sweeping motion, and then he adjusted the way he was sitting.

"I like you here," she told him. She had never really said anything like that to him before, but as soon as it was out of her mouth she knew it was true. She certainly wasn't ready for Hayden to get a job and move away.

"Well, I'm here right now," he said, leaning into the bed and letting their lips meet again.

She groaned deep in her throat as need took her where she hadn't been before. Hayden's weight shifted, and his body pressed down on top of her. Liz's hips swayed side to side enticingly. Her hands found his belt and tugged on it to bring him closer to her.

Her breathing grew ragged as their bodies moved in time together. Between her circle eights and his thrusts up toward her,

Liz felt like her clothes were going to melt off with the heat they built between them. His body kept up the rhythm in a way that made her eyes roll back at the thought of what he could do to her without the clothes on.

And in the dim lighting he seemed to be exploring her everywhere at once. His lips urged her to continue and his tongue made her body tighten in all the right places. His hand jerked in her hair and she felt her legs spread open to accommodate him further. She could feel his thickness pushing against her. His other hand had found the seam of her sweater and was pushing it out of the way. He unclasped her bra and immediately grabbed her breast, kneading it and then pinching her already hard nipples.

Fuck. She was fully clothed and so fucking turned on.

He released her for just a moment before stripping the sweater over her head. The tank top came next, and she didn't even let him bother with the bra; she just tossed it onto the ground. His head dropped down and he sucked on her nipples.

Liz felt her body coming undone at the seams. How had she ever thought she didn't want this? She had been building everything up in her mind for weeks and weeks: How could she give her body completely to someone she hadn't given everything else to? How could she move on?

But as her heart thudded in her heaving chest and her body arched toward Hayden's lips, her nipples demanding his attention, she couldn't imagine not wanting this with him. She was denying herself for what?

She couldn't comprehend the reasoning as waves crashed over her body.

She didn't want to think about anything but Hayden's lips moving farther south. The sound of a zipper made her clench involuntarily. She wanted him to touch her so badly. Her body was practically demanding it, aching for him. He dragged her jeans down her lean legs and pushed her thong aside as his thumb rubbed against her already sensitive clit.

Her body bucked under him, but he took the moan that left her lips as encouragement and licked against her slick folds.

"Oh fuck," Liz cried, her body already pulsing.

He slid a finger into her experimentally, and then another when she allowed it. She tightened all around him, imagining how good it would be in that moment to have his cock fill her. God, she was going to come already.

He started to move in and out of her while he licked and bit and sucked her clit until she was visibly shaking underneath him. She couldn't hold on. She was seeing spots in her vision. Her toes were curling and she was going from the tingly feeling to utter numbness as her whole body tried to take in the enormity of the orgasm pressing in on her on all sides.

Hayden forced her legs open wider with one hand as he continued to work. Gasps left her mouth in between the moans. Oh God, she couldn't hold on any longer. Whatever he was doing right there. Just like that. With his tongue.

Liz's head snapped back and her body pulsed wonderfully as a climax shot through her. Her body moved against his fingers, trying to keep them inside of her even as he slid out. And she just lay there breathing, exhausted and satisfied.

With a deep breath, Hayden rolled off of her before lying back down next to her. He kissed her forehead and pulled her into his bare chest. When had he lost his shirt? She didn't even care right then; she just wanted to curl up against him and pass out.

"Lizzie," he groaned, his breathing still uneven. "I don't want to push you . . ."

He was so used to her saying no that even though she had looked and acted completely willing to move forward, he was hesitant. He didn't want to push her away by pushing too hard. But he wanted her. It was all over his face.

And yet as dirty as she felt thinking about Brady in that moment, it all came back to her: the reason she hadn't moved forward. Brady. She was still hung up on Brady. She couldn't get him out of her head. She ducked into Hayden's chest and tried not to think about Brady, but the image of him only came to her stronger.

She wasn't ready.

Chapter 6
TRUST FOSTERS TRUST

*H*ey, gorgeous, are you out of class yet?

The text from Hayden flashed on her phone just as Liz was packing up. She shouldered her backpack and turned to leave. She was glad that she only had early classes on Friday.

Just got out.

Lunch? I'm starving, and I miss you.

Liz's smile quirked on her face. Ever since that night when she had lost herself in him, she had found something in her changing. Even though they had been dating for nearly four months now, she felt what she could only associate with honeymoon butterflies: when in that initial stage of a relationship, all you wanted to do was spend all your time with the other person, and the mere thought of them made you break into a smile . . . yeah, that was where she was at.

If Hayden noticed the subtle changes in her behavior, he didn't say anything, but he sure responded well to it. They still hadn't had sex, but she didn't have the same reluctance anymore. Now she had waited long enough that she just wanted the moment to be right. She didn't want to walk into his bedroom and be like, *Fuck me.* Though she couldn't see Hayden complaining about that either.

Yes. I need food. Where do you want to go?

Home . . .

Liz cracked a smile. Geez. She was giggly. She needed to work on that, but she knew she couldn't control it.

As she was typing out a response, another message came in, this one from Justin.

Hey, I just got into town. Sorry I'm late. Are we still meeting up today?

She had totally forgotten that Justin was coming in today. She had even forgotten to tell Hayden. She should probably call him to let him know.

Yeah. Top O?

Definitely.

Liz found Hayden's number in her phone and clicked Send. He answered immediately, "Hey. I'm just leaving the paper now. Where should I meet you?"

"Hey. About that . . ." she said awkwardly. She didn't know why she would even let this make her uncomfortable. It was just Justin. There had never been anything romantic between them. And it certainly wasn't like that now. Yet telling Hayden was making her a bit nervous.

She remembered telling Brady about Justin. He had gotten insanely jealous. Their relationship hadn't even developed past sex at that point, but his jealousy had still struck her even then. It had resurfaced later after she had told him that she had gone out with Hayden in D.C. Liz closed her eyes to push out the memories, but the argument they'd had about Hayden washed over her all at once.

It doesn't really matter! Didn't you hear me? He's not you! This isn't a competition, Brady. There's no room for jealousy.

No. She didn't want him in her head. He hadn't been there as much lately. She had buried him deep down inside of her where no one else could reach. It was the safest place for him. She hated the moments when life reminded her of him and fissures broke through her tough resolve.

Because the only thing I felt when he kissed me was that I was glad it was out in public. It wasn't Hayden I wanted. It was you. And if it's not you, then it doesn't matter.

If it's not you, then it doesn't matter. God . . . she forced her mind away from it. She thought about Hayden and filled the crack with memories of his smiling face, his gentle kisses, his attention and devotion and perfection.

It all happened in a matter of seconds, but it felt like an eternity before she finally responded.

"I, uh . . . totally forgot that Justin was coming into town today and that I was meeting him for lunch," Liz told Hayden. She waited for his judgment, his jealousy.

"Oh nice! I hope he's doing all right since the DUI incident last summer. God, that feels like forever ago, doesn't it?" Hayden asked.

Forever ago. Everything from the summer felt equally as if it had happened yesterday and a lifetime ago. But she could remember the whole summer in vivid detail that she was sure would never go away.

"Yeah," she agreed, because she didn't know what else to say. "He's doing a lot better. Working for a computer software company or something. I'm not really sure."

"Well, tell him I said hi. I don't know if he ever really liked me, but I appreciated the work he did for the paper when he was here."

Oh, Hayden. How could she ever think that he would be jealous? He was perpetually good-natured and saw the best in everyone. She appreciated that quality in him more than ever in that moment.

"I'll let him know," she said softly. She didn't want to be senti-mental right now, but it had a tendency to creep up on her. "I have to help Massey with some stuff at the paper before I can head home. Can I see you later?"

"Of course. Come over when you leave the paper. We can hang out then," he told her.

"That sounds perfect. Is the day over yet?"

Hayden laughed softly. "I wish."

"See you soon."

Liz hung up as she rounded the corner to the Top of the Hill, where she was meeting Justin for lunch. It was one of her favorite restaurants in town, with a large balcony overlooking the main city block downtown.

She took the stairs up to the top floor of the building. It was still too cold to sit out on the balcony, so Liz allowed the waitress to direct her to a table. She sipped her water as she waited.

It had been so long since she had seen Justin. She didn't really know what to expect. They had been friends since freshman year, but sometimes it was hard to be friends with Justin. Half arrogant brainiac, half douche frat boy made for a hard combination. But he was fiercely loyal and had never blamed her for the incident last summer, even though she carried part of the responsibility. She had been wasted at one of Justin's frat parties and he had offered to drive her home. Unfortunately he had been drunk himself, and after driving through a red light had been pulled over and given a DUI. It had lost him his scholarship and he'd had to leave school.

When Justin walked into the bar and saw her, she broke into a smile. God, she had missed him being around, and she hadn't really realized it until then. He had been a fixture in her life at UNC, working for the newspaper and taking classes with her since fresh-man year. She was glad to be reunited.

"Justin!" she said, barreling into him when he got closer.

He laughed and hugged her to him. "Good to see you, Liz."

"It's really good to see you too," she said, pulling away from him and regaining her seat.

Justin looked professional in a way he never had in college in what looked like a brand-new suit and tie. His hair was cut shorter and brushed off of his face. She couldn't see Justin wanting to be in a suit all the time. He was more of a khakis, polos, and boat shoes kind of guy.

The waitress appeared immediately, they ordered food and drinks, and then she disappeared just as quickly.

"You look great," Justin said, a smug look on his face.

Liz managed not to roll her eyes. What did he want? Justin didn't dole out compliments lightly. "Thanks. How is the new job?"

"A drag, but it pays well."

"Yeah?" She knew there was a hitch already. She just waited for him to let the other shoe drop. "What is the company exactly?"

"It's just a software company run by three guys. They wanted to make a program for students and teachers to install on their computers to live-stream from multiple locations on or off campus while still remaining interactive."

"Well, that sounds cool," she admitted.

"Yeah. I was selected online to do some testing for the program to make a few easy bucks. I took what they had redesigned and added a few key features of my own . . ."

"Wow. That's fantastic. I bet professors like it."

"They love it. Or at least, the three universities that have already purchased the software to try in their classrooms love it," Justin told her. "And I'm supposed to pitch it to UNC this afternoon. Kind of ironic, right? UNC dropout sells innovative software to university system." He chuckled to himself. "Anyway, that's not my endgame."

Their orders arrived, and Liz waited patiently for the waitress to leave again, digging her fork into her food. "So, what is your end-game?" she asked.

"I want to own my own company."

"What do you want to do when you work for yourself?"

"I'm working on creating some way to put in place a filtering mechanism on YouTube videos, so I could get past all of the stuff that people watch that isn't actually good and get straight to the good stuff. I designed the reviewing process myself, primarily to see how easy it was to find my own videos through it. I want to take it a step further and give it a social media component, form a central rating system, and then connect that to people's YouTube accounts."

"And you can do all of this? I seriously thought you were just a video expert," she asked, surprised by his genius.

Justin shook his head. "I was majoring in photojournalism because I was already a programmer. My dad's a programmer and I grew up on a computer."

"Well, I think you should go for it." She smiled back at him encouragingly.

"Will you help me?"

"Wh-what?" she stammered. What could he possibly want her help with? Sounded as if he had it all pretty much covered.

"I want to include a blogging component to the site and I need a writer. You and I both know I'm not that good with writing. I can't express my ideas like you can. I know how much influence your pieces have in the paper, and I know you get A's in all of your writing classes. I need someone that I trust to help, to keep people interested, to feed the buzz."

He wanted her to help him with the start-up company he hadn't even started? She didn't know when she would ever find time for that amid her busy schedule.

"I . . . I don't know," she said.

"Come on. You're perfect. And I trust you," he said earnestly.

"Justin, I appreciate you considering me for this, but I'm swamped at school. There's no way I could dedicate the amount of time you would need for this kind of project."

"It wouldn't be that much to begin with."

"Next year I'll be editor." The words thrilled her when they left her mouth. She hadn't said that out loud yet, and it felt right. "I'll have my internship for the Morehead scholarship. It's too much . . ."

"Just think about it. There's plenty of time."

"All right, but I don't think it's going to happen." She didn't like turning him down when he seemed so set on the course of action, but she didn't think she could make it work.

The topic shifted away from Justin's new projects as they finished their meal, but her mind was running a thousand miles a minute. She wished she had more time.

Justin picked up the tab even when she insisted that they split it. He just laughed and paid with a business credit card. They walked out together and he offered to drop her off at the paper, which she declined. It was a short distance, and he had to prepare for his meeting with the university.

She reached the newspaper without remembering anything about the walk. Massey had already left for the day, but Savannah was still milling around the office. Liz waved as she plopped down into the seat across from her.

"Lost in thought?" Savannah mused, typing away at her computer.

"Yeah. Just thinking about something I was talking to a friend about," Liz told her. "Did Massey get through the reports for Monday?"

Savannah laughed. "Hardly. I don't even want to look at the inbox."

"Great," Liz said, as she began working.

People filtered in and out of the office throughout the remainder of the afternoon, but Savannah was a constant presence, sneaking downstairs to get coffee and commiserating about the amount of work left over. Someone turned the television on at some point, but Liz didn't even bother to pay attention to it. She dissected news venues daily in her classes.

But Brady Maxwell's voice snapped her straight to attention. God, how long had it been since she had heard his voice? It had been blissfully quiet up until his induction into Congress at the end of January, and she had managed to avoid him entirely by keeping her TV turned off.

Her eyes followed his chiseled features, those dark brown eyes, the curve of his smile, and the assurance in his black suit, crisp button-down, and blue tie. He was without a doubt the most attractive man she had ever laid eyes on, and she couldn't stop staring. She swam in a mist of emotion that clouded her brain, keeping her rooted to the present, but still trapped in his penetrating stare . . . as if he could see her right now.

Then he was gone, his speech over, and the news outlet flashed a series of pictures of him with the same girl over and over and over. The same skinny brunette she had seen in the green gown on New Year's Eve. He wasn't pictured with anyone else.

Her heart stopped beating. Who was this girl?

Brady's press secretary, Heather, appeared next, standing on a stage, answering questions to a press room in D.C. The clip only showed one question, though.

"Ms. Ferrington, can you comment on Representative Maxwell's bachelor status? He has appeared several times with the same woman, and as we all know, it's not common for the Congressman to stick to just one."

The crowd laughed lightly, but Liz just cringed.

Heather smiled. She had been prepped for the question, no doubt. "Representative Maxwell has no comment but to say that whatever relationship he has with Miss Erin Edwards is business of his own, and he would prefer to keep his personal life personal, ladies and gentlemen."

Liz felt as if her eyes might pop out of their sockets. That was perfectly planned—a stunt by the campaign to spotlight his new relationship. Was it just a ploy, though? It didn't sound like Brady, but Christ, what did she know about Brady Maxwell?

All she knew was the name that was going to be on everyone's lips from here on out: Erin Edwards.

Chapter 7
CONFLICT OF INTEREST

Earth to Liz. Earth to Liz," Savannah said a moment later, waving her hand in front of Liz's face. "Are you alive in there?"

"What? Oh, yeah, sorry. Zoned out, I guess," Liz muttered.

"Happens. I was just about to get out of here. Are you finished?" Savannah walked back to her desk and grabbed her purse.

Liz stared at her computer blankly. Well, she wasn't going to get any work done now. "Yeah, I suppose I am."

She started packing her bag up while her mind worked overtime. Who the hell was Erin Edwards? The girl could be a stunt, but Brady had said that he wouldn't ever let Heather go that far. She couldn't pick someone for him to date . . . for him to marry. He agreed to be set up for events out of convenience, but that was where he drew the line. How had they met? Did he still think about Liz?

No, it clearly didn't matter.

"Is he dating that girl?" Liz blurted out before she could stop herself.

Savannah turned back to face her. Her face was a mask in indifference, and if Liz hadn't worked with her every day for the past seven months, she wouldn't have known the other girl was uncomfortable with the question. Liz knew Savannah didn't like to talk about her family, but she needed someone to tell her whether what they were showing on the news was a false trail . . . or if Brady really had moved on.

"Liz . . . you know I can't talk about it. It's a conflict of interest if I tell you and then you write about it. Sorry."

"No, I know," Liz said. She sighed and looked away, hoping Savannah didn't notice the heat rising in her face. "I wasn't planning to write about it. I mean, no offense, but right now he's old news, with the campaign being over and him a freshman congressman. I was merely curious."

Damn. How had she kept her tone neutral? Brady Maxwell was never old news. He was so hot that she could put him in any paper and make people read about him, but she didn't, because most of the time it just hurt too much. And really, he had just gotten into office, so there wasn't much to cover. Either way, she just hoped she could convince Savannah.

"None taken," Savannah said with a laugh that told Liz she was relaxing. "I will tell you, though, it's so weird having my dad and Brady in D.C. now. I always knew Brady would get there, but I'm not used to him being gone."

"Yeah, I bet that's hard," Liz said. Savannah's father was a sitting Senator in the U.S. Congress, and Brady had followed in his footsteps right into the House of Representatives. She knew they were all close.

"It is sometimes. I know you've heard some of his speeches about not wanting to leave North Carolina, and that's not him spitting bullshit. He really did want to stick close. He made sure to still spend time with me, especially after Clay left," Savannah told her.

"That's sweet of him," Liz managed. She and Savannah had never talked directly about Brady since that first conversation, when Savannah had made it clear that she knew Liz did not agree with Brady's politics. She hadn't wanted to be judged on her brother or by Liz's political beliefs.

Little did she know.

Savannah shrugged and then nodded. "That's Brady."

Yes, it most certainly was.

They both turned to exit the newspaper together, but just before they reached the double doors of the mostly empty office, Liz stopped Savannah short. "Savannah, I don't want you to think that I was digging for material back there or anything. It was just my own curiosity."

Oh man, she was going to go all out, wasn't she?

"And I know what my articles said about him last summer," Liz said. She couldn't believe she was about to do this. "But I changed my mind."

"What do you mean?"

"I was wrong about him and his behavior, and I ended up voting for him in the election."

"You did?" Savannah asked, surprised. "I didn't know that."

"I didn't really talk about it with anyone. It's kind of a personal thing."

"Wow. That's . . . unexpected." She broke into a big smile. "I don't know why, but I feel like a huge weight just lifted off my shoulders. Is that weird?"

Liz laughed and shook her head. "No."

"It feels weird."

"Well, I'm still glad I told you."

"Me too."

"Just don't tell anyone. I'd hate to ruin my reputation as a hard-ass," Liz joked.

"My lips are sealed," Savannah told her, pushing through the double doors.

They walked down the stairs and out to the main lobby. The building looked like a ghost town. Liz rarely saw the Union look so deserted. She knew there was an away basketball game just a town over today, and it was a Friday, but it seemed exceptionally quiet. She walked outside with Savannah and realized why.

It was snowing.

Walking back from her meeting with Justin, she certainly hadn't thought it was cold enough for *snow*. It only snowed in Chapel Hill once or twice a year, and it was never anything dramatic. But for someone who grew up in Tampa and never saw snow, it looked like a blizzard.

Savannah giggled next to her and held her hand out, catching a few flakes on her palm. They immediately dissolved into water droplets and her smile just grew.

"Come on. Let's go catch some!" she said, pulling Liz toward the Pit, where a cluster of other students were milling around and staring up at the sky.

"Um . . . snow and I do not get along," Liz told her. She was already shivering with the cold sinking into her clothes. She hadn't even brought a waterproof jacket and she was in heels, as usual. This was not going to be a fun walk home.

"Why would you wear heels today?" Savannah asked.

"I don't know. I didn't look at the weather."

"Well, we're supposed to get six inches by tonight, and then it's supposed to ice over. Of course, this only ever happens on the weekend."

Liz shuddered. Last winter there had been less than six inches of snow in Chapel Hill and they had closed school for three days, because the roads were impassable. It was a huge problem when the town only had a handful of snowplows.

"Of course, and now I have to walk home in this," Liz groaned.

"Do you want me to give you a ride?" Savannah offered. "I have a parking spot on campus, and the roads won't be bad for a couple hours."

"Oh my God, I would love you forever!"

"It's kind of a walk, but I was just happy I got one," Savannah said, setting off across campus.

Then the thought caught up with her. "Wait, you're a freshman. How *did* you get a parking spot?"

She wasn't sure why she even asked. It was pretty obvious. Savannah had an influential family, so she probably got whatever she wanted. Just like Brady. Ugh! Liz didn't even want to think about him or Erin Edwards right now.

"Um . . . the chancellor and my father are old friends."

"Ah . . ."

Liz wasn't going to argue with their favoritism today. Today she was just glad that she didn't have to walk home.

They reached the parking deck and Savannah located her small black BMW. Liz tried not to sigh. She wasn't surprised that Savannah had one. Brady had a brand-new Lexus. She assumed Clay drove a sports car; it just felt like Clay.

God, why could she not escape Brady? She was surrounded by his family and he was constantly on the news. Just when she was moving past what had happened, he cropped right back up. And she just fucking wanted to know if he was dating that girl. She didn't even care how stupid it was. It made her want to dial his number and demand to know . . . even though she knew she never could.

Liz didn't live too far away. It would have been a bad walk, but it was an easy drive. The snow was coming down harder when Savannah pulled up in front of Liz's house.

"Thanks a lot," Liz told her.

"Anytime. Hopefully this sticks and we don't have school next week, but otherwise I'll see you on Monday."

Liz popped the door open and turned to go, but thought better of it. "I hope you don't think that I'd actually publish anything you tell me, Savannah. I take my job seriously, and unless you're telling me something because you want it in the paper, it would never end up there."

"Yeah. I know. I guess I just clam up when people ask me about my family. I've done it my whole life. It's hard to rewire," Savannah told her. "And it's stupid, really, I mean, why should it matter who Brady is dating?"

Liz could have hugged Savannah Maxwell, if she weren't so pissed at Brady at the mention of the word *dating*. She just tried to keep that feeling under wraps. "He's in the public eye. I think a lot of people feel like they have the right to know his business."

"Yeah, I think a lot more people want to know than really should know. It'll all come out eventually. It always does, but it's not even an interesting story. I mean, Brady was in the North Carolina legislature with her father. They met up at Christmas and started dating. Kind of boring, really."

Liz froze in place. She didn't care that the car door was still open and her right side was freezing cold from the snow. And she didn't care that she was staring at Savannah. She knew that she shouldn't care that Brady was dating someone, or that Erin was from a political family and she would make Brady look good, or anything about it at all.

She was happy with Hayden. Things were going well with their relationship. Brady shouldn't have even been a thought.

Liz took a deep breath, trying to recover. "I'm sure journalists will find a way to make it interesting."

Savannah laughed. "Yeah, that's kind of our job, right?"

"Yeah, it is," Liz said.

"I just feel a little bad for him. All the girls that the media claimed he was dating during the election being held over his head, and then starting his new job in Congress all at the same time as he starts a new relationship."

Relationship. That word felt like a knife wound.

"That must be tough," Liz said, not able to keep the bite out of her voice.

Yes. It must be soooo difficult to have a new dream job and a new dream girlfriend. Liz couldn't imagine how he would ever survive.

"Thanks for the ride again, Savannah," she said quickly. She could see Savannah trying to figure out why Liz was so pissy all of a sudden.

"Sure," Savannah said softly as Liz hopped out of the car. She hoisted her bag on her shoulder and waved at Savannah before rushing for the door. She could not believe that she had almost lost her cool like that. It was so unprofessional. She didn't want anyone to know that she and Brady had been together, and then she had gone and snapped at Savannah when she had said he was dating someone else.

Of course, he had every right. He deserved to move on and be blissfully happy. *She* had left him, after all.

But it didn't keep her from being angry.

It certainly didn't keep her from feeling like an idiot for holding on to those feelings, forestalling her relationship with Hayden, and putting up a barricade at the thought of sex. Brady had moved on, so why shouldn't she? Why did she have to let him make her feel like this before she realized how stupid it was to hold on so fiercely to something that was long gone?

That thought pushing her forward, she quickly changed into warmer clothes and dashed back out to her car. She wanted to get to Hayden's before the snow closed in around her.

Liz arrived at Hayden's house fifteen minutes later. Traffic had been puttering along at twenty miles per hour, because Southern drivers were terrified of the snow. Someone had ended up in a ditch. She assumed that all of the grocery stores were out of water, bread, and milk, as if people thought they weren't ever leaving their houses again. Did these people normally not have shit in their houses? Were they afraid that snow would bring the zombie apocalypse? What the hell was wrong with them?

Suffice it to say, it did nothing for her bad mood.

"Oh my God, people can*not* drive!" Liz said as soon as she walked into Hayden's house.

"Hey, gorgeous!" Hayden rounded the corner with a big smile. "I made dinner."

Liz sighed in frustration. She shouldn't have been irritated that Hayden made dinner; it was just another part of his perfection. And when she looked at him, it did loosen some of the tension in her shoulders, but only marginally.

"Rough day?" he asked, seeing her frown.

She let every comeback she had to that die on her tongue. She was tired of thinking and overanalyzing every moment. She just wanted to get lost in emotion and sensation. Maybe some other time she could let her heart feel what her mind was telling her was stupid, but right now she just wanted to tamp it down and beat it into submission.

Without answering, she walked right up and pressed her lips to his. She wound her hands around his neck and reveled in the way their bodies melded together, the grip of his hands on her hips, the feel of his tongue massaging her own. It was too timid, too tentative. She wanted more, and she bit down on his bottom lip, sucking it between her teeth until she felt him urging her forward, asking for more.

"Bedroom," she growled in between kisses.

Hayden pulled back and looked at her with newfound interest. His eyes roamed her body, hungry yet questioning. She was sure he was wondering where all of this was coming from, but if he was smart he wouldn't open his mouth.

"Lizzie . . ."

"Now," she said. When he didn't move fast enough, she took his hand and directed him to the bedroom. He chuckled but followed behind her.

Hayden closed the door and she quickly started unbuttoning his shirt while she had him backed up against the wall. He let her slide the shirt to the ground and then she immediately reached for his belt buckle.

"Hey," he said, taking her hand. "Slow down a bit."

She shook her head and kissed him again, rocking him into the door. He grabbed her and pulled her backward. She practically launched herself at him, but he held her at arm's length.

"There's no rush. Kevin went home for the weekend. We have the house to ourselves." He turned her around and moved her toward the bed, which she promptly crawled on and pulled him toward her.

She didn't want to stop. She didn't want him to keep holding them back as she had been holding them back. She didn't want one more second to go by where she had to think about anything but him.

"Hayden," she groaned, when he sat down on the bed next to her. "Come here."

He leaned down and their lips locked all over again. Wrapping her arms around his shoulders, she tried to pull him down on top of her. She wanted to feel that passion and longing all over again . . . get lost in it. Why wouldn't he just let loose and give her what she wanted?

His hand trailed down her side and pushed against the material of her sweater. She helped him, eagerly yanking the material over her head. God, she wanted this. But as soon as the shirt dropped to the floor, Hayden sat straight and just stared at her.

"Hayden, please," she whispered, feeling vulnerable and exposed. He looked at her as if he knew exactly what she was thinking. He looked at her as if he so desperately wanted to continue, but that he knew something was wrong.

"Lizzie," he said softly then, stroking her wavy blond hair off of her face, "are you all right?"

"Yes, just kiss me," she demanded, her chest rising and falling heavily.

He placed a chaste kiss on her lips. "Are you sure you're okay? Are you sure you're ready?"

Liz bit her lip and closed her eyes. No. She wasn't sure of anything. Even her sanity was questionable at this point.

Was it so wrong to want to forget? She didn't understand why it all had to be so difficult. Brady had moved on. Why was she still struggling through this? It didn't make sense and she wanted it to stop. She just wanted it all to stop.

Tears streamed down her cheeks before she could keep them from coming. Her whole body shook uncontrollably. She crossed her arms over her chest, feeling even more exposed than ever before. Hayden shouldn't have to see her like this. He shouldn't have to see her break down over something she could never even tell him about. It wasn't fair to him. He was a good man. Perfect.

And she would never be perfect. She was just a woman still holding on to a man she had to give up, to a life she had to let go of, to a feeling that never seemed to leave her. Hayden deserved better than that. He deserved better than someone who had to hold back the truth just to keep going through her day. He deserved someone as perfect as himself.

He would never find that in Liz. He would only find a hollow vessel that had once given everything she had and then was left empty. He could fill in the cracks when she broke apart, but now, when she was completely wrecked, there was nothing he could do to fill the hole.

Then his arms came around her and pulled her sobbing body against his. He didn't ask a single question. He didn't try to tease out what was wrong with her. He just did the best possible thing he could do.

Hayden held her until her tears ran their course, and she fell into an exhausted slumber wrapped in his arms.

Chapter 8
SNOW DAY

Liz woke to an empty bed.

She stretched her fingers in all directions, a groan sticking in her throat as her body came to life. She was stiff everywhere from her cramped position in the bed, and her eyes burned from her tears.

But now that the tears were dried up, she felt . . . alive. Not healed. No, it was too early for that, but better. More like the wound had scabbed over; it was still tender, but she could go about her daily life again.

With a big sigh, she pushed the covers back and stepped out of the bed. Liz fumbled around in the dark for a lamp and then flicked it on. She dragged off her jeans from last night. When she found a pair of Hayden's sweatpants, she quickly shimmied into them and then pulled a track hoodie over her head.

She padded out of the bedroom, but stopped at the first window. Her jaw dropped open. It was a winter wonderland. The ground, the driveway, the trees, the bushes—everything in sight was covered in perfectly white snow. The sun was rising high on the horizon, making the world shine brightly before her eyes. Liz wondered if the temperatures would let the snow hang on or if it would melt away by the afternoon.

She found Hayden stoking a fire to life in the living room fireplace. He had his back to her, so he couldn't see the smile that appeared on her face when she found him still in track pants and a Dri-Fit long-sleeved T-shirt. His hair was damp, whether from the snow or from his early morning run, she wasn't sure. But her heart contracted at the sight of him.

How had she gotten so lucky? She had someone sitting right before her eyes who cared for her so deeply. He just wanted her to be happy, because she was the one who made him happy. It was as clear to her then as if a film had been removed from her vision.

She was ashamed of her actions from last night. It was wrong for her to push Hayden into something based on her own fucked-up feelings. Last night had *not* been the right time, and she was glad Hayden had stopped her, because she knew that she would have regretted it.

"Hey," she whispered, her voice slightly hoarse.

Hayden replaced the poker and closed the screen before turning around. "Hey. Are you feeling better?" He looked cautious and she hated that.

"Much. Thank you for letting me sleep in."

"No problem. I needed to go for a run anyway."

To clear his head. That much was obvious.

"About last night . . ." she began awkwardly.

She knew she needed to say something to clear the air. She didn't want him to be angry or confused, but she wasn't sure what she could say that would help besides the truth about Brady, and actually she was pretty sure that would make it worse. The joking about "their politician" aside, Hayden had never liked Brady. He had always agreed with her early assessment of him, even after she changed her mind.

"It's all right. You don't have to say anything."

She didn't? "Oh."

Hayden looked down at his hands and back up at her. "I'm not sure what happened last night. I wanted what you were offering . . . I still do, but I don't want you to do it because you felt pressured by anything. I'm happy just to hold you every night. All I know is that I never want to see you cry like that again over something like this."

He thought that she had been crying because she had felt pressured to move forward. Her mouth was hanging agape and she quickly closed it. Of course, the frustration of not having had sex with Hayden yet had been some of the drive, but most of it had been Brady fucking Maxwell. It was kind of ironic to think that thoughts of Brady had pressured her into sex with Hayden.

"Hayden," she said, shaking her head. God, it wasn't his fault. He shouldn't share the blame in this. "It's really my fault. Absolutely nothing to do with you. I was emotional last night and thought that sex was the right answer. I . . . God, I'm so sorry. I shouldn't have done that."

She wanted to cry at the absurdity of the whole thing, but her tears had been used up last night. She needed to be strong for Hayden where she wasn't before. She needed to realize how valuable he really was.

"It was stupid. *I* was stupid," Liz said, splaying her hands flat before her.

She didn't deserve him. It was something she knew in her gut, but she didn't care. It might be selfish, but she wasn't giving him up. This was the right relationship, the right direction for her life, and she had been so long looking over her shoulder that she hadn't seen what was right in front of her.

"You're not stupid." Hayden walked forward and placed his hands firmly on her arms. "Look at me." She did. "I would never date someone who was stupid. You're brilliant and funny and headstrong and unbelievably gorgeous. Certainly not stupid," he said soothingly.

Liz managed a smile as she stared up into his hazel eyes so filled with emotion. "You're pretty wonderful. You know that, right?"

"I guess that means you'll keep me?"

"I wasn't planning on letting you go."

"Good." Hayden's lips landed lightly on hers and she smiled into the kiss. The simplicity of being with Hayden compared to the complication of Brady was so starkly contrasting. Liz knew relationships were never easy. They took work, but with so few barriers barring her and Hayden's way, it didn't seem like work at all. The work was keeping Brady out, but after last night, Liz had a feeling things were going to get easier. It was over, long gone, and now he had found someone else.

The time had passed to get over it.

So she would.

They stayed like that until the chill started to seep into Liz and she forced Hayden to go take a shower. Then she curled up on the couch, snuggled in front of the fire, and promptly fell back asleep.

—

The smell of bacon woke Liz and she stared around groggily at the living room, forgetting for a moment how she had gotten there. When she reached the kitchen, Hayden greeted her with a kiss and a plate of food. Her stomach grumbled, reminding her that she hadn't eaten dinner last night.

Shit! And Hayden had cooked dinner. Bad girlfriend 101.

She made up for it by devouring everything on her plate and downing a full glass of orange juice. It seemed she was dehydrated, and she poured herself another.

"So, how much work do you have to do today?" Liz asked, sipping on her second glass.

"No work today. I checked the weather. It's supposed to snow again this afternoon and stick through Monday."

Liz's eyes opened wide. "No school Monday?"

Hayden laughed. "They won't announce until Sunday night at the earliest, but we're snowed in today. I think we should get dressed and go play."

"You want me to freeze my ass off in the snow?"

"I like your ass. You'd better not do anything to it."

"You're the one who wants me to risk it in the cold."

Hayden shook his head. "You really don't do well with cold, do you?"

"Not at all."

"We'll layer you up. You can wear some of my ski gear."

The exuberance on his face at the prospect of playing outside in the snow won her over. She wasn't a fan, but she was sure it would be better to be out there freezing with him than inside refusing him something he clearly enjoyed.

So Liz threw on layer after layer of clothing, several pairs of socks under her boots, and then Hayden added gloves, a scarf, and an oversize beanie. She felt ridiculous, but she was practically sweating inside, so maybe it would do in the cold.

They walked out the back door and were hit with a bitter wind. Liz shivered despite the layers.

"My nose is cold," she murmured under her breath.

Hayden heard and just laughed as he stomped out through the snow.

Liz surveyed Hayden's backyard. It was small, since it was just a college house that dead-ended into a wooded lot. The surrounding houses had fences built around their backyards, so Hayden's looked partially enclosed. Everything in sight had a layer of soft white snow on it. Hayden's footprints were the only things that marred the picturesque view.

"Hey," Hayden called.

When Liz turned toward him, she got a snowball right to her side. She grunted on impact and then gasped. "I can't believe you. Jerk!"

Another snowball hit her and she glared at him before reaching down to grab a fistful for herself. She chucked it his direction, missing him by a few feet, and he laughed at her.

"Come on. You can do better than that," he said, throwing another snowball at her.

She lobbed another misguided snowball his way and growled in frustration. "If I had a tennis racket, I would kick your ass," she yelled, stomping out through the snow toward him.

Liz managed to duck his next throw and scooped up a heap of snow, ran, and tossed all of it into his face. Hayden cried out and feverishly tried to brush the snow off of his skin. Some of it was ducking under his shirt and he hopped up and down as the cold slithered down his chest.

"You're going to get it for that," he said, wrapping his arms around her waist and pulling her in close.

Liz stood on her tiptoes and kissed his cold lips. "I'm already freezing because of you," she said softly.

"No, you're not. Forget about it. We still need to make a snow-man and snow angels and build an igloo."

"I am *not* building an igloo," she said with a shake of her head. "You're nuts." She turned to head back inside. No way could she stand the cold much longer. Her nose was already an ice cube and she hadn't even been out that long.

Hayden grabbed her arm and stopped her progression. "You can't leave already. At least help me with the snowman," he pleaded. His eyes were wide and almost green in the light. His cheeks and nose were flushed pink, and the corners of his mouth tugged up into a smile.

"How do you do that?" she asked.

"Do what?"

"Win."

"I always win," he said. "What did I win?"

"Where do we start on the snowman?" she grumbled.

The afternoon disappeared in the blink of an eye. One minute they were building a lopsided snowman with a pickle for a nose and Oreos for eyes, having a snowball fight, and finding enough extra space to create snow angels. The next minute Hayden was helping her peel off her wet outer layers of clothing while she desperately tried to bring feeling back into her fingers and toes.

Snow started to fall again as Liz snuggled up next to Hayden on the couch. The fire was roaring before them and each had a mug of hot chocolate cooling on the coffee table. They popped in a movie and Liz nestled deeper under the mountain of blankets they had dragged from the closet. Hayden stroked her hair softly and Liz fought sleep.

Despite what had happened last night and how awkward the morning had been, she felt content. She couldn't remember the last time she had been so happy and satisfied. She didn't need anything else in that moment but Hayden's arm wrapped around her while she was lying back against his chest.

She felt peaceful, as if all her concerns had momentarily vanished and she was awash with a newfound belief in her own relationship. She fit with Hayden as perfectly as she did in his arms. It all just made sense.

Hayden's lips found her ear and kissed softly down to her earlobe. He sucked it into his mouth and she breathed out heavily, her body instantly pushing back against his on the couch. His hand trailed lightly down her side as his mouth moved to kiss along the gentle curve of her neck.

Liz's heart picked up tempo quickly. The sleep she had been fighting to hold back disappeared entirely when his hand skimmed the front of her pants. Her body arched against him, urging him to continue. Taking her invitation, he delved beneath the material and slid his finger against the soft material of her thong. Liz swallowed hard, unable to keep her breathing under control. His finger brushed against her clit and she moaned in the back of her throat.

Ignoring the desperate bucking of her hips to get him to return to that spot, he ran his hand slowly up her right thigh and then the left. Her body arched against him. She was already turned on from his teasing kisses against her neck and the way he was moving his hands just out of reach.

Then he was there, slipping his finger under her thong and swiping it against her already wet lips. Fuck! How was she so turned on? She could feel the beginning of an orgasm already rippling through her body, but with those teasing touches, Hayden could hold her off as long as he kept it up.

He circled her sensitive area with his thumb and she dropped her head back. Her eyes closed of their own accord. All she could think about was how close she was. She wouldn't even need his tongue at this point. If he just put his fingers up in her, she would find the release she so desperately craved.

"Hayden," she murmured as he kept up the gentle swirling motion. "Fuck! I'm so close. Finger me."

He turned his head toward her and they started kissing just as he plunged two fingers deep inside of her. She gasped at the feel of him, and he used the opportunity to stick his tongue inside her mouth. They kissed as he started to move in and out while continuing to press her toward the edge. Her body shuddered from the pressure as a climax hit her and she clenched around his fingers.

"You're kind of hot when you tell me what to do," he whispered against her neck.

Liz smiled lazily and adjusted how she was sitting. Her ass rubbed against his dick and her breath caught. Shit! He wasn't kidding. He was rock-hard through his pants.

She rolled over to face him and started kissing him again. Her hand moved into his pants. She gripped his dick in her hand and he groaned her name. It was seductive—she really fucking liked the way he said *Lizzie*. She pumped her hand up and down a few times before brushing her thumb against the tip. He responded instantly, bucking against her hand.

Bending down, Liz started pulling his pants off his hips and down his legs. Then her mouth found the tip and she swished her tongue along the sensitive skin. She brought him all the way into her mouth and then started up a rhythm—in then out, swish, in and out. His body responded wonderfully to the way she pulled all the way back and then wrapped her lips around him until they met the base. He must have been really fucking turned on, because his body was already telling her that he was close.

"Lizzie," he said, stilling her where she sat.

She almost ignored him, but something in his voice made her pull back.

When their eyes met, he smiled with a knowing glint in his eye. Then he rolled her over on the couch until her body was pressed underneath. He pulled her pants down her legs so she was lying before him in just her underwear, and then started grinding against her.

Her legs came up immediately to wrap around his waist as he thrust forward against the thin material of her thong. She was soaking through from her earlier orgasm and all she could think about at this point was the way his dick was rubbing up against her.

"Hayden," she moaned, her eyes closing as the material shifted and he slid against bare skin. Oh God! She could not contain how badly she wanted him in that moment, and she didn't want to. Her fingers brushed at the side of her underwear. He seemed to understand her meaning. He yanked them to the floor, found a condom, and rolled it on.

She brought her hips back up to meet him, so ready to feel him. Her body was shaking with the anticipation.

He moved his cock down before her opening and she whimpered. Four months. She had waited four months. An interminable period of time. She wanted him to take her. She wanted to be his, mind, body, and soul.

His eyes met her for approval and she lifted her hips to meet him in response. Then he slid easily deep into her.

Hayden felt amazing. Perfect. Just as she had always expected him to. And the moment was right. Perfect. Just as she had always wanted it to be with him.

He started up a slow rhythm, feeling her walls expand to let him fill her and then pulling back out. Then he thrust back into her over and over and over again. She could feel her body crumbling, falling apart, giving in to Hayden's every movement. Her breathing was uneven and her mind blissfully empty, save for the passion and energy radiating from her and the need she felt for this man.

Liz met him for each stroke, but both of them were already so close. She could feel her body tightening around him each time, aching to let loose. She opened her mouth to tell him how close she was and then she exploded around him, her lower half pulsing around his cock. Hayden's entire body shuddered and then he came deep inside of her.

He dropped forward and rested his head on her shoulder. Neither one could even begin to try for coherent speech. All Liz could think about was how incredible that had felt.

She knew this changed everything.

But she was glad for the change. Finally glad for the change.

Chapter 9

Q&A

A month after the snow day, Liz sat in front of a crowded auditorium for the first-ever colloquium on political journalism at
UNC. Today was the big day that she and Professor Mires had been
working toward all year. A year of work culminated in one day of
activity, and all Liz could think about was the fact that she had to
give a speech. Her palms were sweating, her throat felt as if she had
swallowed a bottle of cotton balls, and her wavy blond hair was
sticking to the back of her neck. She hated public speaking. Hated
it. She always had.

That was part of the reason she wanted to be a reporter. She was
fantastic one-on-one or even in a crowd of reporters, and even better on paper. But she hadn't signed up to speak in front of a large
group of people and have them all stare at her. She had purposely
avoided broadcast journalism, because she would rather be behind
the camera than in front of it. How did people become so comfortable doing this?

She was about to present her research with Professor Mires to a roomful of distinguished professors in their fields, some prominent reporters for big newspapers, and who knew who else could be in attendance. She thought she might be sick.

Sure, she knew the education policy material like no other, and she had worked her ass off to make everything perfect, but she still felt like a really small fish here. It was a feeling that she didn't like.

"Okay. Let's get started," Professor Mires said, quieting the room. "Ladies and gentlemen, thank you so much for attending this panel in undergraduate research. I would like to start off this session with one of my own students, Miss Liz Dougherty. She will be presenting her paper, 'Education Policy and New Media in Political Journalism,' to you today. Take the floor, Liz."

"Thank you, Dr. Mires," Liz said. She stood demurely and smoothed out her knee-length cream pencil dress, which belted around the middle with a black buckle. She had taken off her matching black blazer, because the room was warm enough without her freaking out. Her black heels clicked across the hardwood floor as she took the stage. Her eyes roamed the room, but she took it all in in a haze.

Somehow she started speaking. The words tumbled out of her mouth in coherent sentences that made the people sitting in the room nod their heads along with her. A few older gentlemen in the middle stared stonily up at her and she quickly averted her gaze. She hoped they always looked pissed off and weren't angry about her presentation.

She had a fifteen-minute time slot, and when she reached the halfway point, Dr. Mires gave her a reassuring smile. It eased more of the tension off of her shoulders and she barreled forward. She could do this. She didn't want to do it every day or anything, but she was doing all right so far.

The door at the back of the room opened and Liz's eyes flicked up to the interruption in her speech.

Brady Maxwell walked into the room.

Her tongue tied, her face flushed, and she stood in front of everyone like a blubbering idiot. He closed the door quietly and stood in the back of the auditorium, his arms crossed, leaning against the back wall.

She couldn't believe he had come to *her* panel. She knew that he was going to be at the colloquium for a politicians' roundtable this afternoon, but she had expected him to attend his event and then be gone.

But no. Brady was currently in the room for her presentation. *Fuck.*

Her memory did not do justice to the man. Even at this distance she could see the contours of his face, the sleek three-piece suit, the confident attitude, those dark brown eyes. Okay . . . maybe she couldn't see those, but her imagination sure filled in the details.

What the hell had she been talking about before this?

Education policy. Right.

Liz broke eye contact with Brady across the room and looked down at the paper she was clutching in her hands with a death grip. She took a moment to collect herself. She knew Brady was watching her. She could feel his eyes all over her, and she felt vulnerable and exposed. How long in her dark times after walking away had she imagined him coming to find her and begging for her to come back? How many times had she thought about that beautiful face, reconstructing it in her mind? How many times had she wanted those eyes on her, assessing her, judging her, loving her?

No. Christ, she couldn't go there today. She couldn't love Brady today. She couldn't love him ever again. She had buried those feelings, buried them in that dark, dank place that she would never be able to access. A drum beat a fast rhythm in her chest as she tried to regain her bearings.

She just had to get through this presentation. Then she could freak out. She could hold it together until then.

Liz cleared her throat and looked back up at her audience. "As I was saying, our education policy as it stands needs to be revamped. Students are skimming by, learning only to take a test, not to think for themselves. Several studies have shown that previous generations performed better in college when the emphasis was on forward thinking and not test taking."

She went through the next few slides, detailing the work of political scientists and journalists who had looked at education policy more closely. Then she outlined her own findings and conclusions about the role of social media and how journalism could improve and refocus the political agenda.

"These changes, with the aid of political journalists in the field as well as the support of politicians, could create major improvements not just in secondary education, but on up through the university system."

Liz concluded her presentation and then took a seat. She felt like a towel that had just been wrung out.

Besides her mishap when Brady had walked into the room, she didn't think the presentation had gone poorly. But Brady hadn't taken his eyes off of her the entire time. In fact, she had felt like those chocolate-brown eyes that had once made her entire body warm with desire were drilling a hole straight through her body. And she was talking about education policy, of all things. She had always been passionate about it.

How many times had she argued with Brady about pushing aside education policies that could have benefited the university for some budgetary measure? And she had thought for a long time that he was favoring the donors he so heavily relied on . . . that he was doing this for money . . . that he just wanted to be in the spotlight. It was a sentiment she had never been able to understand, because she had never wanted those things for herself. But then over time she had realized how wrong she was about Brady.

Too late now. She had left. He was with someone else. She was with Hayden.

She didn't hear the next three presenters as each took up his or her own fifteen-minute slot. She knew what they were discussing because of her assistant work for the colloquium, but the words coming out of their mouths might as well have been gibberish. The only thing she could concentrate on was the person standing stoically in the back of the room.

"Thank you so much to all of the presenters," Professor Mires said as the last person finished. The crowd applauded and she waited for the room to quiet down before speaking again. "All the students have worked tremendously hard, and we appreciate the effort. Since we have a little extra time, I'd like to open up the floor for questions."

A few hands were raised and Dr. Mires called on people. Liz answered one or two questions, as did everyone else. Answering questions definitely wasn't as hard as giving her speech, though as a reporter she was used to firing them off.

Then she saw a hand rise in the back of the room and her heart stopped beating. What could Brady possibly have to ask? Was it even kosher for him to ask a question?

"Congressman Maxwell," Professor Mires called. She sounded surprised. Liz doubted she had been expecting a politician to ask a question.

All eyes turned to stare at him. If they were all as surprised as Dr. Mires was then they didn't show it.

"Yes, I have a question for Miss Dougherty," Brady said formally.

"By all means."

"As I'm a current member of the Education Committee in Congress," Brady began, his voice smooth and strong, "what would *you* personally say from your research is the most important factor for me to take back to D.C. regarding education?"

Liz's stomach dropped out. He was on the education committee? She hadn't been following his progression in Congress at all. She had been purposely avoiding it at all costs. She didn't want to know what he was up to and torture herself any more than she already was.

But what would a man who had balanced the budget in the North Carolina State Legislature, whose father was head of the budget committee in the Senate, be doing sitting on an education board? She knew that freshman Congressmen were placed wherever more senior members chose, but this was Brady. His father's name alone would have moved him up the ranks.

And it certainly wasn't his specialty. He hadn't even run on education reform. He worked in real estate, ran his family business, budgeted properties. He wasn't an educator in the slightest. So then . . . why was he working in education?

It made her want to run back to her computer and look up every single bill that he had been working on to find out what the hell he was up to.

But first she had to get through his scrutiny.

What would she tell Brady to take back to D.C.? Christ, what a question!

Oh, how a part of her wanted to spit back at him not to favor big donor money for budget reforms in place of education policy. Education was a positive speaking point, but it wasn't something a politician could run on. It didn't distinguish them. It didn't make them stand out . . . not like balancing a budget in the current fiduciary climate.

If only Congress would make education a priority instead of a backdrop, then they could begin to see improvements to the system.

But she couldn't say that to him. She couldn't throw words she had spoken to him last summer back in his face like this in public. She couldn't let her answer to the question be personal. Wasn't that what Dr. Mires had been trying to instill into Liz's work all last summer?

"Thank you for that question, Congressman Maxwell," Liz said formally.

They were staring at each other across the room, and she felt her cheeks heating. His face was a mask of indifference, and she was dying to know what he was thinking right now.

"I believe there are probably several answers to this question. Education policy, as you know, is multifaceted and should be addressed as such. So I believe that the strongest thing you should take back to D.C. would be to focus on policy that treats students as individuals. So often they are lost in the standardized tests and labeled as a number, a score; you lose the individual. Finding a way to treat education reform both systematically as well as on an individual level would be a step in the right direction, in my opinion."

Her voice wasn't even shaky when she finished. Because by the end it felt as if it were only she and Brady in the room and she was telling him all over again why this was important to her. The faintest of smiles crossed his gorgeous face before it fell away.

"Thank you, Miss Dougherty. I'll take that into consideration," he said formally.

And then as easily as he had walked into the room, he slipped back out. Liz was left reeling.

The panel concluded without fanfare and everyone filed out. Dr. Mires pulled Liz aside with a congratulatory pat on the back. She knew how much Liz disliked public speaking.

"I have some people I want you to meet," she said, directing her to the back of the room.

Two women and a man stood in a cluster with their heads ducked together, and Dr. Mires guided Liz straight to them.

"Lynda," a woman greeted Dr. Mires. She was a few inches shorter than Liz, with hair graying at the temples even though she didn't look that old. She had keen eyes and a sharp smile. She was someone who wasn't imposing until you caught a glimpse of those eyes, and then they cut you straight through.

"Nancy. It's so good to see you."

The two women greeted each other with a warm handshake.

"Bob. Susan," Professor Mires said, acknowledging the other two people. Bob was tall and lanky, with an air of importance to him that matched his black suit. Susan was the youngest of the bunch, no more than ten years older than Liz. She had short straight hair cut with sharp bangs and she tapped her foot incessantly. "This is my student Liz Dougherty. She's the one I've been telling you about."

Liz turned to look at Dr. Mires, slightly slack-jawed. She had been talking to people about her?

"Pleasure to meet you," Nancy said first, shaking hands just as warmly. "It's always good to meet one of Lynda's students."

"Pleasure is all mine," Liz said automatically, shaking hands with the others as well.

"Liz, Nancy is a senior editor for the *New York Times*. We went to college together at Columbia. Bob works for the *Washington Post*. You've spent, what, fifteen years reporting there?" Dr. Mires asked.

He nodded and shrugged. "Twelve."

"And Susan here works for *USA Today*. Before that she was several years at the *Chicago Tribune*. She was also one of my students," Dr. Mires explained cordially.

Liz smiled on the outside while on the inside she was freaking out. First Brady. Now this. Holy shit! She was meeting people who worked her dream jobs. She would kill to get a job at the *Times* or the *Washington Post*. And Dr. Mires was introducing her to these people as if it were no big deal. In fact, as she looked at Professor

Mires, she realized it *was* no big deal to her. These were her colleagues, her friends, her students. These were the people she was introducing to Liz because Liz was also all of those things.

Liz wanted to be a reporter, and as her advisor, Dr. Mires was ensuring that she didn't just become a reporter, but a damn good one.

"Liz, why don't you come to lunch with us and discuss your work and future aspirations? I'm sure my colleagues would be able to point you in the right direction for your scholarship internship hours next year," Professor Mires said.

"Oh yes, we're always happy to meet with Lynda's students," Nancy said.

"I would love to join you. Thank you," Liz responded. She felt as if all the pieces to her life were falling into place in this moment, and it felt incredible.

―

Liz knew that she shouldn't go to the politicians' panel. She should find something else to do with her time. She had just had lunch with Dr. Mires, Nancy, Bob, and Susan. They had all been interested in her work on the paper and her interests in political journalism. They had even given her their business cards and told her to keep in touch. It was definitely a step in the right direction. Walking into the politicians' panel was the exact opposite of that.

But she couldn't stay away from Brady . . . not when the opportunity to see him was staring her in the face.

Extra credit was being offered to most of the journalism classes for attendance, and when Liz ducked into the back of the room, she picked out a ton of her classmates and a large chunk of the newspaper staff.

Liz plopped down into the seat next to Massey with a sigh. She hadn't seen Hayden all day and prayed that he wouldn't show up to this. She knew that he had class most of the day and his electives wouldn't let him out for the presentations. They didn't care that he got extra credit that he in all honesty didn't need in classes other than their own. He thought it was pretty ridiculous, considering he would be graduating in less than two months. Her heart stopped at the thought, and she pushed it away. She could clam up about graduation until it got closer.

Her thoughts trailed off as a side door opened and Brady walked into the room. He took a seat and she couldn't even remember what she had been thinking.

Massey's sharp intake of breath was enough for Liz to know that she had noticed how fucking attractive he was. "Holy shit!" she squealed in Liz's ear. "He's so hot."

Liz nodded.

"Oh, please, just because you have Hayden doesn't mean you can deny pure male attractiveness. You guys aren't perfect enough for that."

Liz swallowed. "I didn't deny anything." And she couldn't. She couldn't even pull her eyes from his face.

She had missed him.

Christ, she wasn't going to think about that.

"Why is he a politician? He can just come right over to get work done in my bed," Massey said with her sorority-girl giggle. "I promise we'll be more effective than Congress, baby."

Her friends next to her snorted through their laughter, and professors turned around to give them nasty looks. It just made them laugh louder.

"I'll avoid a government shutdown, if you know what I mean," she said, nudging Liz.

"That doesn't even make sense," Liz said, allowing herself to laugh a little.

"Whatever. I'd do it for that body."

"You're ridiculous."

"I feel a little bad for Savannah. Having a brother that hot must suck," Massey whispered, glancing around to see if Savannah was in attendance. Liz hadn't seen her all day. Liz wondered if she was hiding out because her dad and brother were here.

"I doubt she even notices."

Massey rolled her eyes. "Puh-lease."

The room quieted down as Dr. Mires stood to begin the round-table. The main topic was the November election. Each politician gave their thoughts on what had happened, the role of the media in the election, and their early projections for the presidential election next November.

As much as it pained her to think about Brady, she was glad that Hayden wasn't here to witness it. He read her like an open book. She couldn't hide what was warring inside of her. She couldn't lie to him, and she wasn't ready to tell him. She wasn't sure she would ever be ready for that.

It wasn't as bad as Liz thought it was going to be. Brady didn't look in her direction once . . . if he even knew that she was there. It hurt, of course. But really it was for the best. She certainly wasn't going to ask him a question during the Q&A.

"What do you think about asking, boxers or briefs?" Massey leaned in and asked.

Liz swallowed. She had some firsthand experience with the answer to that question. It made color rush to her cheeks.

"Oh my God, Lizzie," she joked. "I'm not actually going to ask him that. I'm not that embarrassing!"

Liz just shook her head and tried to hide her own embarrassment. Somehow Massey managed to pull herself together to get a question out to Brady.

"Congressman Maxwell," she said.

Brady looked over in their direction and Liz felt his eyes flicker over her face. Her heart stopped as her blue eyes met the dark depths of his chocolaty brown ones. She felt her world spin in that one look before he passed over her and turned to address Massey.

Liz didn't even hear the question. Massey had it written down, so Liz could grab it from her later . . . and it probably wouldn't be essential to include in her report anyway. But all she could see were memories flashing before her eyes. The lake house, Fourth of July, the moment he slid his key into her hand, the feel of his hands on her body, the sound of his voice when he said that he loved her. It all came rushing back so perfectly.

She thought about the chain sitting in her jewelry box on her dresser and the meaning of each of those charms inside the locket: an airplane, the number four, a key, and the November birthstone. Brady had given it to her on the beach in Hilton Head as a gift, maybe even a promise of a future that they had never had. She had worn it every day for months. She never took the damn thing off except to shower. Even then she felt lost without it. But after the election she had forced herself to stop wearing it. It didn't make any difference. In that moment, she wished desperately that she was wearing it. Her eyes stung as she fought to hold back her tears.

She hadn't felt like this in months. The last time had been when she found out about Brady's new girlfriend, and before that New Year's. She had moved on. But then why did she feel as if she was being torn to pieces with just one lingering look?

The panel concluded and Liz numbly followed Massey out of the auditorium. She was hanging with a group of sorority girls Liz didn't really fit in with, but the benefit of that was that she didn't have to say anything. They carried on the conversation just fine without any input.

The lobby of the campus conference center was full of people milling around after that last panel. There were two more panels after it, but Liz had assumed they would be smaller. A lot of the students wouldn't be attending them. Liz was only going because she had helped Dr. Mires put the entire thing on, so she didn't think she would be able to sneak away.

Liz caught sight of a head of long dark hair and smiled. Savannah. So she was here. Ever since the day that Liz had told her that she had actually voted for Brady, things had been different between them. Both girls had relaxed around each other at work and the few occasions when they hung out. Liz found that she actually liked Savannah best of anyone else at the paper. They had similar work ethics, and each was more determined than the other to prove herself.

Liz waved to her as she walked over to where Savannah was standing. "Hey, I didn't see you in there."

Savannah shrugged. "I've heard them speak a million times. I didn't need to hear this one."

"You didn't miss much. It was pretty boring," she said softly.

"Oh, I figured. Brady said at lunch that it was going to be."

Liz breathed in and out as slowly as possible. Of course Savannah had lunch with her brother while he was in town. Nothing to freak out about.

"Well, he was right." *As always.*

"Hey, I'm glad I ran into you. What are you doing for dinner tonight?" Savannah asked.

"Um . . . I don't know. Why?"

"Want to come with me? I'll pick you up and everything."

"Are you asking me on a date, Savannah?" Liz asked with a half laugh. "You're not really my type."

"Okay, it's super secret. Like, don't even tell Hayden about it. Just tell him you're going out with me, but we'll have a good time, okay?"

"I haven't even agreed," Liz said, her interest piqued.

"Oh, did you not? I didn't notice. I'll come get you around eight," Savannah told her.

"All right," Liz said with a shrug.

"Brady's going to be out in a second. Want me to introduce you two?" she asked. "I know you guys met on campaign, but I'll introduce you to the real Brady Maxwell. He's actually not as stuck up as he looks." Savannah giggled and started dragging her across the room.

"Oh, no, Savannah . . . that's okay. We've . . . we've already met. It's, um . . . really not necessary," Liz stammered out.

"Come on. It's just my brother. He doesn't bite."

Liz disagreed. He most certainly did bite . . .

"Oh, there he is," Savannah said, just as Brady walked out of a back door from the auditorium. "I had a feeling he'd come this way."

"Oh," was all Liz managed to get out as she stared at Brady standing there talking to his father. She felt as if her legs were made of lead and she wasn't sure how she was dragging them along.

"Brady!" Savannah called as they approached.

His eyes snapped up to Savannah and he smiled. She knew that smile. God, how many times had she seen him look that happy? He loved his sister. They were really two peas in a pod. And then he saw Liz walking next to her and the smile dropped off of his face. Her legs didn't just feel like lead then; her whole body felt like lead, sinking straight to the bottom of the ocean.

Savannah pulled Liz along behind her and kept that smile on her face. "Brady, this is my friend Liz. I work with her on the paper. She was my boss during the campaign. I don't know if I mentioned her."

Brady swallowed, his Adam's apple bobbing. "I don't think you did." He seemed to have composed himself, but his eyes were still hard. She felt two feet tall in the shadow of that gaze. Then he stuck his hand out. "Brady Maxwell. I believe we met on campaign. Yes?"

"We did," she whispered, nodding. She took his hand in hers. Sparks flew as if someone had struck a match between them. It jolted her, and she actually jumped a little on contact. He took in a deep, even breath and then quickly dropped her hand.

"How nice to meet you again," he said, that campaign mask firmly in place. She wouldn't be seeing *her* Brady the rest of the conversation. Not that anything about him was *hers* anymore. "How was the rest of the campaign?"

Liz felt the weight of that question to her very core. "Same old, same old. It took forever to get to November," she all but whispered. "Congratulations on your victory."

"Thank you. I had a great team behind me. They really believed in me and my vision," he said, each word stabbing her like a knife wound.

"That's very . . . fortunate," she said, not knowing what else to say.

Savannah smiled, oblivious to the underlying conversation going on between them. "I'm glad I could reintroduce you," she said brightly. "I know Liz voted for you in the election and spent a lot of time ensuring students on campus voted."

"Is that right?" Brady asked, his gaze shifting to Savannah.

"I know how you like to talk to your constituents," Savannah said with a pat on his arm, as if he weren't some big politician. To Savannah he was just her brother. "I'm going to go find Dad. Find me after, Liz, okay?"

Savannah traipsed away to find her father before Liz could say anything. And then she was left alone with Brady.

They stood there together awkwardly. How many times had she envisioned what she would say when she finally saw him? How many times had she thought that she would beg his forgiveness, yell at him for never coming after her, throw herself at him? But none of those things happened. They just stared at each other.

Liz knew that she should say something. She even opened her mouth. But what could she say? They were so far removed from where they had been last August. She just wanted to apologize, to explain, but she couldn't. Not here. Not like this.

"There you are," Liz heard from behind her. Her stomach sank. *Shit.*

She broke Brady's gaze and turned to see Hayden walking toward her. He was in a navy sport jacket and khakis with a striped shirt underneath. His hair was perfectly tousled and his hazel eyes were almost green as he smiled at her.

He walked right up to her and kissed her softly on the lips. She didn't think she even responded.

"Hey, Lizzie," he said when he pulled back.

Liz stepped away from him, feeling terrible at the realization that Brady was watching. *Fuck.*

"Um, hey," she said awkwardly.

Hayden noticed who she was standing by and straightened up immediately. "Oh, you must be Brady Maxwell," Hayden said, having the sense to look slightly embarrassed. Though she wondered if he had kissed her on purpose. No. This was Hayden. He didn't have a bone in his body that wasn't good and decent.

"That's right," Brady said.

Hayden thrust his hand out. "Hayden Lane. I'm the editor at the college newspaper."

Brady took it, keeping his campaign mask firmly in place, but Liz could see the fire brimming in his eyes as he stared at Hayden. His gaze shifted to Liz and she could see precisely what he was thinking in that moment. *You're with this guy now?*

Brady knew *exactly* who Hayden was. She had kissed Hayden in D.C. while she had been seeing Brady. Their picture had shown up in the newspaper when school started.

"Nice to meet you," Brady responded. "If you'll excuse me, I have a meeting to get to."

And without another second's pause, Brady turned and walked in the opposite direction. She was left alone with Hayden, but she might as well have been all by herself all over again . . . because her heart had been ripped out of her chest with Brady's departure.

Chapter 10
BIN 54

The rest of the day passed in a blur of Brady Maxwell. It was like the seven months that she had gone without him had just been a haze and those precious moments with him were her clarity. She remembered all too clearly what it felt like to walk through the world feeling as if she had walked out of Technicolor into black and white. That was life with and without Brady.

By the time she was supposed to meet with Savannah for dinner, Liz was just happy to have an excuse not to have to be around Hayden. He knew she was off. Her focus was shot, and half of the time it felt as if she were listening to him underwater. She told him that she was having dinner with Savannah, which got her raised eyebrows from Hayden.

"Where are you going?" Hayden asked curiously.

Liz shrugged. "I don't know. She just asked if I wanted to go."

"Strange."

"Is it?" Liz asked, wrapping her arms around her middle. She couldn't seem to get herself straight.

"I mean, I know y'all are friends, but I didn't think you guys really hung out like that."

Liz shrugged again. She didn't know what else to do. "She asked me. I said I'd go."

"Are y'all meeting anyone else?" he asked. He seemed to be trying for casual, but they had been together too long for her not to get what he was asking.

"I don't think so." She really had no idea.

"Not her brother?"

Liz's eyes bulged. There was no fucking way that was happening. "No. Why would you think that?" she sputtered.

"He was just . . . looking at you is all."

"People tend to do that when they're introduced," Liz said, trying to brush it off.

"I don't know," Hayden said, taking her nonchalance for it not meaning anything. But of course it meant everything. "I'm probably crazy and way off base, but I didn't really like the way our politician was looking at *my* girlfriend." He pulled her into him and kissed the tip of her nose.

She laughed lightly, hoping that she sounded disbelieving. She was sure she failed, but he couldn't see her face, so maybe she pulled it off. "We're talking about a congressman. A man who works for the House of Representatives. I'm pretty sure he wouldn't look twice at a college reporter. You, Hayden Lane, are just imagining things."

There. It was her first direct lie. How had she managed it so flawlessly?

"Well, you do look pretty gorgeous today."

"Thank you," she said, nuzzling into his chest to hide her face. She felt like a total shit. She didn't deserve him.

Liz ended the conversation as quickly as she could and hurried back to her house. She had no idea what to wear to dinner tonight. It felt weird obsessing over clothing options just to hang out with Savannah, but she had a pretty kickass style and it made Liz want to dress nice. She decided on a high-waist navy-and-white striped skirt with a navy tank top tucked into it. She paired it with a pair of brown sling-back platforms that made her calves look killer.

For a second she thought about pulling out Brady's necklace and wearing it, but it felt too strange. She had put it away for a reason. One afternoon in his presence wasn't going to change that reason.

Savannah showed up just after eight o'clock in her shiny BMW. Liz was out the door before her friend even got out of her car. Victoria was on a date with Duke Fan and she wouldn't be home until later, so Liz locked the house up tight. She teetered to the car in her heels and then sat down in the passenger seat.

Liz felt better about her choices after assessing Savannah's outfit. She was in a knee-length black dress with several strands of pearls and oversize Ray-Bans. Her long dark hair was pulled off of her face into a loose bun at the base of her neck.

"Are you sure you're not going into politics?" Liz joked in greeting.

"Don't even get me started," Savannah said, pulling away from the house and off onto Rosemary Street.

"Where are we going anyway?"

"Have you ever been to Bin 54?"

Liz shook her head. "No."

"It's a steakhouse just off of Raleigh Road before Meadowmont." Meadowmont was a community where groceries, shopping, and fine dining were walkable from the apartments. It was too far away from campus for Liz's taste, but it was still a nice concept.

"All right," Liz said. She wondered what the pricing was going to be on a place like that.

They drove the ten minutes to the restaurant and Savannah pulled into the parking lot. She took a spot and cut the engine.

"Okay. So, before we go inside I thought I'd just fill you in on why I'm being so weird and secretive." Liz arched an eyebrow. "You know I don't really talk about my family."

"Yeah . . ."

"Well, I love them. They're pretty awesome. But I don't get to share them with many people because they're in the spotlight. Since you and I kind of . . . I don't know . . . bonded over that fact, I feel like I can trust you."

Oh, no.

"So, don't take this weird, because my fam is cool, but we're having dinner with them," Savannah said quickly.

Dinner with the Maxwells? Liz was pretty sure that was the worst idea she had ever heard. If it had been awkward to have those few minutes with Brady . . . what would a whole dinner be like? And with his parents!

"You can't report about it or anything, obviously," Savannah went on, oblivious. "I just thought it might be cool to have someone else get to know the real me. I kind of feel like you're the only one who is even close."

Liz didn't know what to say. On one hand she was happy that Savannah trusted her enough to do something like this. On the other hand . . . she was freaking the fuck out.

Did that mean Brady was here? Would she have to sit through dinner with him? Could she pretend not to know him?

Shit! What if Clay was there? That might be even worse. Not to mention the fact that he knew her as Liz Carmichael. How exactly would she begin to explain that?

Not good.

"Liz," Savannah said, twisting at her ring as she did when she was concerned. "I didn't mean to freak you out. I can take you back if you want. I just thought . . ."

"It's okay. Sorry, just had to wrap my mind around meeting someone's parents," she said with a laugh that sounded more like a cough. She didn't want Savannah not to trust her. But she wasn't sure how to keep that acceptance and still get through the evening.

"They're totally chill. I promise," Savannah said, popping open the driver's-side door as if that were all settled.

Well . . . great.

Not seeing another alternative, Liz got out of the car. She smoothed out her skirt and adjusted the shirt she had tucked into the waistband. At least she knew that she looked pretty hot. There was that. She would have probably died if she had shown up wearing jeans to meet Brady's parents . . . to see Brady.

At least she knew that there was no way in hell that she was going to break Savannah's confidence, because she most certainly was not going to tell Hayden about this. Especially not after he had sounded kind of jealous about the way Brady had looked at her at the colloquium. She hoped it wasn't as obvious to everyone else tonight.

They walked in through the front entrance of Bin 54. The entire restaurant was gorgeous, with elegant circular tables, low lighting with candles, and mood-setting red walls. Savannah gave her name to the hostess and she directed them down to a private dining room in the wine cellar. The walls were lined with bottles and bottles of expensive wine, and in the heart of the room was a long rustic wooden table set for ten with large black chairs. Candles littered the cellar, casting a soft glow around the room.

Everyone else was already seated when Liz and Savannah entered. Liz braced herself for the look that Brady was about to send her way, but he didn't glance at her when she walked into the room. He was deeply engrossed in conversation with the person sitting next to him, and Liz was glad that he didn't see her when she got a glimpse of the people in attendance.

Despite the fact that she knew that it wasn't just some big publicity stunt and Heather had all but confirmed that Brady was in fact dating the girl he kept popping up in pictures with, she hadn't truly believed it until the moment that she saw Brady sitting next to her, chatting with her, laughing with his parents.

Liz felt her already fragile heart drop out of her chest and watched as Brady stomped on it. She knew it was ridiculous to feel like that, but she couldn't help it. She had walked out. She was the one who had let him go. But she truthfully hadn't believed their relationship would go anywhere past that summer. She hadn't wanted him to have to choose between her and the campaign. He couldn't give up his career for her, and she couldn't let him be the one to choose his career instead.

But she hadn't ever wanted to be in this position. To meet the new girlfriend.

Her throat was dry. Her fingers felt tingly. She wasn't going to cry. No, this wasn't that kind of moment. This moment wasn't one to be mad or sad or pitch a fit. She couldn't even muster those emotions. The only thing she felt was the one thing that she had never wanted to feel: regret.

"Hey, y'all," Savannah called, drawing everyone's attention to her with a wave.

Here goes nothing.

"This is my friend Liz Dougherty. She works with me at the paper," Savannah said as an introduction.

Brady turned around so slowly that if she didn't know better she would have thought he was uninterested. But instead she could just tell he was struggling for control. His eyes met hers across the room and she managed a smile without thinking about it. He looked so fucking gorgeous. It seriously was heart-stopping . . . if she'd still had a heart.

He didn't smile back. He looked at her as if he was asking, *What the fuck are you doing here?*

"Come on; you can sit by me," Savannah said, taking a seat.

Liz followed behind her and sat down in the last open spot . . . directly across from Brady. The only positive to this entire thing was that Clay wasn't here. Only good thing she could think of at the moment.

Besides the Maxwells and Erin, there were four people she didn't recognize at all. Family friends, or maybe another politician or something if she had to guess.

"Liz, these are my parents," Savannah said, pointing them out. "And I already introduced you to Brady earlier." Liz didn't even glance over at him. She couldn't. "This is his girlfriend, Erin."

She did assess his girlfriend, though. Judged her was more like it. Liz couldn't tell how tall she was, but she guessed a bit taller than her by the pictures she had seen. She looked classy in a red dress with gold buttons up the front and a gold belt at her waist. Her hair looked like a freaking Disney princess—long, dark, curling at the ends, shiny, silky smooth, with all sorts of luscious body. She had almond-shaped dark brown eyes lined in onyx, and perfectly curled black eyelashes. Her lips were on the thin side, but whatever dark pink lipstick she was wearing didn't make them stand out as much. Her skin was tan as if she lived at the beach, but Liz knew that she didn't . . . so it must be fake. Unless Brady was taking her to the lake house . . . or the beach.

Whoa. She needed to stop that train of thought right now.

Liz tore her eyes away from Erin.

"These are the Atwoods. Close family friends," Savannah explained, gesturing to the couple seated at the opposite end of the table. Liz couldn't figure out why Atwood sounded familiar.

"Matthew and Lisa." Savannah pointed out the parents, then gestured at the brother and sister. "Lucas and Alice."

Lucas was seated next to Savannah and looked about Savannah's age. He was handsome in an unconventional way: tall with a kind of lanky frame and overgrown hair. He looked as if he would be more comfortable in athletic gear than the sport coat he was wearing. His sister, Alice, looked as if she was in middle school or at the oldest a freshman in high school. She seemed lost in her own world and twirled her honey-blond curls around her finger the whole time.

"I thought Chris was coming," Savannah said, addressing Matthew and Lisa.

But Brady answered. "He's still in New York. Couldn't get away from work for the weekend."

Click. Chris was Brady's best friend. He was the only other person who knew that Liz and Brady had been together last summer. She had gone with him to one of Brady's galas and he had engineered for her and Brady to be alone together afterward. These were Chris's parents, his brother and sister. It made sense why they were best friends—the two men had grown up together.

"That sucks," Savannah said sullenly. She really looked like the baby of the family in that moment. As if with her family she could ease into the person she always had been instead of the person she pretended to be in public. She clearly did trust Liz to see the real her if she had half as many of the precautions built up around herself that Brady had.

Personally, Liz was glad that Chris wasn't there. She didn't want to deal with his knowing looks any more than Clay's.

The waitress appeared shortly after introductions. Liz ordered a glass of water. There was no way she was going to drink in front of Brady's parents. She was sitting directly across from him and she couldn't even look at him. She didn't trust herself to drink.

Brady's father ordered red wine for the table anyway. Liz almost groaned, but instead she just smiled like a gracious guest. One glass. No more than one glass.

"So, Liz," Brady's father addressed her, "Savannah says you work with her on the paper. How did you get into that?"

Now she wished that she had the wine in front of her so that she had something for her hands to do. Instead she put on an easy smile and tried to remain casual. "Well, I decided a long time ago I wanted to be a reporter. My mom works for the state of Florida and my father is a professor at South Florida, and they always had an interest in politics. So I guess I got that from them," she said. She knew she was rambling about a simple question, but she didn't know where to stop. "I joined the paper when I got to school."

"Are you a senior?" Brady's mother asked.

"Junior. I graduate next year," she said softly. Her eyes drifted up to Brady's for the first time since she started talking. *Separated by another year of school.*

"Don't let Liz fool you into thinking she's just someone at the paper. She ran the campaign division and is going to be editor next year," Savannah explained. "She organized the colloquium y'all were at this afternoon."

"Really?" Brady asked. Neither of them had pulled their eyes from each other, and Liz knew it was dangerous to address him directly.

"Yeah . . . I did."

"That's a major accomplishment," Erin said cheerfully. Liz glanced over at her to see if there was any malice on her face, but of course there wasn't. Erin didn't know who she was.

"Thank you."

"How did you get a job like that?" Erin asked.

Liz cleared her throat. "Last summer when I was following the campaign, I worked with my major professor to improve my writing. She liked the transformation I made over the summer so much that she offered me the job."

A muscle in Brady's jaw tensed at the mention of last summer. She didn't blame him. She hadn't even meant to bring it up, but it had just slipped out.

"What do you do, Erin?" Liz asked quickly as the rest of the table broke into their own side conversations. She would do anything not to directly address Brady again.

"I'm a morning anchor for *Baltimore Mornings* on channel 11," Erin said with a smile that showed exactly why she was an anchor at such a young age.

Broadcast news. Not something Liz had ever been interested in. Of course, *Baltimore Mornings* sounded more like a morning talk show than a news program.

"That's how we met, actually," Erin said, placing her hand on top of Brady's and lacing their fingers together.

Liz sat ramrod straight as she watched Brady turn to look at Erin and smile. Liz didn't know how to deal with all of this. She was just ready to leave. Her wine couldn't have come at a better time. She took a long gulp to avoid speaking further.

Erin seemed to want to tell the story anyway. "Brady worked with my father in the North Carolina state legislature, which is how I got the contact to interview him over Christmas on my morning talk show." Erin's smile brightened as she talked. Liz's diminished.

"Didn't I tell you it wasn't a newsworthy story?" Savannah said, nudging Liz. Liz hadn't even realized that Savannah had been paying attention. She had been talking to Lucas nonstop.

Brady arched an eyebrow, and Liz just opened and closed her mouth like a fish flopping around out of the water.

"Definitely a story we don't want in the news!" Erin said with a giggle. "It seems everything is in the news. I feel like relationships should kind of be off-limits. I don't see why it matters that Brady and I are together. But I don't think it's been too bad. Do you?"

"No," Brady said. His voice came out easy and confident. Another mask. "I don't think it's been too bad being out in the open like this. I'd never want to hide a relationship anyway."

Liz's blood boiled at the blatant lie. She wanted to stab him with her fork. *He* was the one who had wanted to hide their fucking relationship in the first place.

He could probably see her seething at the comment, because he sent her the first fucking gorgeous smirk since they had seen each other this afternoon. It only made her want to lunge across the table more. She would throttle him before the end of the night. She was sure of it.

"Erin handles the spotlight like a pro. Don't you, baby?"

Oh, fuck, no! Was he using the name that he used for Liz on purpose? Two could play at this game.

"I love the spotlight," Erin said again with a smile. "I think I always wanted to be an anchor, just like you always wanted to be a reporter, Liz."

"That's wonderful," Liz said, finishing off her first glass of wine. "Did you two fly here?"

"Oh, yeah. Into Raleigh," Erin confirmed.

"How was the flight? I know there's been some nasty weather lately. I sometimes get freaked out flying into that," Liz said boldly.

Savannah giggled. "Brady has the worst time flying. So I hope that there weren't any storms."

"You have a hard time flying?" Erin asked. Her eyebrows crinkled together in confusion. "I didn't know that."

"I used to have trouble," Brady corrected quickly. "I don't have trouble with airplanes anymore. That time in my life has passed."

That time in his life had passed. Meaning Liz was out of his life. She understood. She wished it were all that easy. It had taken her forever just to feel as if she could move on to dating . . . let alone to anything else with Hayden. God, she hadn't thought of Hayden since she had walked into the building.

As frustrated as she was with Brady for goading her, she didn't want to continue to have painful conversations with him. She would rather pretend he didn't exist again than to have this pain rush through her body.

Liz let Savannah and Erin guide the conversation from there. Both she and Brady were relatively quiet, answering questions only when they were asked them. He seemed to have the same idea as Liz. They always had been in tune.

As much as Liz wanted to hate Erin, the other woman did seem genuinely nice. Besides her work as a morning anchor, she also helped run a charity that benefited inner-city schools in the Baltimore and D.C. area. She had claimed to be a philanthropist at heart, something she said she had cultivated at her time at Brown.

For all intents and purposes, Erin was exactly the kind of person a young up-and-coming politician should be dating. She was smart, outgoing, successful, charitable, beautiful.

Dinner was expensive and rather extravagant for a small location in Chapel Hill, but the Maxwells insisted on picking up the entire tab. They ordered another round of wine for the table before finishing up, but Liz declined the drink. She had promised herself only one. Brady still had a glass sitting in front of him untouched, and Erin was on her third or fourth.

"Savannah," Liz said, tapping her friend on the shoulder. She was talking to Lucas again feverishly.

"Yeah?"

"I have to get home."

"Oh, damn, really?" she asked, glancing back at Lucas and biting her lip.

Shit. How hadn't Liz noticed before? Savannah liked Chris's

brother. That was what that look meant. Of course, Liz had been a little hung up on Brady, so she hadn't been paying all that much attention.

"Yeah. Sorry."

"Do you think you could call Hayden to get you?" Savannah asked. "Oh, wait—damn, he's not supposed to know you're here."

Liz's eyes found Brady at Savannah's comment. She could see his ears had perked up at the comment, but he just stared forward as if it didn't matter to him.

"I guess we could call a cab or something. I'm not ready to go just yet," Savannah said, her eyes pleading for understanding.

"No problem. I'll just take a cab."

"Maybe Brady could take you," Savannah said, sending her brown eyes over to Brady's direction.

Liz's head snapped to the side. Brady could not drive her home. This was a terrible idea. She couldn't be alone with him.

Brady raised his eyebrows at his sister. "Me?"

"Well, you're the only one who hasn't been drinking, and I feel bad making her take a cab," Savannah said, adding a pouty lip for good measure.

Brady cleared his throat and turned his attention to Liz. "How far do you live from here?" He already knew the answer.

Liz bit her lip. What the hell was he thinking? Why would he even act as if he was going to agree? The worst part was she couldn't even object to him driving her without looking suspicious. "Ten minutes. But really, it's not necessary. I don't mind taking a cab."

Brady shrugged nonchalantly. "It's not a problem. I could take you home if you want and then swing back by the restaurant."

"Yes!" Savannah rushed out. "That would be perfect. You're the best older brother ever!"

Liz opened her mouth to say something and then closed it. *Alone with Brady. This could be interesting.*

"Um . . . thank you," she said.

Brady kissed Erin on the top of her head, and then walked right out of the restaurant with Liz. In public. Together.

But not together.

Liz should have picked out his Lexus in the parking lot on the way in, but she hadn't been paying attention. She walked over to it without his directing her. Her heart was thudding in her chest, and she wasn't sure what the fuck she was supposed to do. Today was the first day in seven months that she had seen Brady and now she was going to be completely alone with him. Her hands shook as she reached for the door handle. She needed to get herself together if she wanted to get through this car ride.

After they piled into the car, Brady peeled out of the parking lot. He sat ramrod straight as he turned back toward campus. He didn't glance in her direction once, but it was clear that there was something on his mind. He hadn't agreed to drive her home for no reason. She was terrified to know where this was going.

Liz shifted her gaze to Brady's face, trying to read him. He was completely stoic and blatantly ignoring her. She opened her mouth to say something and then closed it. She didn't know what to say. Before today, they hadn't spoken or seen each other since the day that she had walked out of his primary victory party. Her body was itching to be closer to him, to run her fingers through his hair and feel his lips against her skin. But she knew she couldn't have any of those things and that she shouldn't want them.

And even though they had only the ten minutes alone . . . the first ten minutes they'd had alone since August . . . neither of them spoke. Liz remembered the time he had come and picked her up to talk about finding her and Hayden on the cover of the newspaper. *And if it's not you, then it doesn't matter.* That was the last time they had been in a car together. Her heart ached just thinking about it. No matter what she did, thinking about Brady and their time together always hurt.

Brady pulled up in front of her house and put the car into park. The car idled quietly beneath them and still Liz didn't get out. She knew she needed to say *something*. Anything. She took a deep breath and drummed up the courage to speak.

"Brady . . . ," she whispered, finding her voice.

"I don't know what you're trying to accomplish by coming here tonight," Brady said gruffly, not looking at her across the car.

"I wasn't trying to accomplish anything. Savannah just invited me."

"Look." He finally turned and faced her. His eyes were hard, his campaign mask firmly in place. "I don't know what you thought you could get out of seeing me today, but please don't come back. You already walked out once. It shouldn't be hard to do it again."

Liz felt the knife twist in her chest as his words issued a death strike. She put her hand over her heart as she felt her body collapse in on itself. Walking out on Brady had been the absolute hardest thing she had ever done in her life. She still couldn't believe that she had actually done it. But she had. It killed her to hear him say things like that to her.

It also pissed her off. Those words combined with everything that he had said at dinner tonight just made all of the pent-up anger burst out.

"I didn't even fucking know that you were going to be here tonight. If I'd known, I wouldn't have come at all," Liz snapped. "Okay? Does that make you feel better?"

"Much," he growled.

"Good. Because the bullshit comments about being happy with having a public relationship and being over airplanes were really just unnecessary."

"Oh, and kissing your boyfriend in front of me and bringing up airplanes in the first place wasn't unnecessary, Liz?" he demanded.

"You called her baby!"

"You're dating the guy you left me for!" he said, reaching out and grasping her shoulders roughly between his hands. Her mouth popped open. She stared up into his big brown eyes and felt her whole world narrow down to this one second. That face, those eyes, those lips. Only inches separating them. It would be so easy to just get swept away by their mounting anger.

And then the second passed.

"You should go," he said, dropping his hands.

"You're right." Her breathing was uneven and her whole body was warm. The places where he had touched her were on fire.

Liz cracked the door open, stepped out, and turned to go. But then she thought better of it. She turned back around to face Brady.

"I didn't leave you for him," she said softly. "The moment Heather and Elliott told you that you had to ditch me, you left me for the campaign."

Brady opened his mouth to contradict her, but she shook her head.

"Because while you might have told them that you loved me, you never actually told me."

Chapter 11
INTERVIEW

The weeks following the conversation with Brady outside of her house almost made Liz feel as if it were August again. Her heartbreak was still prominent all these months later, and she had only spent a few hours with Brady. Only fifteen precious minutes alone. Seeing him, talking to him, having him touch her, she felt the rush of lingering emotions once more. And everything was just as fresh as if she had just walked out of that primary all over again.

Hayden didn't say anything. But Victoria told her that she was acting weird frequently enough that Liz knew he would have to be an idiot not to notice. And Hayden was anything but an idiot. He had been the one to spot *his* girlfriend being looked at by Brady in a way that he didn't particularly like in the first place.

At least he didn't ask about her change in behavior. It was the only good thing coming out of the situation. Because if he had asked, she didn't know what she would do. She didn't want to have to lie to him. She didn't *like* lying to him. It made her feel dirty . . .

dirtier than she was already feeling about how easily she had allowed Brady to seep back in.

And it was hard enough keeping Savannah's secret about dinner; it felt like a lie of omission. A part of her just wanted to tell Hayden everything that had happened. She didn't know how he would react. She knew how she had reacted to his dating Calleigh, and those two had broken up because Hayden wasn't interested anymore. That most certainly was not the reason she and Brady had stopped seeing each other.

"Hey, gorgeous, are you even listening?" Hayden asked, waving his hand in front of her face from his seat next to her on his couch.

"Oh, no, I'm sorry," Liz said. She shook her head and tried to bring herself back to reality. She had been lost in Brady Maxwell once again. She wished it wasn't so difficult to get him out of her head. She hadn't seen Brady in weeks, and it wasn't as if she was going to run back to him or anything. He had made himself perfectly clear: he didn't want her to come back.

"I was just asking what you had planned for your birthday this weekend," Hayden said.

Her birthday. Was it April already? When had that happened? School was almost over. Hayden would be graduating soon. She didn't want to think about that either.

"Oh, um . . . no plans. I'd forgotten."

"Your twenty-first birthday?"

Liz shrugged and forced a smile on her face. Shit! Had she actually forgotten her own twenty-first birthday? She had been so looking forward to it before Brady had strolled back into her life. She needed to get her shit together. "I guess I've been busy. I haven't had a chance to plan anything. I'm sure Victoria will want to take me out and get me trashed."

"When doesn't she want to go out?" Hayden asked, slinging an arm over her shoulders and pulling her into him on his couch.

"The girl doesn't need an excuse to celebrate. That's for sure."

"So, I was thinking," Hayden began, planting a kiss on her cheek softly.

"Dangerous habit."

He laughed and tickled her side. She jumped and giggled, pulling away from him as she straightened. She might be torn up about what had happened with Brady, but Hayden seemed to be able to put the smile back on her face.

"I thought we could go to Charlotte on Thursday."

Liz tilted her head and narrowed her eyes. What did Hayden have up his sleeve? "I have class Friday morning."

"I know. I thought you could skip."

She gasped and reached her hand out to his forehead to feel his temperature. "Are you sick? You're telling me to skip school?"

"It's just one class, and it's near the end of the semester," he said, rattling off excuses. "It won't be a big deal."

Liz laughed, placing her hand over his lips. It was nice to forget about Brady and just get caught up in being around Hayden. "I'll skip school for you."

He kissed her hand before taking it into his own and lacing their fingers together. "Good. I have a surprise for you."

"Oh?" Liz asked, raising her eyebrows. "What is it?"

"Not much of a surprise if I tell you, silly."

"So."

"I'm not telling."

"What are we doing in Charlotte? Is that part of the surprise? We could always go to the coast instead," Liz suggested. Not that she wanted to think about the time she had flown to Hilton Head to see Brady, but she preferred the ocean to, well . . . everything. Maybe if she went to the beach with Hayden, she could make new memories that didn't hurt as much as the ones about Brady.

"Well . . . it's part of the surprise, but I'll tell you now," he said, beaming at her. "I have a final interview at *Charlotte Times* for an entry-level reporting position."

"Oh my God, that's great!" Liz said, bouncing up and down with excitement.

Hayden had applied to positions at newspapers all over the country. She knew that he wanted to be at a top paper, but those positions were few and far between. He'd had a phone interview with the *Washington Post*, but he had heard earlier this week that he hadn't gotten the job. He had received an offer to work in the press office where he had interned over the summer, but it wasn't exactly what he wanted to do. So he was keeping his options open until then. He would always prefer a reporting job, and as he told her over and over again, he wasn't moving that far away from her for anything less.

"When is the interview?" Liz asked.

"It's Friday morning. I thought we could drive down Thursday afternoon and get a hotel in the city. I'll have my interview and then we can go out after for dinner for your birthday."

And that was how she ended up in Charlotte that Thursday. Her birthday was technically Saturday, but she liked that they were going to go out in Charlotte, far removed from all of her memories in Chapel Hill. Maybe she would actually jolt herself out of her Brady Maxwell stupor.

Plus this gave Victoria the opportunity to throw her a birthday party Saturday on Franklin Street and get her fucking wasted for her twenty-first. If Liz knew Victoria, she was going to want to steal Liz and take her to every bar for a birthday shot. It wasn't going to be pretty.

⟜

Hayden pulled off of I-85 and into the heart of downtown Charlotte. Liz hadn't been here since the Jefferson-Jackson gala, when she had left with Brady. She hadn't known how much her life would change that night. Now she was on her way back to make new memories.

He followed his GPS instructions and veered down the street. Liz was getting more excited; she had never stayed in a hotel with Hayden. It wasn't that it would be any different from staying at her place or his place, but there was just something to the exclusivity of it that heightened her excitement.

But that was only until they pulled up in front of their hotel.

Liz's stomach dropped to her feet. Of all the places for him to choose to celebrate her birthday, he had to choose *this* hotel.

She stared up at the hotel that she had stayed in that first night she had agreed to go home with Brady after the Jefferson-Jackson gala. Her mind just couldn't grasp the fact that she was here again . . . with Hayden.

How could he choose this place?

"Wow," she whispered, just to break the silence. "This looks fancy. How did you find out about it?"

Hayden chuckled softly. She wished she found it half as amusing. "I'd heard all of the rooms were named for various political positions. Considering our profession, it seemed fitting. I read that the rooms range from a representative suite all the way up to presidential."

Liz's face colored as she remembered what exactly had gone on in the presidential suite. "What kind of room do we have?" she asked, not sure she could handle the answer.

It was Hayden's turn to look a bit sheepish. "Well, I didn't get us a suite, but I think it will be nice to have our own room with a king-size bed and everything. Don't you think?"

Phew! That made sense if Hayden was covering the costs.

"Yes," she admitted, pushing Brady to the back of her mind as best she could. "I think that sounds really nice."

Hayden looked so happy to be doing this for her. There was absolutely no way she could ask him to move hotels. She didn't have a good enough explanation as to why without spilling everything about Brady. Plus, he had clearly put in some time scouting out the right hotel. She couldn't possibly take that away from him.

They parked the car and then walked into the very familiar hotel. Hayden got a key from the front desk and then took them up to their room. It was nothing fancy in comparison to the presidential suite; actually, it looked like every other hotel. A king-size bed took up the majority of the space, and there was a large armoire with a flat-screen TV inside. The bathroom was small, but had a decent size walk-in shower. It was a nice change of pace from Chapel Hill.

She should be happy that she was here with Hayden, that he had taken the time to be with her on her birthday, to plan something like this. It was clearly very thoughtful. Perfect. Classic Hayden.

No matter what had happened with Brady, that door was closed. It didn't do anything for her to live in the past and dwell on what could have been when she had something incredible right in front of her.

They spent the night wrapped in each other's arms and tangled in the hotel sheets. She fell asleep tucked into Hayden's chest, lost in the steady rhythm of his breathing.

The next morning, Hayden fretted over the suit that he was wearing to the interview. He ironed the already flawless white button-down until it was crisp, and the lines down the front of his black pants were stark. He tied and retied his green tie a dozen times until the topknot was perfect. It made his hazel eyes stand out sharply, and when he smiled at her through the mirror as she was fixing her makeup, she remembered exactly why she had fallen for Hayden in the first place.

He was confident, but not arrogant. He was charming, but not conceited. He was intelligent, but not egotistical. He wanted to be there, to be with her, to take care of her, but he didn't have to be overbearing to do it. He respected her decision to not be with him immediately, not to have sex with him immediately . . . to communicate and trust her and believe in her. It was almost too much to feel all at once.

Hayden slid into his black suit coat and buttoned the top button. "How do I look?" he asked, turning in a slow circle.

"Can you lift that jacket up in the back?" she asked with a giggle, tilting her head to the side to check out his ass.

"I doubt I'm going to get judged on that."

"You never know."

He shook his head, then grabbed her around the middle and pulled her against him. "I think you've been spending too much time with Victoria."

"I'm going to tell her that you're not calling her Vickie anymore."

"Don't you dare," he murmured, before bringing his lips down to hers.

She laughed lightly as she moved her arms around his neck and intensified the kiss. He groaned into her mouth and it just made her smile more.

This. This was exactly what it was supposed to be like.

"You're going to do great today," she whispered, opening her eyes and staring up at him.

"I could conquer the world with you at my side."

And in that moment, she believed him.

It was only a short drive to the *Charlotte Times* office from their hotel. The building itself was kind of stark, boxy and boring. It was a basic square warehouse-type building with the words *Charlotte Times* written in scrawling font that mirrored that of the *New York*

Times. The parking lot was massive, and they managed to find an open spot at the back.

Liz didn't have anywhere to be, so she figured that as long as they had somewhere for her to relax while Hayden was upstairs she could catch up on work or read a book. Otherwise, Hayden had given her the keys to his precious Audi and told her to be careful with his baby. She kind of wanted to take it out for a spin, because he got so flustered at the thought of her driving it.

The interior of the building was a thousand times better than the bland exterior. The lobby was a soft powder blue with white tile floors that clicked under her heels. A prominently featured staircase led all the way to the top. A large black desk took up space and three women sat behind it. Two of them were on the phones, answering, asking people to hold, and transferring them over to other lines. The other lady looked up when they entered.

She smiled brightly. "Welcome to the *Charlotte Times.* How can I help you?"

Liz held back as Hayden moved forward. "Hi. I'm Hayden Lane. I have an interview with Ted Moore at eleven."

"Ah! Mr. Lane. Right on time. If you'll take a seat, I'll let Mr. Moore know that you are here."

"Thank you," Hayden said, before turning back to Liz and gesturing for her to follow.

They took seats in the waiting area across from the front desk. Liz tapped her feet anxiously. This wasn't even her job interview, and she was so worried for him. She knew Hayden had an impeccable résumé, and that the *Charlotte Times* was a step down from where he *wanted* to work. But it was better to have a job and get some experience than to graduate without anything.

Hayden's hand landed on her knee. "Hey. You're going to start making me nervous."

"Sorry," she whispered, trying to keep from bouncing her leg.

A man appeared out of the back room. He was balding and it made his ears appear to stick out from his head. But he seemed jovial enough and even had a spring in his step. "Mr. Lane?"

Hayden smiled that heart-stopping smile and stood. "That's me, sir."

"Nice to meet you. I'm Ted Moore." He walked over and extended his hand to Hayden.

"Great to meet you too, sir."

"Please call me Ted," he said casually. "If you'll follow me back, we'll get started with your interview. I do have to say it's good to have you here. Your file has come highly recommended."

Hayden beamed. His recommendations were beyond solid after working four years on the paper, with a year and a half as editor. All of his professors liked him. Who was she kidding? Everyone liked Hayden Lane.

Hayden turned back and picked up his messenger bag that he had dropped on the ground. He gave her a confident wink, and she smiled up at him through her nerves. "I'll see you after, gorgeous. Wish me luck."

"You don't need it," she murmured.

"You're right. I'm already the luckiest guy in the world. I have you."

Liz bit down on her bottom lip and held in her sigh as Hayden walked down the hallway. How was she supposed to respond to that? He was too perfect. There was no way that she could ever compare.

She pulled out her tablet from her purse and started messing around on the Internet, checking emails and responding to messages about the upcoming articles she and Massey were focusing on for the paper.

About forty minutes into Hayden's interview, when Liz was finally wrapping up her G-chat conversation with Tristan about next week, she heard footsteps coming in her direction.

Liz glanced up at the interruption and then immediately wished that she hadn't.

Calleigh Hollingsworth walked toward Liz. Her red hair hung loose in big waves, and she looked every bit the exotically beautiful queen bee she was, with dark makeup and a skirt suit with a plum top underneath that showed off her cleavage. Liz had a visceral reaction to her appearance: she kind of wanted to claw her eyes out.

Calleigh had briefly dated her boyfriend, and acted like a Class A bitch ever since Hayden had shown an ounce of interest in Liz. But Liz was pretty sure her aversion to the other woman went deeper than that. It was the innuendo that Calleigh made about Liz and Brady at the primary that really irked her.

Why hadn't Liz put two and two together before? Calleigh had said from the beginning that she could get Hayden a job at her paper if he wanted. Now he was here.

"Liz! I didn't know you were going to be here today," Calleigh said in greeting.

"Oh, Calleigh, hey. I forgot that you work here."

"Did Hayden not tell you that I helped him get the interview?" she asked, batting her eyelashes.

No. In fact, he hadn't. She didn't even know that they were still talking. Of course, Hayden had made it blatantly clear that he had no interest in Calleigh, but Liz still didn't like it.

"Oh, yeah, he did mention it. I guess we were just so lost in our own world that it slipped my mind," Liz said with an equally pointed smile. She didn't even care that it wasn't true.

"I just know that he'll be a valuable asset to the team."

"Hayden would be a pretty valuable employee anywhere," Liz agreed.

"I think Ted will like him." Calleigh's eyes flashed with mischief. "How are y'all going to do when he moves here?"

When. Not if. Liz tried not to cringe. "We'll be fine."

"I just . . ." Calleigh began, taking a seat next to Liz. "Well, I'm sure you already know that Hayden and I were involved."

Liz narrowed her eyes. Where was she going with this?

"Well, the man isn't good with distance. He just couldn't handle me being far away. It's why we broke up in the first place."

Uh-huh. Not the story she had heard at all. But who was she to contradict Calleigh? It was clear what her game plan was. The fact that she was airing it like this was pretty dumb on her part. Liz wasn't going to be scared off like the frightened sheep she had been a year ago. She had fucking brought a Senator to his knees . . . she could handle Calleigh Hollingsworth.

"Well, thanks for the advice. I guess. But we'll be fine. You don't have to worry about us, Calleigh," Liz said, reaching out and patting the woman's hand. "We have a really strong relationship. No worries."

Anger flashed in Calleigh's green eyes for a brief moment before it disappeared. "Oh, I'm sure you do. Of course you do. I just wish someone had warned me is all."

"I'm sure it wouldn't have made a difference," Liz said offhandedly.

"What does *that* mean?" Calleigh snapped, rearing back.

"Things happen for a reason. You guys broke up so long ago and never got back together, so it must have been for the better. Hayden told me all about it actually," Liz said, batting her eyelashes right back at her. "I'll learn from your past mistakes."

Calleigh stood abruptly. "We'll see."

Not until the woman stormed back down the hallway did Liz realize her mistake. While it had felt amazing to tell Calleigh off, she had just sent that loose cannon out into the world with something to prove. And if Hayden got the job here, then who would she be trying to prove it with . . . ?

Liz didn't have much time to think about it before Hayden returned. He looked as if he was walking on cloud nine. The interview must have gone well. Not that Liz had expected anything else.

He shook Ted's hand once more and they exchanged a few words before Hayden returned to her side. Liz stood hastily as he approached.

"Ready to go?" he asked, tossing an arm across her shoulders and directing her to the door.

"Yep. How did it go?"

"Amazing." Hayden opened the door for her when they reached it and she walked through it. "I got a job offer!"

"That's great," she said softly.

"I just told you I had an amazing interview and was offered a job and you sound sad," Hayden said, stopping her in the parking lot.

"I'm really excited for you!" she said, but the enthusiasm wasn't there. She had been so excited and proud and nervous for him before Calleigh had gone and ruined everything.

"Yeah. Liz, you're kind of an open book when you're unhappy," Hayden said. "I was only gone for an hour. What could happen in an hour?"

"Nothing. It really doesn't matter," she said, brushing her hand aside. "Tell me about the interview."

Hayden took her hand and without a word walked her back to the car. Even when she probed him to talk about it he didn't say anything. When they reached the car, she walked with him to the passenger side to let him open the door for her as usual. Instead, Hayden pushed her back against the car door and leaned forward into her.

"Wha . . ."

"I don't know how I can make this clearer to you, Lizzie," he said, brushing her hair off of her face. "What is going on with you matters to me. What you are feeling—happy, sad, exhausted, emotional, frustrated—it matters to me. I know you've been kind of out of it recently, and I know that *you* know that I've noticed. But

I've let you have your space, because it seemed like that was what you wanted. The very last thing I want is for you to try to tell me that something you are feeling doesn't matter, that it isn't important. Because it's important to me."

"You're too good to me, Hayden," she said.

He smiled at that and kissed the tip of her nose. "Well, you're the best thing that's ever happened to me. You know that, right?"

She bit her lip and then nodded. She didn't feel like the best thing that had ever happened to anyone, but she couldn't argue with him.

"So, what happened?"

Liz shrugged and glanced away. She couldn't meet his eyes. "Calleigh."

Hayden blew out his breath quickly. "What did she say?"

"I'd just forgotten that she worked here."

"Lizzie," he said, turning her face toward him, "what did she say?"

"She still wants you, Hayden."

His eyebrows rose. "She said that?"

"Not directly, but she didn't have to. She started talking to me about your relationship and saying that you just broke up because of the distance."

"That's not true!"

"I know," she said conciliatorily. "She just . . . I don't know. I worry that she's going to try something with you . . ."

Hayden laughed and shook his head. "She can try, but she's not getting anywhere. Not with me. That's for sure."

"I know that. I do. She just gets under my skin. It's like this weird girl competition challenge thing," Liz said with a shrug.

"Well, I got the job and I'll be working here. But it's you I'll be thinking about every day. It's you I'm going to be traveling back to

Chapel Hill to see. It's you who makes working this hard worth it." His lips found hers once more. "Just you."

She smiled and leaned into the kiss. She wanted to believe him. She *did* believe him. If he wanted to be with Calleigh, he could. Calleigh was just trying to get to her.

"I was going to do this over dinner," Hayden said softly, reaching into his coat pocket.

"Do what?" she asked, eyeing him cautiously.

He extracted a small black pouch from his pocket and handed it to her. "Happy birthday, gorgeous."

Liz tilted her head to the side and eyed him curiously. What the hell had he gotten her? "You didn't have to get me anything."

"I wanted to."

She took the pouch and weighed it in her hand. It was really light. It didn't actually feel like there was anything in it.

She pulled open the small pouch and tipped it upside down into her cupped hand. A small clear packet dropped out. Liz just stared at what rested inside with a numb realization settling over her.

Charms.

Four tiny charms. A snowflake, tennis racket, the letter *L*, and a diamond.

She could determine the meaning behind each charm clearly. The snowflake for the first time they had been together during their snow day. The tennis racket and *L* were all too obvious. And then a diamond for her April birthstone.

"I didn't get the locket part, because I knew you already had one. You used to wear it all the time. I thought you would start wearing it again if you had new charms," he said with a big cheesy smile. "It looked good on you."

She swallowed. Shit. No. This was . . . she couldn't even . . . she didn't know what to do. This was too much. Too soon. Brady. No, she didn't want to think about him, but of course she couldn't stop. She couldn't wear Hayden's charms. He was so thoughtful, but no.

Liz cleared her throat and tried to remember what she was supposed to say when she received gifts. "Thank you," she managed to get out.

"Lizzie," he whispered, staring into her unfocused eyes, "I love you."

Her mind froze on those three words. The three words she had wanted Brady to say to her so badly. The three words that she had told Brady that she knew about in the car a couple weeks ago. Words she had spoken to Brady.

But Hayden?

Clay's words rang in her ear from the art gallery. *But you don't love him.* It hurt to think about. Brady. Clay. Hayden. They all clouded in her vision and she had to remember to speak . . . to say anything in that moment. She just couldn't say what Hayden wanted to hear.

"I know," she whispered back.

Chapter 12

TWENTY-FIRST

Liz placed another bobby pin in her uncooperative honey-blond hair. She had been putting her hair up and pulling it down for the last thirty minutes, trying to make it look good enough to go out for her twenty-first birthday. Victoria had told her that a ton of people were meeting them. Liz was already tipsy from the Jell-O shots Victoria had made to pregame with, and she was kind of worried about her liver making it through the night.

The weekend with Hayden had gone by so fast, despite the mess-ups. It was as if every time he did something good and cute and wonderful . . . it reminded her of Brady. And then there was Calleigh. Still, Hayden had tried to end their time in Charlotte as best he could. He had taken them to a little Italian restaurant called Villa Antonio's that had spectacular food and a warm, inviting atmosphere. Then they had retreated back to the hotel for another night of fun.

What Liz couldn't understand was how Hayden wasn't upset at all that she hadn't told him that she loved him. She just couldn't seem to get the words out. And as with everything else, he hadn't pressured her or made her feel bad. He had just smiled and kissed her.

She wondered how long that would be good enough.

With Hayden she just didn't know. He always surprised her with the depth of his understanding.

At least for now he wasn't pushing her. In fact, he was playing the designated driver for her and Victoria for the night. He had been planning to go out with them, but Victoria had put her foot down.

"You stole her all weekend!" Victoria said, shaking her head. "I didn't even get a shot with her at midnight."

Hayden shrugged and kissed Liz's forehead. "She's my girlfriend. I can't help that I want to spoil her."

"Spoil her. Steal her. Same thing," Victoria said. "I'm going to spoil her tonight. And by spoil her . . . I mean steal her."

Hayden raised his eyebrows. "You're saying I can't be with my girlfriend on her birthday?"

Liz rolled her eyes. *Oh brother . . . this was going to go downhill quickly.*

"I'm saying that you already spent time with you girlfriend for three whole days. I want to spend time with my best friend, and I don't need some uptight guy cramping my style. This is about Liz and needing some quality girl time. With me! Don't worry, Lane," Victoria said, patting his shoulder. "I'll take real good care of your girl. I'm super responsible."

"Oh dear Lord, you're going to end up in jail!"

Liz laughed and shook her head. "Ye of little faith! Vickie doesn't get caught."

"Stop calling me that!" she snapped.

They laughed then, but Hayden had eventually agreed to sit this one out. As much as they bantered, Liz didn't think Hayden actually wanted Victoria to dislike him.

"Are you ready, bitch?" Victoria called from the end of the hall. Liz blew her hair out of her face and shrugged. It wasn't getting any better than this.

"I love when you dress like a slut," Liz said when she walked out to see Victoria in a red dress that sheathed her voluptuous frame and mile-high spiked heels. She was busting out of her top and her already thick makeup was darkened and heavy, with bright red lipstick to match.

"What? This is like every day," Victoria said with a wink.

"Uh-huh."

"At least you look fabulous on your birthday."

"Is that a compliment?" Liz asked, glancing down at her outfit. She had chosen a short lace dress in white with skinny straps that cut down into an eye-catching square neck courtesy of her balconet bra. She knew she had a nice rack, but she didn't normally show it off. Tonight was not one of those nights. Vibrant blue heels gave her an additional four and a half inches on her frame and accentuated her already toned legs.

"Don't get used to it."

Liz laughed just as they heard a knock on the front door. Hayden walked in without waiting for someone to answer, and Liz smiled brighter when she caught a glimpse of him. Clay had told her Hayden loved her over New Year's, but it was different hearing him say it and knowing that he meant it. Whatever she was feeling . . . while it might not be love . . . it was definitely something strong.

"Ready to go, gorgeous?" he asked, pulling her into his arms and kissing her on the lips.

"All ready."

"I'm not sure I should let you go out like this alone. You're going to have people fighting for your attention."

"You're ridiculous. No one is going to be fighting for anything except Victoria and the shots she's going to be buying," Liz said with a bemused look in Victoria's direction.

"Yeah, shots. Let's go so we can have some," Victoria said, shouldering past Hayden. "And I already told you, Lane. She'll be fine in my capable hands."

Hayden glanced over at Liz as Victoria sauntered out the door. "Are you sure I can't convince you to let me stay?"

"You don't have to convince me. You have to convince her," Liz said, pointing at Victoria's retreating back.

He groaned and nodded. "Come on. There's no hope for her."

They all piled into Hayden's Audi and he drove them the short distance to Franklin Street. They lived only about three streets from where the bar was, but in heels it wasn't a super fun walk.

Victoria jumped out of the car as soon as Hayden pulled over to let them out. Liz leaned over and kissed Hayden softly on the lips.

"Have a fun time," he said.

"We will."

"Call me if you need me."

"I will."

"I'll come pick you up at bar close, all right?" Hayden said, his voice earnest. She could see the worry line forming between his eyebrows; the war going on in his head was written all over his face: he was clearly not comfortable letting her go off with Victoria, but he trusted Liz.

"Sure. Try not to worry," she whispered, dropping a hand on his sleeve. "We'll be fine."

Hayden grabbed the back of her head and pulled her in for one last kiss. "I know you will, but I'll be here in case you aren't."

"Thanks," she said softly, before popping her door open and moving to leave. "I'll see you later."

"About time," Victoria said, tapping her foot. "Let's get drunk."

Liz laughed and followed her friend into the first bar. She couldn't even remember the last time it had just been the two of them out. Hayden was usually with them, and she didn't usually drink much when he was around. Before she had started dating Hayden she hadn't gone out at all. She just hadn't been into it. The last time might have been when Victoria came back from London last summer. Brady had picked her up that night and they had met his best friend, Chris. That felt so long ago.

It *was* so long ago.

Victoria strutted straight up to the bar. "Kyle! It's my best friend's twenty-first birthday and she needs to get so fucked up that she doesn't remember anything!" she announced to the bartender loudly enough for anyone else to hear.

Liz groaned. This was going to be a long night.

Kyle looked up at Liz, who took a place next to Victoria. His eyes lowered to her chest and then back up to her face. Liz felt the color rushing to her cheeks, but he just smiled and winked at her. "Shots coming right up."

That was the beginning of the end.

Liz wasn't exactly a lightweight. But by the time Massey showed up at the bar, Liz had had enough drinks in that short time frame that whatever concoction she was drinking tasted like fruit punch.

Victoria just laughed at her. "It's not Kool-Aid, I swear."

"What is she even drinking?" Massey asked with a giggle as she fluttered her fingers in Kyle's direction.

"I don't know." Victoria shrugged. "Kyle, what is she drinking?"

"Kool-Aid," Liz answered immediately.

"It's a 3AM and vodka mixture with cranberry," he called back to Victoria.

"See, not Kool-Aid."

Liz thought she shrugged, but her eyes felt heavy and she wasn't sure what her body actually did. "What's 3AM?"

"Oh my God, who let you drink this much?" Massey said, covering her mouth and almost shaking with laughter.

"3AM is caffeinated vodka," Victoria explained.

"Yeah, it's what the bartenders drink to stay awake," Massey followed up.

"It tastes like Kool-Aid."

"No it doesn't! It tastes like shit!" Massey cried.

"Here, try it. It's so good," Liz said, shoving it into Massey's hand.

"Um no . . . I'm more of a Maker's Mark kind of girl. You should probably slow down if you want to be coherent. Where is Lane? Shouldn't he be taking care of you?"

Liz rolled her eyes. "I don't need anyone to take care of me. I'm totally fine," she slurred, and hugged the glass back to her chest.

"And the point is that she shouldn't be coherent on her twenty-first," Victoria corrected her.

"You know he would freak if he found you like this."

"He'll get over it. I'm barely even drunk," Liz said.

Massey snorted and laughed. "Yeah. Okayyy."

Liz moved forward and put her drink on the bar. "I'm going to the bathroom. Watch that."

"One, don't put your drink down. Someone could roofie it. Two, you shouldn't go anywhere alone. Hello, have you heard of rape?" Massey asked, rolling her eyes. "I'll come with."

"Oh my God, you baby her," Victoria said, rolling her eyes.

"I'm fine, Massey. Just stay here and keep someone from fucking Victoria!"

Victoria burst out laughing. "Why are we keeping someone from doing that?"

"Because you're drunk," Liz said as she started laughing for no reason at all.

"What the fuck have I gotten myself into?" Victoria groaned.

"Come on. Bathroom," Massey said, directing Liz in the opposite direction. "Watch her drink!"

"Fine!" Victoria said.

Liz stumbled to the back of the bar with Massey assisting her. The more she walked the sicker she felt. She really needed to sit down. Maybe she was a little drunk.

"Please do not throw up," Massey grumbled when they walked into the bathroom.

"I'm not going to!" Liz replied defensively.

Well . . . she wasn't going to *now*.

She fumbled with the door and walked into the bathroom stall. Once she locked the door, she pulled out her cell phone. She had three texts from Hayden.

Liz shrugged and scrolled through them. *Be safe.* Blah, blah, blah. Same stuff. She would answer him later. Maybe.

That made her giggle.

She clicked over to Facebook and scrolled through her newsfeed, commenting randomly on different statuses. Not anyone she really wanted to talk to. No. The person she wanted to talk to probably didn't even have a Facebook. Or at least, he probably only had an official page.

That made Liz laugh again. She had never checked whether Brady had an official page. She had always gone to his website instead. But he had to have one. Only made sense.

She typed his name incorrectly three times into the box before getting it right. There it was. Yep. Nothing interesting. Same as his website. It's not like he was going to be posting pictures of him and his *girlfriend*. She rolled her eyes.

Whatever. Girlfriend.

Stupid word.

She could probably still get ahold of him if she wanted. *Girlfriend be damned.*

Liz searched her phone for the various numbers programmed into it. She didn't know if the line he had used on campaign for his office was still active, and he changed his work number frequently enough because of people tapping into his line that there was no way that one still worked. Plus, he didn't take work calls this late.

That left his personal number. The one he reserved strictly for family.

It was amazing that even through her addled mind the details of his personal schedule from the summer came back to her clear as day. She didn't think she would ever forget that time of her life. Even if it only hit her in moments now.

Liz bit her lip and clicked the number. She started typing out a message before she even had a chance to think about it.

It's my birthday and I want to cash in my congressional favor.

She giggled and placed her phone back into her purse. After relieving herself she hurried out of the stall.

"Jesus, what took you so long?" Massey asked, typing away on her own phone.

"I think I'm drunk," Liz said while washing her hands.

"Um . . . yeah."

The girls walked out of the restroom and back to Victoria, who was standing and talking to Savannah.

"Savannah!" Liz cried, giving her a big hug.

Savannah raised her eyebrows at her. "Um . . . hey. Happy birthday."

"Thank you."

"Let's do shots and then head to a bar we can dance in," Victoria announced.

Kyle poured five shots full of something that smelled like lemons. He passed them across the bar and kept one for himself.

"Just close me out."

"Anything for you, V."

Victoria pushed one over to Savannah, who shook her head. "Oh no, sorry. I'm not drinking."

"Um . . . I just bought you a shot. So you're drinking."

"Come on!" Liz called. "It's my birthday."

"Um . . . maybe just one. But nothing after this."

"Don't be so uptight, Maxwell," Massey said, nudging her in the ribs. "It's okay to have a good time in college. You'll still get into Congress even if you drank underage once."

Savannah's cheeks heated as she took the glass in her hand.

Liz reached out and shoved Massey. "Don't be a bitch. She doesn't even want to go into politics. Don't you know your newspaper staff?" Liz asked through her drunken haze. She didn't like anyone messing with her friends, especially after Savannah trusted her. All the alcohol kept her inhibitions down. "Don't be rude!"

Massey's eyes practically popped out of her head. "Feisty much, Liz?"

"Well, I wouldn't have to be if you weren't being an asshole."

"Whoa!" Victoria said, raising her glass up to silence them. "Drunk Liz wants to get into a fight."

Massey shrugged. "I was only joking," she said to Savannah.

"It's fine," she said tightly. "Let's just do the shot."

"Agreed," Victoria said.

Liz felt her phone vibrate in her purse and butterflies flew around her stomach. Had Brady actually responded? What had she even said to him? It hadn't been that long ago, had it? God, she didn't even remember.

"Happy Birthday, Liz," Victoria called.

Everyone raised their shot glasses and cheered her. Liz realized what was happening and held her shot glass up too. She tipped the glass back and let the liquid slide down her throat.

Whoa! That was strong.

They set the glasses back down on the bar and as they waited for Victoria to close her tab, Liz pulled her phone back out to check her messages.

One new message.

Carmichael Personal read on the screen.

Brady. Her stomach flipped. He had responded. She couldn't believe it.

And what favor could a congressman offer to a girl on her birthday?

Liz's heart stopped. Was he . . . teasing her? Shit! What had she said to get Brady to tease her? Liz reread her other messages and then Brady's once more. Yeah . . . he was totally teasing her. She jotted back another drunken message immediately.

I can think of a few things.

I can think of more than a few. Perhaps you could be more specific.

"Are you drunk texting Lane?" Massey asked, coming up next to her as they walked in the street.

"What? Oh no," she said quickly.

"Oh my God, you so are. What is he saying?"

"Nothing!"

"Is he sexting you? Because you are totally blushing."

Liz's face colored deeper at the accusation. "You think Hayden sexts?"

Massey wrinkled her nose. "No. You're right. He probably doesn't."

"Are y'all talking about Hayden?" Savannah asked, listening in on the conversation. "Because that's gross."

"He's not gross!" Liz defended him.

"No, he's not! I didn't mean it like that," Savannah said automatically. "I just don't see him like that. To me he's like the boss."

"Liz is fucking the boss," Massey said giggling.

Liz rolled her eyes and hid her phone as she responded to Brady.

Things your sister wouldn't approve of me discussing with you right now.

I bet she wouldn't be the only one.

She bit her lip at the message. Somewhere in the dark recesses of her mind, something was telling her to stop talking and not continue on this conversation. There was a reason that she shouldn't be saying these things. Both of them shouldn't. It wasn't a good idea, and it wasn't going anywhere. But she'd had too much alcohol to care at the moment. So she jotted out a text.

Please tell me you're in Raleigh without the uppity nuisance.

She giggled to herself about her jab on Erin as Victoria directed them into a bar on the corner. Liz followed at the back of the pack, waiting for Brady's response to her jab about Erin.

Uppity nuisance, huh? I'm in D.C. Don't make me fly down there and remind you why he's just a boring fill-in. I do believe we own his desk, after all.

Oh shit! She gasped loud enough that Savannah turned around and looked at her. Liz stuffed her phone back into her purse and tried not to look scandalized at the thought of she and Brady sleeping together on Hayden's desk. Then she quickly pulled it out again and typed out a reply.

You wouldn't.

Baby, are you asking me to prove it?

"Who are you texting anyway?" Savannah asked as they walked into the club Victoria and Massey had selected. Savannah looked concerned, but Liz couldn't figure out why. Did she look that drunk?

"No one," Liz said.

"We're going to go dance," Victoria called back to them as she and Massey threaded through the crowd.

"Someone should take your phone away from you," Savannah said. "You can't be forming coherent sentences with anyone at your level of inebriation."

Liz glared at her. She didn't want anyone to take her phone from her. Brady was talking to her. But as drunk as she was, she still didn't say anything about that.

"I'm so totally fine."

Savannah rolled her eyes. "Why don't we just go dance with Victoria and Massey? It might do you some good to sweat out some of that alcohol."

"Seriously, Savannah. I'm fine," Liz said as she stumbled forward and nearly tripped over her own feet.

Savannah grabbed her arm. "I know it's your twenty-first, and I mean this with love, Liz, but please don't do anything stupid. I really, really don't want to have to call Hayden for you."

"Um . . . yeah. No."

"I mean, he can probably already tell how drunk you are from your texts."

"Probs," Liz said with a shrug as she pushed forward to the center of the dance floor to find Victoria. She didn't want to continue that conversation. The alcohol felt as if it was sloshing around inside her head, and everything was getting jumbled.

Liz sent another quick message as she was walking.

So what if I am?

"Put that thing away," Victoria cried over the music.

"Fine," Liz snapped, shoving it back into her purse. "You guys are no fun."

"The reason we left Lane at home is so that you'll have fun with us. You can't have fun with us while you're messaging him," Victoria told her.

The girls spent the next couple hours loading Liz up with more booze and dancing the night away with each other and any available hot guys. As much as Liz was dying to check her phone, she had a sneaking suspicion that she wouldn't get away with it again.

And as the night grew longer, her head got heavier and heavier. She felt pretty sick, but the dancing seemed to be helping. Maybe there was something to Savannah's comment about sweating out the booze.

Savannah dipped out first. She claimed that she had a test to study for tomorrow and she would call to check on Liz after. She didn't suspect Liz would be awake before then. Massey left about an hour before bar close. She found a hot fraternity guy that she knew and they disappeared with a hasty good-bye.

Liz and Victoria danced until Liz felt as if her feet were going to fall off. And that was saying something through her buzz.

"Let's get out of here," Liz yelled over the music.

Victoria nodded and gestured to exit the dance floor. She was wobbling on her heels too. If they had drunk enough for Victoria to be unsteady, then Liz knew she was well past drunk. Luckily the sick feeling had passed and she just wanted to walk off the rest of the haze in her mind.

"Close out?" Liz asked.

"Yeah," Victoria agreed. "Call Lane and tell him to come get us."

Liz shrugged and fished her phone back out of her purse. She hadn't checked it in hours. There had been no room on the dance floor. Her fingers fumbled on the keys as she tried to figure out what the hell she was doing. What was she supposed to be doing anyway?

Two new messages.

As good a place to start as anywhere.

Okay.

Okay what? Liz scrolled up through the conversation. She had told him to prove it and he had said okay. Fuck. What was the next text?

See you soon.

Liz panicked. Fire alarms were going off in her head. God, she wanted to see him. She really, really wanted to see him. But seeing him was a bad idea. Hayden. She was supposed to be calling Hayden. She couldn't call Hayden if Brady was coming to see her.

She did the first thing that came to mind. She clicked the number to dial Brady's phone and prayed that he wasn't already on a plane . . . or maybe that he already was. She didn't know how she felt in that moment.

Drunk. She felt drunk. And sick. The sickness was coming back.

She started walking. Out of the bar and onto the sidewalk.

The phone rang twice before the line picked up. She held her breath. She wasn't sure what she had been expecting, but all along she hadn't thought he would answer.

"Hey," he said, his voice as sexy as she remembered it.

"Hey."

"You called me on my personal line."

"You were texting me," she said, finding a bench and plopping down.

"I've been drinking."

Oh.

"How much?" she slurred.

He laughed, and it was one of the best sounds she had ever heard. "Not as many as you, apparently."

"More than one, though."

"Many more than one," he agreed.

"I'm drunk."

"I can tell."

Victoria's voice rang out behind her. "Liz, where the fuck did you go?"

"Hold on," she told Brady. She stood and waved at Victoria. "Over here."

"Jesus! Don't do that!" Victoria said. "Are you talking to Lane? Is he picking us up?"

"Let's just walk home. I want to walk off all this booze," she crooned, and started walking away without waiting to hear what Victoria had to say. "So . . . what was I saying? Oh, you can't come visit."

"I can't or you don't want me to?" That was the first line where she actually heard the alcohol in his voice.

"Liz, are you kidding me right now?" Victoria yelled. "Who the hell are you talking to?"

"Who is that?" Brady asked.

"My roommate. She doesn't want me to walk home."

"You shouldn't walk home. I'll come get you."

"You're not here," she said, drawing out the E dramatically as she wandered aimlessly down Franklin Street.

Victoria grabbed her shoulder and halted her in place. "Who are you talking to? Give me the phone. We're not fucking walking home!"

"Chill out, Vickie," Liz said, swatting her hand away.

Victoria dodged her easily and nimbly grabbed her phone. Liz stumbled as she tried to reach for it. She couldn't let Victoria talk to Brady!

"Hey, who is this? You know what—it doesn't matter. Liz is really drunk and she has to go now. She'll call you back some other time," Victoria said into the phone and then ended the call. Liz's heart sank. She had just hung up on Brady in the middle of their call.

"I'm calling Lane," Victoria said, finding his number and dialing.

Liz plopped back down on the bench and tried to keep her head from spinning. It wouldn't stop. And she felt so out of control. All the booze seemed to be hitting her at one time and she thought that she might be sick.

There was a trash can to the side of the bench, and Liz just made it as she unloaded the contents of her stomach into the bin. She retched repeatedly until it felt as if she had nothing left in her entire body. She felt the tears spring to her eyes and she tried to swipe them away, but it made her stomach clench. She hadn't thought that she had anything left in her, but she doubled over and puked again.

"Fuck!" she heard Victoria cry behind her.

Her friend was at her side in an instant, holding her hair back, cleaning her up the best she could, and sitting her back down on the bench. Hayden arrived not long after that and drove them back to her house. Liz had enough sense to grab her phone back from Victoria before crawling into bed. But lying down was a bad move, and soon she had her face buried in the toilet.

Hayden stayed up half the night with her as she got sick over and over until she passed out into a delirious, dehydrated, exhausted slumber.

Chapter 13
SLIP THROUGH THEIR FINGERTIPS

Liz awoke the next afternoon with a headache from hell. Her eyes were puffy, her throat was swollen, and she felt as if someone had run her over with a Mack truck. She was equal parts starving and never wanting to eat again.

Why oh why had she ever allowed herself to drink as much as she did?

Rolling over slowly in bed, she peeled her eyes open and tried to let them adjust to the light in the room. Her head spun and she wondered briefly if she was actually still drunk from last night. Moving onto her other side, Liz stared at a little slice of heaven.

A glass of water. A bottle of Gatorade. A thousand milligrams of Tylenol. And a note from Hayden letting her know that he was going to pick them up some lunch. Not that she had any intention of eating anything.

After taking the medicine, she sipped on the Gatorade, trying to drink as much as she could without feeling sick. Last night had been a very bad idea. Fuzzy memories came back to her slowly. But she didn't remember a lot of what had happened after Massey got there.

Something.

Savannah.

Right. Savannah had shown up. That was so nice of her. She should text her a thank-you.

Liz reached for her phone and stopped just before grabbing it. "Oh no," she whispered.

Now she remembered.

Brady.

She had texted Brady last night. And he had answered. They had talked back and forth. Had she even called him? Fuck, what had they talked about?

She snatched the phone off the nightstand and pulled up her text messages. Scrolling through them made the sickness she'd had all last night come back full force. Had she actually said those things to Brady? Had she asked him to fly to Chapel Hill to see her? Had he encouraged her?

Oh God. Oh God. Oh God. What the hell was she supposed to do?

Liz dropped the phone into her lap on the bed and covered her eyes. She was a fucking idiot. A terrible fucking idiot. She had left Brady eight long months ago. So what was she still doing obsessing over this?

Brady had been drunk and fucking with her last night. No matter what she felt or what she had felt last August . . . that part of her life was over.

And Hayden.

Oh, Hayden . . .

What if he had read the messages? What if he had seen what she had insinuated? What if he had seen how stupid she had been? She didn't think he had, based on the merry assortment of hangover fixers on the nightstand, but God, what if he had?

Hayden was the nicest person she had ever met. He was a complete gentleman and treated her exactly the way she deserved to be treated. He loved her. And she didn't deserve him. Not with the way she had acted last night. Not by a long shot. She knew that she had been drunk, beyond drunk, but it wasn't an excuse. She couldn't use that to excuse her behavior.

The reality check slapped her in the face.

She couldn't do this to Hayden. She couldn't allow herself to become *that* person. She had never in her life been that person . . . the person she had been last night. It wasn't an acceptable manner of behavior. She couldn't live with herself.

Hayden loved her, and maybe she didn't love him right now, but how did she know that feeling would never flourish if she gave it a real chance? She wasn't giving Hayden a chance, much like Brady had stifled theirs. It hadn't been fair to her, and it certainly wasn't fair to Hayden, who was a much better person than she was.

She never wanted Hayden to have to make the choice that she had made with Brady. She needed to pull back, reevaluate herself.

She owed Hayden a fresh start.

Liz pulled up Brady's numbers in her phone with trembling hands. She slowly went through each of them and deleted them. She knew his work number by heart, but she doubted that one even worked anymore, so it didn't matter. She couldn't have pieces of Brady floating around and reminding her.

She could never take back the words she had shared with Brady last night, but she could learn from what happened. Live and learn from her mistakes.

━

Graduation came and went without big fanfare.

Hayden's parents came to town for the week to celebrate and attend the ceremony. Jamie and James flew down a couple days after

Hayden's parents just in time for graduation. Hayden dressed in Carolina-blue graduation robes, and Liz wore a blue dress to match. Hayden had frowned at her bare neck and asked if she was going to wear her birthday present. She had blushed and told him it didn't go with the outfit. She didn't want a reminder of Brady at Hayden's graduation. Easily appeased, Hayden left to find the rest of his class, while Liz entered Kenan Stadium with his family to watch from the bleachers. She had a hard time believing that the time had already come for Hayden to graduate, and that she would be in the same place within a year.

Liz had an amazing time with his family, who were unbelievably welcoming and accepting. She really felt at home with them, and that was encouraging all around.

Jamie and James dropped on everyone that they planned to elope in Hawaii at the beginning of June. They kept insisting that no one else had to attend, but of course everyone told them that they would be there. Liz understood their wanting a small intimate get-together rather than a big affair. That seemed like Jamie.

That left her and Hayden a whole month together where neither of them had school or the paper or anything at all to do besides relax and enjoy each other's company. Hayden would officially start his job at the *Charlotte Times* the Monday after Jamie's wedding, and as much as the two of them tried to hold on to time, it seemed to slip right through their fingertips.

Soon enough their blissful month together came to a close and they were on a plane to Hawaii. Liz had never been before, and was excited to spend some time with Hayden on the beach as much as to see Jamie and James get married.

They arrived in Honolulu late the night before the wedding just in time to see the sunset over the island. The sky lit up into the most gorgeous reds, yellows, pinks, and oranges that Liz had ever seen. She was sure that a sunset never looked more beautiful than in Hawaii, and was so thankful that she was able to experience it.

Hayden grabbed her luggage out of the back of the taxi as soon as it pulled up in front of their resort. It was a gorgeous twenty-story construction on a secluded area off the north coast of Oahu and boasted private beaches, snorkeling excursions to nearby waterfalls, the luxury of a big resort, and the exclusivity and intimacy of a smaller one.

Liz felt a little awkward sharing a room with Hayden, knowing that his parents were going to be in the same hotel. Not that they had connecting rooms or anything. As far as she knew they weren't even on the same floor. Hayden thought she was being ridiculous. It wasn't like his parents didn't know that they were sleeping together. Which of course made sense . . . because they were college students and all. Still it did nothing to alleviate her stress.

The gorgeous view from the tenth floor overlooking the ocean helped make up for it.

As soon as they arrived, though, they had to change and meet everyone in the lobby for an informal rehearsal dinner. The only other people who had flown all this way for the wedding were Meredith, Jamie's maid of honor, and Nick, who was the best man. After they'd had a great time with friends, good food, and some choice wine, jet lag began to set in, and she and Hayden called it an early night.

Because of the six-hour time difference, Jamie had planned an early-morning wedding on the beach. Liz woke up at the crack of dawn to get ready for the big day. She was practically bouncing up and down on her toes with excitement. She really liked Jamie, and she was so glad to be here for her.

Liz had brought with her a plain coral sundress that flowed down to her ankles, and strappy gold sandals. It wasn't extravagant, but then again none of this was. She left her hair down in natural beachy waves, pulling one section back with a bobby pin. Her face was sun-kissed from the extra hours she had put in playing tennis in her month break from school, so she only needed light makeup that highlighted her skin.

When she caught a glimpse of Hayden as she exited the shower, she just smiled. He was in khakis and boat shoes with a green polo that accented his eyes. She couldn't have picked out an outfit that suited him more.

"You ready?" he asked, his eyes roaming her figure.

"Yeah. I'm excited for Jamie. Do you think she's nervous?"

"She's probably running around like a maniac, as usual," Hayden said, shaking his head. "But I think my sister knows that James is the right decision."

"Oh, I know she does. I kind of love that she didn't want to plan a wedding. It's super romantic that they just jet off to a resort for this little private ceremony. Don't you think?" Liz asked dreamily.

Hayden shrugged, pulling her into him. "I don't know. I'm a bit more traditional than my sister. I kind of like the idea of a big wedding. Have it all planned out and the anticipation of the event only bringing us closer."

Liz flushed under his scrutiny as the words washed over her. He was talking about *them*. Of course, he wasn't talking about them getting married anytime soon, but she could see in his eyes that he was interested in that. That it was something he wanted.

She hadn't really thought about it until that moment. What would a lifetime with Hayden be like? She could just see how it would be. He would love her unconditionally, always put her first, plan out their lives. She could see the requisite two and a half kids with a house in the suburbs, a white picket fence, and everything. She could see Hayden's smiling face greeting her day in and day out. She saw herself happy there.

She had never had that thought with anyone before. At least, not like this. Not realistically.

"What do you think? I would guess you have your dream wedding all planned out," Hayden said.

"I . . . yeah. I mean, I've thought about it. I just thought it would be nice and stress free. Not that eloping is for me, necessarily," Liz corrected. "I guess I always wanted a big wedding too, with all of my family and friends."

A broad smile grew on Hayden's face the longer she spoke. When she finished he leaned forward and kissed her passionately. "You are perfect for me."

Liz laughed and tried to play it off as if it didn't matter . . . as if he hadn't just said that they had the same dream wedding. "Come on. We don't want to be late to your own sister's wedding."

He kissed her once more lovingly. He leaned back and trailed his fingers along her collarbones. "Are you going to wear your necklace?"

Liz bit her lip and tried not to look guilty. "I left it at home."

"Oh," Hayden said, disappointed. "Maybe next time."

Liz swallowed and wished she had the strength to tell him she could never wear it again.

They exited the hotel room and took the elevator downstairs. His parents were waiting for them in the lobby. His mom came forward and gave her a hug. "Thank you so much for being here with us today. It means so much to us."

Liz smiled and looked down at the ground. "I wouldn't miss it. I'm so happy for Jamie."

"We're so happy for her too, dear," she said warmly. "Come on, y'all. Let's go down to the beach to wait for the bridal party."

Liz and Hayden followed his parents out to the private beach where the ceremony was going to be held. The pastor was already in place. James's mother had flown in on the red-eye that morning from

New York City and was already standing on the beach in a black dress when they arrived. Liz had heard mention that his parents were divorced and neither James nor his mother spoke to his father anymore, and his mother had become somewhat of a recluse ever since. She had wondered last night if that had been part of the reason for the elopement, but considering Jamie, Liz kind of doubted it.

There were no chairs, and Liz let her feet sink into the white sand as she waited. She wiggled her toes and watched her feet bury themselves. Hayden reached out for her hand and laced their fingers together just as the bridal party arrived.

Jamie walked forward in a short, flowy white sundress that floated out behind her in the breeze. The dress cinched in at the waist with a multicolored sheer print sash that bowed in the back. Her black bob was straight almost to her shoulders, and she had a circle of small white flowers in her hair. She was barefoot with no jewelry aside from a slender gold bracelet on one hand that her parents had given her the night before. Her mother had worn it at her own wedding and passed it down to her daughter for her wedding day.

James was dressed in khakis and a loose linen button-down. They couldn't have been more perfect for each other if they tried.

Meredith and Nick followed behind Jamie and James to the pastor standing in a suit in the hot sand. He smiled at them all and then began the service. It was short and to the point. They exchanged vows, slid simple bands on each other's fingers, and then before Liz knew it the pastor was announcing that James could kiss his bride.

Everyone cheered as they kissed and then the short ceremony was over. Jamie flitted from person to person, thanking everyone for coming even though there were only nine people in attendance including the bride and groom.

Her arms wound around Liz's neck and she pulled her into a hug. "I'm so glad you could be here."

"I wouldn't miss it for the world, Jamie," Liz replied.

"I know it sounds crazy, but I already feel like you're family."

Hayden rolled his eyes and sighed. "Jamie . . ."

"I love you too, little brother," she said with a huge smile plastered on her face as she strangle-hugged him.

Liz laughed at Jamie and Hayden acting like typical brother and sister. She didn't even know why Hayden had sighed so heavily. She liked that she already felt like family to Jamie. She really loved her. She was so much fun and such a free spirit. It made Liz want to loosen up a bit herself. But to Jamie, Liz was fifty times less stressed than her uptight brother. Liz's smile grew at the thought.

After thirty minutes of pictures, the wedding party retreated to a small private dining room for the small reception brunch. Mimosas and Bloody Marys were served and the whole table toasted the young couple to many years of happiness. When the plates were cleared, the drinks gone, and conversations were dying down, Jamie and James said their good-byes and retreated to their hotel room. No one had any specific plans until tomorrow, so everyone went their separate ways to change and head out to enjoy the sunshine.

When they made it back up to their room, Hayden slid his arm around her waist. "I have plans for us, gorgeous," he murmured against her ear.

Liz shivered at the soft touch of his lips against her ear. "Plans?"

"I thought you would want to do something after the wedding, so I scheduled something for us."

"What is it?" she asked, biting down on her lip.

He kissed the side of her neck. "Surprise. Get into your bathing suit. We have to head out soon."

Liz turned around and backed farther into the bedroom. She tugged the zipper down the back of the dress and slowly inched the straps down her shoulders. His eyes followed the loose material as it revealed more and more of her skin. "Should I bring anything else with me?"

The dress dropped to the floor. Desire was evident in his eyes as she stepped out of the pool of material at her feet and reached back to unclasp her strapless bra.

"I have everything else covered," he said, taking a step toward her.

She smirked at him and snapped the hook and eye open. His eyes fell to her breasts as they dropped full and perky out of the bra. His hands were on her in an instant, pulling her nearly naked body against him as his lips found her.

"My girlfriend the tease," he groaned.

"I would never." Her voice came out breathy, and she was pretty sure that if he kept that up they weren't going to make any plans.

"I like it."

His fingers hooked into her soft lacy underwear and slowly dragged them to the ground as he knelt before her. He leaned forward and placed earnest kisses down her stomach. Her breathing picked up as he drew nearer.

His lips touched her most sensitive skin, and he chuckled at her sharp intake of breath. He brought his fingers up and ran them gently across her folds. She shuddered as he eased her open before quickly retreating.

"Now who's the tease?" she managed to get out.

He smiled up at her and gave her another kiss before standing. "That would be me. Now go get dressed."

Liz stuck her bottom lip out. "Really? Now that I'm all riled up?"

Hayden pulled her close again and melded their lips together. His tongue ran along her lip, entering her mouth when she moaned, and met hers. "I promise to make up for it when we get back."

"The anticipation is going to kill me."

"It will be worth it."

Liz sighed through her sexual frustration and turned to change. It wasn't as if she and Hayden hadn't had sex the night before . . .

or the night before that, but a part of her just wanted him to grab her, throw her over the bed, and take her. Not that she needed that by any means. They had amazing sex. It was just different, emotional rather than primal.

She slid into a hot-pink bathing suit and threw an oversize white eyelet tank on top, and then followed Hayden out of their hotel room. They took the elevator to the bottom floor and veered through the lobby to the back entrance. They trekked through the sand to a small white catamaran docked near the resort. Six or seven other people were already on deck, beers in hand, music playing through the speakers.

"Oh my God," Liz whispered into the breeze.

"Do you like it?"

"It's a great surprise!"

"This is only part of it," he said, taking her hand and helping her onto the boat. "Wait until you see what else I have in store."

Liz's eyes lit up as she stared at the man before her. Damn, did he love her. And she could see reflected back in his eyes that the only thing he wanted in this moment was for her to be happy. He made her happy.

Once Hayden hopped on board, they were promptly greeted by the catamaran tour captain. All food and beverages were included and they were strictly ordered to enjoy themselves.

With drinks in hand, they found an open spot at the front of the catamaran just as they set sail. Their guide sailed them around the North Shore, which, unlike Honolulu, was mostly gorgeous natural habitat and known for bigger waves and isolated alcoves that had been featured in Hollywood films such as *Blue Crush* and the television show *Lost*. Liz stripped her tank off and let the rays sink into her skin. Hayden stretched out next to her and they spent the majority of the afternoon enjoying each other's company and the beautiful natural seascape before them.

"And this is where we're going to be stopping for a couple hours," the captain announced.

He turned the boat into a small private lagoon obscured from the rest of the island by cliffs on one side. The water was crystal clear blue, and a white sandy beach was visible on the coast.

"This area is only for tour participants, so you shouldn't be bothered by a constant stream of tourists. If you got the snorkeling package, see me after we dock and I'll explain everything you need to know."

The captain docked the boat and helped the passengers out, where they were immediately greeted by Hawaiian women in traditional grass skirts, bra tops, and multicolored leis. Liz moved to follow the rest of the partiers, but Hayden stopped her.

"I got us snorkeling gear. I wasn't sure if you would be into it, but I read about some amazing caverns and even a small waterfall in the area. I'd love to check it out with you," he said.

"I love snorkeling. You think there's an actual waterfall nearby?" she asked excitedly.

"In fact, there is," the captain said when he walked up to them. "I can give you two directions to get there. Just off of one of these cliffs. Beautiful sight. Just let me get you through the safety guidelines and you'll be free to go."

The captain instructed them on how to use the equipment, which was pretty self-explanatory, all things considered, and then explained where they could and couldn't go.

"Have a good time," he said with a wave as he walked back over to his seat. "I have to pick up the next tour. I'll be back to get you all in a few hours!"

They grabbed their snorkeling equipment and exited the catamaran right before it set sail. After they found a place to leave their stuff, they headed back out into the warm water with their flippers and masks in place. Liz simply couldn't get over how clear the water was and how much marine life was in the little lagoon. She had a mini panic attack thinking that she might see sharks, but Hayden just laughed at her and told her that he would protect her. Luckily, they didn't see any.

Hayden gestured for Liz to follow him as they swam in the direction that the captain had instructed to see the waterfall. They rounded a corner into a small closed cavern. After overcoming a momentary panic from closed-in spaces, Liz followed Hayden at an easy pace through the cavern until it opened up to an even smaller lagoon with a waterfall. It was surrounded on three sides by the cliff and then one side had a flat area, which it looked like people over the years had used to rest.

They swam over there and Hayden helped Liz out of the water. She pulled off her flippers, tossed her mask to the side, and lay back in the most stunning natural environment she had ever encountered.

"Now, *this* is a surprise," she murmured.

Her eyes drifted from the waterfall to her boyfriend standing shirtless over her. He ran his hand back through his wet hair. His biceps were defined as he held his arms over his head, and she could make out each line in his abdomen as the water ran down his body. His little tease from earlier came back to her in full force, and she felt her body warming just from looking at him.

"I thought you would like it," Hayden said, sinking into the space next to her.

Liz nuzzled into his chest and slid her hand down the slick surface. "About you making it up to me," she whispered huskily.

Hayden laughed deep in his throat. "Is that where your mind is?" His hand trailed the length of her body.

"Is that not where your mind is?"

"Oh, it is," he said, rolling over on top of her and pinning her back against the ground.

As he pressed his body down against her, she felt him stiffen through the thin material of his swim trunks. His mouth crashed down on top of hers with none of the hesitancy that he usually exhibited. They were alone in their own world out here, and the exhilaration of being out in the open like this fueled their passion.

His fingers wound into her hair and she exposed her neck to his mouth. Her hands found the waistline of his swim trunks and it took every ounce of effort not to just rip them off. She gripped on to them for dear life as he ravaged her neck, down to her collarbones, and found the strap of her bikini.

"Hayden," she groaned. "I want you."

Not having any more willpower, Liz started tugging on his trunks and dragging them down his thighs. Hayden sat up and pulled them off as she easily stripped out of her bikini, baring herself before him.

"God, you're gorgeous," he said, leaning back over her.

Their lips met hungrily as he pushed himself forward inside of her. Her eyes fluttered closed and she groaned at the feel of him filling her. It had only been a day and it felt like forever. She felt insatiable; she couldn't figure out why she had waited so long initially, and now that she had tasted him she couldn't get enough. She wanted to explore every inch of his skin. She wanted him to trace every curve.

Her heart swelled as Hayden pulled back slowly and then lunged into her swiftly. She met his rhythm, always craving more, desiring more from him. And he gave it to her over and over again. She felt her body giving in to the intensity and elation of the moment.

She didn't even think about the rocks digging into her back or the grass scratching up her arms and legs. What mattered was this feeling, this right here. Knowing that Hayden had done all of this for her, and that he was going to keep doing things like this for her. Knowing that they created their own memories, they had control of the future, not the past, and they were doing that together. Knowing that in love, the strongest emotion of all was the connections . . . in proving to someone day in and day out that this was what they deserved and accepting nothing less. That was what Hayden was giving to her.

Liz's back arched off of the hard ground as he drove forward into her forcefully enough to scoot her backward. All pretenses of taking her slowly were gone, and he was demanding all of her. And she was giving it back.

Her body spasmed with climax as he pushed into her once more. He pumped a few more times before grunting and coming with her.

"Fuck, Lizzie," he murmured against her neck.

"That was amazing." The words were wispy and she suddenly felt as if she was floating on a cloud.

Hayden collapsed on the earth next to her and she buried her head into his chest. Their breathing began to slow as they lay there recovering from the intensity of what had just occurred. Liz tried to wrap her mind around what she had just felt and experienced.

She had been giving Hayden everything she had for a month now. She knew that wasn't a very long time, but she was glad that at least she had figured it out. She had wasted too much time obsessing about something that was never going to happen, never going to go the way she wanted. When the thing she had wanted for two years, the person who had been giving her everything for months and months, was right in front of her. And to be honest, the last month had been better than all the others combined. She felt them grow and mature with each other in a relationship . . . in a healthy and sane way.

And she knew what this feeling meant that was bubbling up inside of her. She had known for a while, but it was never clearer than now, when she was lying in a secluded area in Hawaii, surrounded by nature, listening to the beat of Hayden's heart and the sound of the waterfall splashing.

"Hayden," she breathed, sitting up on her elbow and staring down into his hazel eyes. They were practically gold in the sunlight, and it made her shiver at the sight.

"Yeah, gorgeous?" he asked, pushing her hair off of her face for her.

"You know I love you, right?"

He smiled that brilliant smile up at her and nodded. "Yeah, I know. I'm glad you finally figured it out."

Chapter 14

EDITOR

Liz spent the majority of her summer in Hayden's new one-bedroom apartment in Charlotte. She wasn't taking any classes, and the paper practically ran itself; Hayden had been absent all last summer and it had still continued just fine. She knew that once school started she wouldn't have as much free time to come see him, so she wanted to spend as much time as she could with him now.

Right before the summer ended, Liz met with Professor Mires and her scholarship advisement committee to determine how she was going to spend her scholarship intern hours. Liz had been planning to work with the *Raleigh News* reporting staff that she had contacts with, but Dr. Mires had something else in mind. She had gotten in touch with her colleague Nancy from the *New York Times* and had secured Liz a spot working with their team on a political journalism reporting portfolio. It included some travel to and from New York City to meet with the team and perfect on-site reporting skills.

Liz was floored that Dr. Mires had gone to that much trouble for her. Dr. Mires insisted that Liz had earned such a position. Nancy had been so impressed with her work on the colloquium in the spring that it had made it an easy choice. Liz would be flying up to New York at the beginning of September for her first meeting.

Fall rolled around all too soon and she kissed Hayden good-bye and returned to Chapel Hill for her senior year of college. She had a busy year ahead of her. It made her a bit dizzy to think about it: editor, internship with the *New York Times*, research hours with Dr. Mires, not to mention that she was still taking a full load of classes, had a boyfriend, and had tried to keep up with regular tennis lessons. She wasn't sure she was going to have any time to breathe, let alone think. Of course, she couldn't complain; she had basically gotten everything that she wanted.

Liz walked into the newspaper office on the second floor of the Union on campus. It felt a bit surreal to have spent so much time away from the place over the summer. She had practically lived there the three years prior.

It was the first week back to school for her senior year. The paper had already gone out and only division leaders had to be in the office that afternoon. They had the full meeting for everyone interested in working on the paper that evening. Liz had prepared for it best she could. She just hoped she had half of Hayden's charisma.

She walked into her new editorial office and sighed. It was one of the few offices in the building that had a door and a lock that actually worked. It felt a bit surreal to be in here again; she had commandeered the office last summer while Hayden had been away.

She ran her hands along the desk that she knew she would never be able to keep as clean and meticulous as Hayden did. She had helped him move his stuff out of the office this summer, and it had barely taken any time, even though he had occupied the space for a year and a half. By the end of the first week, she knew it would be a mess that she would never be able to get back under control.

A knock on the door jolted her from her thoughts. "You're early," Savannah said with a smile.

Liz checked her watch. Still thirty minutes before the meeting. "I'm editor. I'm supposed to be early. What are you doing here?"

"I just got out of class. You've had Professor Mires before, right?"

"She's my advisor," Liz told her.

"Is she as difficult as everyone says she is? Her classes are always packed, but I know a bunch of people who want to drop because she grades unfairly."

Liz snorted. "She just makes you earn your grade. It's worth it to be on her good side. She helped get me an internship with the *New York Times* for this year."

"Nice. It's who you know, not what you know," Savannah said with that knowing Maxwell glint in her eye.

"Usually," Liz confirmed with a shrug. If anyone had connections it was Savannah Maxwell. "How was your summer?"

She shrugged, but had an unmistakable giddy smirk across her face. "Pretty good."

"And what's his name?" Liz asked, leaning back against the desk.

"I mean, I'm talking to this guy named Forrest," she said, the look disappearing.

Uh-huh. That clearly wasn't who had caused her to get all flustered.

"Forrest and Savannah. Not getting much more Southern than that," Liz joked, wondering if she should push for the real story.

"It's not serious or anything. He's just a guy I met at the gym."

"Did you see Lucas this summer?" Liz asked, diving in.

Savannah's cheeks colored, but she clearly tried to play it off. "Yeah. Some. Over the Fourth of July my family goes to Hilton Head, and his family came with us this year."

Liz already knew about the Fourth of July, of course. Brady had postponed going to Hilton Head last summer to stay with her an extra day. She was glad Savannah had had a good time.

"Right. And you still like him?" she asked her friend.

"I don't really know. I've known him . . . forever. I don't think he feels the same way about me."

"Have you looked at you recently? He would have to be dumb or blind or both not to be interested in you, Savannah," Liz said. She knew Lucas had to be into her. The guy was related to Chris, Brady's best friend, so he couldn't be stupid.

Savannah laughed. "Thanks for the ego boost. He's dating someone else, though."

Liz deflated. Damn. Savannah seemed so happy about him. "Really? That sucks."

"I mean . . . don't tell anyone," Savannah said, biting her lip conspiratorially. "He kissed me on the beach."

"Oh my God, really? What happened? When did it happen? Did you kiss him back? Did it go further?" Liz asked, going into full-on girl mode in a matter of seconds.

"We kissed in the sand for like two hours at sunset. It was incredibly . . . insane. I don't know how to explain it."

"So, why isn't he interested in you? I'm so confused."

Savannah shrugged with a sigh. "He said that he didn't think we should keep doing what we did that night. He goes to Vandy, so he probably wouldn't want to do the distance thing. And the part where he has a girlfriend . . ." She trailed off.

"You're Savannah Maxwell. Said girlfriend might as well not exist."

"Well, she exists, so it doesn't matter. Let's talk about something else. Lucas is like a distant summer memory," she said entirely unconvincingly. "How about a big thank-you for putting me as the coleader for the Washington division!"

Liz knew Lucas was far from a distant memory, but she knew that she wouldn't get any more dirt now. She hoped that Savannah figured out what was best for her.

"You totally deserve it," she told her.

"I'm excited to get started. I have some big shoes to fill."

"I don't have that big of feet," Liz said, glancing down at her high heels.

"Knock-knock!"

Liz groaned as Savannah turned to see who was entering the office. Meagan appeared around the corner with an oversize Vera Bradley bag on her shoulder and a big smile. She ran the kvetching column, which was essentially gossip and complaining, but the majority of the student body really loved it.

And with Meagan's introduction the fun girl time officially became the paper division meeting. Savannah gave Liz an amused look as they turned to listen to Meagan talk about her summer.

$\sim$

Nearly every day Liz and Hayden had left the paper and walked together to his car parked in the space reserved for the editor— which was now reserved for her. It felt so strange walking out of the newspaper building that evening having just completed her first-ever paper meeting and walking down to her car without Hayden.

Victoria had planned a back-to-school party at their place that night, and Liz anticipated it being in full swing before she even got there. And in all honesty she just wanted to take her time getting home. Maybe she would call Hayden and see how he was doing.

He seemed to like his new job. They didn't push him enough, and she knew that he wanted to do more, but he always wanted to do more. He just wanted a break to prove himself, but as with most people in an entry-level job, Hayden was suffering from the problem of having to work his way up the company ladder.

Hayden answered on the third ring. "Hey, gorgeous! How was your first meeting? Do they all love you as much as I do?"

"I miss you," she murmured softly into the phone.

"I miss you too, Lizzie."

She sighed heavily and then tried to let the feeling pass. Long distance sucked. It was why she and her last boyfriend hadn't worked out. Of course, her last boyfriend hadn't really cared either. She didn't think this was even close to the same situation, and she wasn't worried about Hayden. But it still sucked.

"The meeting went well," she told him. "Everything is in place and now I just have to be there to make sure it runs smoothly."

"I'm sure it will. You had a pretty good mentor."

Liz reached her car and slipped inside. "I'm just glad I now have my mentor's parking spot."

Hayden laughed through the line just as she turned on the car and backed out. "I wish I were there to drive you to and from school. I'm going to miss that."

"Me too."

"And our secretive smiles across the office."

"Mmm."

"And having you curled up against me when you sleep."

"Hayden . . ."

"And whispering your name when we make love."

"You're not making this any easier," she groaned.

"Come visit."

Liz shook her head even though she knew he couldn't see. "I just left."

"I'll come visit you then."

Liz giggled. "You have to work tomorrow."

"I just want you in my arms. Is that too much to ask?" he asked.

"Never," she murmured as she pulled up in front of her house.

The ride was too short. She barely got any time with him, and as she had suspected, Victoria already had the party going.

"Wow, it's loud wherever you are," Hayden said.

"Victoria is throwing a back-to-school party. I didn't realize it had already started. She knew I wouldn't be back until late."

"Well, have a good time and tell Vickie I said hi. I'm sure she'll be thrilled."

"Will do. I'll call you later. Love you," Liz said, popping the door open and exiting the car.

"Love you too."

Liz hung up the phone and sauntered into her house. The music was blasting and a crowd of people took up her living room. She was nearly tackle-hugged as soon as she walked in the door. She screamed as she was picked up and spun around.

"What the fuck!" The guy who was holding her just laughed louder as she tried to get free. "Put me down!"

"All right. All right," he said, catching her and setting her down on her feet. She smacked him on the arm when she regained her balance.

"Justin!" she yelled, throwing her arms around him. "What are you doing here?"

"Such a kind welcome. I haven't seen you in months and you're already smacking me around," he said, laughing at her still-shocked expression.

"You deserved it. Picking me up like that! I had no idea who you were." She just shook her head as Justin smiled down at her. "What are you doing here anyway?" Liz nodded toward her room, and Justin followed her back there as they continued talking.

"Victoria invited me," he told her.

"She's just full of surprises, isn't she?"

"Nice," he said, sitting down on her bed and crossing his ankle over his knee. "So, how have you been? Are you still with Lane?"

"Yeah, he's in Charlotte working as a reporter. I'm editor now and working internship hours with the *New York Times*," she said, slipping out of her heels.

Justin whistled low. "Someone is fancy."

"What about you? Where are your big plans taking you?"

As Justin filled her in on what was going on in his life, Liz retreated into her closet and picked out an acceptable outfit for the party tonight. He told her that the company he had been working for had gone under over the summer, and he had been out of work for a little while when he finally found an investor for the business he had been working on since they last talked. After he had a source of revenue again, the project had hit the ground running. He asked Liz again if she would be interested in working with him as a writer for the company, but she turned him down and, as other people showed up for the party, they left it at that.

She sought out Victoria, who was regaling a small crowd with one of her ludicrous stories. Liz only caught the tail end of it.

"So two Australian firefighters and a scuba instructor later and I had the perfect Aussie sandwich. I know that I'll be going back to Australia. That place should not be a one and done kind of thing. There's a reason their population started off as criminals," Victoria said with a wink. She shifted into her right hip and took a drink out of her red Solo cup.

Liz just shook her head. Victoria and her adventures in Australia this summer for study abroad had been a constant stream of conversation since she returned. Liz had heard about how Victoria had been triple-teamed by the three Aussies at least twice. She was most proud of that story.

Why she insisted on telling it to complete strangers was beyond Liz's mental capacity.

"Hey, bitch!" Victoria said when she saw Liz. "About time you got here."

"I've been here for a while. I was talking to Justin. Thanks for inviting him."

Victoria twirled her finger in the air and took another sip from the cup. "You're friends and all that. Plus, I'm secretly hoping you'll find someone other than your Hayden Lane," she said with that teasing lilt she always got to her voice when she got the opportunity to make fun of Hayden.

"Oh, yes, so many better options at this party. I guess I should go back to Australia with you."

"Don't be jealous of my abilities. I don't know if you can handle three," she said, patting Liz on the arm. "You have a hard enough time with one."

"Oh my God. Why am I friends with you?" Liz asked.

"Because I'm awesome, obviously."

Liz couldn't deny that her best friend was awesome, and she was happy that Justin was in attendance even if she was missing Hayden. She wandered into the kitchen and poured herself a glass of the red hunch punch sitting in a cooler. The party picked up pace as everyone fed off of the post-summer energy that took over the room.

Massey showed up at some point with a bunch of her sorority friends. She and Justin seemed to know each other. Soon enough he had his arm around her and was regaling her friends with stories. Tristan appeared shortly after that. Liz wasn't even sure how he had found out about it, but he only stayed for a grand total of fifteen minutes before making some excuse about homework and leaving. It was the first day of school. There was no way he had any homework.

Savannah arrived late as usual. Liz was pretty sure she had never been to anything except the paper on time. She had a guy with her who couldn't seem to stop touching her ass even when she swatted his hand away. He was pretty hot, super tall, with buzzed dark hair and a tattoo peeking out of the sleeve of his black T-shirt. He must be the aforementioned Forrest. All Liz saw when she looked at him was the exact opposite of Lucas. A very clear rebellious act.

At the first opportunity, Savannah ditched the guy and veered over to Liz. She was standing off to the side debating on whether or not she wanted a second glass of the hunch punch.

"Hey! Sorry I'm late," Savannah said in greeting.

Liz chuckled. "I wouldn't expect anything less."

"Sorry—years of making fashionably late entrances never wore off, I guess. Also, my brother's in town."

"Understandable," Liz said, ignoring the part about her brother. "Is that your Forrest?"

Savannah glanced back at the beefy guy she had walked inside with. She tilted her head and smiled. "Yeah. That's him."

When Liz glanced past Forrest, she saw Justin had Massey's back against the wall and his tongue down her throat. Liz laughed and pointed it out to Savannah. "Well, he certainly moves fast."

"So does she, apparently," Savannah said.

Liz shifted her gaze back to Savannah with a smile. She liked having her around. She was different from most of Liz's other friends, and she appreciated how easily their friendship came to her.

"What were you up to before this?"

"Ugh! I had family shit after the newspaper meeting," Savannah grumbled.

"Did you take Forrest to your family stuff?" Liz asked with a giggle, imagining the large, tatted man in front of her in the Maxwell house. It pinched at her heart to think about Brady being in town, but she tried to dismiss it. It wasn't as if she were going to see Brady, and anyway she had moved on to Hayden. That was what was important now.

"No! Are you crazy? My family would take one look at him and tell me to stop acting like a teenager," Savannah said indignantly.

"And I was getting enough of that shit this summer from my brother's stupid *girlfriend*."

The way she said that almost made Liz laugh. There was only one person that Savannah would think was the *stupid* girlfriend in the Maxwell family. "Andrea?" she asked without thinking.

Savannah raised her eyebrows sharply and Liz realized her mistake. There was no way that Liz was supposed to know that name. No way she was supposed to know anything about Clay, let alone Clay's girlfriend.

Shit! Shit! Shit!

How could she backpedal out of this one? Liz knew there wasn't stuff about them in the papers. She had checked and rechecked all of her sources last summer. Clay Maxwell didn't even have pictures appear online that weren't from when he was a kid, and the man had sure grown since he was a boy.

"How do you know Andrea?" Savannah asked curiously.

"Um . . ." Liz said, racking her brain. "I met her at an art gallery opening in D.C. over New Year's," she blurted out.

"Really?" Savannah asked. "I remember her mentioning buying a bunch of artwork, but I normally tune everything she says out. Have you met Clay? They're an odd pair, but normally together."

"He was there with her," Liz confirmed. That was completely a true statement and yet didn't answer Savannah's question. How many times had she met Clay? How many times had he propositioned her to go home with him? Um . . . yeah she had met Clay.

"Huh," Savannah murmured, clearly mulling it all over. "Well, anyway . . . no, not Andrea. She's a nut job, but she's always been that way. You get used to it. It's Erin . . ."

Liz swallowed and cleared her mind. Nothing to think about. Nothing at all.

"What happened with Erin?"

Savannah rolled her big brown eyes to the ceiling and pulled all of her hair over to one shoulder. "She just . . . mothers me! Like I think she really, really wants to be my friend, because Brady and I are close. But she was at Hilton Head with us, and found out about the thing with Lucas. She wanted me to play buddy-buddy and have me confide in her. She kept saying things like, 'I feel like we're sisters.' Um . . . I'm sorry. I don't know you like that. We're not sisters. I don't *have* any sisters, you know?"

"Sure," Liz said softly.

"Anyway, once I told her what happened with Lucas, she started telling me how I was like a bad person for kissing him and that if he really liked me then he wouldn't string me along and all this. Which, okay . . . she's right. Fine. It's not exactly what she said, but how she said it. In this holier-than-thou voice with her finger sticking out and scolding me. And she has treated me like that every time I've seen her since. When I'm around her, I swear I'm about to go crazy."

Liz nodded, her mind drifting off. She felt bad for Savannah having to deal with someone like that. And she really wanted to think that it didn't matter that Savannah didn't like Brady's girlfriend.

But it made her smile devilishly anyway.

Chapter 15

DROPPING THE BALL

Liz landed back in the Raleigh airport after three days spent in New York City working with Nancy at the *New York Times* over fall break. She had never worked so hard, but also had never had a better experience in journalism. Nancy had a knack for utilizing people's strengths, and Liz had been knee-deep in the political reporting area at the paper. She had shadowed various people, assisted in research, writing, and editing, and had even gone out into the field with a seasoned reporter.

The experience further solidified that she was really doing what she loved. She was so often locked away in the academic setting that she didn't always see what it really felt like to be out there. The college newspaper, while an incredible publication, was nothing compared to starting a career at a professional newspaper.

The only downside to her being in New York for her break meant that she didn't get to see Hayden. They visited each other as frequently as they could, but as his job grew more demanding and midterms rolled around, they found less and less time together.

It wasn't the end of the world. A part of her just wanted to drive to Charlotte and shirk her responsibilities. But that wasn't like her at all . . . She hadn't been able to do any work for the school newspaper while in New York, and she had homework on top of that. So at least she would be keeping herself busy.

As soon as she got home, she changed into jeans, a three-quarter-sleeve blue button-down, and her knee-high brown boots. She twirled a pink chevron scarf around her neck and grabbed her North Face jacket and laptop before heading right back out the door to the paper.

She parked in her normal parking spot reserved for the editor and trekked up the stairs and into the Union. Liz plopped down at her desk and fired up her computer. She had a million emails regarding editorial work, newspaper design, next week's stories, and on down the line. She would be up all night sorting through the mess.

A while into her email binge, Liz heard the office door opening. She checked her watch and saw that it was already eight thirty at night. She suspected she wouldn't get out of here until well past midnight. She actually considered pulling an all-nighter. But she hadn't thought anyone else would show up at the paper on their fall break.

"Hello?" she called, standing and walking out of her office. A smile broke out on her face as she saw Hayden standing in front of her. "What are you doing here?"

She rushed forward and wrapped her arms around his neck. He drew her into him and kissed her cheek. "I got two days off and knew you would be back from New York today."

"You could have called!"

"Nah . . . it's better to see that beautiful face when I surprised you," he said, cupping her cheek and kissing her lips.

"I just can't believe you're here. I really didn't think I'd get to see you until next weekend. How did you know I would be here, anyway?"

Hayden shrugged and gestured for her to walk back into the office. "I called Victoria and she told me."

"Ah, makes sense," Liz said, taking a seat her desk. "Well, if I'd known then I wouldn't have started all this stuff." She gestured toward the cluttered desk and her open laptop.

"It's all right. No rush. Do you want to just finish up and then we could head out? Maybe we could get dinner at Top O," he suggested.

"That sounds great. There's no way I'm finishing all of this tonight anyway," she said. The piles of emails would still be there tomorrow for her to take care of.

"What do you have to do?" Hayden asked, walking over to her computer, reading over her shoulder.

"Just some basic stuff. Layout, editing, new material. The usual."

Liz began to pack up her other stuff as Hayden scrolled through the mass of emails she had neglected while working in New York. She had so much other stuff to do on top of the newspaper that she probably should have just stayed, but how often did she get to see Hayden these days?

"You have a lot here," Hayden said.

"Yeah. I've been pretty swamped the past two weeks, and then the *New York Times* on top of all of that," Liz said, shrugging. "I'll get through it all."

She heard Hayden sigh as she tidied up her desk and pretended to put it into some order. If she had known he was going to be here, she would have made some kind of effort to make it look presentable.

Now she was just doing it out of habit because she knew that he liked things tidy.

"Liz, you know I really don't like that you're dropping the ball with this kind of stuff," he said, his voice carrying the edge of authority he used when he had been editor of the paper. She had always thought that voice was commanding in a gentle, nudging way. Right now . . . it didn't have that quality. It sounded a whole hell of a lot more like her boyfriend was about to reprimand her.

"Dropping the ball on what?" she said, turning to stare at him, her hands on her hips. She didn't know why the comment immediately made her defensive. She was editor of the paper now, not him, and she was doing just fine. In fact, sometimes she thought she was doing a better job than Hayden had, because she didn't have to micromanage people.

"You have about a hundred emails in here. Things that really need to get taken care of. I know you have this big internship lined up at the *New York Times*, but that doesn't mean you can let my paper turn to shit."

Liz froze, her blue eyes narrowing. "Excuse me?"

"Look, I picked you for this position because I thought you could handle juggling everything at once. If you can't, then maybe you should think about how that affects the newspaper and not jeopardize its reputation for your other projects."

"You think I'm jeopardizing the reputation of the newspaper by having a few unread emails?" she asked, crossing her arms over her chest.

"Stop making this sound bad. I'm just saying that you should consider the impact of your carelessness. I would have never let this go on like this," he told her.

"Well, I'm not sure if you noticed, Hayden, but I'm not you," she said, rounding on him. "And the only reason anything is being *neglected* is because my boyfriend took a job hours away. So sorry if you wanted to see me."

He quickly tried to backtrack. "This isn't about us."

"No. I think this is very much about us and actually has little to do with the paper. So perhaps you could just spell out to me what's going on."

Hayden shook his head in frustration. "See, this is it. I built this paper into a well-oiled machine. I took what a bunch of other editors had done and made it all run like it was on wheels. I laid the foundation and now you're trying to dig away at what I created by being as selfish as all the other editors before you."

Liz's eyebrows rose sharply. "Selfish?" she said in a strangled voice. "I'm being selfish by pursuing my career? I'm being selfish by visiting my boyfriend who wants me to see him? I'm being selfish by not being you?"

"Lizzie . . . , calm down, please. It has nothing to do with our relationship."

"You keep saying that, but it's not what I hear. All I hear is someone who is pissed off and jealous because his girlfriend is interning at the *New York Times* when you stood no chance at the *Washington Post*, and reminiscing about the good old days in college. And now you're being an asshole to me when I don't deserve it," she spat.

"I'm not *jealous*. That's fucking insane. I got internships in D.C. too; that doesn't mean you'll get a job at the *New York Times* out of college, especially not with the way you're running this newspaper," he retorted harshly.

"Fine," she snapped, shaking her head. "You know what? I'm going home."

She slammed her computer closed, stuffed it into her bag, then grabbed it and started walking out of the office.

"Lizzie, come on. Why are you leaving?" Hayden asked, reaching for her.

Liz wrenched her arm back. "Stop it."

"I came all this way to visit you," he said earnestly.

"Then you should have considered how you were going to treat me. I'm not a punching bag for your emotions."

She turned on her heel and stormed toward the exit. He didn't even follow her this time, and that just fueled her anger.

They had never had an argument in the almost year that they had been dating, and her whole body ached at the thought. She hated being angry with him, but he deserved it. Tears stung her eyes as she shouldered open the heavy double doors.

Liz wasn't sure why, but as the door slammed behind her, her thoughts strayed to Brady. He would have never belittled her career like that. In fact, he had always been interested in where her life was headed.

She ground her teeth together to try to hold herself together. It didn't matter what he thought. That ship had long since sailed.

Liz wrapped her scarf around her neck and braced herself against the cold. Winter was rearing its ugly head a little too early for her Florida fancy. She didn't like the cold, nor was she used to it, and she wished in that moment that she had remembered her gloves. They were stowed away in her glove compartment, little good that did her.

Rubbing her hands together, she tried not to think of Hayden and his jealous, antagonistic attitude. Every time she tried not to think about her boyfriend, it brought her full circle to Brady, another person she didn't want to think about. She had been doing so well on that front for so long that it was weird that her mind immediately drifted there. Why couldn't she just forget about these boys and focus on her career?

Yet, all she wanted to do was talk out her anger with someone. Victoria would lynch Hayden before the full story even left Liz's mouth. Liz was close with Massey and Savannah, but it was break and she just couldn't bring herself to ruin theirs after Hayden had just ruined the end of hers.

Brady. She just kept coming back to Brady for some reason. Her stomach tugged and she felt a prickle travel through her lower half just at the thought. Groaning, she tried to forget his name, his presence, his damn smirk, and that insufferable way he had of never really leaving her life.

Liz reached for her phone and ran her index finger across the touch screen. She had deleted all of his numbers from her phone in the spring after her twenty-first-birthday escapade. She didn't have a way to get hold of him other than the office number she had used all last summer. She doubted it would work anyway.

It had just been so long since they had talked . . . really talked. What was the last thing he had even said to her? She couldn't remember. She had been drunk on the phone. But she could remember clear as day the last thing he had texted to her before leaving the primary. *You know this can't be anything else right now. Just don't forget, okay?* He had been antagonizing her, just reminding her over and over that they could never really work out, never be more than a secret affair.

But how could she forget? How could she forget anything when Brady always clouded her consciousness? How could she forget when he was still around, when she was always near his sister, when everything from the very desk that she sat in day in and day out at the paper reminded her of him and how they hadn't worked out?

Liz shook her head. She needed to get herself together, but she didn't feel as if it was worth it tonight. Hayden's harsh words had struck a chord with her, and she didn't know how to stop playing to his tune. She was too emotional, and she just wanted to get away from it all—her "perfect" boyfriend, her perfect school, her perfect life. She wanted to go back to that summer when she hadn't been Lizzie.

Against her better judgment she typed in the number.

Her heart hammered in her chest and her body warmed despite the ever-cooling temperatures. She walked briskly across the leaf-strewn sidewalk with her phone pressed tightly to her ear. She chanced a glance behind her to confirm that the door to the Union was still sealed shut. Hayden hadn't left. He wasn't going to follow her. He wasn't running after her.

"Congressman Maxwell's office."

Liz felt a rush of adrenaline pump through her body as she remembered their summer exploits and the thrill of being someone else for a while. She hadn't thought that this number would be working any longer. But he must have kept a local office open in the district for when he was here on business. Still, it shocked her a little.

"Yes," she said her voice shaky. "I'm trying to reach the Congressman. Is he in this evening?"

Her hands trembled. It had been a while since she had done this. She knew it was a long shot, but maybe they could connect her with the D.C. office. It was invigorating and terrifying how much she reveled in the rebellion.

"Yes, he's in, but the Congressman is occupied. May I take a message?"

Liz's heart leaped. He was here . . . in North Carolina. At least, that was what she assumed the lady meant.

"Can you tell him Sandy Carmichael is on the line," she murmured, the strength renewed in her voice.

The woman paused. "Yes, Ms. Carmichael. Please hold."

Liz chewed on her lips as she waited. The wind picked up and tore through her hair, whipping it into her eyes. She tried to brush it out of her face, but the wind was relentless. She could empathize with its ferocity tonight.

Jogging the last few feet in her knee-high brown boots, Liz made it to her car and quickly ducked inside out of the cold. She was still shivering as she waited . . . and waited . . . and waited. Would he answer? She hadn't spoken to him since her birthday in April, and it was now the end of October. Had she made a mistake in calling?

The clock told her it was only nine o'clock. Last summer felt like so long ago. Just as her mind drifted to nights at his lake house, stolen nights in hotel rooms, and fancy cocktail dinners, where mere looks across the room were enough to push them into deliriously dangerous circumstances, the line clicked over.

"The Congressman will be right with you," the woman said, pausing briefly, before adding, "Ms. Carmichael."

A second later, Liz heard a buzz on the line. Her heart leaped out of her chest with anticipation, and she felt a stirring between her thighs. She was already turned on, and she hadn't even heard his voice. It was wrong, so wrong that just a buzz on the other line could make her throb. She didn't want to admit that the waiting riled her up as much as he did. She had tried to forget all of these things.

"Sandy?" Brady's intoxicating voice murmured the name they had always used in public. She almost groaned aloud at the seductive quality it carried. He didn't talk like this on the radio. She started to squirm and pressed her legs together.

"Brady." She sighed into the phone, forgetting all of her worries with the sound of his voice. She slumped back against the seat and closed her eyes, remembering easier times.

"Are you okay?" he asked, his voice showing what she knew was a hint of desperation. She hadn't called in months; of course he would be concerned.

Or would he? God, she didn't know right now. All she knew was that she wanted to forget her argument with Hayden. She wanted to get lost in Brady. If all she could have was his voice to soothe her aches, then she would take it.

"Yeah . . ." Tears fell down her cheeks unbidden. Where had they come from? How had just his voice opened the floodgates? She choked back a sob, bringing her knees up to her chest. She was overreacting. She knew it, but it all felt like too much with Hayden right then. She wanted something . . . else.

"Where are you?" he demanded.

"At the newspaper," she choked out.

"I'm coming to get you."

"What?" she cried jumping out of her seat, her legs smacking the steering wheel.

"You don't call me crying in the middle of the night after not speaking with me for months, and then tell me I can't see you. I can't handle it, Liz," he growled. She gasped lightly at the way he said her name. "I said I'm coming to get you."

The phone went dead in her hand.

Chapter 16
NOTHING ELSE EVER HAD

L iz crashed back heavily into her seat.

What had she *done*? Brady couldn't come here. Over a year had passed since they had last been together like that. She felt as if she was losing her mind even considering it.

Her head snapped to the still-closed newspaper door. Hayden was inside. He had acted like a total asshole and pushed her away. The way he had treated her was completely unacceptable and it just set her off. How could he act like that after the last year? She was clearly motivated, independent, hardworking, and a dozen or so other power adjectives. The thought of him saying otherwise to her just infuriated her further.

She ground her teeth together. She had to make up her mind. If she decided to go with Brady, then she needed to move her car. Hayden would know something was wrong if it was still parked in the lot after she had told him she was leaving. And at the moment the last thing she wanted to do was talk to him.

Liz turned over the engine without thinking more about the consequences of her actions and drove her car into the parking deck. It was located behind a row of dorms off the back of the Union, which was good, because Hayden would never think to check there. The only problem was that she couldn't see the main newspaper parking lot from her new location.

That was where she had told Brady she would be, so unfortunately it looked as if she would have to suffer through the cold again. Liz didn't understand how it felt like a winter storm was about to rip through North Carolina any second when it was only October. It didn't help that she had mistakenly left her jacket in the office. Rummaging through her backseat, she found a Patagonia pullover, threw that over her button-down, and added a pair of gloves out of the glove compartment.

As she eased the door open, the wind whistled through the opening, stinging her eyes. It was too damn cold.

Grunting, Liz shoved the door open all the way and locked her car up tight. She walked briskly across the pavement and took a seat on the damp hill that led to the Union. From her vantage point she could see everything—the main parking lot, the newspaper entrance, the entrance where she would anticipate Brady . . . if he actually showed.

Light streamed out of the back entrance to the Union and Liz's eyes darted to the brick building partially obscured by century-old trees. Hayden walked out and into a circle of light from overhead. He ran his hands back through his hair and looked disgruntled . . . maybe even pissed off. She had never quite seen him look like that. It was sexy, and that made her angry. They wouldn't even be in this position if he wasn't acting like such an idiot.

She didn't want to watch him, but at the same time she couldn't tear her eyes away. It was like watching someone else. A stranger. Her Hayden was always calm and collected.

He held the door propped open, clearly lost in deep thought. Liz narrowed her eyes as he reached into his pocket. She watched him pull something out, but he had turned partially away from her, so she couldn't see what it was. As she tried to figure it out, her phone buzzed next to her. She jumped and grabbed at her cell phone, not wanting him to notice the light in the distance.

Liz debated answering it, but after a second she silenced it. She didn't really want to talk to Hayden right now.

The call ended. She watched him hang up the phone and place it back into his pocket.

After a second he dug something out of his other pocket. In shock, she watched the Zippo lighter from across the parking lot as the cigarette flared to life in his hand. Her mouth was hanging open as he took a long drag from the cigarette, breathing in deeply. His chest expanded and his head dipped back ever so slightly, as if he had just tasted a piece of heaven.

Her mouth went dry. This wasn't Hayden. He would never smoke. He abhorred the dirty habit. Christ, he was a runner! How the hell could he run for miles if he had cigarette smoke clogging his lungs?

She watched, completely astonished, as he drew another long drag on the cigarette before almost viciously throwing it off to the side. His hands visibly shook before fisting angrily into his hair. She could have sworn he cursed, but she couldn't hear him against the howling wind.

His hands fell out of his hair, but stayed in fists and slammed uselessly against the metal door. Violent. Not a word that she would have ever used to describe Hayden. He shook out his fists, seeming only to grow angrier.

Clearly debating with himself, he pushed the newspaper door closed before storming across the parking lot to his car. The lights to his Audi came to life right before he recklessly peeled out of the parking lot.

His car disappeared, and she felt as numb as the cold surrounding her.

Their argument was spiraling further and further out of control. She could see the pieces of the puzzle laid out before her as to how to fix this situation, but instead of moving them into place she tossed them off to the side. She stood up. Today she was bereft of the willingness to make it right.

And she was strangely okay with it all. Of course, she was shaken by Hayden's reaction. What was he doing with cigarettes in his pocket? That wasn't some freak accident. He'd had them with him. How long had he been hiding it from her? It made her wonder what else he was lying about, and made her sick to think about what had transpired between them. Yet, despite that, she couldn't help but *want* him to suffer for how he had treated her. Her heart contracted, but she couldn't shake the feeling.

Headlights blazed across the now empty parking lot, and Liz scrambled to her feet, brushing the crumpled leaves from the dark denim of her jeans. Her feet carried her down the hill, across the street, and out into the open lot. Her body was warming for a reason that had nothing to do with the cold and everything to do with the anticipation of seeing Brady, being alone with Brady.

Brady. What the hell was she going to say when she saw him? So much time had passed. How would he even react? The last time she had seen him, he had told her to just stay out of his life. The last time they had talked, he had said that he would fly from D.C. to see her. She didn't know which Brady she would see tonight. It made her stomach knot in anticipation.

His black Lexus slid evenly across the black pavement straight toward her, the bright lights the indication of his approach. She didn't even notice until it glided right up to her that her hands were shaking.

The tinted window slowly rolled down, revealing the all-black leather interior that she had spent a good deal of time in. She glanced around anxiously even though she knew that the only other person nearby had left in a rage minutes beforehand.

"Hey," she murmured softly, leaning forward through the window and getting her first up-close look at Brady in what felt like a lifetime. He was flawless. It was undeniable. Whatever had gone on between them, whatever had ended it all—it didn't change how attracted she was to him. How attracted she had always been to him.

"Get in the car," he said, unlocking the doors.

"Brady . . ." She trailed off. She couldn't believe that he was here right now. She couldn't believe she was staring at this beautiful face and that she was talking to him. She couldn't believe she'd had the guts to call him and that he was here. She just wanted to stare at him, but instead she said the only thing that she could muster enough courage to say: "I don't think we should do this."

"Get in the car."

"Look, it's not a good idea. I'm really messed up. Calling you was impulsive and thoughtless of me. I shouldn't have freaked you out. But driving away with you right now would be even worse," she told him, hugging herself tightly. All she wanted to do was say the exact opposite of what was coming out of her mouth. She wanted to drive off into the sunset with him and never look back. She always had.

"Get in the car, Liz."

"I'm still dating him, Brady. Think about what you would feel if you were him. Think about how much it would hurt if he knew about this—about what I'm thinking of doing," she said even softer than before, her whole body nearly trembling with the anxiety.

"Liz," he growled. "Get. In. The. Car."

"I can't. I just can't get in the car with you," she said. She made the mistake then of lifting her eyes to meet his deep chocolate orbs. Fuck! His eyes were so intense and commanding. She just wanted to get lost in those eyes forever. She swallowed hard and licked her bottom lip. "It's not a good idea."

"Goddamn it, Liz. Get in the car!" he yelled. "I didn't get out of my meetings for the night and drive thirty minutes out of the way for you to tell me to go home. Now get in the car."

"Seriously, shut up," she cried, pushing off of the car door. "I made a mistake. People make mistakes." The car jerked into park and he popped the driver's-side door open. "What are you doing?"

"I said get in the car, Liz, and you're going to listen one way or another," he said, walking around the front of the car.

"What the fuck does that mean?" she asked, narrowing her eyes. "I'm trying to have a conversation with you. I'm not in the right frame of mind tonight, and being around you is a *bad* idea."

"I like bad ideas," he said, standing before her.

"Well, I don't!"

Brady shook his head, a gorgeous smile replacing the glare he had been shooting at her. Dear Lord, he was too attractive for his own good. She could hardly even concentrate when she looked up at that face. Liz tried to find her words again to tell him to leave, but in that moment, he moved forward and stood a mere inch away from her. She could feel his body heat radiating toward her. She stood ramrod still at his nearness. He moved forward as if he was going to touch her, and then at the last second he pivoted quickly and threw her easily over his shoulder.

She screamed in protest, completely caught off guard. "What are you doing? Brady Maxwell, put me down. Put me down now!"

"I told you to listen, and you didn't." His arm held the back of her legs easily in place to keep her from moving as he opened the back door of his Lexus.

"I didn't think you were going to act like a caveman," she said, muffled in the back of his suit coat.

"Well, now you know better, huh?" he asked, tossing her into the backseat and slamming the door shut in her face.

Liz reached for the door, yanking the handle back and forth uselessly. "You have fucking child locks on these doors?" she screamed into the empty car as he slowly strolled back to the driver's side.

She shoved her entire body into the movement anyway, wrenching her shoulder with the extra effort. Releasing the handle, she fell backward, the cool leather cushioning her body upon impact. She quickly righted herself and climbed into the front just as Brady eased into his seat.

"I can't believe you!" she yelled, sliding her body into the passenger seat and reaching for the door. Pulling the handle several times in frustration, she discovered it too was locked. She moved to grab the lock and pull it up, but Brady's hand caught her wrist and put it back at her side. "Seriously?"

Brady smirked. "You should have gotten in the car from the beginning."

"You're kidnapping me," she growled, glaring at him.

"Listen here," he said, reaching across her body to grab her hands. She tried to pull away from him, but he held her hard and fast, pressing her back into the seat. "I want you to remember that you called me crying in the middle of the night," he growled. "You were the one who used that line. You were the one who used that name. You were the one who fell back into old methods. So don't you fucking pull this shit on me. Did you or did you not call as Sandy Carmichael?"

He waited.

"Yes," she grumbled through gritted teeth.

"Did you or did you not typically call that line for me to fuck you?"

He waited again.

She tilted her head up and refused to look at him. She was not going to have this conversation right now.

"Liz," he growled, tightening his grip on her hands.

"Yes," she yelped. *Well, sort of.*

"Then stop acting crazy. I don't have time for this. I'm going to let your hands go, and you are going to act like a normal person again. Are you ready?"

She nodded her head with as much dignity as she could manage as he let her hands go and put the car into drive. Liz didn't say anything as he pulled away from the newspaper. She was fuming. First Hayden's accusations, and then when Brady showed up he acted like a maniac. She really should have just gone home and cried into her pillow.

Except now that she was here . . . with him, she didn't actually want to be anywhere else.

"Where are we going?" she asked.

His brown eyes cut over to her momentarily and she had to keep from sighing. Christ, the man did things to her body she didn't understand.

"A condo."

"You have a new condo?" she asked.

He smirked. "Something like that."

"Sounds ominous."

"You've always been safe with me."

"Yeah. Who's going to mess with a congressman, right?" she asked with a soft chuckle.

"Plenty of people, I'm sure, but I don't think we'll be bothered tonight."

Tonight. That word. As if he didn't intend for her to leave.

She didn't even bother contradicting him. She didn't trust herself alone with Brady for an entire night. Not in his condo, where there were probably beds and couches and doors . . . and other things they'd had sex on last summer. But clearly telling him to take her home was out of the question. He had thrown her over his shoulder earlier just because she wouldn't get into his car. She had a feeling tonight was on his terms . . . as most things with Brady were.

Ten minutes later, he pulled into the winding entrance to a new complex on the outskirts of town. The buildings were in various stages of construction. Some were only partially built, others just had the frames, and some were complete but missing windows. Only one building had the entire brick framing with all the other fixtures and landscaping complete. Liz thought that was odd.

"Is this the right place? It doesn't even look finished," she said, peering out the windshield.

"It's not. It's still in development. But it's owned by a division of Maxwell Industries, and so I have access to it."

Huh. Liz knew how Brady's family had earned their fortune over the generations. It started out with large tracts of land and had developed into an immense real estate venture coupled with the political side. She hadn't known about this particular project, though. Granted, she hadn't been following his career as closely as she had before.

Brady parked the car in front of the one building that looked finished and killed the engine. "We have a fully furnished open house for potential buyers," he explained when she just stared at him quizzically. "There aren't any cameras on the premises."

"Oh," she whispered. Brady, always thinking ahead about who could see them together. This felt all too familiar and made her voice come out harsher than she intended. "Why didn't you just take me to a hotel?"

He popped the door open and answered without a backward glance. "Because I like to fuck you in different places."

Liz's mouth dropped open at the comment. He had to be joking. She sputtered and tried to collect herself, but it wasn't working.

He chuckled softly when he saw she was still staring up at him slack-jawed. "Come on, Liz. Don't make me come get you."

She scrambled out of the car. Holy shit! This was not happening. She was not following him up the stairs and into a condo when she knew that he had every intention of fucking her. She wasn't that person. No matter how angry she was . . . she couldn't go through with something like that.

Brady slid a key into the door and turned the knob, letting it swing inward. His hand on the small of her back sent warmth radiating throughout her entire body and she wondered if she even stood a chance at resisting.

She stumbled into the condo and Brady flicked the lights on. It was a nice-looking place, clearly decorated by someone with taste, but from a corporate angle. No imagination. There were stairs right off of the entrance and a kitchen hidden off of the living room. That was all she got to see of first floor before Brady shut the door and started up the stairs without a word.

Here goes nothing.

Even though Liz knew she shouldn't follow him, she did. She was drawn to him. No matter how much she tried to convince herself, she always had been.

There were two rooms, and Liz walked into the bigger of the two, where Brady was standing with his arms crossed, staring at the giant king-size bed that took up the majority of the room.

At the sight of it, Liz deflated. Her emotions were all over the place tonight. She was a wreck. The ups and downs had taken a toll on her, and she kind of wished that she could just go to sleep. She couldn't add another roller coaster to the equation.

"Brady," she whispered, her voice taking on an edge of desperation.

He didn't move for a solid minute. Just stood there and stared at the bed. She had no clue what he was thinking at that point.

Finally, he turned around and stared at her. She could see that whatever mask he had been wearing before had completely dropped away. He looked like *her* Brady—in control, but somehow still vulnerable. She hadn't really thought about it like that before, but when she looked at him now after all that time apart, she knew that that look of desire that so often crossed his face was a vulnerability to *her*. He still felt very strongly toward her. It was all over his face, and it made her heart melt.

"Come here," he said, crooking his finger.

She licked her lips before walking over and standing in front of him. She didn't even play around by standing at a distance. She knew that he was in control, and she knew what he wanted. She planted herself directly in front of him and tilted her chin up to look at him.

Brady's strong hands threaded back through her hair. Her eyes fluttered closed at the softest of touches. He ran his hands backward and swept it off of her shoulders. She nearly groaned as his fingers brushed against her ears, neck, and collarbones. But she didn't move or say anything until he cupped her face in his hands, and then she opened her eyes to stare up into his handsome face.

Her breathing was already ragged and irregular. How often had she fantasized about this moment—about him coming back for her?

"What happened, Liz?" he whispered.

His words seemed to break the floodgates again as they reminded her of her argument with Hayden tonight. Tears welled in her eyes as she started babbling. "Hayden surprised me at the newspaper. I'd been in New York for my internship and I hadn't gotten through a lot of my work. He saw it and flipped his shit. He basically said I was irresponsible and should give up the paper because I was running it into the ground. Then I saw him smoking and . . ."

"Liz," he said, cutting her off. A tear trickled down her cheek and he reached up and swiped it from her face. "No. What happened with us?"

Liz opened and closed her mouth a few times as she tried to come up with the answer to that question. "You were going to choose the campaign," she murmured.

"You left before I had a chance to choose."

"I didn't want you to have to make that choice. I didn't want you to break up with me," she said, another tear leaving her eye.

"Why were you so sure I would?"

Liz shook her head softly in his grasp. "You wouldn't let me love you. It was like walking into a brick wall over and over again. I was the liability that you couldn't figure out how to deal with."

"Liz . . ."

"And in the end, Brady . . . I let you have the campaign and Congress. I couldn't let you jeopardize any of that for me."

Brady released a stifled laugh. "You thought I was happy?"

"I . . ."

"Heather basically talked me off of a ledge for the next three months."

Liz stood there as solid as stone. She couldn't believe what he had just said. No way had it affected him that much. No way. She just couldn't see that being the case. He was dating Erin . . . and had been so happy . . . and . . . Shit!

No. She couldn't have walked away for nothing. He hadn't come after her. He hadn't tried to follow her. She couldn't think about those months. She couldn't think . . .

"I wish I'd had someone to talk me off of the ledge," she whispered. She didn't even know where it came from. But she'd had no one. She had been all alone with her misery.

Brady's eyes darkened when she said that. "You mean you didn't have the boring fill-in to keep you company?"

"We didn't start dating until the election was over."

Brady cursed under his breath. "How could you date him?"

"Me? How could you date *her*?"

"You left me, remember?"

"And you pushed me away," she snapped.

"Well, I'm not pushing you away now." He grabbed her by her shoulders and pulled her body against his. Her hands jerked up against his chest just as his lips dropped down to cover hers.

The world stopped. There was only Brady. Nothing else existed. Nothing else ever had. When their lips touched, it was like the fireworks on Fourth of July mixed with the ball dropping on New Year's. She could feel her body wake up from head to toe. Her mind cleared until everything seemed perfectly crystallized. It was as if she had been wading through mud in a dense fog, and suddenly she walked onto solid ground and the sun was shining.

Chapter 17
REMEMBERING HISTORY

She was kissing Brady.

Her hands were gripping his suit coat. His were tangled in her hair. Their bodies were flush together. Somehow they had moved to where he was pressed back into the footboard of the bed. Their mouths were moving in time and tongues volleying for position. She could feel her heart practically leaping out of her throat and her chest rising and falling as the adrenaline coursed through her body.

It had been months . . . over a year since they had last been together. The built-up tension superheated the room until she felt as if she couldn't breathe. It was too much all at once. And still she needed more. She wanted more. She could never get enough.

"Liz," he groaned against her mouth. He moved his hands down her sides and clutched her hips tightly, jerking her into him.

And then her world came crashing down all around her.

"Oh, no," she whispered, shaking her head.

"No. Don't do that." He brought her face back up to stare at him.

"No. Brady, no," she said, pushing his chest and walking across the room. "Oh, no. No. No. No."

"Liz," he said breathlessly.

"Stop." She put her hand up hoping to keep him from saying anything.

"Why are you pushing me away?"

"I walked away for a reason Brady, and you didn't come after me. That door closed a year ago," she whispered. Her chest ached just speaking the words.

"Are you serious? What did you expect me to do, run after a woman who didn't want me? Who left me?"

"I don't know what I would have wanted you to do, but the fact of the matter is, neither of us did anything. Anything at all. The ifs, ands, or buts don't matter, because I left and you didn't follow me. And we did nothing for the next year."

Brady visibly straightened across the room. "So, I'm standing here a year later for nothing."

"Just like you were a year before this," she whispered.

She swallowed heavily and waited for him to contradict her, but he didn't. How could he? They'd been at a standstill then, and they were driving backward currently. This was a terrible, terrible mistake. One that she had not intended to make. One that she had not considered the consequences of when she had called him in her bout of anger.

They stood there in the silence, each waiting for the other to make them stop slipping down this slope. But neither did.

Brady's phone vibrated in his pocket and he broke eye contact with Liz. He pulled it out of his coat, checked the name, and then silenced it and replaced it.

"Not important?" she asked, even though she knew that she shouldn't.

His eyes found hers again. "No."

Liz hadn't checked her phone since she had gotten into the car with Brady. She wondered how many messages she had from Hayden. She knew she shouldn't ignore him. He was probably flipping out, and not responding wasn't exactly the mature way to handle the situation. But she certainly wasn't calling him back right now. Not while she was with Brady.

She hated the distance that stretched between them. She hated that she had to force the distance and that they couldn't just fall into their easy rhythm. But a lot had happened in the time they had been apart. She had spent a year moving on.

"I think you're just being stubborn," he finally said, breaking the silence.

Liz tilted her head forward and looked at him incredulously. "*I'm* being stubborn? You, of all people, are telling me that I'm stubborn? Pot. Meet kettle," she said, gesturing toward him.

"Your sarcasm is a good defense mechanism," he said casually. "It probably works on someone else."

"Your politician confidence is a good defense mechanism," she threw back. "It probably works on someone else."

"It worked on you."

Liz laughed and rolled her eyes to the ceiling. "You think I was taken in by your cocky asshole attitude? I'm pretty sure I saw through that a mile off. I didn't even use your number that you gave to me at the club that first night we met."

"Keep telling yourself that."

"You're insufferable," she spat, pacing away from him.

"You liked every minute of it."

She rounded on him. "What about the time that you left me at Hilton Head all by myself and never called? Or the time that you were pissed off that I wrote the article I wanted to and not yours? Or the time that you brought another girl to the gala you invited me to?"

"Liz . . ."

"Or just keeping me secret. Oh, look, we're at a place without cameras in the middle of the night. How convenient," she drawled, shaking her head.

Brady closed the distance between them and slowly walked her backward until she was pressed up against the wall. Her breath caught in her throat at his nearness. Her whole body woke up. Holy shit! How did he do that?

"You seem to remember history very differently than I do," he said, guiding his hand down the curve of her neck and over her shoulder. His other hand was on the wall to the left of her head. She swallowed. "I seem to remember afternoons spent on the lake, stripping your clothes off in a cabana, holding you close all night when you drank too much, staying with you an extra night on the Fourth of July . . ."

His hand brushed against the side of her breast and her head thudded back into the wall. He smirked and moved his hand to her slim waist.

"Did you forget about those things?" he asked, his eyes boring into her.

Voice. She had a voice. It was there somewhere.

"No . . . no, I didn't," she finally whispered.

"I didn't think so."

Arrogant son of a bitch . . .

"If you tell me right now that you don't want me, I'll stop." His fingers found the hem of her waistline and he slid the fabric across the sensitive skin from one side to the next. Her eyes fluttered as she struggled to find words.

"I'm sorry. I didn't catch that," he teased. His hand dipped inside her pants and played mischievously with the lace of her thong. His lips moved to her ear and he nipped at her earlobe before speaking seductively. "If you don't say anything, I'm going to have to fuck you into tomorrow."

Her body was screaming and moaning and crying out. It was demanding everything that Brady was offering. It was desperate for his perfect brand of ecstasy. But her brain was fighting with her body. It was whispering in the back of her mind, reminding her why she had left, reminding her there was someone else . . . in both of their lives.

In the time that it took for her brain to speak louder than her body, Brady had flicked the button open on her jeans and was sliding the zipper down.

"Stop," she murmured, pulling her hands up. "Brady, you're with someone else."

"I believe you called her an uppity nuisance," he offered with a sigh as he straightened.

"I can't do this while we're with other people. As long as we are, this door remains shut," she whispered. Her body was such a hussy.

"Are you going to stay with that guy after he upset you enough that you called and came here with me?"

"I don't even want to hear this from you."

"Then why the fuck did you call me?" he demanded.

"I don't know, okay!" she yelled, bringing her hands up to her head and grabbing her hair. "I just didn't want to be . . . me."

"I see," he said softly.

Liz took a second to collect herself. While she straightened and smoothed her hair out, his phone beeped, indicating a text message. She watched him check the phone and then replace it into his pocket.

"That was probably your girlfriend anyway," she said after a minute.

Brady just stood there staring at her. She could feel his eyes assessing her, but she didn't want to look up at him. She didn't want to know what he was thinking. He had wanted to fuck her. God! He probably still wanted to, and it would have been so easy to just give in, but she wasn't that girl. How could she jump back into something with Brady without any guarantee that it wouldn't all go to shit again?

How could she even think that he wanted to jump back into anything other than sex? The worst part of all was she just didn't know. She never knew what she was going to get with Brady. There were no assurances. And while that had been sexy, exhilarating, and endearing over their summer together . . . it was flat-out terrifying to think about the future.

"It was," he finally answered.

Liz nodded. She had figured as much. "What did she say?"

He shrugged. "Nothing."

"Uh-huh," she said disbelievingly. "I should go."

"You're not going anywhere."

"Tell me what she said."

"What does it even matter?"

Liz shrugged. She didn't know why it mattered. It just did. "Fine. It doesn't matter. Can I go home now?"

"No."

Liz yanked the bedroom door open and started out into the hallway. Brady caught up to her easily and grabbed her wrist. "Don't touch me," she said, yanking it away from him. "Go talk to your girlfriend or something."

"It was literally nothing," he said, stopping her. "She was just saying good night."

That made sense actually. It still made her stomach turn.

"Read it if you don't believe me," he said flippantly, tossing the phone into her hand.

The message was still lit up and she read it word for word.

Good night! I thought I'd already hear from you but I'm exhausted and going to sleep. I love you!!!

Liz's stomach dropped out. Erin loved him. Well, of course she did. Who didn't love Brady Maxwell? He was entirely lovable under that asshole persona. Liz had fallen in love with him, after all . . . and in a much shorter time frame than Brady and Erin had been dating.

"She loves you." It was all she could get out.

Brady didn't say anything. His eyes just zeroed in on the phone she was holding in her hands. She didn't know why she asked the next question. She was a masochist. She liked to torture herself. She never wanted to be happy again.

"Do you love her?"

Brady didn't say anything at first, and it was all the answer she needed. Oh, God! She clutched her stomach and closed her eyes. This was not happening. She didn't care how hypocritical it was to feel like this about Brady loving someone else. She had told Hayden she loved him over the summer, but this . . . this was somehow different.

It all came back to the fact that Brady had never told her that he loved her. And it was clear from just one text message that he had told Erin. That he loved Erin. It made her head throb thinking about it.

When Brady didn't answer, Liz said the first thing that came to mind. "You know Savannah hates her, right?"

"What?" he asked, clearly caught off guard.

"It doesn't matter," Liz said, shaking her head. "You love her. It doesn't matter."

Liz glanced up at him one more time wistfully. Hayden might be giving her almost everything she wanted, but he wasn't Brady Maxwell. And Brady Maxwell was giving everything she wanted to someone else.

Chapter 18
LOUD AND CLEAR

The ride back to Liz's car was excruciating. She had sat through painful car rides with Brady before, but the silence was deafening. A year of built-up tension had been unleashed between them tonight, and to what end? They were still in the same place they were before. Sure, it had felt good to finally talk to Brady about why she had left, but it certainly hadn't helped anything.

It had only made her more confused. Brady felt strongly enough about her to have nearly gone off the deep end on campaign, yet he'd never once reached out to her. He seduced her and yet loved another woman. How was she supposed to handle the number of paradoxes in their relationship?

Their nonexistent relationship.

That was how she would handle it: as if it didn't exist. Because it didn't. They were with other people. She may have had an argument with Hayden. She might feel hurt, betrayed, and confused about what had caused it, but it was the first . . . the only argument they had ever had. That didn't mean they were over. That meant they had their first roadblock that they had to deal with.

The stuff she had to deal with with Brady was more like climbing mountains. With bare feet. While she was running out of oxygen.

They reached the parking deck and Brady stopped in front of it. Liz wrung her hands in her lap. She felt as if she should say something, but what could she say that hadn't already been said?

That door was closed and it would continue to be closed. She was with Hayden and he was with Erin. She could practically hear the lock clicking into place and securing them on opposite sides. It made her heart constrict all over again.

"Thank you for picking me up," she whispered.

She heard him sigh heavily and practically felt his annoyance at the whole situation. Or maybe just that the situation hadn't gone as he had anticipated.

"I think this will be the last time," he said solemnly.

She shifted her eyes to look at him. His were hard. They had lost all the warmth he had shown her at the condo. Not that they were particularly mean, but they were distant. At that point it basically equated to the same thing.

"I'm not doing this again. Next time he breaks your heart, I don't want to hear about it. I don't want you to call me. I don't want you to think about me. I'm not part of your life. We might as well have never happened," he said, turning to look at her finally.

She wasn't going to cry. His words weren't going to bring her to tears. No. She could control it. She could keep the pain away.

"I understand," she whispered, her voice hoarse. A tear trickled down her cheek.

His hands reached up automatically and wiped it away with his thumb. "No tears for me, baby. Soon enough you'll forget I ever existed . . . just like you wanted."

Liz shook her head, wanting nothing more than to turn her cheek into his palm, to find the warmth and comfort in his touch that she so desperately craved. But instead she withdrew from him, pushed open the door, and walked out. She didn't have a clever retort or a final word this time. Brady had made his point. Loud and clear.

—

Liz should have called Hayden straightaway. They had so much to talk about, but she couldn't face him like this.

He might have been an ass, but her calling Brady and driving off with him had been worse. Kissing him and almost sleeping with him had been much worse. Hayden didn't deserve that. She felt like a coward not facing him after what she had done, but it was the middle of the night, she had no idea where he had gone, and she just wanted to sleep off the depression that was crushing her heart.

Falling into the front seat of her car, she drove home in a blur. She didn't really remember the drive, but she hadn't gotten in an accident, so it didn't matter. Lights were on in her house. Liz checked her watch. Half past midnight. She really thought it was later than that. It felt as if she had been out all night.

The last thing she wanted was to run into anyone looking like this. She just hoped that Hayden hadn't come over here when she didn't respond to him.

With a deep breath, she pushed the door open. Victoria was sitting on the couch in sweats and a low-cut T-shirt, eating popcorn, and watching reruns of some nineties television show. She jumped when she saw Liz walk through the door. She scrambled out of her seat and tossed the popcorn onto the coffee table.

"Where the fuck have you been? I've been calling you for hours!" Victoria shrieked.

"What?" she asked numbly.

"Hayden called me and he came by to try to talk to you, but obviously you weren't here. He told me you guys got into an argument and thought I knew where you would be. What the fuck was I supposed to tell him?"

"That I wasn't here?" Liz offered. What else was she supposed to say? "Sorry you had to deal with that."

"Oh, Hayden, psh," Victoria said, pushing her hands to the side. "I don't care about him. I care about you, and the fact that I had to cover for your ass."

"Cover for me?"

"Where the hell did you go after you guys had that fight if you weren't with someone else?" Victoria demanded.

Liz blanched. No. No. No. No one could know about that. Brady was out of her life. Brady was gone. Whatever they'd had didn't even exist anymore. She couldn't tell anyone about it now.

"I was just driving around . . ."

"Bullshit! For over three hours?"

"What do you want me to say, Victoria? 'Thank you for talking to Hayden for me because I'm not ready to'?"

Victoria shrugged and ran a hand back through her dark hair. "I don't want you to say anything. I just don't want to have to cover for you when you're not even going to give me the juicy details of your sexcapade!"

"It's too late for this," Liz said, shaking her head and pushing past Victoria. "I'm not having sex with anyone but my boyfriend, and after our argument, I'm second-guessing that."

"Wait . . . so are you like actually going to break up with Lane?"

"I think I should sleep on it."

"Wow," Victoria said, clearly stunned. "I never saw that one coming. I thought you two were getting married and having twelve babies on the farm and shit."

Liz narrowed her eyes. "On the farm, Vic?"

"You know what I mean. But what happened?" she asked, walking back and grabbing her popcorn. She stuffed some into her mouth and waited for Liz's response as if she were watching a movie.

"We fought. He was an asshole. He said I was letting the paper turn to shit because I had other things going on. And then when I left I saw him smoking and he punched the door," Liz summarized.

"Hayden smoking?" Victoria asked. "Hot!"

"What? No, it's totally disgusting!"

"Come on! You don't think that Mr. Stick Up His Ass getting a little rebellious and breaking some barriers is hot? Just a little?"

"No," Liz told her flatly. That had been the farthest thing from her mind when she had seen Hayden smoking. She had been disgusted and she felt betrayed. How long had he been smoking? How long had he been keeping it from her? What else was he keeping from her?

"Okay. Well are you going to talk about it with him? I can come with and whip his ass into shape," she said, her eyes lighting up. "Literally."

"Thanks for the offer, but I guess I'll talk to him tomorrow."

"Hey," Victoria said, reaching out and touching Liz's jacket. She actually looked serious for a change. "I'm sorry about what happened. I know you really like Hayden. I wouldn't have made fun of him so much if you didn't. I hope it works out. You know . . . for your sake. I don't want you as sad as you were last fall."

Liz bit her lip. She couldn't think about last fall. That was Brady territory, and Brady no longer existed.

"Thanks," Liz said softly.

Victoria put her popcorn on the ground and pulled Liz into a hug. That broke her down. Tears fell from Liz's eyes as she cried into her best friend's shoulder. They didn't have to say anything else. Victoria just let her cry as long as she needed.

The next morning she didn't even bother sorting through the missed calls, messages, and voicemails. She just pulled her hair up into a messy bun on the top of her head and slid into a pair of yoga pants and a sweater. Then she called Hayden.

He answered on the first ring. Maybe before the first ring finished. He must have been holding it for him to answer that quickly.

"Lizzie . . ."

"Hey," she murmured.

"I'm so glad you called."

"Look, Hayden," she said, burying her head in her hands, "I think we need to talk."

She heard his sharp intake of breath on the other line.

"I'm at Hannity's place. I can come see you if that works for you."

He was still in Chapel Hill. Of course he would still be in Chapel Hill. That only made sense. He probably hadn't wanted to leave until he got to see her again.

"Sure. Come on over."

"I'll be there in ten minutes," he said. "Liz?"

"Mmm?"

He sighed heavily. "Please don't do anything drastic."

"Hayden, can we talk when you get here?" she whispered.

"Yeah. Yeah, I'll see you soon."

Hayden arrived no more than ten minutes later. Exactly prompt. Just as he had said he would be. She hadn't expected anything less, but after last night everything was all out of whack. Normally Hayden was perfectly put together. Meticulous was the best word to describe him, but he wasn't anything like that today.

He looked like a wreck. He looked as if he hadn't slept all night. Or as if any sleep he had gotten had been restless. He wore the same clothes from yesterday, but rumpled, as if he had slept in them. His eyes were slightly bloodshot and he had stubble brushing across his cheeks and chin. She had never seen him anything but clean-shaven.

At the sight of him, her heart softened a bit. He was clearly fucked up over what had happened and realized how much of a mistake he had made. And she had made a mistake. A big fucking mistake. He wasn't the only one to blame in this situation, but he didn't know that, and he looked sheepish when he walked in.

"Hey," he said, closing the door behind him.

"Hi." She crossed her arms over her chest uncomfortably. This was going to be painful.

He glanced over at Victoria's closed bedroom door and then back at Liz. "Can we go talk in your room?"

Liz nodded. "Sure."

They retreated back to the bedroom and Liz took a seat on her bed. She crossed her feet pretzel style and stared down at her hands. She knew that she should start, but she didn't even know where to begin.

"Look, Liz," Hayden said, combing through his hair with his fingers. "I know you said that we need to talk, but I'd really like to go first, if that's all right."

"Um . . . sure."

"I'm really sorry about what I said. It was uncalled for, and irresponsible of me to accuse you of hurting the paper based on a few unread emails. I know you have a lot on your plate, and I just took my frustration with my new job out on you. And it was irresponsible of me as your boyfriend," he said, looking up into her eyes, "to dismiss your feelings so easily."

"Hayden," she murmured.

"No, Liz, please. I don't know what was wrong with me last night. I shouldn't have said the things I said. And I damn well shouldn't have let you walk out of the door angry. That's not the kind of person I am. I should have run after you. I should have stopped you."

"Yeah, you should have," she said softly. Guilt tugged at her even as the words fell from her mouth.

He nodded slowly. "I was stupid to not follow you. I was stupid about a lot of things. But in the year that we've been dating, we've never had an argument like this before. Discussions about our differences, but nothing like this. I think that really says something about us. I can't promise you it will always be perfect, Liz, because it won't. And I can't promise I'll always be the perfect guy for you."

Liz tried to breathe easy . . . normal. All of these things he couldn't promise sounded so familiar . . .

Hayden continued, "I can't promise you that we won't argue or fight or disagree like we did last night. I can't promise you any of these things, but I can promise you, on the record," he said, with that beautiful Hayden smile, "that I'll always be here and I'll never let go. I am not a perfect man, but I'll always be yours, imperfections and all, if you'll have me."

Oh the sincerity. Liz put her hand on her head and tried to process it. She had thought he would apologize, but all of *this*. It was so much.

He was right: they had never had an argument before this. This was a doozy of an argument. Not to mention the bullshit with him smoking. She didn't even know what to make of it, but how could she ask him if she didn't tell him that she had been spying on him and that she hadn't left right away? How was she supposed to explain that away logically?

She knew how to do it. She needed to tell him about Brady, but when she opened her mouth to speak, the words stuck in her throat. She had been holding on to it so long that she couldn't even form the words.

"Do you know what it feels like for someone to take everything they have ever worked for and have someone else tear it all down? You of all people know how much work I put in to become editor, to get this internship, to be on the Morehead scholarship. You know the work I've put into this relationship. And then you took all of that, Hayden, and stomped on it," she whispered, looking up into his hazel eyes, almost brown in the darkness.

"I know I did. It was wrong of me to do that to you. Wrong and selfish. I'm not sure what happened, but something snapped inside of me. I worked so hard in college to get where I was, and then somehow I was stuck in an average reporting position in Charlotte. I was overwhelmed and did the worst thing I could," he said, walking toward her, pleading. He sat heavily on the bed and stared into her eyes. She let him take one of her hands and he stroked her palm with his thumb. "I never should have taken this out on you."

She nodded, but didn't pull back. She was angry with Hayden, but angrier with herself. She had called Brady in her desperation instead of working through her problems with Hayden. Hayden was the one who deserved a second chance . . . not her.

"I love you, Liz. I was an idiot. I'll say it a million times over to prove to you I was wrong," he whispered, staring straight into her eyes. "Just don't leave me. I need you. You're my world."

Liz bit her lip. She knew she should give him an answer. She knew that she should tell him everything she was feeling. But exhaustion nipped at her from all sides. She had made up her mind already anyway.

"Okay," she murmured.

"Yeah?" he asked, his eyes lighting up.

"But, Hayden, if you ever make me feel like that again, it's over," she told him point-blank.

Chapter 19

THE BOUTIQUE

Hayden left for Charlotte that evening. Liz tried to act normal throughout the remainder of his visit, but she was emotionally exhausted.

She knew that Brady was out of her life. She had known it every day since she had walked out on him, but still in the back of her mind she had always secretly hoped that it would work out. Now that hope was gone.

Before that night, she hadn't realized how hard she had clung to that feeling. It hadn't even been a realistic or rational expectation. She had known that, but it was Brady Maxwell. She would have clung to his memory forever. She was sure of it. But he had erased that too. She was supposed to act as if he had never existed.

The guilt of her actions ate at her, though. When she saw Hayden the weight pressed down on her shoulders and tried to crush her. They spent their one-year anniversary over a fancy dinner. Hayden gave her small diamond earrings. She had stared at them in shock. She knew he had a real job now and that he could buy her things, but she hadn't been expecting it. Part of it was him trying to make up for their argument and part of it was just how much he adored her. The itch to tell him about Brady grew a bit each day.

When they talked on the phone, all she wanted to do was blurt out what had happened. Somehow she held her tongue. Even when she was away from him over Thanksgiving and Christmas, all Liz could think about was that one word, the one word that threatened to undo her.

Cheating.

She had cheated on Hayden. One kiss. A drive with Brady. The feel of his hands sliding across the waistline of her pants. Emotional attachment that had lasted far too long.

She had taken Hayden back. She had made him feel terrible for how he had treated her. And what kind of person was she? Harboring feelings for another man, hiding secrets from him for over a year, kissing someone else and never telling him. She was a coward. But she had lost Brady, and she hadn't been willing to lose Hayden too.

They spent their second New Year's together at a bar in D.C. with Jamie and James. Besides the nagging guilt that settled into the pit of her stomach, their relationship was smoother than ever. And she wanted to keep it that way, so she did the only thing she knew how: she buried the guilt and kept her secrets.

She spent the week before school at the *New York Times* and wasn't able to see Hayden once school got back in because she was so busy. Two weeks into the semester, she and Victoria received invitations to a banquet for their Morehead scholarships. It was an annual thing for seniors to thank them for dedicating so much time to the school and the enhancement of their education. It was supposed to be pretty dull, but they were told it had free alcohol so it was always full.

Victoria used anything as an excuse to go shopping, which was how Liz ended up in a dress boutique in downtown Durham looking for the perfect thing to wear to the banquet.

"Okay, bitch, I have fifty dresses and you only have one. How is that even possible?" Victoria asked, holding a pile of dresses in her arms.

"I already have something to wear," Liz said with a shrug.

"You are not wearing that champagne dress in the back of your closet!" Victoria snapped. "I know that's what you're thinking."

Liz bit her lip. No way was she wearing the champagne dress she had gotten for Brady's gala event. That would be torture. "I wasn't planning to."

"Good. Now find a couple more options to try on so I'm not in there alone." With that she turned and walked into the first dressing room.

Liz rolled her eyes. She grabbed two more dresses that she had been eyeing earlier and took the room next to Victoria. It all really was pointless. She had plenty of dresses that she could wear to an event like this that no one had ever seen her in. Well, Hayden had probably seen her in most of them, and he was her date, but that didn't matter. Hayden didn't count.

The first dress was a knee-length black dress with a high neck and slight shimmer to it. She liked it, but it was a little tight through the hips, and she didn't *love* it by any means. Victoria vetoed it immediately. The second dress, a baby-pink lace ensemble, also received an instant no.

Victoria would be trying on her dresses forever, so Liz took her time with the last one, the one that she had liked the most originally. She carefully pulled the zipper down to the bottom and stepped into the silky material. Finding the edge of the zipper, she pulled it back into place.

She stared at herself in the mirror and a sad smile crossed her face. The black dress was exquisitely cut and molded to her body in a way that made it seem it had been made for her. It was cap-sleeved with an extensively beaded bodice that hugged her torso. A soft silk material covered her athletic hips down to just a few inches above her knees. The back created a U shape to the middle of her back.

It was beautiful. Unbelievably beautiful. Probably too beautiful to waste on a scholarship banquet.

Suddenly her vision blurred as tears marred her eyes. Liz saw herself then as a mirage. A woman floating and indistinguishable amongst her surroundings.

It was ridiculous for her to be near tears just from looking at a boutique dress. She hadn't cried since the night of the argument with Hayden. Why was she crying now? She willed her tears away, but they refused, and she got a sick feeling in the pit of her stomach.

She loved Hayden. She adored Hayden. He was everything she ever wanted. Well, almost. Her stomach tightened painfully.

He was everything she ever needed. Taking a deep breath, she accepted that. Listing his qualities would take too long, and she knew what a great man he was. She didn't need to convince herself. Yet as her eyes lifted back to the mirror, a tear trailed slowly down her pale cheek.

The guilt of what she had done was weighing on her heavier than ever. All she wanted to do was tell someone, anyone. But the one person she could talk to about it never wanted to see her again, and the one person she needed to talk to about it would never forgive her. He loved her, but how could he accept what she had done?

"Hey, bitch, check out this one," Victoria said, banging on her dressing room door.

Liz wiped at her face and tried to compose herself before opening the door.

"You look great!" Victoria said, checking out the dress. When she looked back up at Liz, though, she tilted her head and furrowed her brow. "What's this about? You okay?"

"Yeah, I'm fine," she croaked. She wasn't hiding anything from her best friend.

"I mean, it's just a dress, Liz. I think it looks great." The look on Victoria's face made it all too clear to Liz that Victoria knew it wasn't the dress. "Now, what's really wrong?" Victoria demanded, planting her hands on her hips.

Liz shook her head. "Nothing, Vic, I'm fine. No worries. Just a beautiful dress, huh?" she said, lying through her teeth.

"What the fuck is going on?"

"Nothing! Can't I appreciate a good-looking dress?" She turned away from Victoria and looked at herself in the boutique's trifold mirror.

"If it makes you cry that much, then don't get it," Victoria said flatly.

A tear rolled down Liz's face when she stared at her reflection again. She very clearly looked as if she had been crying. God, she needed to get it together.

"Okay. I can't make light of this anymore. What the fuck happened? Just fucking spit it out."

"I kissed someone else!" Liz said, covering her mouth as soon as the words left it. She crouched in the middle of the dressing room and covered her face. Even as her tears continued falling, she brushed them away and looked back up at her friend.

Victoria's mouth was hanging open and she was staring at Liz as if she had never seen her before. Liz shrank in on herself even more at the expression. Yeah, she was a terrible person.

"Oh my God! Was it recently?" Victoria asked, her eyes as large as saucers.

"No."

"Was it that night when you and Hayden got into an argument last October?"

Liz stood up and pushed her hair off her face. She felt clammy and slightly nauseated, but it felt good to get it out for the first time ever.

"Yeah. It was."

"I knew it!" Victoria shrieked.

"Yeah, you guessed it. I'm a terrible girlfriend who cheated on her perfect fucking boyfriend. Yay! So glad you were right," Liz said in frustration. She felt like shit.

"Oh, please, your boyfriend is *not* perfect! He pushed you into someone else's arms. I would have fucked someone else that night. You were totally in the right."

"I was not!" Liz cried. "Are you insane? I kissed someone else while I'm dating Hayden."

"Well, don't tell the whole world," Victoria said, nodding her head into the boutique.

Liz shook her head. She hadn't been paying any attention to what was going on around her. "I'm going to change. I just want to go home."

"Yeah, but you should get that dress."

"I don't want it."

"But it's like your meltdown dress. You need it."

"Whatever," Liz said, walking into the dressing room.

"So, who is the guy?" Victoria prodded after a couple silent seconds.

"It doesn't matter."

Liz took the dress off and put it back on the hanger before sliding back into her jeans and sweater. She was in and out of there in no time at all, but when she walked back out, Victoria was still in her dress.

"But really . . . you're not going to tell me?"

"It doesn't matter."

"Um . . . it does."

"Let's just go," Liz said, placing the dress on the return rack and folding her arms over her chest.

"You have been beating yourself up about this since October, and you're not going to even talk about it with me now?" Victoria asked. She actually looked hurt.

Liz ran her hands over her face and tried to decide what to do. She had already confessed to Victoria, and her friend wasn't judging her. In fact, the only thing she seemed perturbed about at all was the fact that Liz hadn't told her sooner. Maybe she could trust Victoria.

It would be so nice to have someone to talk to about this. It wasn't as if Brady were ever coming back into her life. The secret wasn't even that important anymore. It was just something she had always kept at this point. But really, who was Victoria going to tell? Certainly not Hayden, and anyone she and Brady had been concerned about was long out of the picture.

"So . . . you remember last summer, not this past year but the year before that, how I told you I was seeing someone?" Liz offered.

"Yeah," Victoria said eagerly.

"I called him that night Hayden and I argued. He picked me up and we went to his condo. We made out. I freaked out and he brought me home."

"Holy shit! You're sneaky." Victoria jumped from one foot to the other. "This is so exciting! I'm usually the dirty one."

Liz couldn't help but laugh. What else could she do?

"How could you call him, go to his condo, and kiss, but not fuck? I'm astonished at your self-control!"

"I wanted to, but it didn't feel right. It's complicated," Liz told her.

"Um . . . it's not complicated. You insert his dick inside—"

"Whoa!" Liz said, holding her hand up. "You don't have to give away Victoria's secret."

"Oh, ha ha! You're so fucking original." Victoria rolled her eyes. "So seriously, who is the guy?"

Liz sighed heavily. She couldn't tell. She just couldn't. Especially not out in public.

"Can we talk about this somewhere more private?" Liz pleaded.

Victoria clapped her hands together and dashed into the dressing room. A few minutes later, she had all of the dresses hanging haphazardly on the rack, with her selection and Liz's black beaded dress in her hand. She paid for both through Liz's protests and then quickly hurried Liz out of the boutique.

"Okay," Victoria said when they were finally seated in her car.

"Let's go home. It's probably safer," Liz said ominously. She didn't trust Victoria not to drive them into a telephone pole.

"Seriously?"

"Seriously."

Liz swallowed, her throat constricting the closer they got to home. She was warring with herself on what she could and couldn't tell Victoria. She desperately wanted to confide in someone. It was making her crazy. She had held this in for a year and a half and she didn't want to have to hide anymore. She didn't want to reveal it to the entire populace or anything. In fact, that was the last thing she wanted.

She still valued Brady's career and would do everything in her power to keep their relationship from hurting him. That was the reason she had left in the first place. If she didn't believe in that, then she never would have left.

Victoria pulled into their driveway twenty minutes later and practically skipped to the front door. At least someone was enjoying this.

Once Liz was inside, she took a seat on the couch and tucked her feet up underneath her. While Victoria sat in the chair across from her, bouncing with anticipation, Liz picked at her nails. She didn't even know where to begin or what to say. Maybe she shouldn't say anything.

But the one thing she had learned about the entire situation was that secrets were heavy. Mentally, physically, emotionally—they exhausted her. And she had quite the secret tucked away in her heart.

"Well . . . we're home and it's safe," Victoria offered. "I'm literally dying over here. I've been curious about this guy since you first told me about him, and to think you saw him in October."

"It's really not something to be excited about. There's a reason I've been keeping it all secret," Liz explained.

"I remember you saying that he asked you to keep it secret. Still shitty to me, if I do say so."

Liz breathed out heavily. "I know why you think that, but it's a necessary precaution. I just want you to promise me that you're not going to tell anyone about this. I'm already kind of freaked out. I mean, I think I should tell Hayden about what happened, but God, I don't even know how to do that. I don't want him to hate me."

"He's not going to hate you."

"You don't know that."

Victoria rolled her eyes. "I do too. He's crazy about you."

"Maybe. So, do you promise?"

"Of course, who am I going to tell?"

"Absolutely no one," Liz said, trying to drill it into her head.

"Right. I promise not to say anything. I can't see how it's that big a deal though," Victoria said dismissively.

Liz took a deep breath and then let it out slowly. She didn't have any idea how to start, so she just blurted it out: "Brady Maxwell."

Victoria sat very still for a second. Her eyes were glued to Liz, but didn't give anything away. Then slowly the name seemed to sink in and her eyes gradually grew in size. Her mouth dropped open slightly and she stopped bouncing.

"Wait . . . like Brady Maxwell, Brady Maxwell? Like the congressman you interviewed?" Victoria asked.

"Um . . . yeah," Liz whispered. She felt as if she could breathe properly for the first time in a long while. She had been carrying that secret around for so long. She hadn't known she would feel so relieved now that it was out.

"Whoa!" Victoria said, falling back into her chair. "You were banging a congressman. Is he married?"

"No. He's not," Liz said tensely.

"I just . . . wow. You were right. I wasn't expecting that at all. I definitely thought you were going to tell me one of Hayden's friends or something and that's why it was a big secret. I never in a million years would have guessed you were fucking that hot specimen." She was clearly shocked, because Victoria didn't ramble. "Is he good in bed?"

Liz laughed softly. "Um . . . yeah. Very good."

"So wait . . . a sitting congressman picked you up from the newspaper, took you to his condo, and you didn't fuck him?" Victoria asked, slapping her hands on the armrests. "Are you out of your mind? Are you not attracted to power? Why did it end? What happened last summer? Gah, give me details! I need to know."

Tears sprang to Liz's eyes again without warning. She pushed her palms into her eyes to stop them. "You don't understand," she murmured. "I was a liability to the campaign. I'd written negative stuff about him and they already weren't sure he was going to win. He only won by a slim margin as it was, and if anyone found out we were together, he wouldn't have. Any small slipup had the potential to ruin him."

"So he broke it off? They forced you out?" Victoria whispered. "Bastard!"

"No," Liz said, shaking her head. Victoria hopped off the chair and plopped down into the seat next to her. "I left."

"You left? But why?"

"I didn't think he'd choose me over the campaign and I didn't want him to. I believe in him and I wanted him to pursue his dreams, but after I saw him, he told me that he was as much of a wreck as I was after the split," Liz said, her hands shaking as she finally spilled everything to her best friend.

"Oh my God, then go to him!"

"It's complicated. He's dating someone. I'm with Hayden. Brady closed that door, Vic. He told me that he didn't even want to be a memory to me anymore. I hurt him past the point of recovery and I was too much of a coward to tell Hayden. And ever since I've just felt like complete and total shit."

"Oh, Liz," Victoria said with a sigh. "I really don't know what to tell you. If you feel like you were in the wrong—which, trust me, I don't think you were—then maybe you should tell Hayden."

"You think?"

She couldn't do it. It hurt too much. He would leave her. But maybe she deserved it. Maybe the truth would set her free. Maybe it would lift the weight off her chest.

"What's the worst that could happen?" Victoria asked.

"He would leave me."

"And considering you were making out with a politician a couple months ago, that might not be *that* bad."

Chapter 20
THE BANQUET

Is that your politician?" Victoria asked, coming out of her bedroom dressed to the nines for the banquet tonight. Liz couldn't believe the first month of her last semester had already passed so quickly.

Liz stared at the screen where Brady stood in front of a podium in a three-piece black suit. He looked gorgeous. "Yeah, that's him."

"He's so smoking hot."

"Mmm . . ."

"What's he talking about?" Victoria asked after a minute.

"He's running for reelection. It's not a surprise," Liz told her. "Everyone knew that he would. He's into it for life."

"You make it sound like a prison sentence."

Sometimes Liz thought it was.

"Do you think he'll win? Is he going to come to campus? Are you going to see him?" Victoria prodded.

Ever since Liz had told Victoria about Brady it had been this way. Liz wasn't sure if Victoria was more excited that Liz had done something completely out of character or because it was something that maybe even topped her crazy stories. But as much of a relief as it was to finally have told someone about what had happened, it was wearing on Liz's nerves having to talk about Brady every day. She had been trying not to think about him for over a year. This wasn't helping.

"Yes, I think he'll win. I have no idea if he will come to campus. And no," Liz said in a sad, frustrated tone, "I won't see him."

Victoria shrugged. "Can't hurt anything if you did."

"Oh, yes, it could," Liz murmured.

"Nothing besides your vagina."

Liz rolled her eyes to the ceiling. "I'm not going to sleep with him."

"Not with that attitude."

"Boyfriend," Liz reminded her.

"Details."

"Pretty important details," Liz said, standing up and running her hands back through the tresses she had expertly put curls into. She had completed her hair and makeup for the Morehead scholarship banquet thirty minutes ago, but she wasn't ready to slip into her dress until right before they had to leave. "Especially considering that detail is about to walk through our front door."

"Are you going to tell him?" Victoria asked.

"I haven't decided," Liz said, her stomach dipping uncomfortably. She hated hiding it from Hayden, but telling him about Brady made her even more anxious. "Just don't say anything, okay?"

"I'm sworn to secrecy."

"Good," Liz said over her shoulder as she walked into her bedroom.

She stripped out of her lounge clothes and tugged the boutique dress off of the hanger. She stepped into the dress and pulled the zipper into place. Strapping on silver glitter high heels, she looked herself over in the mirror once. Her hand moved to her neck and she sighed.

She wasn't looking forward to her decision tonight. Should she tell Hayden? Her hand reached for the jewelry box on her dresser, and she gingerly removed Brady's necklace from within. She walked across the room and took a seat on her bed. God, too many questions, and not enough answers.

She was still wavering with indecision when she heard a knock on the front door. "Liz!" Victoria called. "Get your ass out here."

Liz set the necklace on her nightstand before walking back down the hall. Liz stopped where she was standing when she saw the guy Victoria was currently attached to. Liz cleared her throat softly and Victoria broke the lip-lock.

"Oh! Daniel, this is my roommate, Liz," Victoria said as introduction.

Liz raised her eyebrows at Victoria. She hadn't mentioned that she was even still talking to Duke Fan, let alone that he was going to be coming to the banquet with them tonight.

"So nice to finally meet you," Daniel said, walking forward and extending his hand.

"The illustrious Duke Fan," Liz said, taking his hand in hers and shaking.

Daniel chuckled and nodded. "I've heard that's what you call me."

Liz saw the look that passed between Victoria and Daniel. It made Liz smile. Victoria was clearly very happy.

Another knock on the door made Liz turn around and then Hayden was walking through the door. He was in a black pinstripe suit with a crisp white shirt and red tie. He pulled his hand out from behind his back and produced a bouquet of red roses. He smiled that heart-stopping smile, and Liz felt the wave of guilt wash over her all over again.

"These are for you, gorgeous," Hayden said in greeting. He walked up to her and placed a soft kiss on her lips.

"Wow," Liz breathed. "Thank you."

"Let me help you find a vase for those," Victoria said immediately, ushering Liz out of the living room and leaving the guys alone without an introduction.

Their heels clattered against the kitchen tiles as they strode into the room. Victoria plucked the roses out of Liz's hands and went in search of a vase in a cabinet.

"Stop whatever you're thinking right now," Victoria said. "These flowers are no reason to freak out."

"I'm not freaked out," Liz told her.

"Uh-huh. I think you should just take a breath and then let it out."

Liz did what she said as Victoria found a vase and started pouring water into it.

"So I really think you should tell him tonight," Victoria said.

Liz squeaked. "Tonight!"

"It makes sense. He's here, and then you can break up with him and go back to the politician."

Her eyes bugged out. "You are insane. I'm not going to go back to him," she hissed, glancing over her shoulder, "because he doesn't want me. Now would you keep it down so that I don't have to fucking explain myself before I'm ready?"

"Oh, please," Victoria said, slipping the roses out of their packaging and plopping them into the vase. She turned and popped her hip out. "Any guy would be an idiot not to want you."

"Well, *you* didn't hear him. You didn't have him look you in the eyes and say, 'No more tears, because soon I won't even be a memory, just like you want,'" Liz spat. "So stop bringing it up! I'm going to regret telling you."

"Just like *you* wanted . . . not like *he* wanted. There's a difference," Victoria said, primping the roses into formation. She grasped the vase in her hands. "I just think that the fact that you haven't told Lane is telling for your relationship. So why not find out how he reacts and see if it's everything you actually want."

"Just give me those," Liz snapped, snatching the roses out of Victoria's hand and walking out of the kitchen. She plastered on a smile as she walked back into the living room with the roses. "These look beautiful."

Hayden and Daniel were standing a few feet apart in silence.

"I'm glad you like them," Hayden said. He followed her into the living room, where she placed them on the coffee table, and then wrapped her in a hug. He planted a kiss on her forehead as he grasped the soft material between his fingers. "I've missed you."

"I missed you too," she said softly.

"Y'all ready?" Victoria asked, grabbing her coat out of the closet and walking toward the door.

"Yes," Hayden answered immediately. He leaned down and whispered in her ear, "Sooner we leave, sooner I can get you home."

Liz giggled at the implication in his words. This was easy, simple. No need for her to stress or put more thought into it than she needed to. If she wanted to tell Hayden then she would. If the time wasn't right, then she wouldn't. Right now she was just going to enjoy her evening.

Hayden and Liz crashed back into the house several hours later, tipsy from the wine that had been flowing all night, and drunk on the energy of the evening. Victoria and Daniel had stayed at the banquet, since Victoria won the Senior Morehead scholarship award, which provided funding to the genetics project she was working on. Dr. Mires had been in attendance and had talked Liz through all of the reporting jobs that Liz had applied for over break. They were both hopeful that offers would be coming in within the next couple weeks.

It was exciting and exhilarating being at the banquet, discussing the future, and finally realizing that this was the end. This was her last semester of college and then she would be out in the real world.

Hayden's hands slid down the sides of her dress as soon as the door closed. One hand grabbed her ass and the other wound around her waist, drawing her into him. His breath was hot on her neck, and she squirmed against him.

"Bedroom," he whispered huskily.

"Hayden . . ."

He released her waist and spun her around fast. She teetered in her heels, latching on to him for support just before his lips claimed her. That cut off all conversation. After he broke the kiss, Hayden took her hand and walked her back to her bedroom. She staggered forward after him.

They made it into the bedroom and Liz kicked off her heels. She wasn't exactly drunk, but they were dangerous even when she was sober.

Hayden pulled her into him again and started walking them backward. His lips fell on top of hers once more. In between kisses, he murmured, "Bed."

Liz swallowed hard. She wanted to get into this. She wanted this to happen. She wanted Hayden to remind her why she loved him. But as her knees hit the edge of the bed another pair of eyes flashed in her mind. Brown eyes. Big brooding brown eyes. Eyes that consumed her to her very core. The very same eyes of the person she had been kissing a few months ago.

She pulled back with a gasp. Holy shit! She couldn't do this right now with such a heavy heart. They'd had an amazing time at the party. They had danced and drank and celebrated together. She had tried so hard to be what they had been. She had almost been able to forget what she had done. Almost.

"Hayden, stop," she whispered, pushing lightly against his chest.

"I'll close the door," he said in response. He started walking across the room.

"No, that's not what I meant." She took a seat on the bed and her head swam. She wasn't sure if it was the alcohol or the fear of what she was about to do.

Liz had never anticipated telling anyone about what had happened with Brady. She had sworn that she wouldn't. She didn't want to hurt Brady. But she had hurt him anyway and now he was gone from her life forever. She just knew that she couldn't continue with this life she was leading. She couldn't keep feeling the guilt and self-loathing about kissing the man that she had so desperately loved for so long. She just needed to be free.

"I want to talk to you," she breathed.

Hayden shut the door and walked back over to her. His hands found her face, and he cupped her cheeks in his palms. "Let's talk later."

He had never been a sex-first-and-talk-later kind of guy. The alcohol must have been talking. Just as it was giving her the courage to speak up.

"No. Talk first," she encouraged.

He breathed out heavily. "I think we should wait." He eased her back on the bed and started trailing kisses down her neck.

"Hayden . . ."

"Shhh . . ." he whispered, running a hand up her bare thigh. "I just want to feel you next to me."

On any other night, she would have preferred his forthrightness. He wasn't normally this guy. He wasn't normally demanding. And she liked this new Hayden. She found that she actually really, really wanted it. But she couldn't.

"No, Hayden. No," she said more forcefully. She pushed him off of her and rolled off of the bed. She flicked on the side table lamp so she could see his face. "We really need to talk."

The alcohol was sending liquid courage through her veins, and still her stomach knotted with anxiety. How would he take what she was about to say? She had told Victoria that the worst thing that could happen would be for Hayden to leave her. The uncertainty ate away at her. Was he going to blow up on her? Was he going to just be shocked? She wouldn't know until she told him, but as she stood there in front of him, her tongue stuck to the roof of her mouth.

"What do we need to talk about?" Hayden asked, clearly frustrated. He straightened himself, crossed one leg over the other at the ankle, and leaned forward.

She could tell that he had no idea what she was about to throw at him. There was no way she could approach this as she had with Victoria. At that time, she had just blurted out that she had kissed someone else, but with Hayden she couldn't imagine what that would do to him. She couldn't break him.

"Um . . . I've been meaning to tell you this for a long time," she began carefully. "I just didn't know how to say it."

"Didn't know how to say what?" Hayden asked. There wasn't any caution in his voice at all. He had no clue. She hated herself for what she was about to do to him in that moment.

"I know you might be mad with me, but please just let me explain."

That sure captured his attention. He sat up straighter and his hazel eyes narrowed. She could see that he was trying to figure out where this was going, and that he hadn't expected that at all. There was no going back now.

"So . . . two summers ago, I was dating someone else," Liz began.

"You were?" he asked clearly confused.

"Yeah. I met this guy, and we had this secret relationship the summer before my junior year. I was still seeing him when I visited you in D.C."

Hayden's eyebrows rose sharply at that comment. She hated telling him the whole story, but she knew that she needed to. He wouldn't understand if she didn't start from the beginning.

"It was a strange relationship. One that's kind of hard to explain. One that up until last week, I'd never told anyone else about. We weren't exactly exclusive, but . . ." Liz cringed. She wished there were an easier way to explain this. "Anyway, I was with you in D.C. and then sometime shortly after school started, he and I broke it off. Well, I left him."

"Why are you telling me all of this?" Hayden asked, unable to keep the slight tone of anger out of his voice.

She didn't blame him.

"Because I saw him again in October."

Hayden stopped moving. He had only been slightly fidgeting with his suit coat and tapping his foot, but when she said that he stopped everything and just stared at her.

"When in October?"

She could tell that he already knew the answer. Her heart pounded away in her chest. This was going to be even more difficult than she thought.

"When we had our argument," she whispered.

Hayden stood at the statement. He walked to the end of the bed and rested his hand on the footboard, facing away from her. His chest was rising and falling with barely concealed anger and pain . . . betrayal.

"I've been meaning to tell you this whole time, but I never found a way. There was always something else."

"What happened?" he asked, his voice cold.

"He picked me up from the paper. We kissed. That's it," she said earnestly.

Hayden sagged against the footboard. He brought his hand to his head and she saw his shoulders shake. There. She had broken him. And it hurt so fucking bad. She couldn't even see his face, but she knew, she just knew that she had hurt him beyond compare. She could imagine his face crumpled and the hollowness in his eyes at her words.

"I swear it will never happen again. We agreed to never see each other after that," she told him. It hadn't gone exactly that way, but it wasn't as if it wasn't the truth. "I felt so terrible, and I wanted to tell you, Hayden. I really did."

"Then why didn't you?" he asked, his voice the same cold calculation.

"I don't know."

He turned around sharply. "I was a total prick to you that day. I was completely a hundred percent in the wrong. And I owned up to that. I told you exactly everything that I did, and you let me sit there and grovel. I might have pushed you back to him that day, but you had your opportunity to tell me what happened and you chose not to."

"I know," Liz whispered, tears welling in her eyes. She could have told him what had happened. She could have been honest, but she hadn't.

"I felt like absolute shit for months. I tried to do everything I could to be better. Calleigh has been breathing down my fucking throat since I started working there. Why don't I just go back to Charlotte and kiss her?"

Liz gasped. Her hands flew to her face and tears fell from her eyes. "No."

"It wouldn't be any different, would it?"

"No," she whispered, shaking her head. She didn't know if she answered him or if she was just horrified at the thought.

"Did he try anything else?" Hayden demanded, the fire still in his eyes.

Liz shook her head.

"Don't fucking lie to me!" he yelled.

Liz took a step back, startled by the outburst. It so wasn't Hayden. "Yes! Okay! Does it make you feel better?" she cried. "He wanted to fuck me. But I didn't let him. I made him take me back home. All right?"

"Jesus Christ, Liz," Hayden spat. "You had another guy's hands on you, another guy's lips on you, another guy's body against yours . . ."

"I didn't say . . ."

"Who is it?" he demanded.

"Hayden, I can't."

He walked slowly toward her until he was standing directly in front of her. She cowered slightly at the feel of him hovering over her. "Liz, who is it?" he asked, his voice low and deliberate.

"It doesn't matter."

"It fucking matters," he growled.

Liz bit her lip and stared down. She couldn't tell him. No fucking way.

"Is he at the paper?"

She glanced back up into his eyes and shook her head. "No."

"It's not Justin?"

Liz laughed and then quickly cleared her throat. *So not appropriate.*

Hayden glared at her. "Are you actually laughing? Do you find something about this funny?"

"No. No, it wasn't Justin," she squeaked.

"Do I know the guy?"

"Um . . ." she said, deciding on how to answer that. God, she didn't want to be having this conversation. "You've, um . . . met."

He reached out and grabbed both of her shoulders in his hands. She stared up into those eyes and saw a wildness she had never seen before. "Look, I'm not going to confront him. I just *need* to know. Don't you understand? I'm going crazy here. I love you so fucking much. You're my whole world, Lizzie. You're everything to me. I was the idiot who pushed you away, and I swore I was never going to make you feel like that again. If I don't know who the guy is, you're going to make me feel like this forever."

Liz cringed away from the accusation. She didn't want to make him feel like this. It had been eating at her for long enough. She didn't want to hurt him too, but she couldn't tell him. She shook her head, breaking eye contact.

"Really? You won't tell me?"

When she didn't answer, he shook his head and then seemed to consider another option.

"You said I met the guy. Where?" he said, his tone going back to commanding.

"It doesn't matter."

"Lizzie, *where* did I meet him?" he said, shaking her lightly until she looked up at him. "Where?"

"The colloquium last spring," she finally whispered out of guilt. Hayden dropped his hands and just stared at her. *Oh no. Please don't figure it out.* She could see that his brain was ticking away, putting the pieces together, fitting things into place. He was seeing the solution in front of him but not really believing it. He was a damn good reporter, and he hadn't gotten that way without being able to see the big picture from a lot of smaller clues.

"But I was late," he mused aloud. "I didn't meet anyone at the colloquium."

Liz swallowed and remained frozen. If he wasn't seeing it, then she wasn't going to help him out. She couldn't tell him. God, she felt sick to her stomach. Whatever alcohol was inside of her was slowly churning away, eating away at her insides, pushing bile up her throat. She covered her mouth and tried to push down the acidic taste.

"Who did I meet there?" he asked, racking his brain.

Liz shook her head. She couldn't tell him.

Hayden stopped and pointed at her, but he was looking off in the distance. She froze in place with his finger near her face.

"Brady Maxwell. I met Brady Maxwell. But he's a congressman," Hayden said softly. "He's a sitting congressman."

His eyes found hers and she stopped breathing. She was trapped in that look. He was commanding her attention, and all she wanted to do was run away and hide. She had brought this down on herself.

"Two summers ago, he would have just been running for Congress. He was your first reporting job. I was with you. He's *our* politician," he said, the hurt seeping deeper and deeper into every syllable. "Tell me it's not him, Lizzie. Tell me it's not him."

Liz just stood there. What could she say? She couldn't corroborate the story, and she couldn't lie anymore.

"Brady Maxwell," Hayden said as if he still couldn't believe it. "You hated him. You disagreed with everything that he said. You wrote some brilliant articles practically calling for his job and still you fucked him?"

"Hayden . . ."

"Tell me how this happened," Hayden said. "I just don't see how you could go from interviewing him, writing those articles, to ending up in his bed."

Liz bit her lip and glanced away. "I met him at the club we went to after his press conference."

"You met him, fucked him, and *then* wrote those articles?" he asked in disbelief.

"No, no, no. I went back with you that night. But after that, I kept running into him while he was on campaign that summer. We just kind of tumbled into it."

"You did this all summer and no one caught you?"

"His press secretary and attorney caught us, but otherwise no. I went by a fake name, Sandy Carmichael, so it wouldn't be traced back to me," she whispered. When she said it like that it sounded so much worse than what it had been in reality.

"A fake name? Do you realize how insane that sounds?" Hayden spat. "Christ, isn't he like thirty? You weren't even legal to drink when you were together." He fisted his hand into his hair.

"Twenty-seven," she whispered. "He was twenty-seven."

"Don't fucking defend him!" Hayden cried. "The guy manipulated a twenty-year-old college student who wrote a bad article about him to get her on his fucking side."

"He didn't manipulate me," she said, unable to stop herself.

"You're so deep in that you didn't even see it. A dick with a little bit of power sees a young girl with a little bit of backbone and takes that away from her in a few easy fucks." He shook his head. "He used you."

Liz fisted her hands at her sides. She couldn't even think that. No. That wasn't what happened. Brady had loved her . . . at one point. He hadn't used her. She had to remind herself of that. Things had been different. It was easy to see it from an outsider's perspective, to break their relationship down into one line and show her as the victim. But she had never felt like a victim with Brady. Not once.

"No," she breathed.

"Then explain to me what happened in October. He tried to fuck you, you said no, and then you agreed not to see each other again, which I assume means he told you to fuck off. Sounds like he came for what he wanted, but didn't get it."

"Hayden, stop."

"I see it for what it is," Hayden said, grasping her shoulders and forcing her to look at him again. His grip tightened and she winced.

"Hayden, let go," she whimpered.

"Is that why we couldn't be together before the election? Is that why you resisted me for so long? Fuck, is that why we didn't even have sex for *months*?"

She tried to wiggle out of his grasp, but he held her tightly.

"Answer me. You owe me that. Is that the reason? Was it because of Brady?"

Liz cringed at the words. She'd hoped that he would never come to that conclusion. "Hayden, you're hurting me!"

He pushed away from her and paced the room. He rested his hand on the nightstand and reached down. Liz swallowed hard. She wanted to say something, anything to make it better, but there was nothing to say.

"What is this?" Hayden asked. And then Liz saw what he was holding, the necklace she had left there when Victoria had called for her earlier this afternoon. "These aren't my charms."

"I know," she managed to get out.

Hayden turned back to face her brandishing the necklace as an accusation. "Is this his too? Is this why you wore it up until the election and I never saw it again?"

Liz bit her lip and refused to answer, but her non-answer was enough. Hayden threw the necklace across the room where it hit the wall and fell to the carpet. Liz gasped and covered her mouth.

"All of this time I just thought you weren't ready for a relationship and then you weren't ready to be physical. But you were just holding on to him."

"I'm sorry," she whispered. There was nothing else for her to say. She had hurt him, crushed him. There was no coming back from that.

"What are you sorry for? Kissing him? Cheating with him? What about emotionally cheating on me for our *entire* relationship?"

"Yes. I don't know," she stammered. She wasn't sorry for Brady and yet she hated hurting Hayden. "All of it."

He turned back to her, grasped her chin firmly in his hand, and stared down into her glassy blue eyes. "You know what. I see it. I see what he did to you. And . . . I forgive you."

"What?" Her mouth hung open in surprise at the words.

"It's not your fault for what he did to you."

"He didn't do anything to me."

Hayden continued speaking as if she hadn't. "He's a skilled manipulator. He made you see what he wanted you to see."

He sighed heavily, as if the weight was off of his chest, and she just stood there, ramrod still. Hayden thought that Brady had manipulated her. But he hadn't. She had never once thought about it like that. She knew what she was getting into from the start, right? He had set the terms in that diner, and she had agreed. That wasn't manipulative. Right?

She felt all fucked up from what Hayden was saying. On some level she understood the manipulation, but her heart was saying it wasn't. And that made her feel even guiltier.

"Lizzie, I love you," Hayden said, pushing her hair off of her face. "I hate that this happened to you. I hate that you cheated on me with someone who was only using you . . . that you cheated on me at all."

"I'm sorry," Liz cried. "I didn't mean to cheat on you. I just got so angry and stupid. I'm never going to be like that again."

At her words, his lips crashed down on hers. She let him have her. What else could she do? She had lost her fight. And she deserved much worse than a hard kiss. She deserved his fury, and him leaving her.

But he wasn't leaving her. He was kissing her passionately, feverishly. His fingers were tangled in her long hair, pulling the life out of her. One of his hands found the zipper on her dress, and when he pulled it down, the material dropped to the ground in front of him. He snapped the clasp on her bra and she was left standing before him in nothing but her black thong.

"You're mine," he growled against her lips. "All of you. Every inch. Make it like he never touched you."

Liz whimpered as he bit down on her bottom lip and sucked it back through his teeth. His hands were everywhere at once. Caressing, fondling, claiming, owning her body. She hardly even moved as he raked his hands down her skin. He had every right to his anger.

"Turn around," he ordered, directing her until she was facing her bed.

She didn't dare move. She had never seen Hayden like this. A part of her was crazy turned on by it, and another part knew that she should stop it. She shouldn't let him do it. But she couldn't. She deserved it.

Liz heard the zipper of his pants and the swish as they dropped to his feet. Her heart rate skyrocketed in the seconds that she waited for him to act. She could feel her body tingling in anticipation and fear, wondering what was coming next, what he would do to her.

Hayden bent Liz forward roughly at the waist, and she braced herself on her mattress.

"Hayden," she whispered. "Please . . ."

He didn't respond, just knelt behind her before dragging her thong down her lean legs. She trembled at the feel of his hands along her thighs. He helped her step out of the clothing, and then roughly spread her legs apart before him.

Hayden bent forward over her, and Liz turned her head to look up at him. "Shhh," he whispered, collecting her hair in one hand and tugging on it lightly.

Where was this coming from? Nearly her entire body was telling her to stand up . . . to stop him. But she hadn't up until this point, and she wasn't going to now.

Then his dick was spreading her lips and sliding easily up inside of her. Liz gasped with the pressure of him filling her, unable to move with the way he had her pinned down. He gripped her hip with one hand and began to work himself in and out of her. His momentum picked up quickly. Soon he was driving into her hard enough to push her entire body forward into the bed.

She didn't want to enjoy this. She didn't want to derive pleasure from it. She didn't want to feel anything at all. But her traitorous body refused to listen. He was fucking her with vengeance. Not just owning her, but staking his claim . . . asserting his right. He fucked her as if he didn't want anyone else to even think about coming close to this.

And even when she tried to hold it off, her body cracked open for him. She saw black as her orgasm tore through her body. She tightened all around him and screamed her lungs out, until he drove into her for the last time, and emptied himself buried deep within her.

Chapter 21

HE HAD IT COMING

Hayden left the next morning without much more than a good-bye. Liz stayed in bed until well past the time that he walked out. He hadn't left her. That was as much as she could say about their relationship at this point. He hadn't left her, but things were far from okay.

Her brain and her body felt numb. What had happened last night? She had thought the worst thing would be for Hayden to leave her. But here she was lying in bed, feeling worse than she had before. Telling Hayden hadn't gotten rid of her guilt; in fact, maybe she felt worse. He had proven that her guilt was warranted. She had been in the wrong and then lied to him about it for months. It made her stomach turn.

She finally forced herself out of bed, fumbling for a light on the nightstand. She stood and that's when she saw it. The necklace. It was resting on the nightstand as if Hayden had never hurled it across the room. It mocked her from its position as if he wanted to say *Here, take your necklace back, whore.*

She felt her chest sliced open again and it took everything in her to reach for the necklace. She checked it to make sure that it wasn't damaged. Another wave of guilt hit her that she should even care if it was broken. She hastily put it back into her jewelry box and stumbled into the shower. She turned the handle to the hottest setting and stepped into the hot spray.

She was most surprised by the fact that she didn't cry. She didn't shed one tear. It was as if she hurt all over and still she couldn't feel anything.

Victoria had ended up staying at Daniel's house, so Liz had the place to herself. After her shower she shut all the lights back off, crawled into bed, and slept the afternoon away. She couldn't think about her neglected responsibilities when her body and mind weren't functioning. Maybe tomorrow . . .

Valentine's Day was coming up that next weekend. Liz had a hard time focusing on what she was going to do when she next saw Hayden. Their conversations were almost exclusively one-sided over the next couple days. Liz gave her input when necessary, but she had too much else on her mind to really be into it.

All she was doing was making Hayden more frustrated with her. Liz didn't know how to stop it. She felt as if she was self-destructing.

Friday rolled around soon enough. It was the day Hayden was supposed to come back to Chapel Hill for Valentine's Day. Liz had finally forced herself to start acting like a human again. She ate a full breakfast, went to all of her classes, ninety percent of which she had skipped earlier in the week, and made it into the paper. She had never lied to get out of work a day in her life before this week. She had left Massey in charge of editorial work while Savannah took over the Washington division.

The smell and feel of the office kicked her back into high gear. *This* was where she belonged. This made her blood flow and reminded her what she was doing with her life.

Savannah stopped her before she reached her office. "Hey, are you feeling any better?"

Liz smiled at Savannah and nodded. "A bit."

She wished Savannah didn't remind her so much of her brother. Brady was the last person she wanted to think about today. He was part of the reason she was in this whole mess to begin with.

"Good. We were worried about you. Can't have a functional paper without the editor, and Massey is no editor," Savannah said with an easy laugh. They started toward Liz's office.

"I'm sure she held down the fort."

"That's one word for it."

Liz laughed softly. It felt good to laugh. "Well, I'm back. So, no worries."

They reached her office, and Savannah nodded her farewell. Liz stepped inside and shut the door. She wanted peace and quiet and the feel of being in control of something. She booted up her computer and plopped down in her chair.

As the screen came to life in front of her, her phone started vibrating. Liz fished it out of her pocket and stared down at the screen. The *New York Times*.

"Hello?" Liz asked. Normally when Nancy called, it was from her personal line. Liz had programmed the main line of the *New York Times* into her phone along with several other numbers Nancy had given her at the start of last semester, but Nancy had never used them.

It made her jittery with excitement.

"Liz, it's Nancy. How are you?" she said in her thick northern accent.

"I'm doing well, and yourself?"

"Really well up here. When do I see you again?"

Liz furrowed her brow and tried to recall when she was next scheduled to be in New York. She knew for sure the first weekend of her spring break, and that was only a couple weeks away. She told Nancy as much.

"Perfect. That's perfect timing."

"For what?"

"Liz, I'm really very pleased to have worked with you so far this year, and I'd like to extend a job offer to you working as a political journalist here at the *New York Times* starting post-graduation."

"Oh my God," Liz breathed softly.

She had been waiting to hear about her job applications. She had heard back two noes already, but they hadn't been a surprise. And now she had a job offer on the table. Her head told her that she should take some time to think about it and weigh her options, but her gut told her just to take the damn deal.

It would get her out of Chapel Hill. She could start over, move to New York, get a crappy place for way too much money, and just live out her dream. It sounded too good to be true.

"Yes," she said without another thought. "Yes, I want to take the job."

No way was she getting a better offer than that, and even if she did, she couldn't imagine having as good a boss as Nancy. She was ecstatic.

"Wonderful. I can't wait for you to start. We'll be in touch with further details."

"Thank you so much," Liz murmured before hanging up her phone.

She sat in her chair in shock. She had just accepted an offer to work as a reporter in New York City. Holy shit! Her hands were shaking. She didn't even know what to do. It was as if everything was finally falling into place. She couldn't believe it.

The first thing she did was press the button to dial Hayden's number. It was automatic. She had to let him know. He would be excited for her. This was what they had always talked about.

It rang three times before going to voice mail.

"Hey, Hayden, I have some exciting news! Call me back!"

Liz hung up the phone and tossed it down on her cluttered desk. Job offer at the *New York Times*. She had to keep reminding herself it was real. When she had gotten the internship there, she had been freaking ecstatic, but that paled in comparison to what she was feeling right now. She didn't even know what to do or who to tell first.

She opened her email and started sorting through them, hoping that Hayden would call her back soon. She had been so out of it lately that the emails were piling up quickly. She was finding it hard to focus with all the adrenaline pumping through her, but since Massey had taken over, Liz knew she had a lot to do. She would tell Victoria when she got home and they would celebrate with some Patrón, if Liz knew Victoria. Hayden would get there shortly after and then it would all be as it was supposed to be.

Liz stopped on an email that she had from the *Charlotte Times*. She had become a junkie of that paper's ever since Hayden had started working there. She subscribed to his byline, which allowed her to read all of the articles that had his name on them. Not that many did, but she wanted to know when they were there.

The email opened up and Liz froze. Her stomach dropped out, and she was pretty sure that she saw stars. This couldn't be happening. It couldn't.

The headline read, *"Congressman Brady Maxwell's Alleged Affair with University of North Carolina Student."*

Liz's vision dipped and she had to clutch on to the desk to hold herself steady. Oh no. No, no, no. This wasn't happening. This couldn't possibly be happening.

She needed to read the rest. She needed to see what he had written. Her hands shook as she scrolled down the page. She covered her mouth with her hand as she looked at a picture of Brady under the headline. She had been avoiding him at all costs, and seeing his picture now just made her whole body want to curl up into a ball and die. What had she done?

They had given up their entire relationship, everything, so that he could have his career. Now he was going to be faced with their relationship in the papers *anyway*! And he had just announced his run for reelection. This could fuck up everything.

She couldn't breathe. She couldn't even focus enough to comprehend what she was seeing in front of her. All she saw was Brady and how horribly she had fucked everything up.

Her fingers curled around the desk, and she forced herself to read the article. It was all in there. Everything she had told Hayden and every twisted way he had interpreted her relationship with Brady. How she and Brady had met, their sexual relationship, the age difference, the pseudonym Sandy Carmichael, even the fact that Heather and Elliott were aware of the relationship. The only thing that wasn't in the article was Liz's actual name. *She* was the anonymous source to her own nightmare.

Liz reached the bottom of the article, and just when she thought she couldn't hate what had happened any more, she read the byline: Hayden Lane and Calleigh Hollingsworth.

Banging on her office door pulled her out of her stupor. "Come in."

Savannah stumbled through the door and immediately closed it behind her. She was breathing heavily and looked to be on the verge of tears. "Have you seen what your boyfriend has *done?*" she asked.

"Yeah. I just saw," Liz managed to get out.

"Did you know? Did you know he was going to write this?" Savannah looked manic.

"No," Liz said with enough ferocity that Savannah had to believe her. "No, I had no idea."

Savannah sank to the ground and buried her head into her knees. "I can't believe this is happening. Brady isn't that kind of person. He would never just sleep with a random undergrad. He wouldn't do that. I love my brother, but Clay is that kind of person. He would do it just for fun, but not Brady. He's a good man, and Hayden is trying to ruin him."

Liz didn't know what to say. The story was true, but she couldn't say that without explaining how she knew. And after telling Hayden what had happened, she never wanted to tell anyone else ever again.

"Do you know anyone named Sandy Carmichael? I mean, I know he said it's a pseudonym, but maybe it's not," Savannah said hopefully.

Liz shook her head. "No. I don't know anyone by that name."

"Me either," Savannah said with a sigh. "I just don't understand what any of this has to do with Brady's reelection, with what he's done as a congressman. His private life should be private. I know Hayden's your boyfriend, but I want to strangle him."

"No need to apologize to me," Liz said gruffly. "I want to strangle him too."

Savannah turned her head to the side and narrowed her eyes. "Yeah? What's been going on?"

"It's been bad for a while," she admitted. Ever since she had seen Brady again. He sauntered back into her life and she remembered in those fleeting hours what passion was. Her relationship with Hayden had never been the same. "It's over."

"Wow. I'm sorry."

"Don't be," Liz said, shaking her head. "He had it coming."

Chapter 22

MELODRAMA

Savannah left ten minutes later when she received a call from her father. Liz tried not to overhear, but the words *lockdown* and *emergency* were definitely thrown around. Before Savannah walked out of Liz's office, Liz hugged her. She wished that she could tell Savannah how sorry she was and how much she wished that she could take it all back, but it wasn't possible. No one could know what had happened. She still had to protect Brady however she could.

Liz knew the best thing for her to do would be to lie low, keep her head down, and not draw any attention. Hayden's article hadn't mentioned her real name or the fact that she was a reporter. That made the search pretty broad, and Liz wanted to keep it that way.

She couldn't imagine the cross fire Brady was under because of this article. He had just announced his intention to run for reelection, and the last race hadn't exactly been a walk in the park. His opponents would surely use this to try to get him out of office. That was what he had feared last election.

Thinking about it made the numb feeling she had been harboring the past couple days shatter like broken glass. It was replaced immediately with a fury unlike anything she had ever felt. Hayden, her perfect fucking boyfriend, was the most selfish asshole she had ever met.

Without having to speak to him, Liz knew why he had done this. He had been hurt by what she had done, angry and jealous. But that did not excuse his taking her trust and smashing it into a million pieces. She knew Hayden wanted to advance his career, and he had taken the first opportunity to make it happen. He had used her story when she had trusted him. And he didn't even have the decency to call her back.

Liz snatched her phone back off her desk. She had called Hayden only thirty minutes earlier to tell him about her job offer. She had been ecstatic, wanting to share her good news with him. She was calling for a *very* different reason this time.

She dialed his number and waited. As she expected, after three rings it went to voice mail. Either he was purposely avoiding her calls or he was just *that* swamped with calls about the article. Liz doubted that it was the latter.

The line beeped for her to leave a message.

Liz took a breath before speaking. "Hayden. This is Liz. Perhaps you've heard of me. I called you thirty minutes ago with some really super exciting news. I'm calling you back because I have some even more exciting news that I *really* need to talk to you about. Call me back at this number. I don't think you've managed to lose it overnight. But in case you have, don't worry . . . I couldn't think less of you than I do in this moment."

Liz ended the call and threw the phone into her purse. She was so pissed, she was ready to jump into her car, drive right down to Charlotte, and wring his perfect fucking neck. She had been obsessing since October about what had happened with Brady; she finally let Hayden in, and he did this to repay her.

Well, she couldn't stay at the office any longer feeling like this. She wasn't going to get anything done tonight. Liz tore out of her office with her purse slung over her shoulder. She sought out Massey.

"Hey!" Massey said brightly when Liz approached. Then her face fell. "Are you okay?"

"Still not feeling too well, I guess," Liz said, laying it on thick.

"Oh, no. Do you need me to cover for you again?"

"That would be so nice. I just think I'm trying to push myself too hard."

Massey nodded her head and clicked a button on the computer. "You should probably go rest. Don't worry about tomorrow. I'll take care of it too. I'll see you Monday morning, Liz!"

"Thanks a million, Massey," Liz answered sincerely. The woman was saving her life.

Liz bolted from the office and took the steps down to the bottom floor of the Union two at a time. She wrapped her jacket tighter around her body as she stepped out into the crisp February air. The cold air jolted her memories. This time last year had been her snow day with Hayden. She had decided to finally give up Brady after finding out about Erin and had given herself to Hayden for the first time. Now it all felt like a joke. A big, fat joke.

She had never gotten over Brady, she had never given Brady up, and she had never given herself fully to Hayden. Then as soon as he had found out, he had used that against her. The irony of it all was that when Hayden was furious and hurt over their relationship, he had chosen his career over her, which was the very thing she had feared with Brady.

She had walked out, spent over a year missing Brady, pushed him away to the point of no return—for *nothing*. All she wanted to do was call him, try to explain, beg him to give her one more chance.

But she couldn't.

No. She wouldn't.

Brady had shut the door. He had told her not to call him when Hayden broke her heart, and Hayden had done just that. Brady was probably fuming, and the last thing he needed was for her to call him because of Hayden's article. She wanted to go to him and make it right, but the way to make it right was to remain invisible.

If he wanted to reach out to her, then he would. But she doubted he would. Brady wasn't the type to go back on promises. How often had he told her that he didn't make promises he couldn't keep? Wasn't that the reason he hadn't told her he loved her? Even thinking that word sent a stabbing pain through her chest. Love. What a joke.

Liz sped home, parked the car in the driveway, and burst through the front door. "Victoria!" she called, slamming the door behind her. "Where are you?"

She stalked down the small hallway and banged on the door. "Vic, are you in there?"

"Yeah, I'm busy," Victoria choked out. "Can you come back in like fifteen minutes?" There were some whispers from the other side of the door and then Victoria giggled.

"No. This can't wait. Not unless you want to find your roommate with her veins open on the bathroom floor in fifteen minutes."

Liz knelt in front of Victoria's door and pushed her hands up into her hair. Her whole body ached and just wanted it all to stop. She knew she needed to get herself together, but she couldn't see or think or feel anything through the fury. All she saw was Hayden's face when he found out, when he asked her for details, when he maliciously fucked her for the mistake that was never a mistake. Had he known then? Had he known that he was planning to ruin her . . . them . . . Brady? Was the sex a good-bye? That thought only pissed her off more.

"Melodramatic much?" Victoria called.

There was shuffling from the other room and then the door popped open. Victoria was dressed in skinny jeans and an oversize sweater. Her hair was a hot mess and she was trying to wrangle it into a ponytail as she exited her bedroom. Liz assumed Duke Fan was on the other side, but assumptions with Victoria were a very bad idea. Victoria pulled the door closed and stared down at Liz expectantly.

"Well, Miss Melodrama? What is so goddamn important?"

Liz stood and walked into the living room. She didn't want to have this conversation where Duke Fan could potentially hear her. Victoria huffed loudly, but followed behind her.

"You know how we agreed that the worst thing that could happen when I told Hayden about Brady was that he would leave me?" Liz asked as she pulled out her phone.

"Yeah." Victoria glanced over her shoulder to her closed bedroom door.

"We were wrong."

"What?" Victoria asked. Her head snapped back to Liz. "What do you mean?"

Liz pulled up the article on her phone and passed it to Victoria. "He wrote about it," Liz whispered.

"Fuck!" she cried. "Holy fuck!" Her eyes scanned the article. "What a fucking bastard! I'll cut his balls off!"

"I wouldn't stop you."

"Oh my God, Calleigh's name is on this too," Victoria said, stunned.

"I know. They must have planned this together."

Victoria shook her head and scrolled back up through the article. "What the fuck are you going to do? Have you called Brady? Have you spoken to an attorney? Fuck! What can I do? How can I help?"

Liz fisted her hands at her sides again and turned away from Victoria. "I don't know what I'm going to do. I haven't done anything yet, because my name isn't in the article. He just put me down as Sandy Carmichael. I think it's better if I lie low. If I act rashly then someone will piece it together, and the last thing I want is to be in the public eye."

"Have you talked to Hayden? God, why would he do this?"

"I haven't talked to him. He won't return my calls."

"I never liked Lane, but I didn't think he was this much of a fucking pussy," Victoria cried.

Liz shrugged. "Me either."

"Okay. Okay. Sit down for a second," Victoria said, ushering her to the couch. She dropped Liz's phone on the coffee table and plopped down next to her. "Let's chat. The important thing here is you. How are you? Do *you* need anything?"

"I'm fine."

"Psh! You're far from fine. Talk to me."

Liz sighed heavily and wrapped her arms around her knees. "I'm angry. It feels like everything that I did was for nothing. No Brady. No Hayden. Nothing," she said. "Oh, wait, I accepted a job offer at the *New York Times* today."

"Oh my God!" Victoria squealed. "Congratulations, bitch! That's perfect. All of this shit will blow over, and you can start a new life in New York City!"

Liz managed a half smile, but it quickly fell off of her face when her phone started buzzing noisily on the table. Liz snatched it off the table and stared down at the screen.

"Hayden?" Victoria asked softly.

Liz shook her head. She didn't know the number. Her heart rate picked up with fear. Was it a reporter? Had they already found her? Her throat constricted as she debated answering the phone. Maybe it would be better if she didn't.

Curiosity got the better of her.

"Hello?" Liz asked, pressing the phone to her ear.

"Hello. I'm trying to reach Liz Dougherty."

Liz's heart stopped in that moment. No. Not a reporter. No one had found her who didn't already know that she existed. The voice on the other end of the line was unmistakable.

Heather Ferrington, Brady's press secretary.

The last time Liz had been near Heather, she had told Brady to end it with Liz, and Brady had told her no. She was a fierce woman who had been with Brady since the start of his career and did whatever she could to protect him. Liz was not looking forward to this conversation.

"Who is trying to reach her?" Liz asked carefully.

She didn't want to talk to Heather, but maybe this was her ticket to Brady. She tried not to let herself get excited for yet another letdown. This one was pretty much a guarantee.

"This is Heather Ferrington with Congressman Maxwell's office."

Liz sighed.

"This is Liz. How can I help you, Heather?"

Victoria looked at her with questions in her eyes. Liz mouthed, *Brady's office.*

Victoria's eyes bulged and she whispered, "Are you going to talk to him?"

Liz shook her head and tried to focus on Heather rather than Victoria.

"Miss Dougherty, I would like to keep this conversation brief and private. Strictly off the record, if I can get your guarantee on that," Heather said formally.

What did she have to lose?

"Of course," Liz whispered. If Heather thought Liz was going to write about this, then she was out of her mind.

"I don't know what possessed you after more than a year and a half to divulge the information of your . . . *relationship* with

Congressman Maxwell." Heather said the word as if it physically pained her. "But whatever it is, you won't accomplish it. And I would suggest to you, Miss Dougherty, to not further divulge any information without realizing that you are risking your own career, which I believe is quite important to you."

"Is that a threat, Miss Ferrington?" Liz asked, seething.

"Hardly. Perhaps I should make myself clearer. Brady doesn't want you. Your pathetic attempt at ruining his career isn't even a blip on his radar. You are *nothing*."

"If I'm not even a blip, then why are we speaking?" Liz spat back. She wanted to reach through the phone and slap Heather straight across the face. Liz knew that Heather was only trying to protect Brady, but her methods weren't always that effective.

"We're talking because any and everything related to the Congressman *is* on my radar. I didn't trust you the summer you hid your relationship and I don't trust you now. My job is to minimize problems. You're a problem, and I'm minimizing."

Liz ground her teeth together. What the hell was she supposed to say to that? She was a problem for Brady. Heather was only doing her job. Liz would do the same thing if she were in Heather's situation. She saw the problem for what it was and went straight to the source. No beating around the bush.

"So the best thing for you to do going forward is to do absolutely nothing. You gain *nothing* by revealing yourself further."

"Does he even know that you're speaking with me?" Liz asked softly. She didn't have to tell Heather that she wasn't going to say anything else. She already felt as if she had died a thousand deaths knowing that it was in the papers. Heather would deal with the article however she felt best anyway.

"Congressman Maxwell knows everything that he needs to know in this situation."

"So no," Liz said, disappointed.

"Whether or not he knows doesn't matter to you, because he no longer matters to you as anything more than a congressman in your district. And I'm going to say this once, so listen closely. If you ever cared for Brady at all, then you'll think twice about what you do from here on out. Are we clear?" she snapped.

"Crystal."

"Glad to see we're finally on the same page. Try not to do anything to gain another phone call from me."

"I'll do my best," Liz said sarcastically.

"You'll do better than that."

The conversation ended and Liz dropped the phone into her lap. Her hands were shaking. She felt anger bubbling up under the surface. She wanted to release it, but there were only two people she could blame for what had happened: herself and Hayden. Hayden wouldn't return her calls . . . so that left herself.

Then again, she had the sneaking suspicion that she could blame Calleigh Hollingsworth too.

"So . . . that didn't sound good," Victoria said. "Who was that?"

"Heather Ferrington, Brady's press secretary. She was telling me not to do anything else stupid."

"Does she think you're an idiot?"

Liz bit her lip. "Yeah . . . I think she does."

"Well, bitch needs to step off," Victoria cried. "And Brady? Are you going to talk to him?"

"She told me not to do anything stupid, Vic. Calling Brady is probably the stupidest thing I could possibly do right now."

Chapter 23

TRYING TO FORGET

Hayden never called.

Liz held her phone in her hand all evening waiting for him to call her back, but he never did. She knew that he had ruined their relationship, that he had sacrificed her trust and chosen his career over her. Still she wanted to talk to him. She wanted to know *why*. Why would he do this to her?

She and Brady kissed once while she was dating Hayden. Everything else that had happened was before she and Hayden had even gotten together. She knew that he wasn't happy that she had hidden it from him, but he'd had no reason to know until she had kissed Brady that night. And now Hayden had ruined everything.

When no one seemed willing to move from the living room, Daniel went out to get dinner for all three of them. He knew that something was wrong. He returned with a plastic bag full of Chinese food and a bottle of Maker's Mark. Liz smiled when she saw it and reached for it. Victoria got to it first and snatched it out of her hands.

"I'll just get us some glasses. Eat," Victoria said.

Liz groaned, but let Victoria take her liquor into the kitchen. She couldn't keep it hostage forever. Daniel handed her a box of Chinese, and Liz flipped the lid open. She swirled the food around in her takeout container, took a few bites, and then set it back down. She was too jittery to eat. Her stomach couldn't take it.

Victoria returned with three glasses of Maker's on the rocks in her hands. She passed one off to Daniel and then set hers down on the side table.

Liz brought the glass to her lips and, taking a long swig, she cringed at the taste and set it back down. "That's disgusting."

"It's delicious," Daniel said. "Don't hate on my favorite drink."

Victoria rolled her eyes at him. "You should probably eat more before drinking more anyway."

"I'm fine," Liz lied. She tipped the glass back again. This was going to end poorly.

Two drinks later and the alcohol was numbing her pain. Somehow she convinced Victoria and Daniel that heading to Franklin Street in her condition was a good idea. She wasn't sure if they actually believed her or if they were just going along with whatever she wanted. She was so pissed off at the entire situation that she really just didn't care. She would have walked out of the house and gone drinking alone if they hadn't wanted to come with her.

Wanting to do anything but think about what had happened, Liz took extra special care curling her hair and applying her dark smoky makeup. She changed into the sluttiest outfit in her closet, a skintight black-and-white patterned strapless minidress, which she had to pull down when she was walking, and six-inch leather strappy high heels. Even Victoria would be proud of her.

Liz assessed herself in the mirror and then decided that red lipstick was in order. It wasn't her normal routine, but, well, she wasn't really feeling like herself tonight. She was feeling like total shit. She had walked away from one relationship, tried to love another man, been used for the advancement of his career, and still there was no way she could go back to what she had originally walked away from. So, for tonight, nothing really mattered. She just wanted to get rip-roaring drunk and forget that today ever happened.

As she was about to walk out of her bedroom to see if Victoria was ready to go, her phone started ringing loudly from where she had thrown it on her bed. Liz dashed for it, her heart racing. Was it Hayden? Could he finally have manned up? Her heels skittered across the floor and she crashed down onto her bed, snatching the phone off the comforter. She stared down at the screen. Not Hayden. Another number she didn't know. She hoped this wasn't a reporter, because the two glasses of bourbon weren't making her friendly.

"Hello?" she said into the phone. She crossed her legs and sat up straighter.

"Liz, it's been too long," the smooth, seductive voice said through the line.

Liz's eyes bugged as she pressed the phone to her ear. "Clay?"

"And I thought for a minute you might not recognize me."

"Of course I recognize you." No chance in hell that she wasn't going to recognize Clay Maxwell. Why was he calling her now?

"So, how have you been? Did you have a nice day?" he asked casually.

Liz narrowed her eyes. No contact for over a year and now he was acting all buddy-buddy.

"What do you want, Clay?" she asked.

"I can't check in on an old friend?"

"You've never called me before."

"Well, I am now," he said.

"So, what do you want? I don't assume that you're calling me for no reason."

"I read an article today in the newspaper about my brother. Have you seen it?" Clay asked.

Liz's mouth went dry. "I saw it," she said.

"But do you know what I couldn't stop thinking about, Liz?"

"No," she whispered.

"You. Liz *Carmichael*. The girl who showed up at the Fourth of July event and the gala and Hilton Head. Seemed a bit . . . convenient once I started thinking about it."

Oh shit! Liz couldn't breathe.

"But when I looked up the UNC registry, there wasn't a Liz Carmichael either, and the only Liz at the UNC paper was a Liz Dougherty. Strange that you should tell me that your last name was Carmichael. Don't you think?"

Breathe in. Breathe out.

"I never told you that was my last name," she whispered.

"Ah. Right. The valet mentioned it at the gala . . . the event that you were at with Chris. Perhaps it's just me, but the pieces don't seem to fit," Clay said. She could almost see the dimples in his smile.

"What do you want, Clay?" There had to be a catch, some kind of point to all of this. He knew. But what did he *want*?

"I want to see you tonight."

"I'm not sleeping with you, Clay," she responded immediately.

"Whoa! I never even insinuated that you would. Someone is jumping to conclusions."

She could hear the laughter in his voice. She knew exactly what he was after. He had always been after one thing.

"I'm not stupid."

"No, you're not. But you also don't have anything else to lose by coming to see me. The reporter was your boyfriend, right?"

"Ex-boyfriend," Liz quickly corrected. She didn't even want to *think* about Hayden. She just wanted to knock some sense into him.

"Exactly. So tonight?"

What the hell did she have to lose that she hadn't already lost?

"Well, I'm going to be on Franklin Street in about twenty minutes. If you can find me, then you can see me." She doubted that he would ever find her. There were a ton of bars on Franklin Street, and why would Clay go through that much trouble?

"Any hints?"

"I'll be drinking," she said before hanging up the phone.

That was it. She wasn't going to answer her phone the rest of the night. Each call just brought more and more drama that she didn't want to have to deal with. The only people she actually wanted to speak with hadn't called, and she didn't think they were going to. So she resigned herself to getting blackout drunk.

It actually took thirty minutes for Victoria and Duke Fan to get ready to go out. They started at their usual spot, which was packed with people, since it was Valentine's Day weekend. Heavy dance beats filtered through the speakers, and groups mingled together near the bar. The bar had specialty drinks for the occasion and a giant red-and-pink heart-shaped piñata.

Liz leaned over the bar, her breasts nearly spilling out of her top as she flagged the hot bartender down.

"What'll ya have?" he asked, eyeing her chest appreciatively.

At least someone was enjoying the view.

"Whiskey sour," Liz told him.

"Sure thing."

He filled a glass almost entirely with whiskey. She normally would have cringed, but tonight she didn't care.

"What kind of candy is in the piñata?" she asked him as he added the sour.

"No candy. Condoms, suck and blows, lube, and other fun treats," he said with a wink as he passed her drink across the bar. She went to hand him her cash and he winked at her again. "On the house."

Liz bit her lip coyly and dropped the money into the tip jar. She must look good tonight to warrant free drinks from the bartender. "Thanks."

"Come back and see me."

Liz nodded and went to find Victoria.

"There you are!" Victoria cried. "Did you order? Kyle is working at the other end of the bar. I could have gotten it for free."

"I got mine for free," Liz said, taking a sip of the liquor.

"Look at you! You look totally fuckable tonight."

"Are you encouraging her?" Daniel asked.

"Butt out," Victoria snapped. "Or I'll send you straight home."

"You're not my mother!"

"We can role-play later, baby," she said, slapping him gently across the face twice.

Daniel rolled his eyes and sipped on his drink. Score one for Victoria.

"So . . . you know what they say . . . the best way to get over someone is to get under someone else," Victoria said.

Liz tilted her head and laughed. "I don't think that's the expression."

"It should be."

"I think it's 'find someone else.'"

"It amounts to the same thing. And all I'm saying is that you look fuckable and you've never had a one-night stand. Tonight is the *perfect* night for a threesome!"

"Victoria!" Liz said, shaking her head. "That doesn't even make sense."

"Which part?"

"All of it!"

"Why not make the night memorable?" Victoria asked. "You're trying to ruin all of my fun."

"I just want to get wasted drunk and black out in the safety of my own house."

Victoria shook her head and turned to survey the room. "Hmmm. No. No. Maybe. He probably has back hair though . . . so, no. No. We'll find you one," Victoria said. "This is the perfect night for this. It's like a breeding ground for singles who want to get fucked, because they didn't have a date for Valentine's Day."

"You are the most insensitive person I've met in my entire life," Liz said, tipping her glass back and trying to quell the urge to throw it at her best friend.

"What?" Victoria asked as if she didn't know. "Oh, Lane? I don't consider him a human being anymore."

Liz laughed. Sometimes Victoria was a bitch, but at least Liz wasn't on her bad side. She couldn't imagine what that would be like.

"Oh, oh, oh!" Victoria cried, clapping her hands. "Found him. That one walking into the bar."

Liz's eyes followed Victoria's finger as she pointed out the guy across the bar. She froze in place. No fucking way. How the hell had Clay found her? There weren't a trivial number of bars in downtown Chapel Hill. It would have taken him longer than this to search her out unless he had just gotten fucking lucky. But still she hadn't expected him to actually come find her.

"Yep," Liz said to Victoria. "That one."

"Really?" Victoria shrieked.

"Yeah."

Their eyes met across the bar. Shit! He was too fucking gorgeous. How did everyone in his family have such good genes? He was in a black suit with a white button-down underneath it undone at the neck so he looked more relaxed than stuffy. His dark blond hair was styled and as his mouth rose into a smile, she could see the dimples that she knew were there.

Liz strode deliberately across the room, dropping her drink off as she passed the bar. She didn't stop until she was directly in front of him and she could see the blue eyes gazing mischievously back at her.

"Found you," Clay said.

Liz shrugged. "How are you, Clay?"

"Probably better than you." His dimples showed as his eyes crawled her body.

"Probably." She found it hard to argue that point.

"So, this whole time you were fucking my brother," Clay said with a shake of his head as if he should have known all along.

Liz bit back a snide retort and breathed out slowly. "Could we maybe talk about this somewhere else?" she asked, realizing just how public they were.

Clay nodded. "Yeah, let's get out of here."

Liz followed him out of the bar and out onto the sidewalk. He latched on to her arm and smiled at her. "You wouldn't let me take you home before. Come with me now."

Liz pulled her arm away from his. "I'm not like your girlfriend; you can't just yank me around."

Clay smirked. "No, you're nothing like Andrea."

"How long before you're married anyway?" Liz asked, deflecting that statement.

"As long as I can postpone it," he told her, walking up to the valet and handing over his ticket.

"How did you find me?" Liz could feel the alcohol from that last drink clouding her mind. "There are too many places I could have been."

"I asked Savannah where she would go," he said with a shrug.

Liz's eyes widened. "Did you tell her you were coming to see me?"

"Um . . . no. Why would she care?"

She opened her mouth and then closed it. She wasn't sure that she wanted to disclose the information about how close she and Savannah were, but it seemed too late now. "We're friends. We work on the paper together."

"You seem to be affiliated with everyone in my family somehow."

"All of you by accident."

"Well, it's not an accident tonight," he said with that same smile.

A sleek black car pulled up in front of them. The valet hopped out of the car and handed Clay the keys.

Of course he has a Porsche.

"After you," he said, holding the passenger door open for her.

Liz walked up and stood directly in front of him. "Why are you even with Andrea if you don't want to marry her?"

"Why did you fuck my brother when you knew you had no chance together?" Clay shot back.

"Those two things aren't even comparable," she said with a shake of her head.

Clay smirked. "Just get in the car, Miss Carmichael."

Whatever. It wasn't as if she had anything better to do. Brady wasn't an option. Hayden had fucked up royally. She was drunk and couldn't think of a reason not to go with Clay.

"Fine," she grumbled, looking over her shoulder to make sure no one heard him use that name.

She sat down on the plush leather interior and Clay shut the door in her face. She watched him walk around the front of the car, open the door, and take the seat next to her. Clay revved the engine and then pulled away from the bar. Liz didn't even know where they were going, and at that moment she didn't care. It was nice to not think for once and go along with whatever was happening.

"My roommate is probably freaking the fuck out," she said, leaning her head back against the seat.

"Why is that?"

"Because she picked you out in the bar and told me to go home with you."

Clay cracked up laughing. "She has good taste."

"Usually. I'd say she was questionable on this choice."

"You're cute when you're lying," Clay said with that cocky attitude. "So, how did it all happen?"

"How did *what* happen?"

"You and Brady."

Liz cringed. It was too fresh to even think about them like that. Things had gone all wrong.

"Coincidence. Serendipity. All that," she managed to say with a shrug, glancing out the window. "You read the article. We met after he announced he was running for Congress."

"How remarkable. Starting a clandestine affair off of a chance encounter."

"What does it even matter to you, Clay?" Liz asked, turning back to face him. "You wanted to fuck me, and your big brother got there first. You lose again."

She didn't even know where that had come from. What the fuck was wrong with her?

Clay chuckled softly. "You know, I always knew there was something different about you. That first time we met on the Fourth of July and every time after that. I knew that you weren't some abject drone following my brother around because you believed in his stupid policy speeches or, worse, his pleas for attention by speaking about personal issues. I went and read your articles about Brady from two summers ago, and I think that you were right. You said the things I was telling you about Brady all along."

"That was before I knew your brother."

"Exactly. Back when you saw him for what he really was, not what he wanted you to see. Tell me something. Do you honestly think that he didn't fuck someone else when you guys were together?" he asked, glancing over at her.

"Do you have a point?" she snapped. She couldn't think about that. It didn't even matter.

Clay turned a sharp corner and began to weave down back streets. "With me you know exactly what you're getting. With Brady you never know."

"Is the lawyer trying to tell me that he's honest?" she quipped.

"The lawyer is trying to tell you that after everything he still wants to take you home and he still wants to fuck you. I doubt Brady is saying that."

Liz choked back a gasp at his frankness. "You just want me because your brother had me."

"Correction: I just want you *more*."

"So what? You want to get me out of your system so you can go back to your heiress?" Liz demanded.

Clay smirked and shot her a devious grin. "Lucky for me, I have a pretty insatiable appetite."

Liz knew that she was at a low point in her life. She had never felt so completely and totally destroyed. And at this point, she just didn't care what happened. And maybe, even a small part of her knew that if she couldn't have Brady then she just wanted to be close to him however she could. Even if it was a completely fucked-up notion. Clay was as close to Brady as she was ever going to get again, and it was good enough for her in that moment.

"Fine."

"Fine?" he asked, scrunching up his eyebrows.

"If you think you're better than your brother, prove it." She sat back in the soft leather seat and crossed her arms.

He didn't say anything for a while. She clearly had thrown him for a loop. He probably thought that he was going to have to fight her on this one, but she didn't have any fight left in her.

"Are you . . ." he trailed off. "I don't want to misinterpret you."

Liz's eyes shifted to him briefly. "I think you get my meaning."

"I'd rather you make it very clear."

"I want you to fuck me until I forget Brady Maxwell ever existed," Liz said bluntly. Until he wasn't even a memory . . . just like Brady had said that night last October.

"Shit," he muttered under his breath.

"Unless you can't do that," she challenged.

"I can do that." Clay reached across the car, took her hand, and placed it on his cock. She could feel the hardening length through his suit pants. "I can definitely do that."

Liz squeezed then ran her hand down to the tip and back. His breathing hitched; then she pulled away with a smirk.

"I sure hope so."

Someone needs to.

Chapter 24
MISTAKES WORTH MAKING

Clay turned his Porsche down a long winding driveway about fifteen minutes later. They passed through an overhang of trees before the lot finally opened up to reveal a ranch-style brick house. It was beautiful in its simplicity and completely secluded.

"Is this yours?" Liz asked, staring out the window at the property.

"Yep."

"Courtesy of Maxwell Industries Real Estate, I presume?"

"Someone's done their research," he said, his eyes shifting to hers. "Or do you have experience with other Maxwell properties?"

"I'm a reporter. Give me some credit," she said, trying not to think about all of the other Maxwell properties she had been on.

He parked the Porsche in the driveway and they both stepped out of the car. Liz followed him around to the front door. He kicked over a flowerpot and found a key sitting underneath it.

"High security," Liz observed.

Clay chuckled before he inserted the key, twisted the knob, and opened the door. Liz's body buzzed with adrenaline as Clay stepped inside. She fought to keep her hands from trembling as she followed him. She had decided to do this and she needed to keep the tone light if she was going to go through with it.

"Where are you now anyway?" Liz asked, walking inside. "You graduated from law school last May, right?"

"I'm clerking at the federal level. Once my year is up where I am, I'll move up to clerking for the Supreme Court." He shut the door and tossed the key on a table in the foyer.

"Wow. Ambition runs in the family."

"Are we done talking now?" he asked, slightly annoyed.

"Are you going to be an asshole?"

Clay arched an eyebrow and smirked at her. "Absolutely."

He was before her in two powerful strides, grabbing her roughly around the waist, their lips colliding. He had soft, demanding lips that prodded hers open. He slid his tongue into her mouth and Liz almost sighed with the faint taste of honey. Damn, he was a good kisser. He wasn't Brady, but he would do . . . for now. His hands guided her arms around his neck and she held on to him for support. He drew her body in until they were flush against one another. She could feel his defined chest through the thin material of her dress.

It was easy to get lost in Clay because she didn't have to do anything. He took control of her, teasingly kissing, sucking, and licking her lips, tasting her, devouring her whole. And she let him. She let him cloud her mind with the help of the whiskey still pumping through her veins. It was easier than thinking about the train that had wrecked her life or the consequences that she would have to face in the morning.

His hand slid up her bare arm and she shivered against him. The alcohol had kept her warm against the February chill, but Clay was sending goose bumps up her arm. He found her hand and grasped it in his own.

Their lips finally broke apart and he had that same self-satisfied smirk on his face.

"Come with me," he said, pulling her through the house and toward the back. He opened the door, still facing her, and tugged her lightly into the large master bedroom. A king-size bed took up the center of the room, covered in a fluffy red comforter and a collection of throw pillows.

Holy shit! She was actually going to do this. But what else did she have to lose? Everything else had been stripped away.

"You look like you're thinking too much," Clay said, dropping his mouth down onto hers.

"Guess you're not doing your job," she whispered against his lips.

"We'll see about that."

He started walking them backward to the bed. His hands slid over her shoulders, trailed down the curve of her breasts, down her waist, until he was gripping her hips forcefully.

She arched an eyebrow at him in challenge. This was easier. It was easier to taunt him into action. She could get through this. She wanted it. Clay was fucking unbelievably hot and his lips were like sweet honey. She wanted him to explore her.

His hands slid down to the hem of her minidress, and he ran his fingers softly under the material. Her breathing hitched and she felt her body warming at his touch. Without warning he picked her up and set her down easily on the bed. His hands spread her legs in front of him so that he could lean his body between them and capture her lips once more.

"I bet all you're thinking about right now is me fucking you," he groaned, pressing himself against her.

Liz pretended to yawn, trying to keep up the game they were

playing. "Brady's probably getting a nice sympathy fuck from his girlfriend, and you can't even keep me entertained."

Clay chuckled. His hands ran up her bare inner thighs. She tried to squeeze her legs together as if she were going to stop him, but all she did was tighten her grip on his hips.

"The only thing that's going to be entertained tonight is my dick in your pussy," he said, his finger inching closer and closer to her heated core. "Because Brady doesn't have a girlfriend."

"What?" Liz snapped, straightening and pushing his hand away. "What did you just say?"

"My dick is going to be entertained in your pussy," he said seductively.

"No, after that!"

Clay narrowed his eyes. "Uh . . . Brady doesn't have a girlfriend?"

"Shut the fuck up!"

"What?" he asked, trying to put his hands back on her, but she pushed him away.

"When did they break up? What happened?" Liz demanded.

"I don't know. It doesn't really matter." He tried to lean in again.

"No. Stop," she said, ducking out of the way of his kiss. "When the fuck did they break up?"

Clay rolled his eyes and took a step back, clearly seeing he wasn't going to win this battle. "A few months ago. October maybe? Why does it even matter?"

Liz's mouth dropped open. "Did you just say October?"

"Yeah. Brady just dropped her one day. I don't know what happened, so don't fucking ask me. We're done with the Q&A session. Can we get back to fucking?" he asked, annoyed again.

"No! Are you out of your mind? I'm not having sex with you," Liz said, scooting off of the bed and fixing her dress. "You need to take me home—or better yet, to see Brady."

"What?" he practically yelled. "I'm not taking you anywhere, especially not to see my brother. What the fuck?"

"Just shut up!" she shrieked. "Don't you understand anything? It's Brady. It's always been Brady. Stop trying to be your brother, because you'll never be Brady."

"You don't know what you're talking about."

Liz shook her head. "You're walking in a shadow, and fucking me isn't going to make that any better. I need to talk to Brady tonight, and I'm going to do it whether you take me home or I have to walk all the way to your parents' house in Durham myself."

"Do you think it's going to help him for you to show up at the house the night after the article breaks? Do you think you'll actually be helping him by corroborating the story your boyfriend wrote?"

"Ex-boyfriend," Liz snapped. "And I don't care. I just need to see him. We have to be able to fix it. There has to be a way."

"Why don't you stop and think for a second? Think about what happens if I take you to my parents' house, and you walk into that lockdown war zone. You're not just talking to Brady. You're talking to my parents, his staff, Savannah, everyone. Tell me you want to walk into that."

"Did you not hear me? I. Don't. Care. I need to see him."

"You're insane. You think anyone is going to let you near him when they find out that you're Sandy Carmichael? What happened in October anyway? You flipped out over that," Clay observed.

"Nothing," she answered immediately. He just raised an eyebrow. "Fine. I saw him again, but nothing happened and we parted ways."

"Parted ways. Knowing my brother, I doubt that went over well," Clay said. "Okay, so tell me this then. Why did you agree to see me? Why didn't you speak to him before? And don't give me some bullshit about his girlfriend, because I don't think anyone thought she actually mattered."

"Why?"

"Do you want me to take you there?" he asked.

Liz glared at him. "You're such an asshole."

"What you see is what you get, babe."

"He told me not to speak to him again," Liz said softly. She hated admitting it out loud. Brady's angry words still echoed through her mind all these months later.

"And you're going to anyway? Don't you think he said it for a reason?"

"Yes, I do. I think he said it because he was angry, and he had every right to be. But I clearly *don't* care anymore." Liz brushed past him and started for the door.

"Where are you going?" he cried, following her down the hall.

"I told you that I'd walk home if you didn't take me," she said stubbornly.

Clay humphed behind her. "You can't go tramping through the woods in a minidress and heels."

"Try to stop me!"

Liz made it halfway down the driveway in the middle of the woods, at night, freezing her ass off when she heard the soft hum of the Porsche behind her. The headlights flashed as Clay approached. He rolled down the passenger window and stared at her in frustration.

"Get in, crazy."

She opened the door and sank back into the passenger seat. As soon as her door shut, Clay jolted the car forward.

She sighed as she relaxed. She had been determined to walk home, but realistically it had been a dumb move. She was relieved that Clay had given in and picked her up.

"Thank you," Liz whispered.

"I'm not taking you to my parents' house," he said sullenly. "If you want to do something stupid, you can do it on your own."

Liz nodded. She wasn't surprised that Clay wouldn't take her to Brady, and barging into the Maxwell house didn't exactly sound like the best plan. It was just the first that had come to her. Perhaps the alcohol was still talking. She would have to find a better way to get to him.

"Um . . ." she began, biting her lip.

She didn't say anything for a second and Clay asked, "What?"

"Do you think I could get Brady's number from you?"

"I'm turning around," he said, easing on the brakes.

"What? Why?"

"There is no reasoning with you."

"With me? You're the one who wanted to fuck me because I'd been with your brother."

Clay shrugged. He slid open the compartment between their seats, placed his phone inside, and then purposefully shut it tight. "That makes more sense to me than giving you his phone number."

"I only ever tried to reach him on the campaign line, and unless you think it's a good idea to do that now, perhaps you should give me his personal," she snapped. Well, besides the time she had used his personal line last year, but she had deleted that number and it did nothing to bring that up with Clay right now.

"You called him on the campaign line?" Clay asked, shaking his head. "For being smart, you two are fucking idiots."

"Just get moving. I'll figure it out myself," she said, turning to face the window again.

A million scenarios ran through her mind on the drive back to her house. How the hell was she going to get hold of Brady? Her earlier tactic had always been to call the office, say she was Sandy Carmichael, and poof! Brady answered the phone. Well, she couldn't call as Sandy now. And she doubted they would be taking any calls, especially not from reporters. She could make shit up about knowing who Sandy Carmichael was, but Liz was sure that would only get her as far as Heather. She didn't trust Heather to get her through to Brady. She could have called Savannah, but she wasn't sure she was ready for her friend to know that she had been with her brother, and with Clay not cooperating, she really didn't have another choice.

Liz glanced down at the compartment that held Clay's phone. She wasn't stupid enough to try to get it out of there. But if there was another alternative, she wasn't seeing one.

Clay shifted gears as he veered toward her house. Liz had to make up her mind. The worst thing that could happen was that he would notice her reaching for it. She could live with that.

She had been staring out the window most of the drive, and she slowly turned her body to face Clay. "Hey," she whispered softly.

"Oh, are we talking again?" he asked.

"No need to be rude," she said, leaning forward and resting her forearm on the center compartment. Most of her body covered the compartment so that when he was looking at the road, she was pretty sure the only thing he saw in his periphery were her breasts spilling out of her tiny dress. "I just wanted to say thank you."

"I can keep driving if this includes road head."

Liz laughed melodically. Clay would always be Clay. She just needed to keep him entertained, keep him from seeing what she was planning.

"I don't think so," Liz said, pressing the button on the side of the compartment softly. "But I was kind of a bitch when I said that stuff about you and Brady."

His eyes shifted to hers and she stopped moving. "I'm still not going to take you to see him, Liz."

"I didn't ask you to."

"Road head might convince me," he said, his eyes darting back to the road.

Liz shook her head as she slowly, almost painfully slowly, began to slide back the edge of the compartment. "You think I'm going to suck your dick and *then* go see Brady?"

"At least I'd get off."

Yeah, he deserved this.

The hole in the compartment was just wide enough to stick her hand in. She licked her lips and tried to take even breaths. They were so close to her house, and she needed to time this just right.

They stopped at a red light and Liz for sure thought she was going to start sweating when he turned to look at her. She held his gaze perfectly, though, not wavering once. If she did, she was sure that he was going to notice that something was amiss . . . like the fact that she was leaning into him and the compartment containing his phone was open.

"So what do you say?" Clay asked with that same dimpled smirk.

"I still think no," Liz responded.

The light changed and they were off again. Liz breathed a soft sigh of relief when he had to look where he was going again. Her fingers slowly inched into the compartment, then her palm, and then her hand all the way to the wrist.

"Your loss."

"What, like giving you head is a privilege?" she managed to ask with a disbelieving laugh.

"It is."

Liz scoffed. "Men. Always thinking with the wrong head."

Her fingers brushed against his phone and she slowly lifted the device into her hand. Now to get it out of there.

"As if you weren't thinking about my dick when you let me take you back to my place."

When Clay turned his head at a stop sign to check for traffic, Liz lifted the phone out of the compartment and with a gulp pushed it down under her leg. She pressed her finger on the button to the compartment, gingerly clicked it back into place, and then righted herself.

"That was then and this is now," Liz said with an uneasy shrug.

Holy shit! She had his phone. She couldn't believe it. Her stomach was in knots with anticipation and worry about the last couple minutes of the drive.

"Women. So fickle," he grumbled. "Where am I taking you anyway?"

Liz gave Clay directions for the last few turns, and then he pulled the Porsche up in front of her house. She saw Victoria's and Daniel's cars in the driveway. If they weren't already in a sex coma, she was sure they were going to have a million questions. But first she needed to get the fuck out of Clay's car.

"Thanks for driving me," Liz told him before popping the door open and sliding the phone into her hand.

"I couldn't let you try to *walk* back."

"I thought you might let me."

"No farther than the end of the driveway. Long enough for you to realize how stupid it was," he said. The dimples in his cheeks were visible as she hastily stepped out of the car. She moved her hand behind her body to keep it from his vision.

"Night," she said, moving to push the door closed with the other hand.

"Hey!" he called, stopping her.

The blood pumped through her veins. She was this far. He couldn't know. She was this close!

"Yeah?" she murmured.

"You forgot your purse," he said, pointing at the small bag on the floor.

Liz breathed out heavily. Oh thank God! She grabbed the purse off of the floor of the car, slammed the door shut, and practically sprinted into her house. She shut the front door and leaned her back against it, breathing in and out heavily, her chest heaving.

"Holy shit," she whispered into the quiet house.

She slid the lock into place carefully before taking the phone back into her bedroom. She kicked off her high heels, stripped out of her party dress, and then threw on some sweats. Taking a seat on the bed, she opened the phone, swiped her finger across the touch screen, and it lit up in her hand.

She was in.

Her hands trembled as she searched Clay's contacts for Brady. There were four numbers listed: D.C. office, N.C. office, personal, and work. Since she had gone to the trouble of stealing Clay's phone, she transferred all of them into her phone, even though the only number that she was planning to use tonight was his personal one.

Liz placed Clay's phone down on her nightstand before pulling back up Brady's personal number and clicking Send. She could hear her heart beat in her ears as she waited for him to answer. It rang four times and then went to voice mail. Liz ended the call. She couldn't leave him a voice mail.

All of that trouble, and he didn't pick up her call.

She sat on her bed for a solid minute, just staring off into space wondering what the hell her life had become. How the hell had she gotten to this place? All she wanted to do was find a way to make it right, and still she couldn't do that. She had blown her second chance and didn't deserve another one. But that didn't mean she wasn't going to fight for that.

Then the lightbulb turned on. Clay's phone. He would answer Clay's phone. She would have to do some major explaining as to how she acquired the phone, but at least she would get to speak with Brady.

Liz snatched the phone back off of the nightstand, found Brady's personal number, and dialed. Her foot tapped anxiously on the floor.

Ring.

She could get through this. She just needed to talk to him.

Ring.

She didn't know what she was going to say, but it didn't matter. She would wing it. It was Brady. She had to do something.

Ring.

He wasn't going to answer. She had done this for nothing . . .

"Clay," Brady's gruff voice scolded through the phone, "where the *fuck* have you been? We're on lockdown over here. Everyone is freaking out and you just disappear. This is so like you. Why can't you do one thing that would make someone other than yourself happy?"

"Brady," Liz whispered into the phone.

There was a pregnant pause on the other line. Her heart skipped a beat.

"Liz?" he breathed in disbelief.

Chapter 25
TALK FIRST

Hey," Liz said softly. All of the bold words that she had been planning to say to him flitted out of her mind at his smooth, sexy voice.

"You're calling me from Clay's phone," he said, confused.

"Yeah."

"How did you get Clay's phone?"

Liz bit her lip. Well, this was going to be fun. "It's kind of a long story. I had to get hold of you. I really need to talk to you. Can we meet up?"

"What?" he asked, and then seemed to realize what she had asked. His voice turned cold. "No. I think that is a terrible idea. I told you." He took a deep breath and then whispered, "I told you not to call me again, that I wasn't going to be there when he hurt you."

"I know, but . . ."

"I don't make promises that I can't keep, Liz. You know that."

She swallowed. She knew that perfectly well. It was the reason he had never said I love you. Not because he didn't. That thought pushed her forward.

"I know. I know you did. And I'm sorry. I'm sorry for everything. For leaving, for being with him, for telling him, for ruining things, for hurting you."

"Liz, I really don't want to hear it," he said.

"Well, I'm going to tell you anyway," she cried desperately. "I fucked up. I didn't mean for things to happen like this. And I have so much that I need to tell you. Just please, please . . . meet me in person. If you didn't care about me, then you wouldn't have broken up with Erin. I know I don't deserve another chance, but give me one anyway. Please."

Brady sighed heavily into the phone. "Who told you about Erin? I've kept it out of the news entirely."

"Um . . . Clay," she whispered. She had so much to explain to Brady. She just desperately wanted to do it in person.

"Why do I have the sinking suspicion that I don't want to know how you are suddenly this well acquainted with my brother."

"Clay is . . . whatever. He doesn't matter. Actually he probably wants to kill me right about now, because I stole his phone," she mumbled.

"You did what?" Brady cried. "You stole Clay's phone?"

"I said it's a long story!"

"You didn't tell me the story involved theft!" he snapped back.

"Brady Maxwell losing his cool," she said softly. "How often does that happen?" He remained silent. She could practically see him pacing and trying to calm down after her retort. "It's because it's me. It's me, Brady. I'm the one who makes you lose your cool."

"You say that as if it's a good thing."

"It means there's fucking passion, and it means you fucking care. If you wanted to end this conversation then you would have done it as soon as you heard my voice. But you didn't. And I know why you didn't. It's the same reason that I haven't been able to get you out of my head since the day I walked out of the conference room. I tried! Lord knows I tried to forget you, but I didn't. And I can't. And I don't think you can forget me either."

"What's the point of all this, Liz?" he asked with a heavy sigh. "We're not going back to last year."

"I don't want to. But I can't sit here knowing what hand I had in this getting revealed to the public, knowing how you feel, knowing how *I* feel, and not try to see you. You deserve an explanation. Hell, you deserve so much more, Brady," she whispered. "Can't we just start with that?"

"Not tonight," he said resignedly.

Liz jumped off of her bed. She couldn't believe it. He was actually going to see her.

"Tonight would be best," she managed to get out.

"Am I supposed to just get away from everyone?" he asked. It was a rhetorical question, but she sure as hell wasn't leaving it that way.

"Yes. You're a fucking congressman. Tell them to fuck off."

Brady laughed and it was the most beautiful sound she had ever heard. God, how she had missed that.

"I'll phrase it exactly like that."

"That's smart."

"Heather is going to have a fit when she finds out I left."

"She's not your mother," Liz said, rolling her eyes. She'd had enough of Heather for one night. "Wait, you're really going to leave?"

The pause made her uneasy. She wished that she knew what he was thinking in that moment. She wanted so desperately to get him to understand, to have a shot at making amends. She wasn't going to take no for an answer.

"I think it's better that I come to you," Brady finally said in answer.

"I'm slightly intoxicated, so that might be a good idea."

"Why does this not surprise me?"

"Hey, I broke up with my boyfriend today. Alcohol is allowed," she said, trying to make light of the situation.

"I bet that was a fun conversation," Brady said tersely.

"When you come pick me up, I'll tell you all about it."

"You do realize you are the most infuriating woman I have ever met, right?"

"That means I'm unforgettable," Liz said with coy smile.

"Now, that is spin from a reporter, if I've ever heard it."

"I didn't get a job at the *New York Times* for nothing."

"The *New York Times*?" Brady asked with a low whistle afterward.

Liz preened a little at the recognition. It was a good job, a really, really good job. She was proud of it, and she hadn't even gotten to celebrate.

"I'll tell you all about it when you come to get me."

"Just don't go to sleep," he said firmly. "I'll get there when I get there."

—

Brady was coming. He was actually coming to see her. This wasn't like the last time, when he had picked her up outside of school. While she had the same emotions swirling through her about Hayden, she was no longer denying how she felt about Brady.

It made her body hum with anticipation. She couldn't sit still and she ended up changing her outfit half-a-dozen times. She finally decided to go casual in a pair of dark jeans, a red V-neck sweater, and black riding boots with gold buckles. Her hair and makeup were still done up from going out with Victoria earlier that night. That already felt like forever ago. It was hard to believe it had only been a few hours since her world had shifted. The job offer, Hayden's byline in the newspaper, Clay revealing that Brady was no longer with Erin, and then finally she was going to get to see Brady. Her body could hardly keep up with the highs and lows.

Every time a car drove down her street, she jumped up and looked to see if it was the familiar Lexus pulling up to get her. But after a couple hours, she was starting to wonder if Brady had lied to her. That wasn't like him at all. He would have just told her that he wasn't coming if he actually wasn't going to come see her. But still . . . she couldn't keep from getting frustrated as the hours ticked by.

Headlights flashed in her window and Liz jumped up, hoping, praying that he was finally here. She glanced down at her phone to check the time. Three twenty-seven in the morning. Christ! If it were anyone but Brady, she would have probably already passed out.

The car turned into her driveway. Liz's heart leaped. Brady! He was actually here. She grabbed her purse, threw it over her shoulder, and then dashed out of the house. Before Brady could even kill the engine or get out of the car, she was already sprinting around the front and pulling the door open. Liz ungracefully plopped down in the passenger seat and slammed the door.

"Hey," she said breathlessly. She needed to play more tennis if a short sprint knocked the wind out of her. Or maybe it was Brady's gorgeous face staring back at her.

His hair had grown out a bit since she had last seen him. He was probably due for a haircut, but it couldn't look bad on him. His brown eyes were shadowed in the night. His full lips as tempting as ever. Liz was surprised to find him in casual clothes as well. It was after three in the morning, but still, this was Brady. He had on jeans, a dark fit T-shirt, and the Arc'teryx jacket he had worn that day at the diner when they had agreed to pursue this relationship. She just wanted to reach across the car and kiss the life out of him.

He shook his head at her breathless entrance. "Hey."

"It's good to see you," she whispered, biting her lip.

Brady's eyes roamed her face, down her body, and then back to the windshield. He shifted the car into reverse before backing out of her driveway. "I'm going to have a lot of people angry with me in the morning," he said in response.

Liz didn't know what she had been expecting. Here she was putting herself out there again, and she was dealing with the same cold Brady. She hoped that once they got wherever they were going, his ice would thaw.

"Does that mean we won't be back in the morning?" Liz asked hopefully.

"We'll see."

Well, this was starting off promising.

"I . . . Look, Brady . . ."

"Let's save the conversations for when we get to where we're going," Brady said.

"Okay," she said softly. "Where *are* we going?"

"You'll see," he told her. "You should try to nap now. It'll be a while."

Liz raised her eyebrows. Her interest was piqued. He was taking her somewhere far enough away that she could sleep on the drive. He must be trying to go somewhere that reporters wouldn't think to find him . . . them. Yeah, if they were seen together tonight, the night the story broke, it wouldn't be in anyone's interest.

"All right," she said before settling into her seat and turning her body to stare up at him. It had been so long since she had just been able to look at him that if she was going to be here for a while without talking, she was going to take advantage of the opportunity.

Twenty minutes into the drive her eyes started fluttering closed and she wasn't sure if she was going to be able to hold on to consciousness for much longer.

"Brady," she whispered into the silence. She moved her hand across the car and covered his with hers.

"I thought you were asleep." But he didn't move her hand away. "I'm sorry."

He sighed, lacing their fingers together. "I know. Go to sleep."

—

The soft click of a door and the feel of her body being held by a rather strong, capable man woke Liz up. Then her mind latched on to what had happened. Brady. Brady was carrying her. Oh God, she could die happy. She must have been really out of it for her to sleep through him lifting her out of the car and carrying her nearly all the way inside.

"Mmm," she groaned softly as she came to. She leaned into his body and wrapped her arms around his neck.

"Good morning," he said, coming to a stopping point and setting her gently back onto her feet.

When she was set down, she wobbled slightly as she tried to wake up. Brady held her steady and she leaned forward against him.

"Good morning," she murmured. All she wanted to do was rest her head against his chest, have him wrap his arms around her, and fall back asleep. She could not think of anything she would want to do more than that in this moment. Okay . . . maybe one thing.

"You look dead on your feet."

"Just . . . tired," she said through her yawn.

"I've no idea why. It's only five in the morning."

"Where are we?" she asked, looking around for the first time.

Liz took in her surroundings and her eyes lit up when she realized where they were. The lake house. She couldn't believe he had brought her here. The last time had been Fourth of July weekend two summers ago. She only had good memories here. She hoped it stayed that way.

"I see you approve," he said with a small smile. "Why don't you camp out on the couch? I'm going to make a fire to try to heat this place up and then we can talk about why you called me."

She nodded her head forlornly. She was not looking forward to this conversation. There was so much to say, and she didn't know how much of it would make a difference. He obviously cared about her enough to leave everything behind and take her to the lake house to get away. But that didn't mean that things would suddenly change between them . . . that everything would be better.

Fifteen minutes later a fire was roaring in the fireplace, and Brady dropped down into the seat next to her. Her eyes opened wide. She hadn't even realized that they had been closed.

"You're sleeping again on me, baby," he said softly, brushing her hair out of her face.

Baby. He had called her baby. It was such a small gesture, and yet it meant so much. His touch sent butterflies through her stomach. She had craved it for so long. And it happened so unexpectedly. She had expected him to be angry, to yell at her. Yet here he was being gentle and caring and open. She wished that she knew what it all meant.

"Sorry. I'm so tired, but we need to have this conversation."

"You know," he said, taking her face in his hands and staring down at her deeply, "I'm not normally a talk-first-and-act-later kind of guy."

Liz's heart skipped a beat. Was he . . . ? No. He wasn't suggesting . . . She opened and closed her mouth a few times, unable to come up with a response to that.

"I'm going to be really frank with you right now." Liz licked her lips at Brady's words, preparing for the worst. "I'm pissed at you. I'm so angry that it hurts me to look at you. Thinking about you is more painful than a sucker punch. You fucking train-wrecked through my life, and I can't get rid of you. But at the same time, Liz, my entire body is aching to touch you. I just want to taste your lips and breathe you in, and bury myself inside of you. I feel like I'm going insane, that I'm splitting in two. Because everything tells me I should run headfirst in the opposite direction, but then I look at you, I hear your voice, I see those pleading blue eyes and I'm lost. I forget everything I should do, and I just know what I want to do."

He pulled her forward until their lips were merely an inch apart. Her breathing was ragged. Her heart beating out of her chest at his declaration.

"And this is all I want," he whispered before claiming her lips for his own.

Chapter 26
ACT LATER

Liz couldn't have imagined a more perfect kiss. Brady's lips, which were normally so demanding, moved with hers sensually, evocatively, captivatingly. They were joined as one, lost in each other's tender embrace. It was just a kiss, and yet it was so much more than that. It held the promises that Brady didn't speak.

Her arms wrapped around Brady's neck as he pushed her gently back into the sofa. She knew that they needed to talk. There was so much left unsaid. But for now she let their bodies do the talking and knew the words would come when they were needed.

Brady's hands slid under her sweater and ran along her firm stomach. She groaned at the feel of him. His touch sent shocks throughout her body. Her mind was lost to this man and this feeling, which she had never really been able to give up.

Heat radiated from their bodies as they moved against each other. More than a year's worth of pent-up sexual frustration coaxing the fire between them. Liz's fingers tangled in his dark hair as his tongue met hers and they massaged each other. Her legs bent almost subconsciously and pushed her pelvis up against him. Brady moaned into her mouth and she felt his weight shift until she could feel the hardness through his jeans.

He broke their kiss to pull her sweater over her head and then took a moment just to stare down at her torso with her breasts spilling out of the skimpy black balconet bra she had chosen. She hadn't known what was going to happen with Brady, but she sure as hell had decided to come prepared. He playfully snapped the strap of her bra with a dirty smirk on his face.

"Black lingerie?" he asked, arching an eyebrow.

"It's what you wear when you want someone to see it." She ran her knuckles down his jawline. "I wasn't sure if you were going to, but just when I think that I have you all figured out, you surprise me."

He grabbed her hand in his and kissed each knuckle softly. "Funny. I find that you surprise me constantly."

Brady placed her hand on his shoulder and then dropped his hands to the waistline of her jeans.

"Sexy."

He popped the button.

"Smart."

The zipper dropped to the bottom.

"Funny."

His hand slid under the material and dragged them down her legs.

"Kind."

He placed light kisses up her calf, over her knee, and across her inner thigh.

"Delectable," he murmured, nipping lightly at her black lace thong.

Liz groaned and pressed her hips up invitingly. He was going to drive her mad. "You sound like you're going to eat me up."

He moved the lace aside and swept his tongue gently against her folds. "I am."

"Oh fuck," she moaned.

Her whole body pulsed at his words. She just wanted him. All of him. As she had never wanted anyone or anything else in her entire life. Walking away had been the hardest thing she had ever done, but being with Brady was the easiest. It was just right. Like all the pieces fell into place and the world was singing to their tune and the entire universe was in alignment.

Her thong met the same fate as her jeans. His tongue swirled around her clit and she bucked against him. Brady forced her hips down roughly as he continued his work, sucking her clit into his mouth and nibbling lightly on the small bead. Her moans increased in volume and he took the opportunity to trail his index finger down her wetness.

He kissed her once more before pulling back and glancing at her panting on the couch. "Someone wants me," he said, twirling his fingers in a circle over her opening.

"You think?" she groaned, throwing her hands up and gripping the armrest.

"I wasn't sure. I think you'll have to beg me for it, baby." He planted another teasing kiss on her.

"I'll do whatever you want," she murmured. "Just please, please . . ."

"Please what? Do you want to come?"

"Yes," she whimpered. His fingers stilled and she nearly cried out in frustration.

"I think you're going to have to do better than that. Your body is throbbing underneath me and I haven't even fucked you. I'm not sure you really want me," he said, enjoying holding all the power.

"Brady, just fuck me. I want you to make me come. I want to surrender to you. I want you to make me see stars," she pleaded with him. "Please take me. I'm yours."

He smirked at her with that gorgeous fucking smile and then answered her pleas. Brady's fingers delved into her wet pussy as his tongue licked and sucked at her clit. Her back arched off the couch as she felt the first wave of orgasm hit her full-on. She had been anticipating him touching her so long that her body couldn't even hold out for him. She felt his fingers work a come-hither motion against her G-spot and she lost it. Her walls closed around him as pleasure rolled through her body.

Brady left her legs trembling and hastily stripped out of his shirt and jeans. He sat down next to her, grabbed a fistful of her hair in his hands, and brought her face up to his. Liz stopped breathing as she stared into those commanding eyes, that commanding presence. She knew then that she would never be able to resist this man again. And she never wanted to.

"Do you want to see how good you taste?" he whispered, brushing his nose against her.

"Please," she murmured.

Their lips met softly even as he held her in place. It was a beautiful contrast, just like their relationship. Hot, fiery, and demanding. Soft, intense, and emotional. When they collided, neither could escape the gravitational pull.

She could taste herself on his lips, and she felt her body reacting all over again. There was absolutely nothing Brady could do that would make her uncomfortable. She just wanted this man so badly that all else was lost to her. And he was lost to everything but her.

Brady's hand trailed down her back and snapped her bra off. He eased her back down on the couch and covered her body with his own. One of his hands kneaded her soft breasts while the other remained tangled in her hair. She wiggled her hips temptingly, trying to get to his cock. But he wasn't going to give her an inch until he was ready.

"Demanding little pussy," he said as he shoved her hips back into the couch again.

Liz just whimpered in defeat. She was demanding, and she wanted him so badly. The buildup was torture, pure, beautiful, blissful torture, but torture nonetheless. Her body was all built-up tension again already, and she just wanted him to drive his dick deep within her and never look back.

"I haven't explored enough of your body yet," he murmured against her neck. "I think I should kiss every inch first. What do you think?"

"Brady," she groaned.

He chuckled as he trailed kisses down her neck and across her collarbone. "This is mine," he told her. "And this."

He left kisses down her chest and then latched on to her breast. "Both of these."

His hands sent butterflies through her stomach as he gripped her hips and settled his cock against her opening. She wanted to move and try to ease him into her, but just the feel of him against her was sending her into a frenzy. She didn't want him to pull back.

"I'm going to erase every memory you ever had tonight, baby."

"Not the ones of you," she managed to get out. "I always keep those safe."

He smiled brilliantly at her. That was the right thing to say.

Brady plunged down into her roughly in one swift motion without any warning. Liz cried out as he stretched and filled her gloriously. As promised, Liz saw stars. She was sure nothing else had ever felt this incredible before.

He started a slow rhythm that she was already anxious to increase as he thrust deeper and deeper into her. Liz arched her back again, trying to give him as much room as she could, but she had forgotten how big he was. She was going to be wonderfully sore in the morning, and still she wanted more.

"Harder," Liz gasped out. "Fuck. Brady, fuck me harder."

Brady grabbed her leg and placed it on his shoulder before driving into her harder and faster. She whimpered as he stretched her walls to capacity. He took her so roughly that it was borderline painful, and she was clawing the couch to try to get more leverage.

"Baby, your whimpering is going to make me come," he growled.

"Oh God," she moaned.

He smirked and leaned forward to fuck her even harder. She was almost there. She felt a layer of sweat coat her body and her walls tightening unrelentingly around him.

"Open those legs for me," he said, pushing her leg off of his shoulder and onto the couch. She obliged him by unbending her other leg and spread-eagling before him.

With just that added bit of room, Brady drove down into her and she felt her walls shake. "Right there, yes, oh God," she yelled, and then she shattered.

Her legs trembled mercilessly as he plunged into her one more time before crying out and filling her. Brady collapsed forward on top of her and she wrapped her arms and legs around him. They were both breathless and shaking from the exertion, but unbelievably, unequivocally sated.

As their breathing evened out, Brady propped himself up on his elbows and brushed her matted hair out of her face. He kissed her lips once and when he pulled back, she couldn't keep the megawatt smile off of her face.

"You know, baby," he whispered, "I've been angry at you for so long that I just don't think I have it in me anymore. It takes too much effort. Loving you takes so much less effort, and it means I get to see that smile."

Liz's mouth dropped open in shock. Had he . . . had he just told her that he loved her?

He laughed softly and then kissed her button nose. "Happy Valentine's Day, baby."

Chapter 27
OATMEAL

Liz woke up the next morning to feel Brady's strong arms wrapped around her waist and her face buried in his shoulder. The soft comforter covered their still-naked bodies as light streamed into the bedroom from the upstairs window. In that moment, Liz just let herself feel all the joy and happiness that came with where she was and what she was doing.

Brady Maxwell. She was in bed with Brady Maxwell.

And in the early-morning sunshine, half-delirious from lack of sleep, aching in all the right places from last night, she felt as if she was exactly where she needed to be. She knew that they'd had a rough time getting there, and she was sure that the road ahead wasn't going to be easy. But at least right here and right now, she could let the rest of the world fall away, pretend that they didn't have Hayden's article to face or a public ravenous for a scandal, and just be here with Brady.

She nuzzled into him and left a soft kiss on his neck. "Mmm," Brady murmured as he came to.

"Morning," she whispered.

He tightened his grip on her waist, pulling her closer to him. "I had the most amazing dream last night."

"Oh yeah? Was I in it?" Liz asked, tangling their legs together under the covers.

"You were. I dreamed I brought you to my lake house and had sex with you all morning," he whispered into her ear.

"Hate to break it to you, but that wasn't a dream."

"I know," he said, nipping at her ear. "I think I have another dream coming on."

"Am I in that one?"

"It's me fucking you all afternoon too."

"Oh," she whispered. "I feel like I'm having that same dream."

He chuckled softly and then rolled her on top of him. Liz leaned her breasts against his chest and braced her hands on his shoulders. His hand slid between them, parting her lips and touching her teasingly.

"No begging this time," she groaned, evading his playful fingers and pressing herself against his erection.

"The begging is my favorite part." He found her lips and kissed them softly.

Liz smiled and broke their kiss before slowly lowering herself onto him. "The begging or the whimpering? Or was it when you came?"

Brady grabbed her hips and forced her all the way down onto him. Liz gasped at the unexpected movement. "It's when *you* come."

Liz couldn't argue with that assessment. Every time he made her come, he quickly followed, until both were spent and unable to move. Their bodies were perfectly in tune as if there had never been a pause in their sex life.

Even though she was on top, she let Brady set the pace. His hands guided her body up and down on top of him. Their hips met at a perfect angle. Her breasts bounced with the movement, and all they did was stare back at each other. She had missed this. Missed him. The emotions trapped between her and Brady intensified every touch, taste, feel as they reexperienced everything they had missed in the past year and a half.

Climax crashed over her in waves almost without warning, and Liz dropped over onto his chest again. Brady kept thrusting into her as she rode out her orgasm. She felt him grasp her hips forcefully at the last thrust and his eyes closed as he came.

"This is the best way to wake up," she murmured softly.

"With you."

"Mmm, with you."

Brady kissed her temple and ran his hands up and down her back. "How about you hop in the shower?"

"Join me?" she asked, already almost falling back asleep from his hands on her.

He laughed lightly. "We both know how that will end."

"So, yes?"

"You shower. I'm going to see if we have anything to eat. Didn't think that one through."

"Who are you and what have you done with Brady Maxwell?" she muttered.

"Cut a guy some slack. I wasn't expecting to spend the weekend at the lake," he said with a kiss on her cheek as he rolled to the other side of the bed.

"I'm glad you did."

Brady kicked his feet over the bed and stood in the buff. "Me too."

Good Lord! The man was the definition of sexy. Muscular arms, broad shoulders, washboard abs. It really wasn't fair to the rest of the world, but she didn't mind the view one bit.

He found a pair of black boxer briefs, basketball shorts, and a long-sleeve T-shirt from the closet and reappeared covering everything she had been assessing.

"I'm turning the water on," Brady said, walking into the bathroom.

"Okay. Okay." Liz hopped out of bed and followed him.

Brady placed a towel on the counter for her and turned the water on full steam. She grabbed his T-shirt and pulled him in for a kiss before he could leave. "You should stay," she murmured.

"You're going to need food."

"Yes," she said, touching him through his shorts. "I am."

"I'd bet you're a little sore. I wasn't gentle," he said. "And I don't want to hurt you."

"You won't . . ."

"Liz, shower." He opened the glass door to the massive walk-in shower and slapped her ass to get her moving.

"Fine. Don't say I never asked," she said, scurrying forward.

"Next time I want you to beg me, I'll let you know." He shook his head and shut the shower door.

Liz laughed as he walked out of the bathroom. She stepped into the hot spray, letting the water run down her body. Truth be told, she was sore. *Very* sore. To say he hadn't been gentle was probably the understatement of the year. He had been as rough as she had asked him to be and then some, but she wouldn't take it back. Not for a second.

She showered quickly and then changed into one of Brady's UNC T-shirts and some baggy sweats she found in the closet. It wasn't the sexiest outfit, but it wasn't as if he had cared what she was wearing last night. She took the stairs down into the living room and saw that Brady had started another fire. She turned to walk into the kitchen when she caught a glimpse of the lake through the sliding glass doors.

The lake was pristine and snow fell softly onto its smooth surface. It was a light snow. Nothing that was likely going to stick, but it was beautiful nonetheless.

"It's snowing," she said as she walked into the kitchen.

"Yeah, it's been doing that since I got down here. Hopefully it doesn't stick or we're not going anywhere anytime soon," Brady said.

"That doesn't sound like such a bad thing."

He smiled and her heart stopped. "I hope you like oatmeal, because that's pretty much all we have."

"Oatmeal is fine."

They ate in a peaceful silence. Both knew that the conversation to come was an important one, but each wanted to prolong the state of bliss they were in for a little bit longer. Brady reluctantly cleared the dishes, and Liz sat there sipping on the water he had poured her.

"So," he said, leaning back against the counter.

"So," she replied.

"We have some things to talk about."

"Yeah."

"Maybe we should start at the beginning."

"Living room?" she asked, standing and backing into the room. "Sure."

Liz took a seat on the couch again, but this time Brady sat across from her. She hated the space between them already, but she knew why it was necessary.

"I guess I should preface this conversation," she began, "by letting you know you probably aren't going to like some parts."

"I doubt I'll like much of it," Brady said, leaning back into the seat and crossing his leg at his ankle.

Well, at least he knew. Maybe he wouldn't kill anything along the way.

"So, the beginning, right?" He nodded and she tried not to avoid those dark eyes. Liz took a deep breath and began. "I guess the story starts after I left your primary. I wanted you to be happy, and I didn't want to jeopardize your election. So I left and was miserable the rest of the semester. I never told anyone what happened, and I never let anyone in. Not even my roommate. I guess after you won I realized there was no hope for us, and I just wanted to try to forget. That's when Hayden and I started talking."

She cringed at Hayden's name, and she saw Brady's jaw clench. She didn't blame him. Not one bit.

"Fast-forward to October. Well, you know what happened that night."

"Yes. I do," Brady said stiffly.

God, she hated this.

"Well, when you closed that door, I decided that nothing else really mattered. It was only the first argument Hayden and I had ever had, so I forgave him and we put it past us."

"Just like that?" he asked, frustrated. "I fucking broke up with Erin the next day and you just *forgave* him?"

"I'm not you, Brady. I made my own mistakes," she said softly. "I thought it would be okay."

Brady shook his head. "You're entirely too forgiving. That guy is a jackass."

"He is. But you have to understand that Hayden had *never* once acted like that with me before. And you were gone." He opened his mouth to say something, but Liz beat him too it. "I know. I left. I know. Trust me. Can I just tell the rest?"

He breathed out heavily. "What happened?"

"Everything was fine with my relationship, but nothing was okay with me. I beat myself up for months about cheating on Hayden with you."

"Over our kiss?"

"You and I both know it was more than that, Brady. We wouldn't be here right now if it was just a kiss."

He nodded, acknowledging her statement, and she continued.

"I had a breakdown and told Victoria. She said that I should tell Hayden, because the worst thing that could happen was that he would leave me. At the time, I really thought that was the worst thing that could happen. I just wanted the weight off my chest. I wasn't going to tell him it was you," Liz said. Her body ached as she thought about what happened next.

"But you did."

"Yes. He figured it out and I don't even know how to explain what happened. He wasn't himself. He turned scary."

Brady's eyes narrowed considerably and looked on edge. "Scary how?"

Liz shook her head. She couldn't look him in the eye. She couldn't relive what had happened. She didn't want to tell him. She just wanted to get on with everything else.

"Liz, scary how?" he demanded.

"It doesn't matter," she peeped.

"I don't like the sound of this," he said gruffly. Standing and striding over to her, he grasped her chin softly in his hands and tilted her face up to him. "Look at me. What do you mean by that?"

Liz's bottom lip trembled as she stared up into Brady's concerned brown eyes. "He just freaked out and demanded details. When I gave them to him, he just . . ."

"Just *what*?"

"He made me feel even guiltier about what happened, had sex with me, and then left in the morning."

Brady stood very still at her words. She couldn't read all the emotions rolling through his body, but she could see underneath it all he was pissed. "Did you want to . . . ?"

Liz swallowed. She wanted to shake her head, but she just stared at him, the fear still reflected in her eyes.

"Fuck!" he cried, dropping his hand and storming across the room. "Fuck!"

"Brady . . ."

"I'll kill him, Liz."

"No," she said, jumping up and rushing toward him. "You can't do that."

"Where are my car keys?" he asked, looking around the room.

"Brady," she pleaded. She pressed her hands into his shoulders as he tried to walk toward the door. "Please."

"You want me to stay here and just let him get away with raping you?" he demanded.

Liz shook her head. That word. She couldn't hear that word. No. That wasn't what it was. It wasn't. It had been different. Just angry sex. Just hate sex. Just guilt sex. Anything but that. She could still hear Hayden shushing her as he pushed her into the mattress. A tear fell from her eyes even as she tried to hold them at bay.

"Oh, baby," he said softly. He wiped the tear from under her eye and pulled her into his arms. "I'm not going to leave."

"You can't go after him," Liz said, wrapping her arms around his waist.

"I want to kill him for ever touching you."

"I know, but I don't think murdering the reporter who is writing an ongoing story about you would get you reelected."

He kissed the top of her head and held her close. "Good to know someone is thinking about my reelection chances."

"Always," she murmured.

Brady walked her back over to the couch, and after her tears dammed up, she started her story again. At least the hardest part was out of the way. Though she knew he wasn't going to like what was coming after that.

"I told Hayden a week ago, and the story broke yesterday. He didn't tell me that he was going to put it in the paper. Everything seemed normal . . . or as normal as it could be." Brady tensed next to her, and she knew he wanted to make a remark about Hayden. "I saw the article in the paper and freaked out. I was actually with Savannah when it broke."

"Really?"

"Yeah, so I guess at least I had someone to break down with," Liz said with a sad shrug. "Anyway, I tried to call Hayden, but he never returned my call."

"Pussy," Brady growled under his breath.

"Yeah. Then I got a call from Heather."

"What?" he demanded.

"I hadn't been planning to call you in the first place, because you told me not to and I wanted to respect what you wanted. Then she called me and told me not to contact you."

"I can't believe she would go behind my back like that."

"Really? After how she reacted when she found out about us, and then with her name ending up in Hayden's article? I'm surprised you didn't think of it yourself."

Brady shook his head, trying to process all the new information. "I guess I should have thought that she would tie up everything she thought was a loose end."

"That's me," Liz said bitterly. "A loose end."

"You know what I mean . . ."

"Yeah. I do. But as you can imagine, after that conversation I decided to get drunk, which is when Clay called me."

Brady looked at her in disbelief. "And how does Clay have your phone number?"

"I gave it to him at your gala event that summer we were together. He'd never used it before, but remember that same night he thought my name was Liz Carmichael."

"So he put two and two together," Brady said, inching away from her. He laced his fingers together and stared down at them as he tried to find words. "I know that Clay has a certain reputation. I'd hope that I don't have to kill my brother too."

"Um . . . no. You don't. He kissed me, but that's all."

"You kissed him?"

"Um . . . yeah."

"And he was satisfied with just a kiss?"

"Well, no, but it's kind of complicated. I thought that I was never going to see you again, so when I went with Clay, I was in a really low place."

"But you just kissed?" Brady asked to clarify.

"Yes. He told me that you and Erin broke up, and something in me snapped back into place. I realized what I should have known all along. You were it for me. Nothing else really mattered. I had to talk to you. I had to get you to see that this could be fixed. I wasn't broken as long as I still had a sliver of hope. Which is how I ended up stealing Clay's phone to call you. And now I guess we're here."

"That's a lot to take in," Brady admitted.

"It is. That's why I wanted to talk to you in person. I never would have told Hayden in a million years if I had thought that he would write about it."

"Didn't you even think to clarify with him that this wasn't on the record?"

Liz tucked her legs up underneath herself and sighed. "He was my boyfriend. We'd been together for almost a year and a half. I never thought that he would do that."

"Goddamn reporters."

Liz shrugged her shoulders helplessly. "I've never hated them more than in this moment."

Brady stood up and paced the room. She could see him trying to process everything she had told him. She knew he already believed her. It would be a pretty elaborate story for her to make up, and what would be the point in that? She was here. She was with him. She wasn't about to start lying now.

He pivoted and stared at her. He took in every aspect as his eyes roamed from her body clad in his baggy clothing up to her messy towel-dried hair to her face, open and vulnerable to him. With everything she was worth, she wished she knew what was going on inside of that head.

"So, the real concern is where to go from here," Brady said, his voice even and level. She could see the mask slipping into place, see the wall slamming down and closing her out.

"Please don't do that," she whispered.

"What?"

"I'm right here. You can talk to me. You can tell me what you're thinking," Liz pleaded. "I'm not the public. I'm not the threat. I don't want you to think that you have to hide."

"How do you do that?" he asked in disbelief.

"Do what?"

"See through me so easily. All I did was look at you and ask a question."

Liz slowly shook her head. "That's not what I see when I look at you, Brady." She brushed her hair off of her shoulder, moving it all to one side. "You're not the campaign with me. You're not a congressman with me. You're just the man I fell for, and that man tried to shut me out once. I'm not letting it happen again."

Brady broke her gaze and let his eyes shift out the window. "I think there was a bit of mutual fault in that instance."

"Yeah. I guess we were both stupid." Liz sighed. There was so much she wanted to know. She didn't even know where to start . . . or where exactly they could go from here. "What was it like not having me at your side at all of those events?"

"What does it matter?" he asked, glancing back up at her.

"I was just curious. Like, was Erin all that great? Why were you with her to begin with? She was out there in public with you, on your arm. It seemed so wrong. And you just let her talk about all of that stuff at the dinner with your parents and I just had to sit there. I mean, a morning talk show host who does charity work with inner-city kids? Really? She must have given really great head, because she sure was boring . . ."

"Are you about done?" Brady snapped.

Liz eeped. "Um . . . yeah."

"Good. Now that that's off of your chest, let's try to put all of that behind us and think about what we're doing right now. I can't change anything that happened the past year, and I can't change any of the circumstances we're currently in. I can only think about the future." As Brady messed with his hair, he walked back over and took a seat next to Liz. "I want to go public."

"What?" Liz gasped, standing abruptly and covering her mouth. She was sure that he hadn't just said that. "I'm sorry. What did you say?"

"Liz, I want to go to public. I've had over a year to think about what I would have done differently. I've missed you enough that I want to do this. I want to try to make it work. The public already knows you exist. Sure, it won't be easy to be out there, but I'd rather it be our choice than the media's. We didn't go public before because I couldn't see anything past my career. Well, now I want both. I should be able to have both."

Liz swallowed. She felt a bit faint. She never thought that she would have this conversation with Brady. Not in a million years. Every time she let herself think about being public with him, she had pushed the thought down and buried it. Now that she was faced with the possibility, she didn't even know what that would look like.

"Um, whoa. That's . . . that's kind of huge, Brady. I mean . . . Hayden and I just broke up. I just got the job offer at the *New*

Yorker. I'm still in school, editor of the paper, and those articles. You're up for reelection."

"Liz, I don't care," Brady said, standing with her. He grabbed her hands and pulled her closer. "I want to do this. All I hear is wasted time. You left. I get why you left, but I was stupid for letting it happen."

"I just . . . I want to, Brady, but . . ."

"No," he said, touching his fingers to her lips. "You want to."

She smiled up at him, but her stomach was in knots. This was exactly what she wanted and it scared the shit out of her. Everything had changed so fast.

"I do, Brady. I want to be with you, but this is really sudden."

"I know. It's kind of crazy," he said. "I'm not normally a rash person. You really do fuck me up."

"I just . . . I know I was the one who wanted to go public last time, so I shouldn't be hesitating about this, but it's a lot to think about all at once."

Brady smiled and then bent down and kissed her on the lips. "I think I'd be more surprised if you were completely okay with everything. It's a big decision. I'm used to the limelight. You'd have to be in it too, baby."

Liz froze. She hadn't thought about that. Well, not really. She had always thought she was better behind a camera than in front of one. She preferred writing articles to working in broadcast. What would it be like to be *out there* with Brady?

"Can we . . . can we wait to see if all of this blows over first? I just don't want to be rash and put us out there, only to be under worse scrutiny."

"I'll do it your way," he said with another tender kiss, "as long as it means you're mine."

"I always have been, Brady."

Chapter 28

AROUND THE BLOCK

Brady and Liz spent the rest of the weekend locked away at his lake house. Not wanting to risk being seen by any reporters who might wander by, they didn't leave the house. But there were few objections from either of them about that. It was nice and peaceful compared to the hellfire they were walking back into when they left the lake. Neither was looking forward to it.

The drive back to Chapel Hill seemed to take half as long as the drive to the lake house . . . and she had been asleep for most of the drive there. Liz chewed on her nails compulsively until Brady slapped at her hands and made her stop. She grabbed his hand, laced their fingers together, and leaned on his shoulder. She wasn't ready for their weekend of tranquility to be over.

"Brady," she began as they turned off of I-40 toward her house.

"Yeah, baby?"

"I'm going to see you again, right?"

His eyes left the road to look at her. "Of course. Why would you ask that?"

"I don't know," Liz said. She really didn't. Fears ate at her from every angle. She didn't want to worry about how they were going to make this work, but she couldn't keep those feelings from crowding in on her.

"There are a lot of unknowns going forward, Liz. But I'll always be your airplane, and you'll always be mine." Liz smiled at the reference. She had said the same thing to him on the day of his primary. "You meant it then, and I mean it now."

"Okay. You're right," she said.

She needed to trust Brady and trust what they had. They would let the storm blow over, and then come to terms with what they were going to do. Thrusting them into the spotlight and expecting everything to be all right sounded to her like a recipe for disaster.

Reporters fed on stories like this. Liz hadn't wanted to jeopardize Brady's career before and she didn't want to do it now. She knew he cared about her, and for now that was enough. They had been apart for a year and a half, so the last thing she wanted to do was be away from him again. However, she knew logically that it would be better for them to wait. Plus she probably needed the time away. After Hayden's deception, jumping directly into a full-on, public relationship with Brady sounded drastic. Everything would work itself out with time.

Brady turned down her street, and Liz's head jerked at the sight in front of her. "Keep driving," she barked.

"What?" Brady asked.

"Just keep driving. Don't stop. Drive around the block."

"Okay," he said, continuing to the end of the street and taking a left turn. "What's going on?"

"That Audi was Hayden's."

Brady slammed on his brakes and they came to an abrupt halt. Liz jerked forward against her seat belt and grunted as it cut into her shoulder. "Jesus, Brady!"

"Sorry. But what the fuck is he doing here? I thought you said you broke up."

"We did. Well, I mean, it's over since he wrote that article," Liz told him.

"Wait, 'it's over'? Have you guys actually broken up?"

"We're *not* together. It hardly matters if I've spoken with him," she told him fiercely. "He refused to take my call all day when the story broke. He had his fucking byline next to Calleigh Hollingsworth's," she spat the name. "To me that means we're over."

"But you haven't actually talked to him?" Brady asked. "And who the fuck is Calleigh Holling-whatever?"

"Brady, how was I supposed to talk to him if he refused to take my call? I couldn't. It's over. He's the asshole who wrote the story about us. It's over." Liz massaged her aching shoulder in frustration. She didn't want to have to deal with this, not with everything else in her head. "And Calleigh is the other reporter who broke the story with him. They used to date and now they're working together in Charlotte."

Brady's grip on the steering wheel tightened and she saw him take incredible care to breathe evenly. "I can't let you go in there. The guy is unstable and dangerous."

"He wouldn't hurt me."

His head snapped to the side. "Are you serious?" he asked. "After what he did to you."

"It wasn't like that. Not *that*."

"Well, whatever it was," he said as if he didn't believe for a second that it wasn't exactly what he had said it was, "it was wrong. He's already hurt you. I'll be damned if I let him do it again. And what kind of guy takes a job with his ex-girlfriend? I'll tell you. Someone who wants to fuck her while his girlfriend is hours away still in school."

"Brady," she snapped, shaking her head. "I don't want to think about that. Ugh! Hayden and Calleigh. I can't."

"I'd put money on it."

"Can we just drive and not talk about that?" she asked. Brady eased down the road again slowly. He clearly wasn't in any hurry to drop her off.

"Can I take you somewhere safer?" he pleaded.

"I'm safe at my house. I just . . . I need to talk to him, Brady. He's there for a reason, and I need to let him know that it's over. He has to already know, but wouldn't you feel better if I told it to his face?"

"Fine. You want to go in there, I'm going with you," he said stubbornly.

"Are you out of your mind?" Liz asked. "Did you forget that you're a congressman and he's the asshole who wrote the story about you? Do you want to give him ammunition to write about you? I certainly don't! I thought we talked about letting the story blow over. I guarantee it won't if you storm into my house and confront Hayden."

Brady ground his teeth together and didn't say anything. She knew that she was right. She needed to confront Hayden about what had happened. Brady didn't. He would only take a bad situation and make it worse. She didn't want anything to get worse than it already was.

"Will you just drop me off on the corner?" Liz asked, pointing up the street.

"Liz," he pleaded.

"I'll be okay, Brady. I'll call you after he leaves," she told him.

He sighed heavily and then pulled over at the end of the street. "You have the right number now?"

"Yeah," she murmured, grabbing her purse off the floor. She found Clay's phone in the bag and handed it to Brady. "Will you give this back to Clay? He's probably wondering how he managed to lose it."

"I can't *wait* to give it back to him," Brady said with a devilish smile on his face.

"Don't be too hard on him, okay?"

"I don't make promises I can't keep, baby," he said, grasping her chin in his hand and kissing her hard on the mouth.

"I know you don't."

"Promise you'll be safe?"

Liz nodded softly. "Promise."

"Good."

They kissed again desperately, like a drowning person gasping for their last breath. Then Liz pulled away and exited the car.

With a heavy heart, she clutched her purse to her chest and started walking down the street to her house. She hadn't checked her phone yet and at this point she was kind of afraid to. Had Hayden called? Did he have some kind of explanation? Not that it would change her mind at this point.

She slid her phone out into her palm. She checked her text messages and saw half a dozen from Victoria freaking out about her leaving with Clay and never returning, then another handful in all caps about Hayden showing up and asking what the hell she was supposed to tell him. Hayden had called and texted her even more than that. The messages started the morning after the article went live and ended only a couple minutes ago, when he had been trying to figure out where she was. She wished she had checked her phone so that she would have been more prepared for his appearance, but there was nothing she could do now.

As she walked up the driveway and to the front door, she steeled herself for what was about to happen. At least Victoria was there.

Liz might have been confident when sending Brady away, but she didn't really want to be alone with Hayden. She didn't think he would do anything, but she had no guarantees.

Liz pushed the door open and walked into the living room, only to find Hayden and Victoria screaming at each other.

"I don't fucking care why you're here, Lane, but she's not fucking here. So get out of our fucking house, you douchebag. Haven't you done enough damage? Just thought you'd come over to inflict more pain on my best friend?" Victoria threw in his face.

"Vickie, just shut up," he cried, spitting out her name as viciously as she had said his. "I've had enough of your shit. I don't even want to talk to you. I'm here for Liz."

"Well, I'm right here," Liz said softly.

"Liz," Hayden said, turning to face her.

"You're back," Victoria said. Her eyes bugged, asking a million questions at once. *Where were you? Did you sleep with that guy? Were you with him this whole time? What's going on? Can I kick Hayden out?*

"I am."

"Where were you?" he asked.

"Like you have a right to ask that!" Victoria yelled, slapping him on the back of the head and walking over to Liz. "You don't have to talk to him, Liz. Just send him packing."

"I had a pretty traumatic Friday. I needed to escape. So I did," Liz said, answering Hayden's question. "What are *you* doing here?"

"I needed to talk to you, to explain," he said.

Now that she got a good look at him, she realized that he didn't look like himself. He had stubble growing in on his jaw and his clothes were wrinkled, as if he hadn't changed them recently. The only time she had seen him this disheveled was last October, when she had walked out on him after their argument.

"I'm not sure what you needed to explain. I think I understand completely what happened," Liz said, completely cool and resolute. Any apprehensions about coming in here had faded. She felt a dose of Brady's confidence fueling this conversation.

"Can we talk in private, please?" Hayden asked, glancing over at Victoria and then back.

"Oh what? Like the *last* time we talked in private?" Liz asked harshly.

Hayden winced. "I—"

"Don't have a good enough excuse for anything. And you never did."

Victoria smirked. "I feel like I need to go pop some popcorn for this."

"Victoria, really not helpful," Liz said, shaking her head.

"Fine. I'll be in the kitchen. If I hear anything at all that is out of place, I will be in here to beat the shit out of you, Lane. Don't think for a second that I'm lying."

He just stared at her with stone-cold eyes as she walked away. She left the kitchen door open, so there was no mistaking that she would be back in a matter of seconds.

"What are you doing here? Just spit it out so we can get this over with." Liz crossed her arms over her chest and waited.

"I . . . I came to apologize for what I did."

Liz started laughing in his face. "Oh, you're serious. How sad."

"What's wrong with you, Liz? Why are you acting like this?" he asked.

"Oh, I don't know!" she said, raising her voice. "Maybe because when I confided in my boyfriend a secret I'd never told anyone but my best friend, he went and wrote about it in the newspaper so now the *entire world* knows!"

"I didn't put your name out there. No one else knows that it's you."

"Right! Because that makes it better and suddenly absolves you from fault! Are you that stupid? Someone could figure it out, and even if they don't, you still betrayed my trust in such a way that could never in a million years be repaired. How could I ever trust you again? You didn't even have the decency to tell me you were doing it or fucking call me back that day to face what you had done!"

"Liz . . ."

"You're the definition of a coward, Hayden."

His jaw clenched and his hands balled into fists. She was pushing his buttons and feeding on his insecurities. He had to have known that this was going to happen. There was no coming back from what he had done. If he thought that she was going to let him walk all over her again, he was sadly mistaken. *That* Liz was never resurfacing.

"I came to explain. Are you at least going to let me explain?" he demanded.

"Sure. Go ahead and try to explain to me how this happened."

"Look, I didn't mean for it to all go this way. I was upset about everything and I ended up talking to Calleigh about you. She tried to comfort me. Told me to throw myself into work. That's when I spilled about the story. I didn't give her your name or anything . . ."

"Ugh! Digging the hole deeper," she muttered under her breath.

"It wasn't like that. You know I'm not interested in Calleigh!"

Brady's words echoed in her mind about Hayden and Calleigh. "Sure seems that way to me."

"Nothing happened, but when I told her about the story, she pitched it to the editor without telling me. Once it was approved, I didn't have much choice but to run with it."

"Right. Try to claim that you didn't have a choice. Make it not about you. See if that works," she said.

"I messed up. I'm sorry. I didn't know how to tell you. I wanted to do it in person, but . . ."

"But what?" she snapped. "You lost your balls and had to go looking for them all weekend?"

Liz heard Victoria snort laughing from the other room. That only ticked off Hayden more.

"Are you serious right now?" he yelled into her face. "I'm trying to apologize to you. Can you take this seriously for a second?"

Liz raised her eyebrows. "If you yell at me one more time, Hayden Lane, I promise that you will never be welcome in my house again. And I don't make promises I can't keep," she said menacingly. Brady sure had an effect on her.

"Sorry," he apologized again. "I'm sorry. I don't know what's wrong with me."

"You're probably itching for a cigarette," Liz said offhandedly.

"What?"

"Oh, you thought I didn't know that either?"

"I don't smoke."

"Lies. All lies. They just build the fire into an inferno," she said, shaking her head.

"I don't smoke!" he said, raising his voice again. "Sorry. I didn't mean to . . . Why do you think I smoke?"

"Oh, because I saw you do it in October when you left the newspaper."

"You were watching me?"

"It seems the only way to get you to tell the truth!"

"I used to smoke," Hayden admitted. "When I was in high school, the other guys on the track team smoked, but I quit. High-stress situations make me crave them."

"How many high-stress situations have you been in lately?" Liz asked accusingly.

"A few," he said stiffly. "But that's not why I'm here. I'm here to try to make things right. How can I make things right?" He splayed his hands out in front of him and took a step forward.

"If you came here to fix things, then you should have never come. You can't make it right. There's absolutely nothing that you could say to me that would get me to change my mind. You've already done enough damage here. I think you should maybe do some soul-searching and see how much you totally fucked up the best thing you'll ever have in your life. How does it feel knowing that you ruined your own life?" she said calmly. "I hope that Calleigh beats you to that promotion and drops your ass. It would be what you deserve."

Hayden's mouth dropped open and he just shook his head. "So I can't make this better?"

"No," she said resolutely.

"There's no reasoning with you?" he asked, pleading with his big hazel eyes for some way to make it up to her.

"I couldn't think of a single thing that you could do to fix this. You broke me. You broke us. It's over," she said, her voice cracking. "And I think you should just go."

Hayden nodded, accepting his fate. As he pulled the door open to exit, he turned back to face her. "I am sorry, and I will never stopping looking for a way to make this right."

The door closed behind him and the energy left Liz in a huff. Emotionally she felt as if she had just run a marathon that she had never trained for. She stumbled to the couch and crashed back into the cushions. She didn't think she would have been able to keep going even if she had wanted to. Her heart felt heavy, but at least she knew one thing: she still had Brady.

Victoria rushed into the room. "Is he gone?"

"Yeah, he just left," Liz murmured. "I can't believe I said all of that. I can't believe it's really over."

"Me either, but the bastard deserved every word. So . . . what happened?"

"With Hayden? Didn't you hear the whole thing?" Liz asked.

"No! With the guy you left with on Friday. I heard you come home, but then you went right back out with him. Was he good? Were you in a sex coma? Why didn't you answer your fucking phone, bitch!" Victoria said, punching her lightly in the arm.

"Oh, Clay. No, I didn't sleep with him. I knew him when I walked out with him."

"No fair! That wasn't the game."

"He's Brady's brother," Liz told her with a sigh.

"You left to have sex with Brady's brother!" Victoria gasped.

"Well . . . originally."

"Holy fuck! I underestimated you. Forget my threesomes . . ."

"Foursomes," Liz muttered under her breath.

"You might be dirtier than me!"

Liz shook her head. "Not possible."

"Are you going to sleep with both of them?" Victoria literally gasped. "At the same time?"

"Victoria, no. You're living out your own fantasies, not mine. Clay is really good-looking, but I have no interest. I spent the weekend with Brady at his lake house."

Victoria shrieked and bounced up and down in her chair. "Oh my God! I'm so excited. Did you guys fuck? Are you back together?"

Liz smiled coyly, her eyes drifting down to her hand. "Yes . . . on both counts."

"Okay. Okay," she said, trying to stay calm but not succeeding. "Tell me all about it. You had sex with a congressman. This is too good to go without details."

"I'm not giving you details! We had sex . . . a couple times."

"Like how many times?" Victoria asked, clapping her hands together.

"I don't know." Liz started counting in her head. "Um . . . like five times."

"That's like fifteen orgasms! Lucky girl!"

"You're ridiculous!" Liz said. "Fifteen orgasms? Jesus, Vic."

"Oh, maybe I'm just that lucky," Victoria said with a wink. "But, girl, you're with Brady. What does that feel like?"

Liz sighed and leaned back into the couch. "Perfection."

Chapter 29

MISDIRECTION

Liz took some Tylenol and then collapsed into her bed. The emotional roller coaster she had been riding the past week exhausted her, and all she could think about was sleeping through the day. Luckily Massey was covering the paper this weekend, so she could be a bum another day longer.

She couldn't believe everything that had happened. All she could concentrate on was Brady. She was with Brady. And not just that, but he wanted to go public with their relationship.

It all felt so *fast*. And she felt ridiculous thinking that. A year ago if he had told her that he didn't want to hide their relationship, she would have been jumping up and down, but so much had happened since then. The thought of being out in the open when she hadn't been with the person more than a weekend in over a year made her nervous inside.

The only thing she knew for certain was that she had tried for a long time to get Brady out of her system and it simply hadn't been possible. That thought was what fueled her forward. She and Brady couldn't get enough of each other. They were meant to be together. It was what reminded her that this was all worth it.

Because frankly, she was scared. She didn't really care what people thought about her and Brady, but there were so many unknowns about their relationship and what was to come. When would they get to be alone? How would this all work with him in D.C.? Was she suddenly going to be swamped with reporters? She was already being portrayed as a scandal in the media. She couldn't imagine what it would be like when her identity was revealed.

She still had to finish her senior year of college, and there was her new job at the *New York Times*. She hadn't been anticipating this relationship or the complications that came with it. That didn't mean she didn't want to go through with it. It just meant that she and Brady had a lot to work out themselves before they went public and their relationship was blasted all over the world for everyone else to scrutinize. Didn't seem fair for everyone to pick apart their relationship before they even had the chance to *have* one.

Not that she could let it sit forever. She didn't want to become an even bigger story than Sandy Carmichael already was. She knew the benefit of beating reporters at their game. Then she got to tell the story, and not them.

If anything, that only added stress to the situation. She felt as if she were in a box and all of the sides were slowly sliding in toward her. Every second wasted deciding what to do only brought them that much closer to being discovered.

Jeez! She needed to cut the stress down a bit. She was back with Brady. *She was back with Brady!* Never in a million years had she thought that this moment would come. So now that it had, she just wanted to lie here and remember what it felt like waking up in his arms, the feel of his lips, the way his eyes met hers. *Loving you takes so much less effort.* He loved her. He had always loved her. That was where her focus should be. The rest would follow.

And rest did follow. With all of those thoughts swirling through her mind, Liz fell asleep. Too much stress had completely wiped her out, and slumber became inevitable.

———

Liz woke some time later to the sound of banging on her bedroom door. She yawned loudly and stretched out the kink in her neck.

"Yeah?" she grumbled.

How long had she been out? She hadn't even remembered falling asleep. Shit! She had said that she was going to call Brady after Hayden left. He was probably freaking out. She didn't want him to think that she had forgotten—or worse, that Hayden was still here. She had made it clear to Brady that it was over with Hayden, but he didn't need a reason to doubt her.

"Are you awake in there?" Victoria called.

"Um . . . yeah. Sorry. I guess I passed out." Liz stood and searched around for her phone. She needed to find out how long she had been asleep and then call Brady.

"Well, get your ass out here. You have a visitor."

Liz scrunched her eyebrows together. Who the hell would be visiting her? She snatched her phone off of her desk and checked the time. Okay, she hadn't been asleep that long. Forty-five minutes or so. Still too long not to respond to the text message flashing on her screen from Brady.

Liz clicked on the text and jogged quickly into the bathroom. As she read the message, she found a hair tie in a basket by the sink and threw her hair into a ponytail.

Haven't heard from you. Everything all right? Do I need to swing back by?

Shit! That had been fifteen minutes ago. Her visitor was probably Brady checking to make sure that Hayden was gone and she was all right.

Liz checked out her face in the mirror and winced. Her nap hadn't done her any good; she looked as if she hadn't slept in weeks. After splashing some water on her face to try to wake herself up, she dabbed some foundation under her eyes to cover the dark circles and then slid her phone back into her pocket. Time to face the music.

"Sorry to keep you waiting," Liz said as she walked out of her bedroom. "I wasn't expecting . . ."

She trailed off when she caught a glimpse of red hair. Her stomach plummeted.

Not good.

What the hell was Calleigh Hollingsworth doing in her living room? Liz wanted to walk over there, snatch the woman's box-maroon hair in her hand, and throw her out of her house. As much as Liz despised Hayden, he had supposedly only gone through with the article because of Calleigh's interference; then her name had appeared next to his byline, and now she was standing here in front of Liz.

Liz couldn't think of a single good reason for her to be here. Not one. Hayden had claimed that he hadn't given Calleigh Liz's name in the whole thing, but how much did Calleigh really know? She had been taunting Liz at Brady's primary about this sort of thing. It made Liz anxious, and she didn't know what the hell she was supposed to do.

"Liz," Calleigh said, turning around to face her. "How are you, doll?"

Liz cringed slightly at the nickname. She hated that. Everything about Calleigh irritated her at this point.

"I'm good, Calleigh. How are you?" Liz asked amicably. Maybe if she acted nice then Calleigh would leave quicker.

"Good. Good. Just been busy," Calleigh said flippantly.

"I can only imagine," Liz said dryly. *Busy ruining lives and such.* "How's Hayden?"

Liz narrowed her eyes. "Why?"

She had a million other questions she wanted to ask in response to that, but that was all that came out. Why? Because Calleigh couldn't get into his pants or because she was testing to see if they had broken up or what?

"Geez, calm down, Liz. I was just asking."

"But why? Don't you work together? I would think you see him more than me right now, since we're both so busy," Liz said, trying to keep her anger about Hayden at bay for a few minutes. If she acted super pissed, then Calleigh would start piecing things together.

"Oh, well, yeah, I suppose," Calleigh said, flipping her hair over her shoulder and smiling coyly. "I just hadn't seen him since Friday, when we submitted that article. Did you read it? We're getting so much interest from it."

"I did read it. It was well written."

Calleigh nodded but looked at Liz as if she was waiting for something. "Thank you. We worked on it together."

"Do you think you're going to get a promotion?" Liz asked. She was itching to pull her phone out and text Brady.

"Remains to be seen, I think. After this I'd say we're in line for whatever is next," she said, smiling brightly.

Liz just wished that Calleigh could be ugly instead of this exotic beauty with long straight hair, high cheekbones, and stunning green eyes. It would serve her right for having such a cold heart.

"Well, congrats!" Liz said, evading the one question she really wanted to ask. *What the fuck are you doing here?*

"Thanks. I just thought I'd stop by, since I'm in the area doing some research," Calleigh said.

She paused as if she were waiting for Liz to say something. So Liz didn't. She just stared at Calleigh blankly.

"I've been through the registrar records and it seems, as I suspected, that no one by the name of Sandy Carmichael ever actually went to UNC during the time we wrote about in the article."

"You did say that it was a fake name or something, right? I wouldn't think you would waste your time looking, or at the very least that you would have checked it over before writing the article," Liz said snippily.

Calleigh laughed softly and nodded. "I just thought I'd double- and triple-check. Cover my bases. But it looks like, as Hayden said, she doesn't exist. And he won't tell me who told him."

Liz stood frozen, not wanting to move or shift or even blink. Calleigh didn't need any kind of indicators from Liz as to how Hayden got his information.

"Well, I'd assume that if he wanted to tell you, then he would have," she said simply.

"Hayden seems to be withholding the information for a specific reason. I mean, he wouldn't have told me if the person told him about it off the record. That's breaking ethical boundaries . . ."

Liz gasped lightly. "Oh my God, are you afraid of getting sued for libel? Careers have been ended for less, Calleigh."

Color drained slowly out of her face and she shook her head. "No. I'm not . . . I'm not concerned about that."

Liz seemed to have thrown her off her rhythm, at least for a moment. The wheels were clearly working in Calleigh's mind. She hoped that Calleigh thought that Hayden had lied to her about how he had acquired the information, or even that there was the potential for the Maxwell family to come back and destroy them. Good-bye, reporting career.

"Has he told you?" Calleigh finally blurted out.

"Told me what?" Liz asked, tilting her head and looking at Calleigh innocently.

"Who Sandy Carmichael is? Has he told you who he spoke with? Y'all have been dating over a year, I would think a strong, stable relationship like that," Calleigh said with a gleam of mischief in her eye, "you would tell each other everything."

Liz just smiled sweetly. "Oh, we do. We tell each other everything."

Calleigh's eyes enlarged slightly and then returned to their normal size. "So then . . . you know?"

"Know what?" Liz prompted. "About Sandy Carmichael or about you and Hayden?"

"Um . . ." Calleigh said, her mouth dropping open. Then she shook her head as she recovered. "I was simply asking about Sandy Carmichael."

"Well, I'm asking about Hayden. Is there anything going on between y'all? Because he told me it was over since he dumped you after you graduated and that he's been happy to fend you off since he moved to Charlotte."

"You can believe that if you want," she said, sticking her nose in the air.

Liz laughed, trying to remain casual. "It's okay, Calleigh."

"What's okay?" she snapped.

"I believe him," Liz said with a smile. "I believe that Hayden wanted nothing to do with you because of me. Because you stood no chance."

"What the fuck?" Calleigh muttered.

"Your threat that day that he interviewed for the job was kind of cute actually. To think that he would go near you. He was appalled that I was even irritated with what you had said."

Misdirection. That was the name of the game. Maybe she could get the other woman frustrated enough to just leave, and then Liz wouldn't have to deal with anything else Calleigh was alluding to. She figured Calleigh was grasping at straws and had just shown up at Liz's door on a whim.

"Wow. Someone is in a bitch mood," Calleigh growled, losing her cool.

"You did wake me up from a nap," Liz said with a shrug. "Which I'd actually really like to get back to. So if you want to just . . . head out." Liz gestured toward the door.

Calleigh shook her head and then started to leave. Liz held her breath. She just wanted her gone.

"I guess this was pointless," Calleigh said.

"Pretty much."

"Are you applying to *Charlotte Times* to be closer to Hayden? I hadn't heard anything about your application."

Liz smiled brightly. At last, one question that she could answer truthfully. "Actually I just accepted a job at the *New York Times*. So I'll be moving to New York after graduation."

"What?" Calleigh asked, stunned.

"Yeah. I've been interning with them all year and I just accepted a position."

"Well, congratulations," Calleigh said through gritted teeth. "How is that going to work with you and Hayden?"

"Oh, I'm sure we'll figure it out," Liz said. She couldn't keep the self-satisfied smirk off her face.

"Great. That sounds wonderful. I guess I'll see you in Charlotte sometime," Calleigh said, opening the door.

"Sure," Liz said. *No chance in hell.*

Calleigh walked through the door without a backward glance and then she was gone. Liz shut the door heavily and then nearly collapsed back against it. Holy shit! That had been so fucking close.

Chapter 30
HIGH STRESS

Liz had her phone out of her pocket in a matter of seconds. She skipped responding to Brady's text message and just called him. She couldn't handle the amount of stress she was dealing with right now, and she needed his reassuring voice to calm her down. Brady would make everything all right.

Liz was just proud that she had been able to redirect Calleigh. If she had realized how close she was to learning who Sandy Carmichael was then Liz was sure that she wouldn't have left so easily. Luckily, Liz had been able to use Hayden to her advantage. Sure, Calleigh might find out tomorrow that they had broken up, but Liz didn't give a shit. That bought her a day to talk to Brady and figure out what they were going to do.

She just needed a day.

"Liz, I've been waiting for your call. What happened?" Brady asked after answering on the first ring.

"Sorry. So sorry. Stressful day. Hayden left a while ago, but I passed out and only woke up a couple minutes ago," Liz told him. Her voice was shaking. She had lost the calmness that she had before her conversation with Calleigh. At least she was able to be herself with Brady.

Brady sighed heavily. "I've been in Chapel Hill for nearly two hours waiting to hear what happened. A text would have been nice."

"I know. Gah, I'm sorry. Just emotionally exhausted, Brady. Hayden and I got into a huge argument . . . more like a screaming match."

"Was he trying to salvage?" Brady asked coldly.

"Yeah, he was. He tried to tell me that Calleigh Hollingsworth—you know, the girl who he wrote the article with—brought the story to the editor without his say." Brady scoffed. Yeah, Liz wasn't sure she believed that either. "And then he said a bunch of bullshit about how he didn't put my name in it and we could work it out. Yada, yada, yada."

"But it's over?"

"Yes. Very much over."

"Well, I can't say that I'm disappointed. I just wanted to make sure I was nearby in case you needed me. I've been working out of a coffee shop. It's kind of peaceful."

"Maybe you should ditch the suit more often," she said with a giggle.

"Not happening."

"Good. I like them," she said softly. "But there is one more thing."

Brady sighed. "What is it? I'd like to hear it all before having to go back and deal with everything I left behind when I kidnapped you on Friday."

"You kidnapped me?" Liz asked. "I went willingly."

"How could you not?"

"Arrogant ass," she mumbled.

"What is it you were going to tell me?"

"Calleigh Hollingsworth stopped by when I woke up from my nap."

"The reporter ex-girlfriend?" Brady asked. His voice was like ice. She was sure he already saw red flags.

"Yeah. I think she might know something. Hayden didn't tell her it was me, but I think she's really close to guessing."

"Did she say that?" he demanded. "Do I need to get Heather on it?"

"She didn't *say* anything exactly. It was what she was implying. I think she wanted to see if I knew who it was or if Hayden had told me, but she kept skirting around it. I wouldn't worry too much about it right now, but I wanted you to be aware. We might have to, um . . . alter our plans if she starts sniffing around."

"All right. I'll mention her name to Heather and see what comes out of it. I'm sure she's already had someone looking into both of them extensively."

"That's good. Yeah," Liz whispered.

"Hey," Brady said, his tone softening. "Are you okay?"

"Yeah. Totally. Um . . . just a little freaked out and overwhelmed and exhausted. I just feel like everything happened really, really fast. Like a year and a half ago I wanted this, then we were apart for so long, and now it's only been a weekend and we're suddenly just jumping into things," Liz rambled on.

"Do you . . . not want to?" Brady asked. It was so strange to hear the hesitance in his voice.

"I do. I do. It's just . . . well, can you understand how insane this might all feel to me? I never thought we would get back together,

Brady. Certainly not publicly. When I left you, I really left. I tried to forget and move on. I wanted you to have the things that you wanted."

"I wanted you."

Liz nodded and wished that he could see. She wasn't trying to push him away, but she didn't want to hold in everything she was feeling either. "I know that now. I want you too. I mean, I wanted you the whole time. It's just hard adjusting to fighting so hard to let you go to this, and then the whole public aspect. I'm just worried. Not about *us*," she quickly corrected. "But about everyone else."

"Well, we can't really do anything about anyone else. I think as long as you're not worried here. Right here. Then we'll figure the rest out," Brady told her.

"That's true. I'm just . . . I don't think I'm ready to go public, Brady."

"We'll figure out when the best time is, but, Liz, if you're going to be with me, that's kind of a side effect. I'm not hiding you anymore."

"I do want that," she said. "I wish this was coming out better. I know that we have to beat the reporters to figuring it out and I don't know how much time we have for that, but I just wish however much time it is that we had more of it. Am I making any sense?"

"You want a normal relationship. I get that," Brady said gruffly. "But you want me and I can't give you that. I never could."

Liz closed her eyes and hung her head back against the door. She knew that. If she wanted Brady there were going to have to be sacrifices, but how big would those sacrifices be? Her privacy? Her career? Her ambition? Deep down she knew whatever the sacrifice, it would all be worth it. But the what-ifs drove her insane.

"I don't want normal. I'm . . . I don't know. It'll take some getting used to."

"I think it does in every relationship. We simply have some additional hurdles."

"You're right. I'm just overly emotional right now. I wasn't happy without you. I'd never be happy without you, Brady," Liz said.

She closed her eyes and tried to imagine continuing on this path without him, and all she saw was darkness. Blank, empty darkness. But being with him was like a shining light, a beacon of hope in the darkness. She wasn't going to let that go for anything.

"Something we can agree on."

"I don't want to have to hide my apprehensions from you," Liz told him. "But we'll get through this, right? It'll be worth it."

"Every second with you is worth it."

Liz sighed. "I should probably let you go so that you can get back to work. Sorry to kind of unload on you."

"It's all right, Liz. Just try to get some sleep. We'll start to figure everything out this week."

They hung up the phone and Liz slowly stood from her position against the door. She had a crick in her neck and really wanted to take a shower to ease some of the stress. She wanted to talk to Victoria about everything that had happened, but she didn't have the energy. As Brady said, they would figure everything else out this week.

Liz took her time in the shower, scrubbing her body clean, and washing her long blond tresses. Once she was finished, she toweled off and changed into a pair of yoga pants and a UNC sweatshirt. She pulled her hair up into a messy bun on the top of her head, because she didn't feel like taking the time to blow it out, then set to work on her neglected homework from the past week.

About fifteen minutes into her journalism assignment, Liz heard the doorbell ring. She hopped up out of her desk chair and strode into the living room. Victoria peeked her head out of her bedroom.

Liz just smiled. "I got it."

"Cool." Victoria nodded and then closed the door to her room again.

Liz yawned and covered her mouth as she reached for the door. When she swung it open, she wished that she hadn't.

"Back so soon?" Liz asked in disbelief.

Calleigh Hollingsworth was standing on her doorstep. *What the fuck?*

"Yeah. Do you mind if I come in?" Calleigh asked. Her megawatt smile made Liz uncomfortable. No way was she coming inside.

"I'm kind of busy right now. Maybe you can come back later," Liz said, looking at her as if she was a bit crazy. She started to close the door.

Calleigh put her hand out to stop it. "I can make this quick if you just have a minute."

"I really don't."

"I think you have a minute for what I'm going to say."

Liz rolled her eyes. What did Calleigh want to talk about?

"Not interested," Liz said. She needed her to leave. Now. Anything that was about to come out of her mouth wasn't going to be good. Fear seeped into every pore. Had she spoken to Hayden? Had he tipped her off? Could she have figured everything out in that amount of time?

Calleigh smiled and started speaking anyway. "When I left here, I got into my car and started driving away, thinking that I had wasted my time. Then I started thinking about exactly what had happened and what you had said. Particularly how defensive you got about everything I was saying. And I know that you don't like me, Liz, but it all felt a little *much* for me coming to talk to you to find out a little piece of information. If you didn't want to tell me, then you could have said a million things. You could have simply said that you didn't know. You could have said Hayden swore you to secrecy. You could have said you just didn't want to tell me. I would have expected those responses," Calleigh said, staring directly into Liz's eyes.

Liz swallowed. Oh, shit! She hadn't thought that she had been defensive.

"But you didn't do that, did you? You continually changed the subject and completely sidestepped every question I asked you. And I realized that you had totally played me. You're kind of a pro at it, really. I'm impressed. I didn't see it for what it was at all."

"I'm not a pro at anything, Calleigh," Liz said. She hoped that she sounded neutral. "I don't even know what you're talking about."

Calleigh smiled at Liz as if she were looking at a caged animal, and then answered as if she hadn't heard a word Liz had just said. "So once I realized what you had done, it got me wondering what exactly it was that would make you try to manipulate the situation. What exactly you're hiding."

Liz rolled her eyes. "Are you done? I'm not hiding anything, Calleigh."

"When I came over here in the first place I had my suspicions, but I thought maybe you just *knew* who Sandy Carmichael was . . . now I'm thinking maybe you *are* Sandy Carmichael."

"What?" Liz gasped.

Oh, fuck! She didn't know what to do. What the hell was she supposed to say to that? She didn't want to lie, but this was Calleigh. After everything Liz had just said to Brady, she couldn't imagine confirming this. It would ruin everything. She would be giving over the reins to the media, and Liz didn't even want to think about what her world would be like if that happened.

She could feel her face heating, and knew that she looked uncomfortable. Calleigh no doubt was reading her body language.

It made Liz's palms sweat just thinking about it, and she shifted her eyes away from Calleigh's face. This couldn't be happening.

Deny, deny, deny.

"You can try to change the subject all you want," Calleigh said, "but I knew something was up with you at his primary on the campaign. It's all but confirmed with me now. So how about you go on the record and confirm, Liz: Are you Sandy Carmichael?"

Chapter 31

BRADY

Brady took a deep breath as he circled around his parents' neighborhood and then pulled into the long circular driveway. He knew after checking his phone and seeing all the missed calls, voice mails, and text messages that there were going to be a lot of questions he was going to have to answer. After the peaceful weekend he'd had with Liz, he couldn't imagine going back into the fray. They would never really have that again. It was kind of a sad notion, knowing that even if they worked everything out, they would never truly be alone.

Nothing he could do about it right now. They had to get to that point before he could worry about anything else.

There were reporters camped out on the perimeter of the house, and as he parked and got out of the car, a few jogged up to him. He had expected it to be like this, but still it was irritating.

"Congressman Maxwell, will you comment on the allegations about your relations with Sandy Carmichael?" one called, thrusting a microphone into his face.

"Congressman Maxwell, who is Sandy Carmichael?" another asked.

"Why are you hiding her from us? What other secrets are you hiding from the people?" still another called out. Cameras flashed and people surrounded him on all sides.

Brady had always known that politicians had to live their lives under a microscope. He had seen that firsthand with a father in politics. But it was one thing to see it from afar; it was quite different to be living it.

Brady shook his head and put his hands out. "No comment. When I want to make a statement, I'll call a press conference. Until then, clear out of my property," he told them stiffly, walking up the front steps and slipping in through the front door.

He closed the door heavily and leaned against it. He couldn't keep running from reporters. It had only been a couple days and he was already tired of it. He heard voices down the hall and walked lightly across the foyer to see what was going on. He didn't get far before he heard Heather and his attorney, Elliott, speaking rather fiercely back and forth. His father's voice rang out, silencing them.

"He will be back when he is. You two treat him as if he's a child. He's a fucking congressman. Do you blame him for taking a mental health day? I don't. We'll deal with it all in time. Until then, perhaps you should find somewhere else to bicker."

Brady cracked a smile. His father sure knew how to cut back an argument. Not that he thought Heather and Elliott had any intention of not bombarding him as soon as they found that he was back. Which he was not going to let them do immediately upon his entering the house.

He only wanted to see one more person before he felt obligated to decide how he was going to bring up the whole subject of Liz to everyone. He was hoping that he would get to talk to Heather and Elliott about it first. He kind of wanted Liz to be there with him when he told his family, but he could understand after her mini panic attack why he should probably do it alone.

The last thing he wanted to do was move too fast. But in this kind of situation, he couldn't figure out how to move any slower. He knew where Liz was coming from. They went from not seeing each other for more than a year to fucking in half a second. Now he wanted to bring her home to the family, tell the press they were dating, and live happily ever after in this mob-style media haze. It wasn't fair to her. He wanted to give her more, but he couldn't before and he couldn't now. He just wanted to give her everything he could.

He loved her. Fuck, he had never stopped loving her.

She had said that she had tried to give him up, but he didn't really think he had ever really tried that hard. She was ingrained in him somehow. She had been since day one, when she had stared up at him completely unfazed and asked him one question that changed everything. How could he walk away from someone like that?

Well, the answer had been simple: he couldn't. If he was honest with himself, and he usually was, Erin had just been filler. A poor man's Liz. And it was cruel to think it, but fuck, she was.

Erin would never be Liz. He had always known, but it had been a nice distraction. Then when he had just fucking dropped everything that night in October at a chance of seeing Liz, just so he didn't have to think about her crying . . . yeah, that had been the tipping point.

One desperate drive out there, one look, one kiss. It had been over.

He had broken up with Erin as soon as his plane touched down in D.C. Erin had cried, and he had felt bad, but nothing compared to how he had felt when Liz had called crying. He had felt like he was dying. That had only sealed the deal.

He remembered how angry Erin had gotten.

I thought you loved me. How do you suddenly stop loving someone? Is there someone else? Is that what this is?

Brady shook his head as he took the stairs to the second floor. There had always been someone else.

He didn't know what he would have done if Liz hadn't ended up calling him. At this point he didn't even want to think about it. He had too much else to worry about.

The hall was clear when he made it to the landing. Brady took a left turn and then opened the door to the first bedroom on the right without waiting for a response. Clay turned around quickly from where he was standing with a phone pressed to his ear.

"Hey, hold on," Clay said into the phone. "What's up, man? Where the fuck were you?"

Brady shut the door. "You should probably end your phone call."

Clay's brow furrowed. "Andrea, I'm going to have to call you back." Clay hung the phone up and tossed it onto the bed. "What's this all about?"

"Clay, I know that we've had our differences in the past," Brady said, taking a step toward his brother. "I know we haven't always agreed. You've gone your way. I've gone mine. I accepted that we were never going to be close."

"What the fuck is this, Brady? Are we bonding all of a sudden?" Clay asked.

"You could say that." He took another step. "Now, as I was saying, I know we were never close. But I thought we had a certain *understanding.*"

"Is this about Liz?"

Brady was on him in two seconds, slamming Clay's back roughly against the wall and shoving his forearm against Clay's jugular. "*Don't* say her name."

"Fuck, Brady!" Clay managed to get out as he was held against the wall.

"You're a fucking piece of work, you know that?" Clay just glared at him fiercely. "There are reasons I have the things that I have in my life. And there are reasons why *you* will never have what I have, Clay. Don't think I'm stupid enough not to know why you went after her in the first place."

Clay swung at him but Brady just increased the pressure on his throat and swatted his hand away.

"She might have been naïve enough to almost fall for your game, but just know that she never will be again. You'll never get close to her. You'll never touch her. You'll certainly never kiss her again. She's mine. And if I ever even get a hint that you're trying to *take* what is mine, I don't think I'll just be using words."

"Fuck you!" Clay spat.

"She did."

After he made his point, Brady lessened the pressure on Clay's throat and started to back off.

"You think I'm the piece of work?" Clay said. "If you care about her so much, then why was she fucking that asshole reporter this whole time? Yeah, probably because you weren't there. You had *no* claim on her. Fair game."

"You have a fucking girlfriend," Brady roared. "Why don't you fair-game her ass and leave everyone else's alone!"

Clay scoffed. "It's just Andrea."

"This, this right here!" Brady said, gesturing to Clay. "How the fuck are we even related?"

"Is Liz your girlfriend?" Clay asked with a snide smirk.

Brady shook his head and then slammed Clay back into the wall again. "I said don't say her name. And I don't ever want to hear you talk about someone else fucking her. Imagine what we would be talking about right now if you had succeeded in your stupid mind game."

"I'm imagining," Clay said defiantly.

"You're imagining yourself dead?"

Clay opened his mouth to respond when the bedroom door swung open again. "Clay, Mom just asked me to . . ." Savannah trailed off as she took in what she saw. "What is this? What's going on?"

Brady growled under his breath and then dropped his arm. He wasn't going to do this shit in front of Savannah. He had gotten his point across to Clay. That was going to have to do. Clay wasn't stupid. He had been trying to do all of this shit behind Brady's back. He wasn't going to blatantly go against Brady once it went public. Clay didn't like to be in the papers. He had to stay out of them if he wanted to be the attorney general one day.

"Nothing, Savi," Brady said, dusting off his hands on his pants and striding across the room. "Don't worry about it."

"Don't tell me not to worry about it. You had him against the wall. Why are you guys fighting? Why are you always fighting?" Savannah asked. "And where have you been?"

"I had to get away. I'll tell you about it later," Brady said. He walked toward the door and was almost out of the room before Clay spoke up.

"That's it! You're just going to leave it at that. Not even going to tell your precious little sister what a terrible guy you really are?" Clay spat.

Brady sighed and stopped in the doorway. Great. He had riled Clay up. He should have just beaten the shit out of him. Then his brother wouldn't have had any comebacks.

"Clay, don't be an ass," Savannah said, rolling her eyes.

"Me? He's the one who was banging a UNC student ten years younger than him, and thought he would get away with it. Everyone thinks he's so innocent."

"What?" Savannah breathed.

"You have no idea what you're talking about, Clay."

"Play innocent. Prodigal son and all that. You fucked up. Now own it!"

"Brady, what is he talking about? All of that stuff about the

UNC student was made up. You'd never . . . You're not that kind of guy." She tried to laugh but cut it off. "Wrong brother. Right?"

"Oh Jesus Christ, you too?" Clay cried, throwing his hands up.

Brady sighed and faced Savannah. "It's true. I was with a UNC student two summers ago before you were even there. She's not ten years younger. She's seven. It wasn't an affair. We weren't with other people. It's not all the media is making it out to be."

"Wow." Savannah's mouth hung open. "Is she still at UNC?"

"I was going to wait to talk about it with everyone," Brady said simply.

Clay started laughing. "You believe he's actually going to tell everyone everything, *Savi*?"

"Leave him alone. He's had a rough week!" Savannah said.

"Defend him like normal. She's a reporter," Clay announced. "Got your attention now?"

"What?" Savannah reached out and smacked Brady's arm. "Are you stupid? Don't you know that's rule one in bad politics? It's like . . . fraternizing with the enemy!"

"Savi, you're going to be a reporter," Brady reminded her.

"I'm different. Who is it? What reporter could possibly interest you?" Savannah demanded.

God, this was not how he had wanted this conversation to go. He knew Liz and Savannah were friends. Good enough friends that she brought her along to dinner with their parents. He could only imagine how this was going to go down. He kind of felt obligated to be the one to tell Savannah, since she was his little sister, but Liz was her friend. He wished Liz were with him.

"Before you punch me, please remember this was before you knew her," Brady warned.

Savannah planted her hands on her sides. "Brady Jefferson," she said, narrowing her eyes. "Do I even want to know?"

"It's Liz," he blurted out.

Savannah's mouth dropped open and her hands dropped to her sides. "Liz? Like Liz Dougherty, the editor-in-chief at the UNC newspaper? Like the Liz I brought to dinner that one time? My Liz?"

"Yes."

"Oh, what, you're not going to beat her up because she claims your girlfriend?" Clay grumbled across the room.

"She didn't try to sleep with her!" Brady shot back.

"Girlfriend? Liz is your girlfriend?" Savannah's eyes were wide as if she couldn't seem to process what he was saying.

"Well, yeah." Brady shrugged. What else was he going to say? He was going to have to have this conversation one way or another. He just hoped Savannah would understand. No way around it. He wasn't giving Liz up just because Savi was uncomfortable.

Savannah wrinkled her nose. "Gross. One of my best friends slept with my brother. I am so going to have words with her! She was the first person I talked to when I found out, and she didn't even tell me that you were sleeping together. And," Savannah gasped, "Hayden . . . were you together when . . . ?"

Brady's eyes turned molten at that name. He couldn't even think about Hayden without wanting to put his fist through Hayden's face and tear him apart limb from limb.

"No. He is so far out of the picture. He didn't find out any of it happened—no one did, until the week before the article released."

"So . . . how is she your girlfriend? And wait . . . did you just say Clay tried to sleep with her too?" Savannah asked. "Can *either* of you keep it in your pants?"

Brady shifted his eyes from Savannah. This was not the conversation he wanted to be having. Getting reprimanded for falling for Liz was out of the question. He had heard it enough from Heather. He had beaten himself up about it. He wasn't going to listen to it anymore.

"She's my girlfriend since yesterday. Everyone is just going to have to get used to the idea. I have to deal with the rest of the world having an opinion, so I just can't take any more shit right now," Brady said sternly. He hadn't meant to snap, but he was so over it already.

"I wasn't trying to give you shit," Savannah said softly. "I like Liz. I'm just shocked. Everyone is going to be shocked."

"I know." He tried to clear his head. "I know. I'm just about to break it to Heather."

Savannah cringed. "Do you want me to come with you?"

Brady chuckled at Savannah. He loved his little sister. He hoped no one ever tried to ruin her goodness. "No. I think I'm old enough to tackle my own problems. But thank you."

He walked back over to Clay, who stood taller as he approached. He probably thought Brady was going to hit him after all. It would be what the asshole deserved, but he wasn't going to actually start a fight when he had won in the end anyway.

"What do you want?" Clay asked.

"Don't leave your phone where reporters can take it next time," Brady said, pulling Clay's phone out of his pocket and tossing it into his brother's hands.

"She took my phone? What a . . ."

"I wouldn't finish that sentence," Brady said. He glared at Clay before turning, nodding at Savannah, and walking out of the room. He did have to deal with his own problems. Clay and Savannah now knew. Two down, the rest of the world to go.

As he walked to the staircase, he wondered about what he should expect from Heather. She had been there since day one, and her opinion had always been important to him . . . until Liz. Heather just couldn't see clearly about his relationship with her. He knew that it was because she saw Liz as a liability. It didn't matter now, though, because there was nothing she could do but accept it for what it was.

As Brady descended the staircase, he saw Elliott standing at the base of the stairs typing away on his iPad. If Brady knew him at all, he was probably trying to get away from Heather.

"Hey, man," Brady said as he approached.

Elliott jumped. "When did *you* get back?"

"Not too long ago."

"Where the fuck did you go?"

"Away, but now I'm back and we can deal with all of this."

"Good." Elliott shut down the iPad and tucked it under his arm. "Heather has been driving me mad."

"Sounds accurate."

"You with that girl again?" Elliott asked all nonchalant as if it didn't make a difference one way or another.

Brady laughed and nodded. "Yeah. I am. You going to help me break it to Heather?"

"I think she's been preparing to slaughter you all weekend. She'll come around." Elliott clapped Brady on the back. "I'm surprised it took you this long."

"Stubborn, I guess."

Brady never knew how to read Elliott. They had known each other a long time. Sometimes Brady thought the man was going to blow up on him, and other times Elliott was completely chill. Brady was glad to have him as a friend on the occasions when he just rolled with the punches. Made him a good lawyer.

"Stubborn," Elliott said with raised eyebrows. "Now who would possibly describe you that way?"

"Everyone."

"Right."

"How'd you know I'd go back to her?" Brady asked him. He crossed his arms over his chest and waited. He hadn't even known that he would go after her. She had his heart, but fuck, she had messed him up. He had struggled with the decision up until the minute she had gotten into his car.

"Do you remember what you said to me the day of your primary victory, when I asked you if you really loved her?"

"I said that it didn't matter."

"Exactly. Frankly it doesn't matter," Elliott told him. "You could have said yes and you could have said no, but you said it didn't matter. Which to me meant it was the only thing that mattered."

"She is," Brady agreed. It had just taken him a while to realize that. Without her, all of his dreams and aspirations seemed flat.

"Let's try to convince Heather of that. My advice, for what it's worth, you might want to just let her get a few good punches in," Elliott said with a laugh. "She'll feel bad about it and forgive you quicker."

"I like where your head's at." This was the reason he kept Elliott around.

They walked together to the living room, where Heather was hovering over the phone. She looked like a wreck. Her blond hair was still perfectly straight, but it was up into a high ponytail that he had rarely seen her do before. She was short on makeup, and her suit looked like it needed a trip to the dry cleaner's. Brady had clearly really stressed her out.

"Heather," Brady said softly.

Heather turned around so fast that she looked as if she gave herself whiplash. "Brady! Oh my God, you're back!"

"Of course I'm back," he said with an easy shrug. He wasn't giving up his career for one scandal.

"Great. Let's sit down. We have to figure out our remarks. I need to know what angle we should take. I think personally denying would just be best, but if you think of something different I could work with that. Then I think we should decide about a press conference. Do we want to call for one or should I just release a statement for you? Would that seem like you're hiding behind the screen?"

"Whoa!" Brady said, holding his hands up. "Just like that? You want to talk strategy? You don't want to chew my head off for leaving?"

Heather stared at him stonily. "What I want and what I think are important for your career are two different things."

"Good to be back, Heather," he said, taking a seat on a chair and grinning at her.

"Don't get the two things confused again. I want to smack some sense into you for leaving me knee-deep in this shit, but I know that we need to address this as quickly as possible. I'll hold back my desire to strangle you until we have some semblance of order again," she grumbled.

"I think order is going to be scarce for a while."

"I know, but still I think we should . . ." Heather trailed off. "Wait, why? You sound like there's a reason beyond just the media."

"It's Liz, Heather," Brady said softly.

"I know that Sandy Carmichael is Liz, Brady. I've already surmised that."

"No. Heather," he said, shaking his head. "I'm back with Liz."

"What?" she shrieked. "Brady, are you out of your mind? Her boyfriend wrote the article. It's libelous. What the fuck are we supposed to tell reporters? Where do I go from here?"

"We'll figure it out. We just need a little time for us to decide what to do and then we'll go public."

"Brady, I kind of have to insist as your press secretary that you shouldn't," Heather said. She was pacing the room at this point. "Think about how this will look!"

Brady was going to respond when Heather's phone started ringing noisily. She snatched it off the table it was resting on and frowned at the number. "Give me a second. It's probably another reporter.

"Congressman Maxwell's office," she said evenly.

Brady sighed and rested back in the armchair. Heather was going to be difficult about all of this. He just knew it.

"No, the Congressman is out."

It didn't matter, though, because the wheels were already in motion. He wasn't going back on what he had said to Liz.

"Congressman Maxwell has no comment on the matter of Sandy Carmichael."

He wondered how many calls like this Heather had dealt with while he had been gone. Sure, it was her job, but he wished that it all hadn't happened quite like this. Of course, if it had happened any other way he might not have gotten back with Liz.

As he watched Heather, her face turned red with frustration. "Yes, Miss Hollingsworth, I know that you want a comment from Congressman Maxwell about your article, but we have no comment. He's currently unavailable. We'll reach out to you if we have anything further to say."

Fuck! That name. Hadn't Liz just said that Calleigh Hollingsworth had come to see her in Chapel Hill?

"Heather," Brady snapped. "Did you say Hollingsworth? Are you sure?"

Heather spoke into the phone. "Hold please." Then looked up at Brady. "Yes, Calleigh Hollingsworth of the *Charlotte Times,* why?"

"I'll take it," Brady said, standing and reaching for the phone.

"What? No you will not. I'm your press secretary."

"Give me the phone, Heather. I'll decide for myself if I should comment."

"Elliott, talk some sense into him!"

"It's going to happen one way or another, Heather. Just give him the phone," Elliott said.

She slowly held the phone out with a sigh, clearly looking as if she wanted to jerk it back at any second, but she didn't. Brady took it from her without any idea what he was about to hear on the other line.

"Congressman Maxwell speaking," he said into the phone.

"Congressman Maxwell, this is Calleigh Hollingsworth with the *Charlotte Times*."

"Yes, Miss Hollingsworth. How can I help you?"

"I've recently discovered the identity of Sandy Carmichael and I wanted your comment on the story. Do you have a comment?"

"If you're trying to bait me into discussing whether or not Sandy Carmichael exists, Miss Hollingsworth, you'll have to do better than that," Brady said dryly.

"I'm not baiting anyone. Sandy Carmichael exists. It wasn't until today that I found out the exact identity of the woman you had an affair with. I personally wanted your comment on the story before I went public with the information."

"Miss Hollingsworth, I don't appreciate your games. You just admitted to writing a negative article about me without having any of the facts, and are now claiming to have the facts, though you have shared none with me, and wish for me to comment on that?" Brady asked. He was tiptoeing around the subject as much as she was. He wouldn't believe she had information until she put it forth.

"No. Congressman Maxwell, I want you to make a comment on Sandy Carmichael actually being the fake identity of Liz Dougherty," Calleigh said snootily.

Brady was sure that he stopped breathing.

"No comment?" Calleigh practically taunted.

"What source do you have for that?" Brady asked. He had to know.

"Primary source, Congressman. Do you have a comment now?"

Liz had told her. When was she going to tell him? Just as he had the thought, his phone started vibrating in his pocket. He pulled it out and saw Liz's name light up the screen. Fuck!

What was he going to do? Had Liz been ready to do this? She had wanted more time. He had been willing to give her more time. God, was *he* ready for this? He was used to the public, but the scrutiny it would bring going out like this . . . he didn't know how he was going to deal with it. All he knew at that moment was that he *would* deal with it.

That meant he had Liz. That meant they were working on this together. That meant they were together . . . finally. It would all be worth it for that.

"Yes, Miss Hollingsworth, I'll make a comment. Liz Dougherty is Sandy Carmichael. We were in a private relationship two summers ago, and we're in a public one now."

Don't miss the final book in the Record series
by K.A. Linde

FOR *the* RECORD

Fall 2014

ACKNOWLEDGMENTS

The campaign is the reason for this series. I could have never written Liz's story without the knowledge I received from working on the 2012 campaign. I started writing it while holding a clipboard and going door-to-door, at a Delta Rae concert while doing voter registration, out with other campaign workers. They are the life and the soul of the campaign. They secure everything behind the scenes, they make sure things are running smoothly, they are the ones putting together eight-thousand-person events with three days' notice so that the politician can show up and talk for a few minutes. I hope I conveyed an ounce of that in these books, but they will always mean the world to me because of that time. So thank you for everyone out there who helped make this book a reality: Meera, Gregg, Alex, Maddie, Kane, Greg, Rob, Mary, Susan, Hannah, Daniel, Olivia, Anna, Ralph, Avani, Kathleen, and Kiran.

As always, I appreciate the people who read early versions of this story and helped kick me into gear when I was staring at a blank page. Jessica and Bridget—thank you for being there every night while I delve into my characters' minds. Also, Trish and Becky for falling in love with my characters as much as me. I'd like to thank my agent Jane Dystel at Dystel & Goderich Literary Agency, who believed in this series and helped me every step of the way. Thanks to my content editor Tiffany and my Amazon representative JoVon for making the story everything it could be. And I could never forget my boyfriend, Joel, who deals with my manic behavior without complaint while I'm writing and helps with our adorable puppies, Riker and Lucy.

ABOUT THE AUTHOR

K.A. Linde grew up a military brat traveling the United States and Australia. While studying political science and philosophy at the University of Georgia, she founded the Georgia Dance Team, which she still coaches. Post-graduation she served as campus campaign director for the 2012 presidential campaign at UNC Chapel Hill. She is the author of eight novels, including five in the Avoiding series and two in the Record series. An avid traveler, reader, and bargain hunter, K.A. lives in Athens, Georgia, with her boyfriend and two puppies, Riker and Lucy.